The Yellow Rose Beauty Shop

ALSO BY CAROLYN BROWN

The Yellow Rose Beauty Shop

CAROLYN BROWN

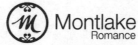

Montlake
Romance

Published by Montlake Romance, Seattle

www.apub.com

Amazon, the Amazon logo, and Montlake Romance are trademarks of Amazon.com, Inc., or its affiliates.

ISBN-13: 9781477830604
ISBN-10: 147783060X

Cover design by Laura Klynstra

Printed in the United States of America

Author's Note

Dear Readers,

Welcome to Cadillac, Texas, where the jalapeño peppers are the hottest in the state and the gossip is even hotter. As you drive into town, take a look at the sign on the church lawn that says, "Pray for My Daughter. She Needs a Husband." Then stop by Clawdy's Café to get lunch. I'm sure they'll tell you what daughter needs a husband and who had the audacity to put her on the Prayer Angels' list.

While you are there, be sure to go into Bless My Bloomers and take a peek at their blinged-out lingerie, and they'll tell you more about Stella Baxter, the lady who needs a husband.

But above all, don't forget to go down to the Yellow Rose Beauty Shop, where all the action is right now. Stella and her two friends own the beauty shop, and she's not a bit happy with her mother or with the sign at the church. But it's there and the gossip is flying about the newest scandal in town, whose name is Stella Baxter and who is no stranger to the hot seat where gossip is concerned! Before the week is over the whole thing will blow up bigger than a class-five Texas tornado, so you might want to stick around for the action.

It takes a village to produce a book. And I'd like to thank the Montlake staff for all their hard work in taking this book from my dream to a reality. To my editor, Kelli Martin, my absolute undying gratitude for the hard work she put in on this to make it a better, stronger book. She deserves a crown made of great big sparkling diamonds. To the publicity crew, y'all are the best of the best. To the folks who designed the cover, OMGoodness, you have outdone yourselves. And to all the behind-the-scenes staff who helped to put this book into my readers' hands, hats off to you all! To my darling husband, who brings hot tea to my office in the mornings and shuts the door behind him without uttering a word, you are special beyond words. And to all of my readers, who continue to buy my books, talk about them, share them with their friends, and write reviews . . . please know that you are appreciated.

As I finish this, the Christmas season is upon us, but *The Yellow Rose Beauty Shop* is set in July and you will be reading it in the heat of the summer. So find a nice cool spot, grab a glass of ice-cold sweet tea, and enjoy!

All my best,
Carolyn Brown

To my editor, Kelli Martin.

It's been said that people come into your path for a reason, a season, or a lifetime.

I'm hoping you are in my path for all three.

Chapter One

I f Nancy Baxter had known that she was turning loose a major shit storm, she would never have put Stella's name on the prayer list down at the church in Cadillac, Texas. But she hadn't had the benefit of hindsight that hot southern night, and she really did want Stella to get married. So when Heather, the president of the Prayer Angels, asked if anyone wanted to add a name to the list, Nancy had spoken right up and said, "Pray for my daughter. She needs a husband."

The Angels took their spirituality seriously, so the praying began in earnest, and before they were done God had been petitioned by a dozen women to send a husband to Cadillac and to earmark him special for Stella Baxter. No one dared to ask why she needed a husband, but they did have their ideas, which turned into juicy gossip by the next morning.

ల్య

Stella hummed a song from a Pistol Annies CD when she opened the door to her beauty shop, the Yellow Rose, that Friday morning. She set the control to the air conditioner back a few notches and swept up a few dead crickets from the waiting area in the front part of the shop.

Hair dryers heated up the small room, though customers liked to be cool. If it was this hot the day before the official first day of summer, then by the end of July it would be even hotter than the famous jalapeño peppers they grew in Cadillac, Texas.

The Yellow Rose Beauty Shop had started out fifty years before as a small clothing store, so it had a big display window in the front. It had taken lots of planning when they were designing the shop, but they'd finally decided to use yellow carpet in the display area and put a white cast-iron bistro set in it. A mason jar with three yellow silk roses and Queen Anne's lace sat in the middle of the table.

They'd left a wide expanse of floor open from the front to the three styling stations at the back. Covered in light-brown tile that shone like glass, it was easy to clean. A soft leather sofa the color of freshly churned butter on one side with a coffee table in front of it took up space on one wall, and a glass-topped table with four chairs around it was across the area on the other wall. Hairstyling magazines were scattered on both tables. Stella stopped long enough to arrange them before she went on back to her station.

To the right of the styling stations, three shampoo sinks with chairs had been installed with a small bookcase separating them from the front area. Above the sinks were posters of her, Charlotte's, and Piper's three favorite movies: *Gone with the Wind*, *Steel Magnolias*, and *Something to Talk About*. A door led into a back room that had once been the place where shoes were stored on shelving. Now it held a weathered wooden table with four mismatched chairs around it. The table was used for folding towels, doing paperwork, and/or having lunch. A washer and dryer sat in the corner with a dorm-size refrigerator topped with a microwave beside it. And the shoe shelves now served for perms, hair dye, shampoo, and racks of towels and capes.

Stella checked her reflection in the mirror while she waited on her first customer of the day. Thank God, only her droopy eyes gave away the fact that she'd slept very little in tangled-up, sweaty sheets after a long night of sex in a motel up in Durant, Oklahoma. If someone could look into her face and see both the happiness and the fear, she'd be in big trouble.

If anyone did notice her tired eyes, she'd pass it off as allergies. She would never, ever admit that she'd only slept a few hours between the time she'd gotten off work the day before and that morning when the alarm went off. Not even to her two best friends and business partners, Charlotte and Piper. She pulled her naturally curly red hair up into a messy ponytail and tied a bright purple scarf around it, hoping that Charlotte and Piper would fuss at her for not fixing her hair and not notice her baggy eyes.

"Hey, are you the only one here?" The bell above the door dinged when Trixie Matthews pushed her way inside. "Ahhh, cool air. We're in for a scorching-hot summer. I love what y'all did with this old building, Stella. It's light and airy and I feel like I'm in an uptown salon every time I walk in here. I know I've said it before, but I wish more businesses would refurbish the old part of town."

Stella waved her over to a chair. "Maybe they will, but this is just a beauty shop. *Salon* sounds like a big-city place. It takes time to rebuild a town when it's got one foot in the grave and the other on a pod of boiled okra. I was just thinking the same thing about this summer."

Picking up a cape and shaking the wrinkles out, Stella went on, "We're due a long, lazy old summer, but it will pass fast and then it'll be time for the jubilee. Tomorrow is the official first day of the season and the weatherman says that today it's going to reach the three-digit mark for the first time this year." She motioned Trixie into the chair. "Have a seat and we'll get you all fixed up. Cut and highlight, right? So what's going on with you and your doctor fellow? Have y'all set a date yet? Oh, and speaking of the jubilee, how's the jalapeño pepper crop coming along?"

Trixie had to hop to get settled into the chair. She pulled off a baseball hat and set her light-brown hair free. She'd always reminded Stella of Ashley Judd in size and looks, but maybe with a few more pounds on her curvy body. "We're taking it slow. Besides, I don't have time to plan my own wedding what with all these other ones going on in town. And Cathy keeps those peppers watered every day. I think she might tell them bedtime stories and that's the secret as to how they get so hot. She might be reading them those erotic romance books that she reads all the time. I read one, and believe me, if she's reading those to the pepper plants, they'll be plenty hot this year."

Stella whipped a black cape around Trixie's shoulders. "You'll be the prettiest bride Cadillac has ever seen when you do decide to get married again. And I wouldn't doubt anything that Cathy does to make those peppers hot. Daddy says they're the best in the whole world."

"That is so sweet, but darlin', I had that big wedding thing once. I don't want it again. A trip to the courthouse is more down my alley. I hear that you're on the way to the altar, too. The gossip is hotter than the peppers this morning up at Clawdy's."

Stella's heart stopped and all the color left her face. The purple scarf didn't even put color into her ashen cheeks.

Trixie reached out from under the cape and touched her arm. "Hey, you look like you saw a ghost. I was just teasing."

After a couple of good solid thumps, Stella's heart went back to pumping and high color filled her cheeks. She'd been so careful the past six months, mostly because she didn't want to jinx something that was so perfect and yet so wrong.

"Why would you think such a thing?" Stella whispered.

"It was the gossip from the breakfast crew at Clawdy's this morning. They said that Nancy put you on the prayer list last night."

"I'm not sick. And what does that have to do with marriage?" Stella gasped.

"Maybe you are lovesick." Trixie laughed.

"I can't imagine why she'd do that," Stella said.

"Gossip has it that she just said to pray for you, that you needed a husband, and they prayed. But this morning everyone is speculating about why you need a husband, and if it's safe to breathe in all these fumes if you are pregnant, and who the father is."

Stella leaned against the counter. "Oh. My. God."

The business. Dammit! The beauty shop would fold. They'd only been open a year. "Everyone in town knows?"

"Probably. Didn't you drive past the church on your way to work this morning?"

Stella shook her head.

Trixie flipped open her phone. "I took a picture."

"Of the church?" Stella asked.

"Of the sign. See."

There it was, right on the big white wooden sign located at the edge of the church lawn in black lettering: "Pray for My Daughter. She Needs a Husband."

Stella blanched then blushed.

"It doesn't say whose daughter or why, but someone put it out there for the whole world to see. I bet the church is packed this next Sunday so everyone can see for sure who is at the top of the list. Preacher Jed reads it every Sunday before the sermon, remember?"

Stella tried to speak, but words wouldn't go from brain to mouth. Her face burned. Her hands shook so bad that she laid the scissors down and ran a comb through Trixie's hair. No way would she trust herself to cut hair until she settled down.

"I'd be pissed if I was you," Trixie said.

Piper came through the back door into the shop. "Who's pissed? They can join my club since I'm permanently pissed. Hey, Stella, have you seen the billboard in front of the church? I saw it when I took the boys to day care. Who's got a pregnant daughter in town?"

Instead of a hairdresser, Piper could have been a plus-size model with her height, sexy curves, and big brown eyes. She pulled off a baseball hat and shook out a thick mane of gorgeous honey-blonde hair that fell into soft curls around her face without a bit of styling. She sat down in her swivel chair, threw one long leg decked out in bright-yellow leggings over the other, and adjusted the collar of a flowing sleeveless blouse printed with huge sunflowers.

Piper looked from Trixie to Stella. "What's going on? I don't think it's ever been this quiet in the shop. The crickets are even quiet."

"Shhh." Trixie put a finger over her lips. "She's about to explode. I can feel it."

"What happened?" Piper whispered.

Trixie adjusted the cape over her lap. "Nancy put Stella on the prayer list down at the church last night. She's the daughter who needs a husband."

"Holy shit! I told you it was a bad idea to come back here. And what happens when we do? Gene divorces me. Charlotte gets all serious about her knitting again. And now you are pregnant. I bet Nancy is ready to do more than shoot you." Piper finally took a deep breath.

"I am not pregnant!" Stella raised her voice. This could not possibly have happened at a worse time. What in the hell was her mother thinking?

"Then why would Nancy think you need a husband? Not that she and I are in agreement on that issue. God only knows if I'd known then what I know now, I damn sure wouldn't have married Gene Stephens when I got pregnant with the twins. Hell, no! I would have just raised them by myself and saved myself the misery. Okay, fess up. Why did Nancy do that?"

Trixie answered, "Morning gossip up at Miss Clawdy's Café says that Nancy wants a grandbaby by Mother's Day, which means that Stella should have a husband by the first week in August. Evidently she wants a legitimate grandbaby."

"That's right before your birthday, Stella," Piper said.

"Who's getting a grandbaby by Mother's Day?" Charlotte called out from the back door.

"Did you drive past the church this morning?" Piper asked.

Charlotte tucked her purse into the cabinet in front of the chair where Stella sat and carried her knitting bag to the sofa. She pulled out a set of circular needles and six inches of pale-yellow baby blanket. "Yes, I did, and what does that sign mean? Who's pregnant? Who is getting a baby by Mother's Day? Boone and I've decided to wait two years to get pregnant. Mama says that I shouldn't start a family when I'm past thirty, but if we wait two years then I'll only be twenty-nine when the baby comes. Now, would somebody please tell me whose daughter needs a husband because she's pregnant?" Charlotte asked.

"Nancy's," Piper said.

Charlotte flipped around, wide-eyed, and slapped a hand over her mouth. "You are pregnant? You didn't tell us you were dating. Dear Lord, you are as pale as a sheet. Have you had morning sickness yet?"

Stella stood up and started to pace. "Some friends you are. I'll say it one more time—I'm not pregnant. I can't believe Mama did this. She's lived here her whole life and she knows how folks talk. This could ruin our business. You know what small-town gossip can do. We don't need a scandal like this."

"Settle down. It'll blow over in a couple of days," Piper said.

Stella kept pacing, fighting back the tears welling up behind her eyelids. "The town is barely big enough for two beauty shops as it is, and we've just now got things built up and . . ." Her voice got louder with each word. The lump in her throat was bigger than a grapefruit, and no matter how hard she swallowed, it would not go down.

"Slow down, girl," Trixie said. "Like Piper said, it'll all blow over by next week. They'll put something else on the sign and the gossip about you will be old news. You know what they do with yesterday's newspaper, don't you? They wrap raw fish in it or put it on the bottom of birdcages."

"We can always sell out and go back to Dallas," Piper said.

"Or maybe we could go to Walmart in Sherman. I hear they're always looking for good help in the beauty shop up there," Charlotte said.

"I'm not going anywhere," Stella declared. "And I don't need a husband and I'm pissed and I could just . . ." She went to the back room; sat down at the table that served as a place to eat, do business, and fold clothing; and put her head on her arms. She wouldn't cry, not with Trixie there, even if she was a friend. She wouldn't. She refused to let one tear fall. But it did, and then a river washed down her face, taking mascara and blush with it but none of the pain.

Charlotte and Piper hurried to her side, pulled out chairs, and patted her shoulder, her arm, and her knee.

"I've never seen you cry like this," Charlotte said.

"Not since that rotten boy ruined your reputation our sophomore year," Piper said.

"I'd almost forgotten about that son of a bitch," Charlotte said.

"You've got every right to be pissed." Trixie laid a hand on her shoulder. "I'll come back later for a cut and highlights. I understand how you feel, but don't worry about the shop. If we've proven anything up at Clawdy's, it's that gossip is damn good for business."

"I'll do your hair, Trixie," Piper said. "I don't have an appointment for another hour, so I can do it with no problem. Just take a seat in my chair and I'll be right there. Stella, pull yourself together. This isn't the end of the world."

Charlotte whispered, "What happens if God answers their prayers? We're right in the middle of planning my wedding. I don't mean to be selfish, but we've barely got started and those Angels are pretty powerful. My aunt is on the team and she's a true believer."

"She can't get married at all and neither should any of you," Piper said. "It's all real good until about that seventh year and then he'll decide he wants to be a bachelor again and he's not ready for those two kids you had. No, he doesn't want to share custody. Every other weekend and two weeks in the summer is fine with him because he and the bitch he's sleeping with are too busy to take care of kids any more than that. Then you'll be totally responsible for six-year-old twin boys and all the bills."

Stella heard them talking. She understood that they had her best interests at heart even if they did disagree. Charlotte wanted her to be as happy as she was with Boone, and Piper wasn't over the pain of a divorce. Stella was happier than she'd ever been in her whole life, but she wasn't ready to tell anyone about her new love . . . not yet.

Keeping a great big secret from them both was hard enough, but keeping it from her mother had been tougher. Mixed emotions shot through Stella. She was pissed—God almighty, but she was pissed—but a tiny little part of her heart understood that her mama only had her best interests at heart. Too bad that little 10 percent couldn't do anything about the pissed-off 90 percent.

Her phone rang and she answered it, "Have you seen that sign?"

"Yes, sweetheart, I saw it. Are you okay? What do you want to do?" the familiar deep voice asked. "You want me to cancel the meeting this morning and come to the shop? You sound like you've been crying. I can't stand to think of you upset like this."

"I'll be okay, and no, a thousand times no, don't come to the shop. We've got to keep this under wraps for a few weeks, and if you walked in the door right now, I'd melt into your arms in a weeping mess."

"I love you, Stella," he said.

"I love you right back. I'll be fine and I'll see you later tonight."

Her forehead made a pop when it hit the table again. Her gut twisted up tighter than a hangman's noose, and she forgot to inhale until her lungs started to burn.

She sat up and said loudly as she headed back into the shop, "I should go down to the church and set that damn sign on fire."

"The more you stir in shit, the worse it smells. Laugh it off when anyone asks you about it. Tell them you're having triplets and Nancy is going to have to babysit them so you can make a living since you don't have a husband. Spread it around that Nancy will be sorry she ever wanted a grandchild since they're all going be red-haired demons," Trixie said.

"I'm only twenty-six. I'm not an old maid," Stella said.

"No wonder everyone in town is so happy to see so many weddings going on. We are known for our hot peppers. We sure wouldn't want that to change to being known for having too many old maids in town," Trixie teased.

Stella slumped down on the other end of the sofa from Charlotte, leaned her head back, and pinched the bridge of her nose with two fingers. It didn't erase the headache but at least she'd stopped seeing red dots in front of her eyes. "I can't go to church on Sunday with that sign out there, and besides, Jed always reads the prayer list."

"Oh, yes, you can and you will," Trixie said. "If you don't go, the gossip will just get worse. They'll say that you are home with morning sickness. Besides, you'll be at the piano, so nobody will turn around and stare at you when he says your name."

Piper finished the haircut and motioned for Trixie to follow her to the shampoo sink. "I agree with Trixie. Pretend it's all a big joke. Sit right there on the piano bench and smile. It will take him three minutes to read the whole list and then he'll start preaching. Everyone will forget the names by the time he gets finished."

Trixie nodded in agreement. "It'll be good for both of our businesses. Folks will flock to the café to gossip and then they'll come by here to make an appointment and take a look at Stella. The minute they walk out the door, they'll call everyone they know to report that you don't have a baby bump yet. You have just become Cadillac's brand-new celebrity."

Stella's hand went from nose to eyes. "What if everyone in town starts trying to find a husband for me? Mama has already embarrassed the hell out of me on more than one Sunday, inviting men over to dinner and expecting me to be nice to them."

She inhaled deeply and whispered, "Dear Lord, what has she done?"

Charlotte's needles clicked as she created a lovely cable pattern on the baby blanket she was working on. "This wouldn't have happened if you'd picked one out. Now she's not the only one looking for a husband for you—the whole town will join in the manhunt. And as far as the preacher reading the list, darlin', I wouldn't care if that man read the dictionary on Sunday morning. I'd drool no matter what he read. He's so sexy it's a shame he's a preacher."

"The preacher?" Piper asked.

Charlotte looked up from her knitting with a twinkle in her eyes. "Yes, ma'am!"

"You are engaged! You shouldn't be looking at other men like that." Stella sat up straight, dry-eyed and unblinking.

"That don't mean I'm dead. I might diet on occasion, but it don't mean I can't look at the ice cream at the grocery store. Mmmmm, ice cream on the preacher's—"

Stella grabbed a bottle of window cleaner and headed toward the front of the shop. "I've got to do something to keep from taking a sledgehammer to that sign."

Piper hollered over the sound of running water, "I just did those windows yesterday."

"I know you did, but my hands are shaking and Charlotte talking about the preacher's equipment isn't helping one bit," Stella said.

"I wasn't going to say his equipment." Charlotte giggled. "I was going to say his Bible. And besides, God is too busy scouring the earth for a husband for you to be busy slinging lightning at me, so come on back over here and sit down."

"You're lyin', girlfriend! The look on your face had nothing to do with the Good Book," Piper said.

Stella didn't see anything funny in any of it, not the Angels, the sign, or the comments. An ominous black cloud hung above her, and the air was static with electricity. The Yellow Rose would have clean windows and a gorgeous display window, but could it withstand all the gossip? Would her clients leave her and go to Ruby's down the street? Worse yet, could her love life withstand the scrutiny? It wouldn't surprise her one bit to be out on the street with nothing but an overdue bank note and a broken heart.

Absolutely nothing could get worse.

And then her mother waved at her from the other side of the window.

"Good mornin', girls." Nancy breezed through the front door. "I had to make an early morning run up to Sherman, so I brought y'all a dozen doughnuts. Why are you cleaning those windows? Didn't Charlotte do them yesterday?"

Stella's jaw ached from clamping it shut so tightly. If she opened her mouth, the words that spewed out would take the paint right off the wall.

"No, ma'am, I cleaned them yesterday," Piper said.

Charlotte put her knitting to the side and made a hasty retreat to the back room to organize the stock shelves.

Nancy set the doughnuts on the coffee table in front of the dryers. "What's going on in this place? All of a sudden it's quiet as a funeral. Y'all know something I don't. Did someone die? Oh, no, has your Agnes Flynn died, Trixie?"

"No, ma'am," Trixie said. "She's alive and well and believe me, she will be meddlin' in whatever happens next in Cadillac. You seen the sign down at the church?"

"What sign?" Nancy asked.

Trixie handed her phone to Piper. She found the picture and held it out to Nancy.

"Oh, no! I didn't tell them to do that. I just . . . oh, shit! The prayer list is confidential . . ."

"Not when they read it on Sunday morning before services," Charlotte said.

"I didn't think about that. Lord love a duck." She gasped her favorite saying.

"I'm really, really pissed off, Mama," Stella said around the lump in her throat and the heaviness in her chest.

Nancy popped her hands on her hips. "Well, I've tried everything else. I've practically dragged men off the streets to find you a husband. *You* won't take care of business, so maybe God and the Angels can. Heather is responsible for that sign, so don't blame me. And I will not apologize for praying for you."

Stella took several steps forward, tiptoed slightly, and went nose to nose with her mother. "That prayer list is for the sick and folks who are needy. Shit fire, Mama! It's not for a husband or a new car or a new boat. What if Agnes did need the prayers and died because y'all were praying for a husband to fall out of the clouds and into my life?"

Nancy pushed back her naturally curly salt-and-pepper hair, but she didn't blink as she stood her ground against Stella. "The Good Book says to ask and it shall be given. It does not say what you can or cannot ask for. It just says to ask believing and the desires of your heart will be granted. I desire a grandbaby and I'm asking. It does not say that you cannot ask for a son-in-law or a new car or a new boat. But don't tell your daddy that. All I've heard since he retired is that his fishing boat is too small since he can go every day now."

"This is not about Daddy's fishin' boat, and you'd better be careful what you ask for. It all could come back around and bite you square on the ass. Everyone in town thinks I need a husband because I'm pregnant. If you want a grandbaby maybe I could arrange that without a husband," Stella said tersely.

"You wouldn't dare." Nancy took a couple of steps back and gasped like a fish out of water. After a long pause, she whispered, "I guess it'd be too much to ask to get my hair trimmed this morning?"

"I wouldn't trust her with scissors if I was you," Piper whispered.

"Then you cut my hair," Nancy said.

"Not on your life. I wouldn't touch anyone's hair who's prayin' for a marriage to take place. I wouldn't wish a damn husband on my worst enemy, and Stella is my friend." Piper followed Trixie back to the chair to do her highlights.

"Charlotte!" Nancy yelled.

Charlotte poked her head out of the door to the supply room. "No, ma'am. I have to work every day with Stella. If I cut your hair, she'll think I'm on your side. I wish Stella could find someone to love her like Boone loves me, but it would be wise if you'd take her name off the list and let her do her own husband hunting."

"This isn't the only beauty shop in town," Nancy said.

"No, it isn't. You go on down to the other one and take your doughnuts with you," Stella said. "I'm going to be mad for a long time, Mama. You should have thought about the consequences of what you were doing. We've got a business to run, and you know how people gossip in Cadillac."

"Sunday dinner?" Nancy narrowed her eyes.

"Won't be at your house," Stella said bluntly.

Nancy picked up the box of doughnuts. "What will I tell your daddy?"

"Tell him he's not going to be a grandfather on Mother's Day. Tell him that he might never be a grandfather if someone doesn't take that shit off the church billboard and my name off that list."

Piper waited until Nancy was gone to light into Stella. "I'm your friend and this is embarrassing, humiliating, and horrible but Nancy is your mother, girl. You only get one mother in this lifetime. Think about it before you cut off your nose to spite your face. I don't want you to get married. Hell, I don't want any woman to get married after what I've been through, but don't blame Nancy for all of it. Heather is in charge of the church sign."

Stella's eyes went to Charlotte, who said, "Don't look at me. I'd probably burn my mama alive if she did something like that."

Stella tucked her chin into her chest. "Charlotte, you are pure genius. We could get some kindlin' and tie Heather to the sign before we set it on fire. Burn the witch at the stake. Maybe that would make everyone who is gossiping at least think about what they're saying."

"Witch!" Charlotte said. "You got that wrong. She's not a witch. She's a full-fledged, card-carryin', bona fide bitch."

CHAPTER TWO

Southern women do not sweat. They get dewy, or in very hot weather they might perspire, but that was said in whispers. It was too damn hot for Nancy Baxter to be getting dewy or perspiring. It was too damn hot for an angry, chubby fifty-plus-year-old woman to be trotting across an asphalt church parking lot. She was downright sweating and that was all there was to it. But there wasn't a single parking spot on either side of the street at Ruby's Beauty Shop, so Nancy had to park a block away in the CNC church parking lot.

Her thighs stuck together but she wasn't about to reach up under her skirt and swipe that away with a tissue. Gossip would have it that Nancy had lost her mind and was wiping her ass right there in the church parking lot because her daughter had gotten pregnant out of wedlock. Who in the hell had authorized that damn sign, anyway, and why hadn't they called her before they did it? She wanted to cry or kick the hell out of something or maybe both.

Heat and fighting with Stella had always jacked up her blood pressure. Stella knew that and she should know better than to argue with her when the day started off at ninety degrees with the possibility of triple digits before noon. It would be all Stella's fault if

Nancy crumpled in a heap of sweat and bones right there on Main Street in Cadillac, Texas, before she ever got a grandchild.

Her ears buzzed and her pulse raced. Hot salty tears stung her eyes. That damned Heather had sweet-talked the last preacher into letting her take care of the church sign when she first came to Cadillac. When he retired and Jed took over, it was like that sign about guns—until they pried it out of her cold, dead hands, no one was getting the box of letters to make words on the sign.

Figuring she'd just about taxed her body to the last degree, Nancy climbed the steps to Miss Clawdy's Café and sat down in the porch swing to catch her breath. Thank God, the Andrews girls had left the porch swing up when they'd turned the old house into a café after their mother died.

How would Stella feel if she just keeled over right there on that swing? Fell forward with her eyes rolled up in the back of her head and her hair needing fixed.

She frowned as she dabbed at the moisture running down her neck and beading up under her nose. She smeared makeup over a tissue when she ran it over her face and across her eyelids. She was not going to apologize to Stella for something she hadn't done, by damn. But she would turn that damn sign into splinters if it wasn't down by noon.

That was, if she lived until noon. Was everything truly ready for her to pass on to eternity? Her hair was a fright but the undertaker could call in Ruby to fix it. She'd rise right up out of her coffin if they let Stella anywhere near her after the way she'd carried on about the prayer list.

It had been weeks since Nancy had plucked her eyebrows. Well, Ruby would have to take care of that, too. She had shaved her legs the night before so there shouldn't be too much flak about that when the old gossips talked about her passing on at such a young age right there on the café porch.

Did her underbritches have holes in them? She couldn't remember, so she discreetly pulled her shirt up and checked. They were the new ones with the good elastic, so yes, she could pass away right there on Main Street if she got too hot or too angry. She had on clean underpants, so not a single woman in town could fault her.

She'd cleaned her house and her oven the day before in case God answered prayers real quick like and Stella brought her new fiancé's parents to visit on Sunday after church. So when the ladies came to mourn, they wouldn't find a nasty oven to heat up the casseroles. She hoped they all brought corn casserole, because Stella hated it.

Just thinking her daughter's name twisted her heart up into a hangman's knot. She'd never liked fighting with Stella, not even when she went through that rebellious stage in high school and wore her skirts too tight and her makeup too thick.

Nancy took a deep breath, banished thoughts of caskets and weeping, and said aloud, "I'm not going to give Stella the satisfaction of me traipsing up to the pearly gates before God sends her a husband. I didn't know they were going to publicize this damn thing, but she can just damn sure get ready to pick out a big white dress and look at wedding cakes."

That's when the tears broke the dam and flowed down her cheeks to mingle with the salty sweat on her neck. She put her hands over her eyes and let them come. Whether in anger at Heather or sorrow at fighting with her daughter or a mixture of the two, they didn't do their job. When she wiped them away with the soggy tissue in her hand, she was still mad and sad at the same time.

She pushed out of the swing and with determination walked the last half block to Ruby's. It had been Ella's Beauty Shop until she retired and her younger sister took over the shop. A blast of cold air met her when she threw open the door, and she inhaled deeply only to start coughing when the pungent aroma of permanent solution and nail polish remover filled her lungs.

It was about half the size of the Yellow Rose, with only one styling station, two dryer chairs, a chair for pedicures, and a table for manicures. Folks who were waiting in line had a choice of one of four folding chairs pushed up under a little round table over in the corner.

"You better sit down," Ruby said. "You look a little dewy, like you're about to pass plumb out. Did you walk through a sprinkler? We heard that you and Stella got into it down at the Yellow Rose. Kids! They're worse than husbands."

"I did not walk through water, and yes, ma'am, kids can be trying, especially when they grow up and think they know everything. And this is not dew; it's plain old sweat that comes from anger and heat. How did you know about Stella, anyway? I just came from there. Can you work me in for a haircut this morning?" she said in a rush, hoping her voice didn't break.

Ruby's honey-blonde hair showed gray at the roots. The bright-red lipstick on her mouth was long gone but that part on the edges had seeped into wrinkles. Her stretch capris bagged on her bony frame and varicose veins twisted down her legs from calves to toes. "We saw the sign and you stopped at the Yellow Rose this morning. It don't take much to figure it out, especially with Stella's temper. And yes, I've got time to cut your hair."

"Need your nails done, too?" Kayla asked from her table.

"Not today," Nancy answered.

Beulah tucked her chin down into her ample chest and picked up the hankie in her lap. It was a perfectly creased little square with no wrinkles, but the day was still young. "Was Stella really angry? Maybe we should take her off the list. Or maybe Heather shouldn't have put up that sign."

Nancy leaned her head back and pinched her nose with two fingers, trying to stop the raging headache. Heather had been at odds with Stella since the day she moved to Cadillac after marrying Quinn. She'd wanted Stella to give up playing the piano for the church so that she could have the job. When Stella refused, it brought out sarcasm and pure old bitchiness.

"Well, there is Heather now," Beulah said. "We can talk to her about it."

Heather slung open the door and smiled at everyone. She wore a floral silk skirt and a pink cotton sweater, and her jet-black hair was cut at chin level, which made her baby face look even rounder. Her brown eyes were set close together and were lost when she smiled. She was slightly overweight and sweat beaded up on her thick neck, but she still wore panty hose and pink high heels.

"Good morning, ladies. I trust you've all seen the church sign. We're serious about our praying, aren't we?" Heather flashed a tight little smile. "Ruby, I just need my nails done today, so don't be looking at the appointment book. I don't come in until next week for a cut."

"Stella is pretty upset," Beulah said.

"Most sinners get angry when they know they're being prayed for," Heather said.

"Stella is not a sinner, and you should have talked to me or at least to Jed before you put that sign up. It needs to come down right now," Nancy said.

"Of course she is. We have all sinned and come short. It says so in the Bible. Brother Jed preached about it two weeks ago, remember. But we can pray and pray until God sees fit to send her a good husband like he did when he sent Quinn to me. He will hear our prayers and answer them if we ask believing. Beulah is here and I see Floy over there getting her nails done, so we should talk about our next step in the program."

Program? Holy hell and damnation! It had gone from a simple prayer request to a billboard and now a program? Nancy wanted to throw herself on the floor and have a tantrum like a two-year-old.

Floy held up her freshly done pale-pink fingernails. They looked out of place with her long-sleeved navy-blue dress buttoned all the way up to her scrawny, wrinkled neck and her tight little gray bun perched on top of her head.

"Heather and I visited a long time after the prayer meeting last night. We've come up with a plan. If we help someone like Stella find a husband, why, there will be dozens and dozens of young women flocking to our church asking for our prayers," Floy said.

Heather took her place behind Kayla's nail table and spread her fingers out. A short, round woman with a thick waist, thin dark hair, and squinty eyes behind tiny little round glasses, she put on her best smile as she looked over her shoulder at the other ladies.

"In a year, we might have our own website where we can enlist the prayers of women the world over for their friends, daughters, and sisters who need a husband." She sounded absolutely ecstatic with joy. "In five years we might have our own television station where we can lay hands on the single women and God will put a man in their lives. And to think, Nancy, it will have all started with Stella. If we can just find a husband for her, why, the sky is the limit. We'll build a bigger church and Cadillac will grow into a city the size of Dallas. I have a vision that starts with Stella. If we can get God to answer our prayers for someone like her, then the world will bow at our toes. So the answer is no, that sign doesn't come down until Stella has a husband."

"Someone like her?" Nancy raised her voice.

"You know your daughter. She's strong willed, has a wild reputation in Cadillac, and lives up to the stereotype of her red hair. I was surprised that they let her play the piano for services after the stories I heard. I offered to take over the job, but she wouldn't give it up. But still . . ." She let her voice trail off a second before she went on. "She is the perfect example to begin my new ministry with. If we can find a man willing to take her for his wife, we can do wonders with other women."

"Take her name off the list and take down that damn sign or I will tear it down with my bare hands," Nancy said.

Heather cocked her head to one side and pursed her thin mouth into a firm line for a second before she answered. "Not on your life. God has spoken to me. He will find your daughter a husband."

"If I was Nancy or Stella either one, I'd be in tears," Beulah whispered.

The whole shop went as quiet as a sinner approaching the pearly gates. Everyone held their breath and waited for Nancy to slap sense into the woman.

Finally after a full thirty seconds, Heather shrugged dramatically. "Tears are the beginning of repentance, Miz Beulah. I'm going to pray night and day for Stella. We will fulfill our destiny. We've got the power of the angels on our side." She tilted her chin up a notch before she went on, "Kayla, I want bright-red polish this week so the Lord can see it when I raise my hands in prayer for Stella. And I've ordered a red banner that says 'Prayerathon on Sunday' to put across the top of the church doors. A week from next Sunday we will have a potluck after services and we will take turns going to the prayer room and praying for Stella."

Nancy was speechless. The shit storm had hit, and there wasn't a thing she could do but duck and cover her head.

Heather went on in her shrill voice, "The Bible says that God helps those who help themselves. So we're going to help him. First thing we're doing is right here in front of Ruby's next Monday morning, we're having a bake sale."

The fact that Ruby motioned her over to the chair was the only thing that kept Nancy in the shop.

"A bake sale?" Nancy asked.

Heather wasn't interested in helping Stella find a husband. She was trying to ruin her business and run her out of town. Well, Nancy might be angry at Stella, but by damn no one else had that right, especially Heather.

Ruby swung a cape around Nancy's shoulders. "I'm closed on Monday and the porch is in the shade, so y'all won't get too warm that way. And I'll donate one of my Mississippi mud cakes and leave the front door open for y'all to have access to the restroom. I don't turn on the air-conditioning until Monday night, so I can't promise cool air."

What would Agnes say about all this? Nancy thought before she asked, "You think God will work faster if we put more money in the church offering plate? Are you crazy, Heather? God isn't interested in money. He has streets of gold. Why would he need money?"

"No, but I think if there's more men for Stella to meet, then she just might see one she likes," Heather answered. "Are men's haircuts down at the Yellow Rose still going for ten dollars a pop?"

Nancy nodded. *Now what, Agnes? What do we do to nip this shit in the bud? She's not sending men down to the Yellow Rose to help my daughter but to embarrass the hell out of her. Does playing the piano mean that much to her?*

"We plan to give a ten-dollar money order made out to the Yellow Rose to every eligible bachelor that we run across. Every dime we make on the bake sale is going into money orders for haircuts. She'll be so busy by Wednesday that she'll wonder if she's a barbershop instead of a fancy beauty shop," Heather said.

"Kind of like that old sayin' about Muhammad and the mountain," Kayla said as she filed Heather's nails.

"She won't know what happened until one of those guys walks in and she's love struck." Ruby grinned.

Nancy sat straight up in the chair. "Do not, and I repeat, do not give one of those money orders to our preacher or to Rhett Monroe."

"I can understand not giving one to Rhett. He's a player, but why not Brother Jed? He's a bachelor even if he is a preacher. He'll feel slighted if y'all don't give him a money order and he already gets his hair cut down there anyway so he'll just be getting a freebie. Lord, I wish I was five or six years older. He's so sexy I could turn into a preacher's wife real easy." Kayla giggled.

Kayla wore her short burgundy hair in a spiked hairdo that seemed to defy gravity. Her nails were purple that day and three sets of pierced earrings dangled up her ears. A heavy gold necklace draped down between two inches of cleavage that peeked out from a low-cut tank top. Ella would never have let her come to work like that. And she would have never allowed her to have a rose tattoo on her thigh, either, but Ruby thought it was all cute.

"Kayla! He's a man of God," Heather gasped.

"He might be, but he's a man, too. And I'd go to Sunday dinner with him at Nancy's any week she wants to invite both of us." Kayla giggled.

"He's too old for you, child," Ruby said.

"Y'all are bringin' God down from heaven when he's got wars and big things to think about just to find a husband for Stella so you can have some kind of marriage ministry. And you think age would matter if the sexy preacher fell for a girl ten years younger than him? I bet he's not a day over thirty and I'll be twenty-one here in a few weeks. Hey, once Stella is married off, will you put my name on your sign, Heather?" Kayla asked.

Nancy sighed. Out of the mouths of babes and a twenty-year-old manicurist with a tat and flapping earrings came the kernel of the matter. She longed to rush back down to Stella's and tell her all about what was really happening, but she had to make this all right before she did a damn thing.

You should have remembered that Heather was president of the Prayer Angels, and that she had control of that damned sign. The sassy voice in her head sounded just like Agnes.

Nancy might not be able to tear down the church sign without spending time in jail, but she could do something. As soon as she got out of the chair she would call Agnes Flynn. If anyone in town could put things to rights, it was Agnes. She was eighty years old and ornery as a rattlesnake, and there wasn't a person in town who messed with Agnes.

Kayla was saying something else but Nancy didn't catch it. She tuned in to the conversation in time to hear Heather's voice raise an octave higher when she said, "I can take my business somewhere else if you're going to make fun of my ministry."

"I'm so sorry. I did not mean to offend." Kayla's voice said one thing but the tone said the exact opposite.

"You are forgiven. Now let's talk about that gold fingernail you fixed for my precious aunt Violet?"

Kayla nodded. "Yes, ma'am."

"I want one. The ark of the covenant was covered with gold. It will be my sign and a pledge of my vow to God that I will not stop praying until Stella is married," she said.

Or until she is run plumb out of town, Nancy thought.

"Which finger? They are expensive, but I've got them in all sizes," Kayla said.

"I think for this time my pinky finger will do fine. When we start charging for our marriage ministry services, I will get a bigger one. Don't you worry, Miz Nancy, I have faith." Heather raised the hand with five red nails toward the ceiling. "The Lord is with the Angels."

Nancy could not leave with half her hair cut and the other part still shaggy and she couldn't rip all those red fingernails from Heather's hand, but she could sure make a phone call to Agnes. Heather was not running Stella out of Cadillac, not on Nancy's watch.

"Y'all have to promise me that you won't give one of those haircut money orders to Brother Jed. Everett cusses worse than a drunk, horny sailor on a good day. If he's mad, his cussin' will blister the paint right off of walls. I'd just die if y'all gave a voucher to Brother Jed and Stella fell for him. A preacher would never come around our place. I want my new son-in-law to be part of the family, and besides, Stella cusses as bad as her daddy," Nancy said.

Heather clicked her tongue against the roof of her mouth, eyes glaring at Nancy as if she were an errant child, and pointed one finger her way. "If Brother Jed fell for Stella, he'd be marryin' Stella, not Everett. But why are you frettin'? He's a man of God. He wouldn't fall for the likes of Stella even if she does play the church piano," Heather said bluntly. "I don't know why they ever let her have that job knowing that she cusses as bad as her daddy and drinks so much."

"My child," Nancy said through clenched teeth, "might cuss, and a beer on Saturday night does not make her a drunk."

Floy spoke up from the corner. "And the new son-in-law, whoever he is, and Nancy have to have a good relationship or he won't let her babysit the grandbaby when it gets here. If he can't go to her house because of the cussin' that Everett does, I don't see him letting her keep his child. But I agree, Heather, we can't slight the preacher. We'll give him a free haircut with the knowledge that God will protect him."

"I vote that Rhett gets one, too. God can always turn his life around just like he's going to do Stella's." Heather turned the conversation back around to the bake sale. "Now let's decide who is making what for the biggest bake sale Cadillac has ever seen."

ร

Stella liked Agnes Flynn. She really did. On any other day she'd be happy to see the old girl and listen to her colorful stories, but not that day. But there was Agnes pushing her way into the Yellow Rose—red hair, bibbed overalls, flip-flops smacking on the tile floor until she stopped and stood under the air-conditioning vent for a minute before she sat down in Piper's chair.

"I need a little color applied to the roots. This short hair is a hell of a lot easier to take care of, but I have to get y'all to touch up the roots twice as often and that's a real bitch. But before you put me in the shampoo chair, I heard that Nancy is down at Ruby's with Heather, Floy, and Beulah. And they are plotting against Stella."

Stella dropped the broom she was using to sweep up hair. "Well, shit!"

"That's exactly what I thought, but don't worry. I've got a connection who feeds me information and here in a few minutes we'll know the rest of what they've got up their sleeves. Who are you knitting that baby blanket for, Charlotte? Is that why Stella needs a husband?" Agnes asked.

"I hope not," Charlotte said. "It's for your niece, Cathy. I wanted to make it pink, but Cathy is doing the nursery in yellow checks. I'm going to add a border of pink and then make little booties, a sweater, and a hat to go with it."

"Why would you tell me what your connection says?" Stella asked.

"Because I can't stand Violet Prescott, and she is Heather's aunt, so she'll be all up in the middle of this soon as she hears. And whatever she's working for, then by damn, I'll be working against. Besides, I figure we got to get you off that prayer list or else they won't pray for me if I get cancer," Agnes told her.

"You're too damn mean to get cancer." Stella smiled for the first time that morning.

"That's the gospel truth, darlin'. And Violet is too big of a bitch to get it, but if she does, I'm joining that angel crew and praying for her." Agnes chuckled.

"You'd pray for Violet?" Piper gasped.

"I'll pray that the devil comes on and claims her soul before she milks all the attention she can get out of her disease. The Good Book doesn't say you got to pray nice prayers." Agnes giggled.

"Well, shit!" Piper muttered. "I lost an opportunity there."

Agnes nodded and went on, "Heather is not stupid, Stella. Chances are if you get married, you'll have to leave Cadillac; then she takes over as piano player at the church. That'll put her a notch higher in this new scheme she's cooked up called the marriage ministry. Who in the hell ever heard of a marriage ministry? Ministry is standing up there in the pulpit and preachin' like Darla Jean does at her church and like Jed Tucker does at his."

Darla Jean was the preacher at the church on the corner, just up the street from the Yellow Rose. Everyone in town knew that she was a former call girl. When she inherited an old grocery store from her uncle, she was in a quandary about whether to put in her own escort business or to start a church. One look at the storefront said that it wouldn't do for an escort business but it would make a right nice church, so she took it as a sign from God.

"I'm not leaving Cadillac," Stella said. "And what is a marriage ministry?"

"Heather has this crazy notion that she's sent to earth from heaven to get all the women in the world married and happy. She probably thinks she'll get rich with her idea. Since you are a spitfire and you don't take no shit off nobody, then it would be a feather in her cap to get you married off first, plus it would put her in the piano seat at the church. Hell, honey, if she can succeed in her mission, then all the little wallflowers will flock to her side and she'll be right important. She might volunteer to play for all their weddings as a side bonus. Besides, she can't stand you because you don't drop down on your knees and kiss her ring," Agnes explained.

Charlotte laid her knitting to the side again. "Remember, they've got God on their side, and now that I think about it, you are really getting into the"—she held up her hands and made quotes in the air—"old maid status."

Stella raised her voice at least five octaves. "Old maid, my Texas ass! I'm not close to thirty and you and Piper are as old as I am. Are y'all old maids?"

"Well, according to our mamas that's getting to the age when you should be starting a family or at least wearing an engagement ring," Charlotte said.

"Some folks don't start families until they are forty these days," Stella reminded her.

Piper waved a hand in the air. "We need to take a lesson from the cat family. Tomcat comes along and screws the mama cat when she's in heat and then goes on his way. Mama cat has the babies and raises them, kicks them out of the laundry basket or wherever the hell she has them when they are old enough, and that's that. She don't have to worry about no son of a bitch breakin' her heart. And while I'm at it, Stella, you need to make things right with Nancy. Things go on too long, they fester, and believe me, if something happened to her tomorrow, you'd be sorry that it ended with y'all mad at each other."

"You finished on that soapbox, Piper? If you are, climb down and let me have it," Agnes said.

"I'm done," Piper said.

"Okay, here's my take, Stella Joy. If you want to get married, then find a husband and do it. If you don't, tell everyone who is prayin' for you to get married to climb on a rusty poker and go straight to hell. It's your decision and you do it in your time and your way to whom-so-damn-ever you please. But it's been slower than molasses in December around Cadillac lately, so I'm ready for some excitement. So don't tell anyone that you ain't goin' to abide by their prayers until we have some fun with this," Agnes said.

Stella wasn't in a very forgiving mood right then and nothing about this whole situation was funny. She fought back another batch of tears and braced herself for her full day of customers. Everyone was already talking about the sign at the church. If they saw her crying, it would add fuel to the fire. She really, really wanted to make a phone call, but the person she needed to talk to was in meetings with his phone turned off.

A rooster crowed and everyone but Agnes looked toward the window.

"That'll be the ring sound for my phone. I hate it when a phone plays music, so I set mine to sound like a rooster. I figure someone must have something they want to crow about or they wouldn't be callin' me." Agnes fished it out of the bib pocket of her denim overalls and put it to her ear. "What have you got for me?" she asked without saying "hello" first.

"Uh-huh. Just what I thought. Don't you worry none. The FBI can pull out my teeth with rusty pliers and I wouldn't rat you out. You just stay in the enemy camp and keep me informed. I'll do the rest. 'Bye now." Agnes put the phone back in her pocket.

"Well?" Stella asked.

Agnes's grin was so wide that it wiped out dozens of wrinkles. "Just as I thought. Heather says the sign stays until God drops a husband into your lap. And they have decided to call out that verse about those who help themselves, so they intend to help God. But don't you worry. We will outwit the whole damn lot of them."

"What have they done?" Stella asked through clenched teeth.

"They're having a bake sale on Monday to raise money," Agnes said.

"And?" Piper asked.

"They're going to give it to the church and hope God drops a husband down from heaven for Stella, right?" Charlotte asked.

"Nope. They're going to take all the money and purchase ten-dollar money orders to give away to bachelors," Agnes reported.

"Why?" Piper raised both eyebrows.

"Ain't that what you charge your men customers for a haircut?" Agnes asked.

"No!" Stella threw her hand over her mouth.

"Want my advice?" Agnes asked.

Stella nodded as she slowly removed her hand. "Yes, ma'am."

Agnes smiled. "They'll have the sale on Monday, count up their money that evening, and go buy money orders down at the post office on Tuesday. It'll be Wednesday before they start finding men to parade through here for haircuts, so Tuesday evening after the post office closes for the day, you put a price increase notice on your door. Effective immediately, due to hell freezin' over, haircuts will now be fifteen dollars or twenty dollars or, hell, a hundred dollars. How many men's haircuts do y'all do in a normal week?" Agnes asked.

"Maybe one or two. Ruby only charges eight dollars, so most of them go there," Piper said.

"Promise me right now that what is said in the Yellow Rose stays in the Yellow Rose, just like that Las Vegas sayin'," Agnes said.

Piper, Charlotte, and Stella all nodded seriously and said in unison, "We promise."

Agnes clapped her hands and giggled like a schoolgirl. "We'll teach them to mess with us. Now, Piper, let's get my hair done. I want it to look real fine for church on Sunday. I may play dumb and offer to take something to their bake sale."

"Not fudge," Stella gasped.

Agnes giggled like a little girl. "I think folks are on to me with the fudge. It was just too damn temptin' not to put laxative in it when I knew Violet would gobble it right down. No, I'm thinking a dozen pecan tarts from over at Clawdy's. Besides, not a thing they'll cook will be as good as Cathy's pecan tarts. As much as I love Nancy's banana bread, it's not as good as tarts."

Stella hugged Agnes. "I love you, Agnes Flynn."

"Us redheads got to stick together." Agnes beamed. "We'll outfox that bunch of bitches, darlin'. Don't you worry about it."

Stella felt a hot burn filling her cheeks but there wasn't a blasted thing she could do about it. She couldn't tell her best friends that she was already married or that she couldn't tell anyone for another four weeks or her new husband might have to leave Cadillac and she didn't want to leave her friends, the shop, or, dammit, her mama, even if she was mad at her. And besides all that, Heather was not about to run her out of town.

CHAPTER THREE

A semicool breeze from off the river ruffled the willow branches, making a lovely canopy above Stella and the sexy man beside her. She could hardly catch her breath after a bout of wild, passionate sex. His naked body was sweaty and hot, both physically and sexually, and somewhere out there in the Red River a catfish splashed in the water and a night owl joined with the bullfrogs and crickets in a concert.

She propped up on an elbow and traced the barbed-wire tat on his bicep. "Why barbed wire?" she asked, still breathless.

"My cousin has one and I always thought it was the coolest thing in the world," he answered.

"Did he rodeo or what was the story behind barbed wire?"

He brushed a leaf from her hair and shooed away a mosquito with the back of his hand. "He's a rancher and raises cattle. His family ranches, too, but they raise prizewinnin' horses in addition to Angus cattle. They live over near Ringgold, Texas. Want to go meet them after church tomorrow? Or do you want to wait and meet the whole family when they show up in church after I sign the contracts?" He kissed her on the tip of the nose. "And for your ears only, darlin', my mama and my dad know that I'm married and they can't wait to meet you."

"Hell, no! That billboard has stirred up everyone in town. They'll be watching me like a hawk to see if the prayers get answered and I understand Heather is determined that she's been called to a marriage ministry, whatever the hell that is," she answered.

She remembered the very first time she looked up and saw him standing just inside the Yellow Rose. That day his curly blond hair, blue eyes, and smile had come close to taking her breath away.

"Can I help you?" she'd asked when she could get words to go from brain to mouth.

"It takes a person with magic in their fingertips to tame my curly hair. I'm expecting miracles from someone as pretty as you," he'd said smoothly.

Major flirting had taken place and she'd found out that he'd just moved to Cadillac to pastor the church where she and her family had gone their whole lives. He'd found out that she wasn't married and asked her to dinner the next week. She'd accepted but the date wasn't sitting across the booth from each other out at the Rib Joint or even at a steak house in Sherman. It was fried chicken on a quilt under a willow tree at the edge of the river.

Bringing her back to the present with a long, lingering kiss, he gathered her into his arms and hugged her tightly. "What were you thinking about?"

"That first time you came into the shop," she said. "I think I fell in love with you on the spot."

"I know I fell in love with you the second that you whipped that cape around my shoulders. The touch of your fingertips on my bare skin about set me plumb on fire," he said.

"We can announce that we got married in May right after my birthday. Mama will have learned her lesson by then and Heather will figure out her marriage ministry is a day late and a dollar short," she said.

He kissed her on the forehead. "Heather has gone overboard with that marriage ministry idea, but if she's got enough rope she will hang herself for sure. Then it will be finished for good. It sounds more like one of those Internet dating things that have a dot-com behind the name. I'm pretty sure that God doesn't appreciate that kind of thinking."

Stella curled up in his arms, not caring if mosquitoes were buzzing around her head. They didn't sink their little beaks into sweaty people, anyway. At least that's what she'd always heard, along with the story about cats and water. Maybe one of them was right.

It had been her idea to keep their marriage a secret until the deacons and the hiring committee offered Jed a full-time position, and he'd agreed. From the get-go, they'd planned to announce it as soon as Jed had signed his contract.

"Now what are you thinking about? Your eyes are sparkling in the moonlight," he said.

"How much I love you."

"I love you, too, darlin'. I promise I didn't know about the sign or that you'd been put on the prayer list until this morning. I'll have it taken down, I promise, and I won't read your name on Sunday. It'll all fade away," he said. "Or we can just announce that we are married and they can pray for the folks in town who are really sick?"

She inhaled deeply and let it out slowly. Agnes wanted some excitement and Stella wasn't ready to tell the whole world she was married to Jed Tucker, the preacher. Their relationship was too perfect and it was only a couple of more weeks before the hiring committee would offer him a two-year contract. Until then he was temporary and could be let go at any given time. And to top it all off, Heather deserved to have to eat a big chunk of crow pie and so did Nancy Baxter.

"Don't take the sign down. Don't take me off the list. I'm going to beat that damn hussy at her own game. She thinks she's going to run me out of town so she can play the piano in church. And darlin', I can't wait to meet your family."

Jed traced her lip line with his finger. "What does the piano have to do with anything?"

"It's a thorn in her flesh that I'm playing it. So we're going to let the gossip go crazy. They'll all feel like fools after you are hired permanently." She brought his lips down to hers for a long, lingering kiss.

He chuckled. "Gossip is like cats. If you take a mean old tomcat off and dump him in someone's yard, make sure that you take him across a body of water if you don't want him to find his way home. Water stops cats and gossips, too."

She traced his lips with the tip of her finger. "But what about prayers?"

He grabbed her hand and slowly kissed each fingertip. "It's a moot point right now, isn't it? You already have a husband. And darlin', if they don't want to give me a contract because I'm married to you, there are other churches."

She cupped his face in her hands. "I don't want to leave Cadillac, Jed. I have my business and my friends and my family, and by the end of your first contract, they'll see that I'm the best preacher's wife in the whole state."

He kissed the tip of her nose. "You do not have to prove one thing, Stella. I wouldn't change a thing about you. I love you, darlin'." A smile tickled the corners of his full, sexy mouth and his blue eyes twinkled in the moonlight. "I am married to the most beautiful woman in the world, who is already an amazing preacher's wife."

Chapter Four

Stella was not looking forward to the next day and hearing her name at the top of that damned prayer list. If she could, she would turn off her phones and put that CD with the rainstorm on repeat in the player beside her bed. That way she couldn't hear Piper and Charlotte when they tried to call or came knocking on the door demanding that she go to church. But she was not giving Heather that kind of power over her. She'd crawl out, get dressed, and play the piano like always. Thank God Heather couldn't carry a tune in a golden bucket and had to sit out in the congregation. At least she'd be far enough away that Stella couldn't rip the belt off the dress she intended to wear and strangle the woman with it.

She parked in the driveway to the east of her little two-bedroom brick home. She'd rented it from the McKays when she moved back to Cadillac with the agreement that if they ever wanted to sell she had first option on the purchase. It had been built for wheelchair access, so there were no steps up to the deep front porch with a white railing around it. With only two bedrooms and one bathroom, it was plenty big enough for a single woman or a couple, but the backyard was small. Thank goodness she didn't have a dog and hadn't gotten around to bringing a cat home from her folks' house.

She flipped the switch right inside the front door of her small house and there were Piper and Charlotte, both wearing pajamas and blinking against the bright overhead light. Charlotte was cuddled up under a quilt in the burgundy leather recliner and Piper was stretched out on the matching sofa with a soft throw over her long legs.

Stella grabbed her chest. "What the hell? You two scared the shit out of me."

"Is it morning?" Piper yawned.

"Where the hell have you been?" Charlotte asked.

"I passed my twenty-first birthday a long time ago and it's not morning by a long shot and I don't have to tell either one of you where I've been," Stella started.

Charlotte held up her palm. "We were there with you when you turned twenty-one, darlin', and we were there when you've had all the rest. We are your best friends, remember? So tell us where you've been and what you've been up to."

Piper sat up and patted the sofa. "We've shared everything since we were babies. Is that afterglow on your face?"

"If this is a damned intervention, you can forget it. I'm going to bed, and yes, I will go to church tomorrow morning so this is all unnecessary," Stella said.

"I'm calling Nancy and telling her to take you off the prayer list because you've got a boyfriend and you are bringing him to Sunday dinner. You really should spend some time with Trixie. She'd give anything to have her mama in her right mind so she could talk to her every day," Piper said.

Stella plopped down on the sofa. "What makes you think I've got a boyfriend? And I love you, Piper, but you are not sending me on that guilt trip."

Piper sniffed the air. "Number one, I smell shaving lotion all over you. Stetson, I do believe it's called."

Charlotte popped the chair up into a sitting position. "And the look on your face says that you've been to bed with the wearer of Stetson in the last few hours. Maybe sooner since it only takes about ten minutes to drive from the nursing home to here at this time of night. Like I said, we're your friends. You can't sneeze without us knowing where you've been and whether there was ragweed there. Just be grateful that you've gotten away with your secret this long, girlfriend."

Stella crossed her arms over her chest. "Have you been stalking me?"

Piper shook her head and stretched. "Hell, no! We wouldn't do that. Besides, who needs to? The gossip comes right to us over a hotline. We know you've been parking at the nursing home to hide your car. And Trixie didn't mean to tattle. She thought we knew you were hiding it there."

Stella slumped down in a rocking chair, shut her eyes, and groaned. "I forgot about Trixie's mama."

"We've sworn Trixie to secrecy. She swears she won't tell Cathy and Marty and for damn sure not Agnes," Piper said quickly.

"So who is he?" Charlotte asked.

"I have been seeing someone. I'm not ready to tell anyone who he is, but I will tell y'all that fate is a bitch. I'm probably the worst woman on the face of the earth for him and it's going to be a secret for a while longer. And all this prayer shit couldn't have come at a worse time," Stella said without opening her eyes.

"Why would you be the worst woman . . . oh, that?" Charlotte said.

"Yes, that. You know small towns. Cadillac won't ever forget or ever forgive. I'm not so sure I can, so why should I expect them to," she said.

"You shouldn't have ever gone out with him," Piper said.

They all three remembered that summer after their sophomore year. A preacher had come to town for a three-month tryout with intentions of staying if the hiring committee liked him. He'd had a seventeen-year-old son—dark haired, dark eyed, sexy as hell and as wild as a Texas tornado. Stella had lost her virginity to that preacher's son on a hot summer night in the back of his pickup truck after they'd both drunk entirely too many beers. And the next day he'd bragged about it to all his new friends in the church.

It took less than twenty-four hours for her to go from a good little farm girl to a slut who'd seduced the preacher's son. A week later the hiring committee decided that the boy's father wasn't what Cadillac needed and they were gone.

Stella had been left behind with a tainted reputation that was still remembered in whispers around town. Cadillac was not forgiving and it never forgot. That's why she was so fearful of telling everyone she and Jed were married until he had signed the contract. Then she'd have a couple of years to show everyone that she wasn't that wild child anymore.

"Good God! Is he another preacher's son? That would serve Nancy right for the way she's been trying to push you down the aisle, but we won't stand by and let you marry a preacher's son," Charlotte said.

"We aren't going to let you marry anyone at all. I'll shoot him and Charlotte will help me bury him if she doesn't want to. You can weep over his grave while we shovel dirt into it, but I won't let my best friend get married. Is that understood? If Charlotte hadn't already bought her dress when I got divorced, she wouldn't be getting married, either," Piper said.

"He's definitely not a preacher's son, so there won't be any long black veils and weeping, or long white veils and walks down the aisle, either," Stella said.

"Hey, you can have all the wild sex you want as long as there is no marriage at the end of it," Piper said.

"Understood." Stella crossed her fingers behind her back.

"And as long as you tell us his name," Charlotte said.

"That ain't happenin'. I will tell you that he used to be a truck driver and he did the rodeo circuit, but that's all I'm sayin'. Now go home."

Piper shook her head. "I'm comfortable right here. My house is empty and lonely since the boys are with their dad tonight. I brought my church clothes."

Charlotte nodded. "Boone called from the riverbank. He and his buddies are having a good night. Fish are biting so they're staying out until morning. I'm going back to sleep here. I'll make biscuits and sausage gravy for breakfast and clean up the dishes."

Stella stood up and started down the short hall to her bedroom. "There are twin beds in the guest room. Y'all don't have to sleep in the living room."

"Well, thank you. We thought you'd never ask," Charlotte said.

"Why didn't you go to bed in there in the first place?"

"We were afraid we wouldn't wake up when you came in," Piper answered.

"If you'll tell us his name, we'll go home," Charlotte said.

"Make up your beds before you leave. I'm not sitting with Mama and I'm not going to Sunday dinner, so don't try to talk me into that tomorrow morning. She can deal with Daddy. And Charlotte, if you giggle when Jed reads that prayer list I'm going to shoot you the bird right there in church from the choir section and everyone will see me," Stella said.

"I'm glad Luke and Tanner will be in children's church. If they heard your name I'd have to answer a dozen questions. And no one would be surprised if you did something like waving around your middle finger, Stella. You are the wild child, remember?" Piper said.

Stella sighed. "Y'all go to bed. I'm going to take a shower. If my alarm doesn't go off in the morning, wake me up in time to get dressed."

"Yes, Mother." Piper yawned. "I'll sleep in your twin bed. I'll clean up my mess after breakfast. I'll fold up the quilt I used on the sofa and I don't blame you for not going to Sunday dinner. But just for the record, your daddy adores you and he only gets to see you on Sunday most weeks. Why does he get punished because you are mad at your mama?"

"She's right. Invite Everett to dinner at the Longhorn Café so y'all can at least talk," Charlotte said.

"Or better yet, forgive your mama and put an end to this," Piper said.

"Best friends aren't supposed to lay a guilt trip on their friends," Stella snapped.

"Best friends tell it like it is. Good night and I'm glad one of us had sex tonight." Charlotte giggled.

∽

"What the hell?" Piper mouthed as she saw her boys bounce out of her mother-in-law's van and come running toward her.

"Where's your daddy?" she asked.

"Gene had plans for the weekend," Lorene said right behind them. "So he brought the boys to my house. We made cookies. They insisted that we bring some to you." She held out a small brown paper bag. "What's that sign all about?"

"Nancy put Stella on the prayer list."

"That should cause a war in Cadillac," Lorene said.

Piper hugged her sons. "Won't be the first one and probably won't be the last."

Lorene shook her head slowly in disbelief. "Might be the biggest, though. What was Nancy thinking? It'll be a riot before it's all done and over. See you guys in a couple of weeks. Come give Grandma a hug."

They left Piper's side and quickly wrapped their arms around Lorene's waist. She kissed them both on the forehead and waved out the window until they couldn't see her anymore.

Piper's jaws ached from clamping them shut so tightly. It wasn't Lorene's fault, and truth was that the twins probably had a better time at her house than they would have with Gene and his girl-friend. Still, it made her so mad that she could have hanged that man from the nearest pecan tree with a barbed-wire noose.

They weren't identical twins. Tanner had blond hair, big blue eyes, and a thin face. Luke had a square face like his father, green eyes, and brown hair. Even though they didn't look alike, they were true twins who thought alike, finished each other's sentences, and slept in the same position.

Tanner grabbed her hand and pulled her toward the church. "Mama, guess what. Grandpa took us fishin' in his pond and Luke caught a perch and I caught a bass and Grandma cooked them for us. And it was like the fishes that Jesus had. They made a whole platter full of fish and we had all we wanted and there was some leftovers and it was the best fish ever. I can't wait to tell Preacher Jed all about it. He's teachin' our Sunday school class now and I like him a whole lot."

Luke held her other hand and skipped along beside her. "He's the neatest preacher we've ever had. I wish he could go fishin' with us. I bet he'd show us how to catch great big fishes."

Piper led them into their class and nodded at the preacher, who was sitting on the floor with children all around him. Luke and Tanner quickly found a place as close to him as they could get. Instead of going to her classroom, she went back outside and leaned on her car. She dug her cell phone out of the bottom of her big purse and dialed the all-too-familiar number. Gene picked up on the fourth ring.

"Why are you calling this early? Didn't Mama bring the boys back to you on time?" he asked gruffly.

"Why the hell didn't you tell me you didn't want the boys this weekend? You don't have to take them and I miss them when they're gone," she said.

"Mama didn't mind watching them. She and Dad get a big kick out of them and Rita and I had plans. We took her two nieces to Six Flags," he said. "I don't have time to argue with you this morning, Piper. I'm making pancakes for all the girls and they're having breakfast in bed."

That dirty bastard knew just how to push her buttons, and it took every bit of her willpower not to fry the airwaves with words that would melt the asphalt in the church parking lot.

"Anything else?" he asked.

"Nothing I can't handle," she answered.

The phone went dead in her hands and then rang before she could get it back into her purse. She groaned when she saw that it was Lorene. Lord, she'd had enough of Gene and his family, more than enough for a Sunday morning. She looked up at the church sign and mumbled, "I guess it could be a hell of a lot worse."

She said, "Hello, Lorene. Did the boys forget something?"

"I wanted to talk to you but the boys were right there and I didn't want to ask in front of them because it might have made it hard on you to say no and . . ."

A long pause and then Lorene went on to say, "Gene is our son and we still love him, Piper, even if we don't understand or agree with what he is doing with his life. You've been a big part of our family for the past seven years, too, and we don't want to cause trouble of any kind, but we do love having the boys. And, well," she stammered. "Would you consider letting us have them on Saturdays? Or . . ." Another long pause. "I know they go to day care in the summertime and school is out and that has to cost a lot."

Gene's parents had been very quiet about the divorce. Lorene had called her once and begged her to give her son another chance, but it hadn't been Piper's decision to get the divorce and Gene had never asked for a second chance. If he had, Piper would have told him to go to hell.

"Yes, it does, but Gene does pay his child support and I use it for the day care center. In the fall, they'll be in school all day and it costs only about half as much during that time," Piper said.

"We'd like to keep the boys for you. I could pick them up in the morning before you go to work and their grandpa would be glad to bring them home in the evenings. Or you could just let us know each day when your last appointment is and we'll deliver them to the shop. We get pretty lonely out here on the ranch since we're both retired. We wouldn't charge you anything, so you could put the money up for their education or use it to buy their school clothes and supplies this fall. Would you just think about it for a week?" Lorene spit out the words in a steady stream without catching her breath.

Piper held the phone out from her ear and looked at it. Was she hearing things?

"You still there?" Lorene yelled.

"I'm sorry. Did you just offer to keep the boys for free?"

"Yes, I did," Lorene said. "Will you just think about it?"

"That is so sweet of y'all," Piper said.

"I know you are off work on Sunday and Monday, but we could have them from Tuesday through Saturday, right?" Lorene asked.

"And on Gene's weekends?" Piper asked.

"If he wants to see them or if he wants to take them, we can do that from right here," Lorene said. "You wouldn't have to deal with him. I think his papers say every other weekend from Friday night at six to Sunday at six, right? Of course, if we have them, we'd be glad to bring them home whenever you say on the weekends like we did this morning."

"That would make it real easy for him to just run by and say hello, though, and not have much responsibility," Piper said.

"I realize that, but we've told him we'll take them any time that he has plans. We really want to be part of their lives, Piper. You'll let us know your decision, then?" Lorene asked.

"Yes, I will think about it and I'll talk to the boys about it. They have made friends at the day care, but I promise we will discuss it."

"That's all I can ask. If they decide to stay at the day care this summer, then please remember we are available any time if one of them doesn't feel well or if they just want a day at the ranch," Lorene said. "'Bye now. I'm at my church and it's time to go inside."

Piper looked up at the sky after she'd dropped the phone in her purse. "Well, how about that? Did some of those prayers for a husband for Stella get diverted my way?"

౭౨

Charlotte had just taken her seat in church when Boone slid in beside her. His jeans were starched and ironed and his shirt had perfect creases down the arms. His cowboy boots were so shiny that she could see the reflection of her shoes in the sides of them. His brown eyes looked tired when he yawned.

She kissed him on the cheek and asked, "Good mornin', darlin'. Did you catch a lot of fish?"

"We've got enough to have a big fish fry at the park. Bring Piper and her boys and Stella. We've invited Everett since he didn't get to go with us last night," Boone answered.

"What time?" she whispered.

"Six o'clock. Don't bring a thing. This is on us. Wade and Marty are bringing desserts from Clawdy's and Cathy and John offered to bring gallons of sweet tea and beer. I can't wait to see you." He stretched his long legs out under the pew in front of them. "I missed you last night, but believe me, I'm going to make it up to you tonight and neither of us has to work tomorrow, so we're going to spend all day in bed. Speaking of which, right after lunch I'm going to take a long nap or I won't be able to stay awake to cook fish or make wild passionate love to you either one," Boone said.

Charlotte smiled. "Sounds like a plan to me."

The noise level settled down immediately when Jed stepped up behind the podium and cleared his throat. "Good morning, everyone. It's a fine morning, isn't it? And aren't we glad that the air-conditioning works this morning as hot as it's turned out these past few days. I suppose you've all seen the sign that Heather has put up outside and most of you know that it's our own pianist, Stella, that it is talking about. Nancy thinks she needs a husband."

It started as a soft giggle somewhere in the back of the church and quickly turned into full-fledged laughter. Jed gave it a minute then held up his hand. "I don't reckon we should limit the powers of God, so y'all feel free to pray for Stella if you want. Now I'll take a minute and read the entire list."

"Stella Baxter," he said.

Stella rose up from the piano seat, waved at the whole congregation, and did a perfect curtsy.

Heather glared at Stella.

Stella blew her a kiss before she sat back down.

"Thank goodness she didn't show them her middle finger," Piper whispered to Charlotte.

"Good God, Nancy, what have you done?" Everett said out the side of his mouth.

"I'm doing what I can to fix it," she answered.

Immediately after the last amen was said, Stella went to the ladies' room, put the potty lid down, sat down, and put her head in her hands. She'd vowed she wouldn't let that black-haired hussy, Heather, see her crying or upset, but keeping a smile pasted on her face during the sermon had been pretty damn difficult. Especially with Heather shooting mean glares toward her all during the services.

Stella had never been an emotional person. In every situation she grabbed the bull by the horns, looked him right in the eye, and he backed down. But there she sat on the church potty, tears streaming down her face, a damn hole in her panty hose with a bubble of skin poking out and sticking to the other leg.

She stood up, removed the hose, and tossed them into the trash can. As much as she wanted to strangle Heather with them, it wouldn't be fitting for the preacher's wife to do such a thing. She wrapped toilet paper around her hand and dabbed away the tears. Ruined panty hose, everyone talking about her, worry over Jed's contract and her business—damn Heather's jealous soul!

The first time she eased open the door she could still hear the buzz of conversation in the choir room next door, so she repaired her makeup and waited. The second time all was quiet, so she started back through the sanctuary. She took her place behind Charlotte and Boone and hoped that her best friend didn't see the sparks dancing around when Stella shook hands with Jed.

"We are going to a fish fry tonight and your dad is coming to it so you can talk to him. I couldn't catch Piper, but doesn't she usually take the boys up to McDonald's in Sherman after church for dinner? Think you could get in touch with her and tell her to bring the boys to the park at six o'clock?" Charlotte asked.

Stella nodded. "Sure thing. I'm not going to Mama's for dinner, so I'll just drive up to McDonald's. Oh—Daddy winked at me when I waved. And Heather shot daggers at me."

"You've got balls the size of an elephant's even if you are a girl," Boone whispered.

"Just determination not to let them win." Stella smiled.

Charlotte laid a hand on Stella's shoulder. "You should call Piper and then go to your mama's for dinner. Your daddy loves you and besides, we only get one mother, lady. They might not be what we want and God knows they ain't never perfect, but . . ."

Stella tucked her chin and rolled her eyes up toward Charlotte. "I'm not ready to talk to her yet and you don't get to preach at me. I might get over this after my birthday comes and goes or I might be pissed off all the way through eternity."

Charlotte took a couple of steps forward. "Hey, don't get mad at me. Nancy might have gone about it the wrong way, but she wants you to be happy, so don't be too hard on her."

"Happy doesn't have to mean married, does it? I can be happy without a marriage license and a man in my house twenty-four/seven, can't I?"

"Happy in my world means I have to be married," Charlotte said.

"I wish you both a lifetime of wonderful bliss," Stella said.

"Can I borrow your phone?" Charlotte changed the subject.

"What's the matter with yours?" Stella asked.

"She's probably going to see who you've been talking to," Boone laughed.

Charlotte slapped him on the shoulder. "Tattletale! I betcha I could have found out who her boyfriend is in five seconds."

Stella zipped the top of her purse and hugged it close to her body. "You are not getting anywhere near my phone."

"If I knew how to hack into a computer, I bet I'd find out who he is in a hurry," Charlotte whispered as she stepped up and held out her hand toward Jed. "That was a wonderful sermon, Brother Jed. And very timely in view of what's on the church sign this week."

"Thank you. I hope it fell on the right ears." Jed smiled. "Hello, Stella."

She put her hand in his and sure enough, a tingle went from her toes to her nose.

"You are taking this very well this morning," he said.

"If you can't lick 'em, prove 'em wrong." She smiled.

"I'll call later today," he whispered.

She squeezed his hand and hurried out to her car.

❧

Piper and the boys were already in a booth at McDonald's when Stella arrived. She waved, went to the counter and ordered, and then slid in beside Piper across from the twins.

"Hey, guys. What's going on?" she asked.

"We got to get big people meals today instead of Happy Meals. And guess what, we went fishin' yesterday with Grandpa and we cooked the fish and two little fishes fed us all and we told Preacher Jed about it this morning. And guess what else?" Luke stopped to suck in more air.

Tanner picked up where he left off. "Grandma says that we can stay at her house and not go to day care and Mama says that we can if we want to so we're going to sleep on it and then make up our minds. And if we eat our big people meal we get ice cream for dessert. If it was breakfast time, we would eat pancakes. We like pancakes. Daddy used to make them for us sometimes."

Piper's eyes misted over and she turned around so the boys couldn't see her expression. Stella could have easily shot Gene. God wouldn't put the murder charge on her tab. He might give her some extra credit and forgive her for blowing kisses at Heather.

She pointed to the McDonald's fun house. "I bet y'all could eat a big ice cream cone if you played out there when you get finished eating. I see Aunt Charlotte coming, so she's going to want to eat and then maybe we could all have ice cream together."

"Wow! This is the best weekend ever, Aunt Stella," Luke said.

They polished off the last of their fries and ran out to the play area. Stella threw an arm around Piper's shoulders. "Coffee?"

Piper nodded and brushed at the tears. "I'm sorry. Sometimes it just gets to me."

"I know exactly what you mean. All I have to do is think of that damn sign and I want to cry all over again or strangle Heather," Stella said.

Piper cleared her throat. "Yes, I'd love a coffee. You know before Mama died last year, she told me that time would fly and soon the boys would be grown and I should spend every minute I could with them. Her one regret was that she had to work and didn't have chocolate chip cookies on the table for me after school. I remember that Nancy always had cookies or banana bread for you. And I'm not trying to guilt you. I just wish I could talk to her about all this and I can't because you are my friend and you are more important but, oh, hell, it's all tangled up and I can't express what I'm trying to say." She pushed back her half-eaten burger.

"Hey, what's going on? You both look like you are about to cry." Charlotte set her food on the table. "Are the boys playing?"

"Yes, they are, and don't discuss anything until I get back. I'm going for coffee," Stella said.

She wished she could talk to her mother, too. She wished that she could tell her that she didn't need a husband because she already had one but first they had to make sure that Jed's job was secure. In two years the church would be used to Stella as the preacher's wife, but letting the cat out of the bag now could be a disaster. She'd seen it happen when she was a teenager, and Cadillac hadn't changed all that much.

She didn't have to stand in line, so in just a few minutes she returned with two large cups of coffee. "Now tell us both, what's that bastard Gene done now?"

"It was the pancakes. I held it together until one of the boys mentioned pancakes," Piper said and went on to tell them what Gene had said. "He never, ever brought me breakfast in bed. Not one time. Not even when we were first married."

"He's probably just saying that to rile you up," Charlotte said.

"Well, it worked. Especially the part about taking her nieces to Six Flags."

"He really is a sorry bastard for doing that. He should have taken Luke and Tanner," Stella said.

"Boone and the guys are all cooking fish tonight at the park and he said to invite you and the kids. They'll get lots of attention there and it'll be more fun than an old amusement park, anyway. It's Gene's loss, believe me," Charlotte said.

Piper wiped her eyes and a smile broke through the tears. "What time and what can I bring?"

"Not a thing. Boone said it was all covered," Charlotte said.

"Oh, no, I need to do something, and cooking helps calm my nerves and keeps me from cussin' in front of the boys. I'll make potato salad and baked beans. You call Boone and tell him I'm bringing enough of both to feed an army."

Luke and Tanner ran back to see if Stella and Charlotte were finished eating. "We done slid down three times and we're ready for ice cream."

"You guys want to go to a fish fry at the park tonight? Boone and Charlotte have invited us," Piper asked.

"This for sure is the bestest weekend ever. I'll bring my Frisbee and baseball," Luke said.

"Hey, Mama, can we I borrow your phone?" Tanner asked.

"Why?"

"I want to tell Boone thank you and to tell him to bring his ball glove," Tanner said.

Charlotte handed her phone to Tanner. "Use mine. It's speed dial one, honey. He should answer real quick. He was going home to get everything ready and finish cleaning the fish for tonight and then take a nap, but he's not asleep yet."

Luke followed his brother to the far corner of the restaurant, made the phone call, and then bet his brother he could beat him to the car. They barely stopped long enough to give the phone to Charlotte before the race was on.

"Competition. Mercy heavens, it's always a competition between them. They're in such a hurry they forgot ice cream," Piper said. "See y'all this evening, and thanks."

"For what?" Stella asked.

"For being here for me when I cry over pancakes."

Chapter Five

Stella's small white frame house with a picket fence around the yard was located three blocks south of Agnes's big two-story that sat right on Main Street. Her beauty shop was two blocks east of Agnes's house and the park was two blocks east and one north of that. It was a hot summer night but she hadn't gone for a run in more than a week and although she wouldn't dream of showing up all sweaty to a fish fry with her friends, it wouldn't hurt her to walk eight blocks. Besides, her mama said that southern women might get all dewy but sweating was for menfolks, not ladies.

A pang of sorrow washed over her. She missed her mother and the Sunday dinner and she wanted to tell her all about that rotten Gene and invite her to the fish fry, but she couldn't. Damn Heather and her precious Prayer Angels, anyway!

She dressed in denim shorts, a bright-red tank top, and her walking shoes, put on a baseball cap, pulled her curly red ponytail out of the hole in the back, and shoved her house key into her pocket. A hot wind picked up sometime during the second block. She passed a house with little kids playing in the water hose and wished that she was four again so she could romp through spraying water in her underpants.

Thirst had set in by the third block. She'd just proven for absolute certain that dew was something that appeared on the grass and had nothing to do with pure old sweat.

"What in the hell are you doing walkin' in this weather, tryin' to kill yourself? Get yourself up here on this porch with me before you drop down dead with a heatstroke, girl," Agnes yelled.

Stella didn't have to be told or invited twice. She climbed the steps out of the blistering-hot evening sun and sank into a chair. Agnes poured a glass of ice-cold sweet tea and handed it to her.

"Drink and don't come up for air until it's half-gone. You damn kids don't have a lick of sense. You don't go out walkin' or runnin' in hun'erd-degree weather. You sit on the porch and drink sweet tea. Where are you goin', anyway? Shop is closed today and tomorrow both," Agnes asked.

Stella gulped several times before setting the glass back down on the small table between the two chairs. "Boone and his buddies are having a fish fry at the park. I haven't run in several days and I thought the exercise would be good for me."

"Well, this ain't the day to start again. We've got our first real heat blast of the summer. Weatherman said it was up more than a hundred degrees, but the sumbitch lied. It's only five degrees cooler than hell. Drink some more. If you die on my porch, Nancy will come huntin' me down, thinkin' that I done let you die before she got her grandbaby. I'd hate to have to kill your mama with my old shotgun in a showdown right out there in the street," Agnes said.

"I'm not going to die," Stella said.

Not now that she'd been rehydrated with sweet tea, bless Agnes's heart.

"Of course you ain't. I saved you. I told you, us redheads got to stick together," Agnes said.

Stella looked at the two glasses on the table. "How did you know I'd be walkin' past here today and need a glass of tea?"

Agnes smiled. "I didn't. I always bring two glasses because Beulah has a sixth sense and knows when I come out for a breath of fresh air. I got tired of going back in the house to get a glass for her, so I just go on ahead and bring out two."

Stella glanced over at the house across the street. "Why isn't she here, then?"

"Jack and Carlene took her out for a snow cone up in Sherman. She don't drive anymore and she loves snow cones. They invited me to go with them. I'm glad I didn't since I had to save your hide this evening. Drink the rest of that and I'll drive you on down to the park," Agnes said.

"Miz Agnes, I can walk that far. It's only five blocks," Stella argued.

"Not on my watch. If you die, they'll shut up the beauty shop until the funeral is over and I won't get to see them women's faces when they realize they done sweat through a bake sale for nothing. Besides, my black suit is too little and I ain't buyin' another one at my age so I'm not going to no more funerals and it would sure look bad if I didn't attend yours since we're both redheaded and all," Agnes told her.

"You wouldn't go to Violet's funeral if she died? I thought y'all had a bet going as to who was going to outlive the other one," Stella asked.

"Yes, I'd go to that old bat's funeral, but I'd go in my overalls and my flip-flops just to see if I could get her to rise up out of that coffin." Agnes giggled again. "Now you sit right here and I'll get my truck keys. Piper or Charlotte can take you home. You got to take care of yourself, girl. We got us a war fixin' to start come Wednesday mornin' and I can't wait for it to get going."

"Only way I'll let you take me to the park is if you stay with me and drive me back home when the fish fry is over," Stella said.

"Well, hell, I thought you'd never ask. I ain't been to a good out-door fish fry in years. Fold up your lawn chair and mine and throw them in the back of the truck so we'll have something to sit on. I'll get the keys and my purse." Agnes didn't leave any room for argument.

"How about the tea and the glasses?"

"Let 'em set there. It'll draw in a bunch of ants and mosquitoes and drown 'em. There'll be less to pester me the rest of the summer. Meet me at the truck. I'll come through the kitchen door," Agnes said.

Stella had just tossed the chairs into the back of the truck when she heard rubber flip-flops slapping against the hot concrete drive-way. She crawled into the passenger's side and gasped.

"Leave the door open a minute to let the hot air out. Feels like a bake oven in here but there ain't no need in turnin' on the air-conditioning since it won't kick in cool until we get there, so roll down the window. It's still better than walkin' or runnin', for God's sake." Agnes threw her purse on the wide front seat and hopped up into the driver's seat. "I'm tickled to get to go. Ain't a damn thing on the television that I like on Sunday night. Don't tell me that self-righteous Heather is coming or I'm going back home and watchin' them flies drown."

"I hope Heather isn't there. I can't imagine who'd invite her," Stella answered.

"Well, Quinn does go fishin' sometimes with Boone and Rhett, so I didn't know. It's a good thing she's not coming. She'd prob-ably die of heat exhaustion in them panty hose, anyway. I did offer to bring something to their bake sale tomorrow but she told me I wasn't on the prayer committee and they didn't want anything from me. I guess they're afraid of my prayers."

Stella smiled. "That might be a compliment. Have you ever heard of a marriage ministry before?"

"Hell, no! I heard of a singing ministry but not a marriage one. That's the biggest crock of bullshit I ever heard." Agnes giggled as she stopped at the only red light on Main Street, looked both ways, and went on.

Stella grabbed the armrest and held on until her fingers turned white. "That light wasn't green yet."

"Nothing was comin' and I ain't got time to sit there and wait for it to turn green when the fish is fryin'."

"Miz Agnes, if you don't obey the law, they'll take your license away from you."

Agnes harrumphed loudly. "I don't give a shit. Hell, I'll give my license to them or cut it up right in front of them. I don't need a damn license to drive. Hell, girl, I was drivin' a truck when I had to sit on a pillow to see over the steering wheel back when I wasn't but nine years old. Daddy needed an extra field hand to bring in the hay and I wasn't big enough to throw the bales up on the truck, but I could damn sure drive. So they can have my license. I don't need it to drive."

"Yes, ma'am," Stella said.

"Here we are. Take a deep breath. If that ain't the best-smellin' fish I've got a whiff of in years, then my name ain't Agnes Flynn." She bailed out of the truck and looked over her shoulder. "You bring the chairs. Well, would you look at that? Preacher Jed is here. Did you invite him? How come he didn't bring you if you did?"

"I did not invite him, and why would he bring me to the fish fry?" Stella said.

Agnes turned around and came back to the truck. She leaned on the fender and whispered, "Well, you should have. I heard that your mama said they could give them money orders for haircuts to anyone but Preacher Jed or Rhett Monroe. The preacher is the one I think you should set your hat for. That'd really be the highlight of the war."

"Why wouldn't Mama want me to marry Rhett or Jed?" Stella asked.

"One's a skirt chaser, which might make her grandbaby a skirt chaser, too. The other one is a preacher and you know what they say about preacher's kids bein' the meanest kids in town. I don't reckon she wants either one, so she'd best be tellin' God some real specific instructions about that husband you need so bad," Agnes answered.

"Agnes!"

"Well, they would." Agnes giggled. "Come on, girl. Let's go have some fun. Tomorrow I might just let it slip at Clawdy's when I go over there for breakfast that I saw you and the preacher flirting. Or maybe I'll start a rumor that you are seeing both Jed and Rhett and that you might be sleeping with both of them to see if a holy man or if a devil in tight blue jeans does it better."

Stella stopped in her tracks. "Agnes!"

Agnes slapped her thigh. "I'm just jokin'. I don't care if you have a feller but don't tell nobody who it is. Well, you could tell me but nobody else or it would end all the fun."

Stella grabbed the chairs. Her father waved so she had no choice but to head toward the picnic table where he and Jed sat. Everett met her halfway and took the chairs from her, carried them the rest of the way, and popped them out.

"Boone invited Preacher Jed to the fish fry. I didn't know that he was a fisherman until tonight. We're going out tomorrow evening on my boat after it cools down to see if we can catch some crappie. I hear they're runnin' pretty good," Everett said.

"That mean we might have another fish fry before long?" Agnes asked.

"If we catch enough, we'll get Boone to bring his fryer and have one in a couple of weeks at my place. That way Nancy can be there. She's at some kind of church foo-rah tonight talkin' about that prayer shit they do on Thursdays. Looks to me like one night a week would be enough. Just pray and leave it in the good Lord's hands, but oh, no, we got to talk about prayin' before we do it," Everett said.

Jed touched the tip of his baseball cap. "Miz Agnes. Miz Stella. I believe summer has arrived."

"It damn sure has. How long are you going to leave that sign up down at the church?" Agnes asked.

Stella fought the blush turning her cheeks bright crimson, but she lost.

"Heather takes care of that sign, so you'll have to ask her." Jed smiled.

❧

"Brother Jed! Brother Jed!" Piper's boys jumped out of her car and went running before she could make them help her carry food and paper plates to the pavilion where Boone and Charlotte were frying fish and hush puppies.

Piper saw both Charlotte and Stella wore jean shorts and tank tops. Why hadn't she called them before she went to all the trouble to iron the red-and-white-checkered dress that made her feel like she was wearing a picnic tablecloth now that she was at the park? Charlotte had pulled her brown hair up in a short ponytail and Stella had a baseball cap on.

Piper had curled her hair and now it was sticking to her neck. She'd put on makeup and was sweating it all off. All she needed was a bow and a quiver of arrows on her back and she could be one of those Amazon women from the jungle who'd overdressed for a damn picnic in the park.

"They're too excited to see Jed to help me carry things and y'all should have told me to wear shorts," she whispered when they arrived to help carry the food to the picnic table.

"You look great," Charlotte said. "The way that Luke and Tanner are all excited about the preacher, maybe you should use the fact that you're the prettiest one here tonight to flirt with him."

"I should've worn shorts," she whispered.

Stella picked up a huge bowl of potato salad. "We feel like ugly ducklings up beside you. Maybe we should go home and change."

Using two oven mitts, Charlotte picked up the oversize Crock-Pot of baked beans. "These smell scrumptious. Wait until the preacher realizes that you cook as well as you look."

"Stop it right now. I'm tellin' you I'm not through being mad at Gene and it's not time to start a new relationship even if my boys think Jed has wings and a halo," Piper told them.

All that talk about getting Stella married off must have put the ringing of wedding bells in her two best friends' heads. She could understand Charlotte trying to play matchmaker, but not Stella. That redhead was on a mission to prove her mama wrong, so she shouldn't be pushing her toward the preacher.

Whoa! Wait just a damn minute. Hold the horses and don't fire the cannons. Stella was flushed and her eyes were twinkling like they did when she was hiding something. New boyfriend was in their midst; Piper could feel the vibes and the sparks. Now it was just a matter of figuring out which one of those single men was the one. She scanned the group as she started back toward the picnic table and bit back the gasp.

Sweet Jesus! Stella had to be sleeping with Boone's older brother, Rhett, who was over there helping fry fish. He had done the rodeo rounds and he'd driven a truck back when he was in college and she'd said that her secret boyfriend had done those things. That's exactly who it was and she didn't want to tell anyone because Rhett had always been Cadillac's resident bad boy. Nancy was going to go up in flames if that praying business netted her Rhett Monroe for a son-in-law.

Well, dammit! Charlotte and Stella would be sisters-in-law—would that leave her out in the cold? No, but it could change the dynamics among the whole bunch of them.

"How did Agnes get here?" Piper asked to take her mind off the idea of being a third wheel in the family.

"She waylaid me with sweet tea when I was about to have a heat-stroke and offered to drive me the rest of the way," Stella answered.

"And which one of these cowboys are you sleeping with? I know it's one of them, so fess up. I can feel the vibes comin' off you like a heat wave and it don't have a thing to do with the hundred-degree weather, either. Is it Rhett?" Piper said.

Stella set the potato salad on the table with a thud. "What makes you think I'd be interested in Rhett?"

"You said the worst choice in the whole world. Nancy is going to pass plumb out when she hears that you are sleeping with Rhett. She might refuse to keep a grandbaby if he fathers it."

Stella gasped. "Shhh . . . ?"

"No one heard me," Piper said. "But believe me I will be watching you. I wish your mama was here rather than spending time with that bossy Heather tonight. She'd be smart enough to figure out who your boyfriend is."

"What if it is Rhett?" Stella said.

"What about my future brother-in-law?" Charlotte asked after joining their circle.

"He makes the best fish in the whole county. We should have a fish festival instead of a chili cook-off," Stella said quickly.

"That ain't about to happen. The chili cook-off is a tradition and you know how the old folks in Cadillac are about tradition. But guess what I heard this afternoon?" Charlotte said.

"What?" Piper whispered.

With a head motion toward Piper's car, she mouthed, "Follow me."

"Man, those beans smell good," Rhett said.

"Mama's special recipe." Piper smiled. "Fish about ready?"

Rhett flashed a brilliant grin. "Oh, yeah. We're going to start servin' it up in five minutes, and you look mighty nice this evening, Miz Piper."

Rhett was even sexier than his younger brother, Boone. Both of the brothers were tall, dark, and handsome, but Rhett had an air about him that drew women like a flame brings in the moths. His eyes were darker brown than Boone's, his face more chiseled, and that cleft in his chin flat spelled danger.

Charlotte had fallen for the right Monroe boy back in high school, though. Boone was the steady one, the one who'd make a good husband and father. Rhett had the reputation of never sticking around in a relationship long enough to get past the third or fourth date. Suddenly, Piper wasn't sure she wanted to be right about her best friend's new fellow, but being Stella's best friend, it was her job to find out more about Rhett before she passed judgment.

"Thank you, Rhett. I've got to go unlock the trunk of my car so we can get the napkins and extra paper plates." Piper smiled.

"Need some help?" he asked.

"No, Charlotte and Stella are already headed that way, but thank you."

The two women had their heads together, whispering, and Piper couldn't wait to find out what it was all about. She pushed between them and looked from one to the other.

"Okay, what'd I miss? My Lord, Stella, you are white as a ghost," Piper asked.

"I just told her what Agnes found out from Beulah a couple of minutes ago," Charlotte said out the side of her mouth. "I happened to be standing close enough that Agnes told me when she finished talkin'."

"She didn't. They didn't. My God!" Stella said.

"What? Who did what?" Piper asked again.

"It has been decided that Cadillac needs something more formal than the chili cook-off and the Fourth of July thing at the football field and the jubilee," Charlotte said.

"A fish festival after all?" Piper asked.

Agnes joined them. "Did you tell Stella?"

Charlotte nodded. "You can fill Piper in on the news."

Agnes leaned against the fender of Piper's car. "The war has taken a new turn. On the last Saturday night in July there's going to be a ball in Cadillac. All the details have not been ironed out, but it's going to be something like a debutante ball for everyone, but mainly for the women who aren't married and who should be. Stella is the prime target, because it's been officially named the Yellow Rose Barbecue Ball but any woman that ain't married is fair game. Heather says that this is a giant leap for her new marriage ministry." Agnes lowered her voice to a whisper. "And on the other side of the gossip fence I heard that Charlotte was seen buying pink yarn at Walmart and that Stella is far enough along now that she knows it's a girl."

"Shit! How many stories are floating around?" Stella asked.

"A bunch, but that's the two I like best, and before you ask, I'm going to the ball. I wouldn't miss it for the whole world. It'll be the perfect time to show the whole damn bunch of them that I'm still the boss of Cadillac," Agnes said.

"I'm damn sure not going," Piper said.

"I didn't give them permission to use my beauty shop name in their idea," Stella said.

"They say it's for 'The Yellow Rose of Texas,' that song that Roy Rogers and Johnny Cash and half a dozen other singers have sung," Agnes said. "But we know it's just Heather slapping you in the face so we have to retaliate. They think they're so damn smart. Well, we'll mow them under like dead grass before the summer is over."

Piper groaned. "I'm not being a part of any such thing. I've got enough troubles of my own right now."

"Bullshit," Agnes said. "They've insulted your friend and you will be a part of it so suck it up, Piper. Put on your armor and get out your army tanks. We're going to war. Praise God! I thought I was going to die of pure damn old boredom."

"Barbecue ball? That sounds like it comes right of *Duck Dynasty*." Charlotte laughed. "And I really was buying pink yarn. I'm ready to put the border on Cathy's baby blanket and make the matching booties and sweater."

Agnes shrugged. "I figured that much out, but you know how people do love to talk. My snitch says we'll get any more news soon as it comes out so we can plan our strategy, but Heather has talked her aunt, who is Violet if y'all will remember, into letting them use her big old barn out on the Prescott place for the ball. They ain't growed cattle out there for years, so I reckon it's full of spiders and snakes. I just wonder if Heather is going to pull off her high heels and help clean it up."

"Now, that's a funny picture in my head," Stella said.

"It is, ain't it? Only thing funnier is puttin' Violet in it with her. Now let's go eat fish. Did you make them beans by your mama's recipe, Piper? I'm going to eat half of that pot full and be damned to the gas it will produce," Agnes said.

"How in the hell do a ball and barbecue get mixed up together?" Stella asked Charlotte.

"Y'all walk slow so I can hear what you are sayin'," Agnes said.

"I could see barbecue and a barn dance, but a ball? A ball means a sit-down dinner with waiters that bring chicken cordon bleu or maybe prime rib, not barbecue," Piper answered. "Barbecue means beer, paper plates, and country music."

"Do we all have to wear white dresses and long white gloves?" Charlotte asked.

"Not me. If I go, I'm wearing a camouflage gown with a hot pink sash," Stella said. "Mama says that redheads can't wear red or hot pink, so I'll fix it up real good."

"Nancy would probably make that dress for you if you just asked her to," Piper said.

Stella shot a dirty look her way.

Agnes stopped in her tracks when her rooster-crowing phone sounded off in the bib pocket of her overalls. "Y'all hold up."

She listened awhile and then said thank you. "Now you can walk again, but keep it slow. I ain't no young chicken no more. That was my snitch. And for the record, girls, you are all three going to the ball. Piper and Charlotte are going to support you, Stella, because they are your best friends and that's what friends do. I'll be there, too, and we'll show them that they've failed in their mission. If I can go to Violet's place, then y'all will go. No arguments."

"What else did your snitch say?" Piper asked.

"Heather is bringing in air conditioners to cool the place down so the ladies won't get too hot and they're going to start designing the interior next week. They say it's going to be something like one of those renaissance fair things down in Dallas, only instead of turkey legs, they'll be serving barbecue. I'm not sure if y'all are going to cook it or if y'all are just supposed to eat it in your fancy dresses. Maybe we ought to borrow them big bibs they use at the nursing home. Barbecue can get messy."

"God help us!" Piper set down the box she'd brought from her car.

"Who is God helping, if I may ask?" Jed raised an eyebrow.

"He's going to help all of us." Tanner nodded his head seriously. "God does that when people pray in church, don't he, Preacher Jed?"

"I think maybe he does, son," Jed answered.

Piper blushed when she saw Luke wink at Tanner. Surely those two weren't playing matchmaker. They'd been devastated when their father left. They'd really acted out when they went to stay overnight with him the first time and Rita had been there. Gene had been so angry at the way they'd treated his girlfriend that he'd told Piper they couldn't come back unless she taught them some manners.

"You look mighty pretty tonight, Piper," Rhett said.

"Thank you, sir." She smiled. "You boys get one of those wipes from the container over there and clean your hands."

"Jed, you want to say the blessing over this food before we start?" Boone pulled off his ball cap and laced his fingers in Charlotte's.

Jed laced his hands behind his back and every head bowed. No one, not even Piper, saw Stella slip her hand over his during grace.

"Amen, now let's eat!" Agnes said the minute he finished.

&

Charlotte sat between Boone and Stella. Piper was across the table beside Jed with the twins bookending them.

"Looks pretty good, don't it?" Charlotte whispered into Stella's ear.

"I always love fish cooked outside," Stella said.

"Not that. Piper and the preacher."

Stella shrugged. "Oh! I don't think she's ready to date."

Jed had kicked his sandal off under the table and ran a foot up the inside of Stella's calf. Her whole body tingled at his touch. She looked across the table and caught a quick wink.

"What are y'all whispering about?" Piper asked.

"My wedding dinner. Shall we have a buffet or sit-down dinner?" Charlotte said quickly. "And the barbecue ball. Can you believe that the prayer group is doing that? Now this whole thing is going to last for weeks, not just until Heather takes that sign down."

"What thing? What barbecue?" Boone asked.

Charlotte leaned over and kissed Boone on the cheek. "Looks like Cadillac is having a festival this summer. It's going to be a formal ball where barbecue is served."

Everett slapped the table. "Don't tell me your mama and those women in that damned club have come up with this shitty idea in hopes of finding you a husband, Stella Joy. Lord, I about burned down the church this morning when I saw that damned sign. I don't know what in the hell your mama was thinkin' but I'll tell you one thing, she's mighty sorry she ever stirred up this pile of shit. She was hoping it would be over after that damned bake sale tomorrow."

Rhett picked up a gallon of sweet tea and filled plastic glasses. "Well, Stella, darlin', you know that you are getting long in the tooth. Lord, how old are you? Forty?"

She pointed a finger at him. "Not even near thirty and you'd better be careful, buster. They might put you on the list next. Marryin' you off would be a real feather in Heather's marriage ministry cap."

"They'd wear calluses on their knees if they started praying for me. Marriage ministry? Sounds like an Internet dating service for the religious folks, don't it?" Rhett laughed.

Agnes blew on a piece of fish and waited for it to cool. "Looks to me like them stupid hussies might as well just round up all the unmarried women like cattle and slap a brand on their asses. I'd ask for your pardon, Jed, but I really don't give a shit what you think of my language. But I'm here to tell you three girls that I'll need bodyguards to keep Violet from killin' me at that barn dance. She'll be all up in the middle of this ball since her niece is ringleading the new wedding preacher shit."

"Well, you can bet your sweet southern ass I'm not going to be a part of such shenanigans," Everett said.

"But Daddy, you make the best barbecue in the whole state and you know Mama has probably already volunteered you to do all the smokin'," Stella said.

Everett's eyebrows drew down in one heavy line across his green eyes. "I'll smoke the brisket if I can tear that damned sign down and use the wood for the fire."

Stella gasped. "It'd taste like shit, Daddy. You have to have your special wood to make good barbecue."

"I'll go without a fuss if you're doin' the cookin'," Boone said. "Only thing I like better than fish is your smoked brisket and turkey. Oh, and your chicken and pork loin, too."

"You might as well suck it up, Everett. Nancy won't give you a minute's peace if you refuse to cook. Smart thing to do is to volunteer before she can tell you that you are going to do it. That way you win and them women lose," Agnes said.

"Well, I'm damn sure not gettin' all dressed up. If I can't go in my jeans or overalls, I ain't goin'," Everett declared.

"Mama," Luke piped up. "Me and Tanner was wonderin' if we could invite Brother Jed to come to supper at our house tomorrow night? We want to show him our train set. I bet he'd just love to play with it."

"Sorry, boys," Everett said. "You'll have to take Jed home with you another night. Tomorrow night me and him are goin' fishin'."

"Well, rats! When me and Tanner get big enough, will you take us fishin' at night?" Luke asked.

Everett chuckled. "I sure will, but you got to be bigger than ol' Roy. He's the biggest, meanest old catfish in the Red River and if you was to fall over the edge of the boat, why, he might get a hold of the seat of your britches and haul you all the way to the ocean before he let go of you."

Luke's eyes were so big that the pupils were completely outlined in white. He brushed back a lock of light-brown hair from his sweaty forehead. "I heard about ol' Roy. My grandpa told me that he's older than God."

"That's pretty old," Jed said.

Tanner nodded seriously. "Grandpa—he knows them things."

Charlotte bumped Stella with her knee. "See, the boys like Jed. It's one of those made-in-heaven matches. We'll focus on Piper rather than finding you a husband and you can just keep having sex with your truck driver. We can tell Heather that her prayers landed on Piper instead of you. After all, we do own the Yellow Rose all together. It's not just your beauty shop."

"Hey, guys, I'd love to see your train set," Rhett said.

"Really?" Luke asked.

"You any good at baseball?" Tanner asked.

"Well, I played when I went to college and they let me pitch."

"Well, we don't go to Grandma's tomorrow and Mama don't have to work, so I reckon you could come see us about six o'clock," Tanner said.

Charlotte poked Stella and whispered, "Did you hear that?"

"I did but I'm not believing it."

"Mama, can Rhett come over and teach us about baseball tomorrow evening?" Luke asked.

Piper smiled at Stella before she nodded at Rhett. "Sure, he can. Don't eat supper before you come, Rhett. We'll grill some hot dogs and make it a real baseball game."

❧

Agnes dropped Stella at her house and said, "Don't worry. We'll fix it up so that this will be the last year they have a barbecue ball. It does sound like a *Duck Dynasty* thing. Got to admit, I do watch that show. I love it when Si gets the best of them younger boys. And when Mama Kay starts cookin', my mouth just waters."

"I hope that it's a big flop and no one but us four shows up," Stella said.

"Oh, I want a lot of people there so they can see Heather and this damn silly idea of hers bite the dust. What do you think of Rhett going over to Piper's place tomorrow night? That upset you or do you think he's just going because she's your best friend and he wants some advice about how to handle a red-haired spitfire?"

"Agnes Flynn, you are nosy. I think Rhett gets a bad rap because he dates so many women, but there's nothing wrong with that, is there? But between us, I'm not seeing him or interested in him."

"Well, shit! I just knew he was the one. You been as jittery as a worm in hot ashes all night. Still, you might forewarn Piper, because she's of the opinion that he's coming over to get on your good side. I still think it would be downright hilarious if you went out with the preacher, if it was only one time. Heather would shit her pants without a bit of my dosed-up fudge to help her along."

Stella's laughter set Agnes off and before long they were both wiping at their eyes.

"I'd forgotten that you dosed up some fudge with laxative and gave it to Violet last year," Stella said between hiccups.

Agnes nodded. "And I'll do it again if she gets out of hand. You want me to sit here until you get inside?"

"No. I'm a big girl and I'm so mad about all this barbecue ball stuff and prayin' shit that I just dare anyone to cross me," Stella said.

"That's my girl. Us redheads, we do have a temper. See you later."

Stella waved as she got out of the truck. "Thanks for the tea and the ride."

"Thanks for a fun evening. It was fun to get out with a bunch of young kids like y'all," Agnes yelled out the open window as she backed out of the driveway.

Stella pulled her keys from the pocket of her shorts and reached around the door to flip the light switch. A big hand covered hers and a deep voice said, "We don't need the lights, darlin'. Just take my hand and let me lead you to the bathroom. I'm thinkin' that we could both use a nice long bath in that claw-footed tub of yours."

"But Charlotte and Piper have keys . . ." she argued as she followed Jed down the short hall.

"They are both too busy to come here tonight," Jed whispered. "Charlotte and Boone could hardly keep their hands off each other all evening. And Piper will be home planning a ball game tomorrow night."

He swung the door open to the cool bathroom. Two jar candles, one on the back of the potty and one on the floor beside the tub, provided enough light that she could see the sparkle in his blue eyes and also that he was stark naked. Rose petals floated on the bathwater. The steam carried the scent of vanilla along with the faint aroma of roses to her nose.

He pulled the tank top out of the top of her shorts and slowly brought it over her head, stopping to kiss her before he unzipped her shorts and tugged them down to her ankles.

Underpants, bra, and shoes all went into a pile with the rest of her clothing. And then he picked her up and slowly submerged her up to her breasts in the deep tub. He slipped in behind her and picked up a sponge, squeezing water down over her back.

"That feels so good," she murmured. "But"—she twisted around so she could look into his eyes—"I just about stood up on the table and told them all that we were married tonight so Charlotte would stop trying to do some matchmaking between you and Piper. And yes, I was jealous."

"I didn't notice Charlotte as much as I did Piper's boys. They're just little boys and they don't cover their tricks up so well." He chuckled.

"Hey, Stella! Where are you?" Charlotte's voice rang out from the living room.

Stella jumped but he wrapped his arms around her, making a shelf for her breasts. "Tell her you are in the tub. She won't come in here," he whispered.

His warm breath caused more shivers.

"I'm in the tub. You stayin' here tonight?" Stella called out.

"Oh, no! Boone is all mine tonight, darlin'. He's waiting in the truck. I'm just bringing some leftover fish for your dinner tomorrow. Want me to put it in the fridge?"

"No, just leave it on the bar. I might want some before I go to bed," Stella yelled back. "Lock the door on your way out."

"Will do. See you Tuesday."

Jed pulled her hair loose from the braid, picked up a cup from the floor, and poured water through it. "Plannin' on workin' up an appetite, are you?"

"We always do."

Chapter Six

Heather and half a dozen of her most devout Angels met on the front porch of Ruby's Beauty Shop and set up for the bake sale just after daylight on Monday morning. According to Heather, folks came early to a bake sale so they wouldn't have to cook breakfast. Heather opened up a leather-bound notebook embossed with gold angel wings, and between customers they wrote down ideas for the ball. Heather, God love her heart, had never lived in a small town before Cadillac and thought she was keeping everything between the covers of her fancy little book. But nothing was ever a secret more than five minutes in Cadillac. If all the gossips died and were buried in the Cadillac cemetery, they'd figure out a way to tell tales from the graves.

Heather was sitting in a cute little fold-out chair with a cup pocket on the side, her gold fingernail sparkling in the morning sun, when Nancy brought six loaves of banana bread and two dozen chocolate chip cookies to the sale.

"How is it going?" Nancy asked.

Heather pointed her brand-new gold fingernail at Nancy. "Today begins my marriage ministry in earnest and I'm so happy. By the end of the summer your daughter will be married and submitting to the will of her husband and I will be on my way to becoming the first marriage minister in history. It's so exciting that I can hardly take it all in."

"I can't see Stella submitting to anyone or leaving Cadillac, either, if that's what you've got in mind," Nancy said.

"Oh, she will, believe me. I never thought I'd submit to moving out of my precious big city and into this podunk town. I just came for a visit to my sweet little aunt Violet. She introduced me to Quinn and I fell in love. Now I see that it was God's plan for me to move here to help women like Stella find her place in God's will. And if that requires that she move away from Cadillac, then so be it."

Nancy exhaled slowly. "You've picked out a name for the ball and you said you were ordering posters to put up all over the county. I talked to Everett last night and he's willing to cook the meat. The Fannin sisters called me and they'll help me prepare the rest of the food and help serve it. I was thinking maybe the admission to get into the ball would be a covered dish."

Heather shook her head. "But if we don't charge admission, then we won't make enough to begin an account for the marriage ministry. To further my ministry, I'll need to be able to cover expenses like having a website and office supplies. We'll have to charge an entry fee but we'll make it worthwhile. For their ticket, they get supper, a partner, and dancing for the evening. Oh, and I heard a story that Stella is pregnant and it's a girl. Congratulations, Nancy, you're having a granddaughter, but now we have to pray harder that the man will come forward and marry her, don't we?"

Nancy put up both palms. "My daughter is not pregnant. That is a nasty rumor because her best friend knits baby things and don't you be spreading it around."

Heather smiled but it did not reach her eyes. "Oh, honey, I never spread gossip. It would be unbecoming to a marriage minister."

Trixie Matthews dashed across the street and picked up a loaf of Nancy's banana bread. "Agnes said y'all was plannin' a big barbecue ball out in one of Miz Violet's barns. Sounds like fun. I haven't had an excuse to wear a pretty formal since my senior prom. I just love those new fancy dresses with the halter straps and all that bling all over them. Here's five dollars. Y'all keep the change since it's going to a good cause. Even if no one gets married, we'll love having a barn dance."

"It's a ball, not a barn dance," Heather snapped.

"Whatever." Trixie grinned.

As soon as Trixie was gone, Heather rolled her eyes toward the ceiling and sighed so heavy that she snorted. "Damn that Agnes. She's going to be trouble. As God is my witness, she will be a nightmare. My sweet little aunt Violet warned me that she might try to sabotage my ministry."

"What on earth could Agnes do? It's your party at your aunt's house," Nancy asked.

Heather giggled and waved her fingernail around excitedly. "You are so right. It's going to be a grand debut, my first big event in Cadillac. I'm so glad that you put Stella on the prayer list and helped me to realize my true service is in creating happy marriages."

A feeling akin to icy water being trickled down Nancy's back chilled her to the bone. All she'd wanted was a few prayers and God's help to get her a son-in-law so she could have a grandbaby. She really hadn't realized she'd fire the first shot for another war in Cadillac when she marched into the Angels' meeting four days before. But the battle had started and there was nothing left to do but see it to the end. She'd just have to trust Agnes to help her throw a wrench in the barbecue ball.

If it had been for anything other than to get her married off, Stella would have stopped by the bake sale and bought a loaf of her mother's banana bread to nibble on as she cleaned the shop. But there was no way she'd help finance that endeavor, not in a million years.

She, Charlotte, and Piper rotated turns cleaning the shop. It wasn't set in stone. If Piper had something she had to do with her boys, then Stella or Charlotte traded with her. If Charlotte had to go to a bridal fair, then someone swapped with her. It all worked out in the end and they managed to keep from having to hire extra help.

She'd just finished folding the last load of towels when the front door opened and her father, Everett, waltzed in with two cold bottles of beer, dripping with water where he'd just taken them out of the cooler.

"Thought you might need something to cool you off," Everett said.

"Have a seat, and thank you, Daddy! I just finished getting this place in order and a beer is just what I need. What are you out doing today?"

"Tryin' to stay away from my gun safe so I'm not tempted to shoot a bunch of angels. Don't know why they'd call them meddling women angels." Everett sat down in one of the chairs around the table and twisted the top off the beer bottle before he handed it to her.

Stella pulled out a chair and settled in across from him. She took several long gulps before she came up for air. "Tastes better than I thought it would. You can't shoot them, Daddy. That would be too easy. Agnes and I will take care of it, I promise."

"I just get so damned mad at the way your mama does all the work for everything. Used to be if Violet Prescott wanted some glory she called on your mama to be part of a committee of some damn kind, and now it's that new woman, Heather. I hear she's Violet's niece and is just as bossy as that old bitch."

"Have you told Mama how you feel?"

"Honey, we wore this fight threadbare when you was just a little girl. We'd fight and it'd be hell to pay around the house for a few days and then we'd get over it until Violet wanted your mother to work her ass off on another project that Violet would take credit for doing," Everett said.

"But Mama has always been better friends with Agnes than she is with Violet. She can't stand Violet," Stella said.

"I know that, but if it's something for the church like dyein' Easter eggs or servin' dinner for anything from funerals to Sunday school meetings, it was your mama who did the work. She'd tell me that it was for the church and she couldn't say no to something for the church." Everett finished his beer and tossed the bottle into the metal trash can. It rattled around, the sound echoing off the walls for several seconds before it settled to the bottom. "I'm going fishin' with Jed. Maybe floatin' down the river with a preacher will keep me from doin' something that ain't right. I kind of like that feller. He's all right for a preacher. He ain't all pompous and holier-than-thou and he don't preach at me when we're talkin'. He's just a good old regular feller."

Stella swallowed fast to keep from spitting beer across the room. "I'm glad you've found a new friend. Don't worry about the Angels, Daddy. When they all learn that their barbecue ball is just a party and not a matchmaking club, it'll blow over and maybe Mama will see what you've been tryin' to tell her all along. Agnes says it's not going to be an annual affair, that she'll make sure of it. So all we got to do is weather this storm. You know there's sunshine back in behind most storms."

Everett chuckled as he hoisted himself out of the chair. "Who are you preachin' at, darlin', me or you?"

Stella held out her hand and he pulled her up. "Mostly to myself, if I'm honest."

"Well, it's a damn good thing that you know that, and don't you say that matchmaking club idea out loud ever again. They'll start drawing up the constitution and bylaws for one and invite Nancy to be the chairman of the board or some such shit. Them old women need to leave you young girls alone and let y'all decide what to do with your lives. Hell, both your grandmas would roll over in their graves if they knew what was going on here. They fought like pit bulls for women's rights and now this bunch thinks they can go back to the caveman days and do them prearranged marriage things with a side order of brisket. Dammit! I'm goin' fishin' before I get riled up." Everett started for the door but then turned around and came back to hug his daughter. At well over six feet tall, he had to bend to wrap her up in a bear hug. "I ain't about to let your mama's doin's keep me from seein' you, kiddo. I'll pop in and out and bring you a beer."

"Thanks, Daddy," Stella said.

He waved over his shoulder and hollered, "See you at the football field on Friday for the Fourth of July celebration if I don't see you before then. We can share a funnel cake like we always do."

❧

Charlotte purred like a kitten as she rolled over and wrapped her arms around Boone that morning. Her eyes flew open when she realized that all she had was a handful of feather pillow, but then she smelled the coffee and smiled. Boone was making his famous straight-from-the-can cinnamon rolls. She shut her eyes so she'd be surprised when he brought the tray to the bed. Her hand touched something that felt like paper so she peeked over the pillow and there was a note attached with a safety pin: *Sorry, darlin'. Thought I had the day off but I have to go in after all. One of the other firemen came down with the flu and it's my rotation for overtime. Coffee is made. Love, Boone.*

Charlotte moaned, pulled the covers over her head, and whined. Now that all her Monday plans had been shot to hell, she might as well go on to the shop and help Stella clean up. She could work on that knitted baby blanket she'd started the week before or finish reading that new cowboy romance by Joanne Kennedy, but neither one sounded as good as gossiping with Stella.

Maybe after they cleaned the shop they could get some lunch at Clawdy's and then run up to Sherman and shop. It would be the perfect day to try on dresses for the barbecue ball Agnes said they had to attend. Truth was that she'd love to get dressed up all pretty for Boone and spend a few hours in his arms on the dance floor.

She slipped a hand out from under the covers and searched for her cell phone on the nightstand. When she found it, she hit the speed dial number for Piper.

"Good morning?" Piper answered.

"I'm going to help Stella clean the shop and talk her into lunch at Clawdy's and then having an afternoon in Sherman to try on dresses for this ball that Heather is planning. You should come with us."

"Can't. Remember, the boys asked Rhett over for supper. I just know he's going to tell me that he's the one who is seeing Stella and he's going to ask a million questions about her because we are her best friends. Don't go shopping for pretty dresses without me, promise that you won't. Why don't y'all come for hot dogs and a baseball game out in the backyard?" Piper said.

"Well, she did say that her feller was the worst man in the whole county for her to fall in love with. So it might be Rhett, but he's not going to tell you anything if she's right there, so get all the information and fill him in on everything about her that you can without telling our private secrets and call me tonight when he leaves. I'll put the thumbscrews to Stella. Between the two of us I bet we figure it out by bedtime."

"Y'all have a good time, but no shopping until I'm there. I'm cooking. The way to a man's heart is through his stomach and I mean to find out just what he's hiding in his heart for our friend," Piper told her.

When life gives you lemons, make chocolate chip cookies and make the whole world wonder what you've been up to. That was what Charlotte's grandmother used to say, and it sure enough applied that day. Charlotte had had the day planned, but now it had taken a ninety-degree turn the other way and she wasn't sad anymore. She and Piper might not agree on the way Stella was keeping her distance from Nancy, but they were united in their mission to find out who Stella was keeping company with. Lord help if Stella's boyfriend was Rhett Monroe, the resident bad boy of Cadillac, Texas. Nancy might crawl up in a casket and breathe her last if that was happening right under everyone's noses.

Charlotte remembered the bake sale when she saw all the cars parked in front of Ruby's Beauty Shop and whipped her vehicle into an empty space. Stella loved her mama's banana bread, so if there was a loaf left, Charlotte intended to use it to pry information out of her about this new feller. She opened the car door to a blast of summer heat and had second thoughts about using food to get Stella to talk. By the time she went from car to porch, sweat rolled down her face, melting all the makeup she'd so carefully applied. She whipped a rubber band from the pocket of her shorts and pulled her hair up into a ponytail as she crossed the yard.

"Well, I sure didn't expect to see you here," Nancy said.

Beulah fanned with one of those church fans with Jesus on one side and an advertisement for a funeral home on the other. "Hot, ain't it?"

"Good mornin', ladies. Y'all got any of Nancy's banana bread left?" Charlotte asked.

"Honey, that was gone within an hour of the time we opened up. We have one of Heather's special carrot cakes," Beulah said. "I'll sell it to you for half price if you want it."

"I'll just look around," Charlotte answered.

Everyone in town knew that Heather couldn't cook. She bought her bake sale donations out of the grocery store freezer section, removed them from the packaging, and put them on a fancy disposable tray before she wrapped them in plastic wrap.

"That peach cobbler is from Clawdy's," Beulah whispered. "I bought it special for the bake sale. And I made the banana pudding myself."

Charlotte nodded and looked around some more. She picked up a couple of caramel popcorn balls and handed them to Beulah with a wink. "I think I'll have this chocolate cake, too, but only if you made it."

Beulah beamed. "Yes, I did, from scratch. It's Jack's favorite, so I made two."

She pulled a bill from her pocket and shook her head when Beulah started to give her a dollar back. "Just add that to the fund. We all want to see Stella happy, don't we?"

Heather wiped her face with a lace-trimmed white hankie. "This is about more than just finding a husband for Stella. It's about the beginning of turning Cadillac from a backwoods, two-light town into something like Tulsa with theaters and a shopping mall as well as a place where we can have an elegant ball—" She stopped midsentence. "Well, hello, Sugar Magee. Where are your sisters?"

"Gigi is parking the car and Tansy is right behind me. Why didn't you tell me the church was having a bake sale? We would have donated something," Sugar said.

"This is for the Prayer Angels. You aren't on that committee. Y'all take care of the Easter egg committee, remember?" Heather said.

Charlotte slipped away with her cake and two popcorn balls as the snippy, sugar-sweet remarks started.

"Hey, where are you?" she yelled at the back door of the Yellow Rose.

"In here getting ready to shampoo my hair," Stella yelled back.

Charlotte set everything on a nearby table and hurried into the shop. "Don't start yet. Sit down in the chair and I'll do it for you and then you can do mine. I want some more highlights and it's hard for me to get the back done right."

"Deal," Stella said. "I smell caramel or chocolate. Don't tell me you went to that damned bake sale."

"I did and I bought two popcorn balls for us to share and a chocolate cake that Beulah made. And the Fannin sisters—strange how folks still refer to them by their maiden names when they're together, even though they've all been married for years, isn't it? Anyway, they showed up just as I was leaving and . . ."

Agnes pushed through the front door, stopped under the air-conditioning vent, and said, "God almighty, but it's hot out there. Do I smell chocolate cake?"

"I bought it at that bake sale. What'd you buy?" Charlotte asked.

"Not a damn thing, but I'm glad you did. It'll throw them hussies off and make them think we're supportin' them. What's the cake for?" Agnes asked.

"It's to eat. Go cut yourself a piece. We got two popcorn balls, too, if you want to share them," Stella said. "I'm not sure I'm going to eat any of it since the proceeds are going to find me a husband."

"Gossip this morning is that you are sleeping with Rhett. He's going over to Piper's tonight to play baseball with her boys and eat hot dogs with them. Everyone says he's being nice to her because she's your friend and he's hoping to learn more about you. You told me last night that you weren't interested in him. You didn't lie to me, did you?"

Stella sat down in the chair and leaned her head back in the sink. "Sure, I did. I'm a good liar. Truth is, I'm screwing Rhett Monroe every chance I get."

Agnes giggled as she headed toward the back room. "I know you ain't screwin' Rhett, because he's been coachin' the little boys' baseball team this summer down at that new field they built. And he was there while your car was parked at the nursing home. I haven't figured out whose car or truck is gone at the same time your car is parked out under that cottonwood tree at the backside of the lot, but I will."

Charlotte's quick intake of air was audible all over the shop.

Was Stella lying, joking, or telling the gospel truth about not being involved with Rhett? If she was telling the truth, then Piper should be warned.

Stella threw up both palms. "I'm busted, Miz Agnes, but could you just let Piper and Mama think it's Rhett that I'm sleeping with? It's the only way we'll get Piper to let a guy into her life and it'll drive Mama crazy."

Charlotte wet down Stella's hair and massaged the shampoo into her scalp. "You flat-out had me going there for a minute. So you think Rhett is interested in Piper? Maybe I should buy some more baby yarn for the next blanket."

"Good grief, Charlotte! She don't know that he's flirting with her. Don't be buying a pregnancy test or baby yarn either just yet," Stella answered.

Agnes came back with a big chunk of chocolate cake on a paper plate. "I may live. I was having a damn chocolate attack. Trixie says

I'm addicted to it, and she might be right. At my age, when sex is out of the question, I guess it's better to be addicted to chocolate than it is to whiskey."

"You mean that when I'm eighty, sex will be out of the question? Well, thank you for ruining my day," Stella said.

Agnes sat down at the table and commenced to eating cake, talking between bites. "Sorry, kid, but it is what it is. Better get all you can before you are eighty and all the men you know dry plumb up. It ain't us women who have to have them pills to get ready. Hell, no! It's the men."

"Who is your snitch?" Charlotte changed the subject.

"A person don't tell them things." Agnes accentuated every word with a poke of the pink plastic fork in her hand.

"Why?"

"Privacy act that some president or 'nother put into law sometime in the past. You can't tell your snitches' names or else you get banned from heaven or the FBI will come haul your ass off to jail and you have to live in orange jumpsuits for the rest of your life. You know how hard it is to get them damn things down to go to the bathroom? And old women have to go real often, so it's a pain in the ass. Besides, my mama always said that redheaded women do not ever, ever wear orange," Agnes said.

"Agnes Flynn, you are full of shit!" Stella said.

"It's what comes with having red hair and being old. You'll get the same privilege someday. Now tell me and Charlotte who it is that you are sneaking off with. We're under that privacy act thing so we're bound by God and the FBI not to tell nobody about it," Agnes said.

Charlotte rinsed the shampoo from Stella's hair and squirted on a healthy dose of conditioner that had extra product in it to keep hair from frizzing. "It's really *not* Rhett Monroe that you're keeping company with, is it?"

"It's really not, but let everyone think that if they want to," Stella said. "I'm not being mean or secretive with my friends. It's a matter of national security. If anyone knew, he could get fired, and believe me, I am protecting Mama. She'd have a stroke if she knew his name. Now let's talk about something else. How's the bake sale going, Agnes?"

"Are you thinking about that past crap?" Charlotte asked.

"That was years ago," Agnes said.

"Yes, but you don't have to be told about small-town gossip. Once it's said, it's gospel for at least a hundred years. It doesn't matter what happens afterward, so I'll be a slut for a long time. Now about that bake sale, Agnes?" Stella said.

Agnes finished off the cake, put her paper plate and napkin in the trash, and moved to the sofa. "My contact says they're sneakin' up on two hundred dollars. That means they'll buy twenty money orders. Y'all got the sign made for the front window?"

"I do," Stella said. "Made it this morning, but we don't put it up until tomorrow at closing time, right?"

Agnes wiped a paper napkin across her lips. "Change of plans. That's really what I came down here for but then I got a whiff of chocolate and remembered that thing about Rhett. You know, he's a handsome young man. It's just that he got the reputation for being . . . what do you call it these days?"

"A player," Charlotte said.

"That's it. Sounds like a dumb thing to call him, but that's the word I was lookin' for. Anyway, they're sending Floy to the post office this afternoon. The bake sale is just about sold plumb out. Folks buy more if they think it's for the church." She looked up at the ceiling. "God, you got to take your hearing aids out and listen to me. You could zap that Heather girl, not enough to kill her, just to make her fall down in the dirt on a fire ant pile, for letting folks think that the bake sale money was going to the church when it's going for haircuts."

Charlotte giggled. "Why, Agnes, are you praying?"

Agnes rubbed her hands together. "Hell, no, I'm talking to God. I don't pray in public," she declared. "Hurry up and get her hair done. We'll go to Clawdy's for dinner. If you'll get a move on it, then they'll see us three together and get all antsy about what we got planned."

"So when do we put the sign up?" Charlotte asked.

"First thing tomorrow mornin'. They'll already have all those money orders bought up and they'll either have to divvy them up between themselves or find some way to use them. I bet they make them door prizes at that ball." Agnes drew her eyes down in a frown and then she chuckled. "We've got to stay on our toes to stay ahead of them, girls. I'll buy our dinner today since y'all saved me from certain death by givin' me chocolate cake," Agnes said.

"But I was going to do Charlotte's hair and you just ate half a cake," Stella told her.

Agnes stood up. "I only ate a fourth of that cake, not half. It was my appetizer. Now I want fried okra and red beans and a couple of pork chops."

"Give me a minute to work some mousse in her hair and we'll go eat at Clawdy's," Charlotte said. "We can do my hair on a slow day next week. But only if we don't talk weddings. My mama is driving me crazy with every detail about my wedding. If you ever do think about marriage, just elope, Stella. Nancy would be twice as bad as my mama because you are her only daughter."

❧

Nancy could almost see Heather's blood pressure rising from the color in her cheeks when Beulah pointed at Agnes coming up the street between Stella and Charlotte. The two hairdressers were dressed in cutoff denim shorts and T-shirts and Agnes wore her newest fashion statement: faded bibbed overalls, a red T-shirt—which everyone in the whole universe knew should not be worn by red-haired women—and rubber flip-flops that cost about a dollar a pair.

"She looks like a bag lady," Heather hissed. "No wonder she's a thorn in my sweet aunt's flesh."

Nancy might be mad at her daughter. Hell, she might be ready to throw in the towel and arrange a marriage for her, but no one was going to call her daughter a bag lady. She took a step right into Heather's personal space, narrowed her eyes, and said, "Don't you ever call my daughter names. I can be mad at her but I'll wipe up the streets with your ass if you say anything mean about her. I don't care how close to God you are. And for your information, she doesn't wear a cocktail dress to clean her beauty shop."

"I was talking about Agnes." Heather blanched.

"You'd best be," Nancy said. "I'm going to buy this poor old lonesome carrot cake so we can go home and get out of this blistering heat. How much did we make today, Beulah?"

"You can have the carrot cake for half price since it's the last item, and that will make us two hundred and ten dollars. Enough to buy twenty-one haircuts," Beulah said. "Y'all got a list of the fellows you are giving them to?"

"Yes, we do," Floy said.

"And Preacher Jed and Rhett Monroe are not on it, right?" Nancy said.

"You are getting almighty picky for a woman who didn't care if her daughter married a poor old feller who pumps gas," Heather smarted off.

"Why not Rhett Monroe? He's got a job and he's very nice lookin'," Floy asked.

"You know his reputation. I want a son-in-law, not a live-in boyfriend. Rhett Monroe won't ever settle down and get married. And good God almighty . . ." Nancy handed Beulah a five-dollar bill and went on, "Stella can't marry a preacher. Everett would have to clean up his language and that ain't about to happen."

"And besides, can't you just see Stella as the preacher's wife." Heather chuckled.

Nancy shot Heather a drop-graveyard-dead look, letting the hussy have the last word. If the cake tasted like freezer burn, it was still the best five dollars she ever spent just to get off that hot porch. Maybe she'd give it to Everett and tell him to mix it up with that stinky stuff he used to make fish bait.

Heather tilted her chin up a notch. "Beggars can't be choosers."

Nancy silently asked God nicely if she could knock a smart-ass woman who wasn't thirty out into the dirt but the only answer she got was a loud booming, "No!" in her soul. So she raised her head and smiled at the ladies. "I'm headed to the house, where it's air-conditioned. Everett and Preacher Jed have gone fishin', so I intend to read a big thick romance book all evening while the air conditioner blows right down on me."

"Your cussin' husband is out fishin' with our dear Jed." Heather's tone said that she was totally aghast at such horrible news.

"Strange, ain't it?" Nancy grinned. "They've formed a pretty tight friendship the last few days. Jed overlooks Everett's cussin' and Everett says he's a serious fisherman."

"Our poor Jed is trying to save his soul, I'm sure. Now please tell me that you don't read those books with naked-breasted men on the front, do you? If you do, I shall have to pray for your sinning soul. I'm sure God does not approve," Heather said.

"Honey, what do you do when you crawl into bed with your husband? Do you have twin beds and have one of those marriages where you don't touch each other? God made men and women different so that when they have sex they can become one flesh. And besides, he's probably busy with much more important things than listening to prayers about what I read," Nancy said.

Heather blushed and stammered, but intelligent words would not come out of her mouth.

"Oh, my! Oh, my!" Beulah twisted at her hankie. "Do they really put stuff like that in those books?"

Nancy laughed. "The one that's made its way to the top of my big stack of to-be-read books is one by Grace Burrowes titled *Ethan*. I just can't wait to get all involved with it. And yes, they describe sex in the books, Beulah. You want to borrow one, Heather? I've got some really descriptive ones that might help you with your marriage."

Heather set her mouth in a firm line that said she was disappointed that a member of the Angels would read anything other than the Bible or maybe one of those inspirational-for-the-soul books. "Don't you dare bring one of those dirty books around me."

Nancy couldn't back down now because she'd promised Agnes that she'd keep her informed of what was going on from inside the marriage ministry camp. But she hadn't promised that she wouldn't take up for Stella while she was infiltrating the enemy's camp. No, ma'am! And Heather had better begin to understand that Nancy's endurance level was getting mighty slim.

❦

Looking out the window at Rhett playing with her sons, Piper wished that she could go by the ranch and tell Nancy that everything was going to be all right. She wished that she could knock some sense into Stella's hard head about the silly fight with her mother. But since she couldn't do either, she'd just bask in the glory of being right about Rhett and Stella.

Luke hit the back door in a blur, dashed off to the bathroom, and then came back through the kitchen on his way out. "We need three bottles of water, Mama. Playin' baseball is tough work. I'm glad Preacher Jed went fishin' with Mr. Baxter. Me and Tanner like Rhett better."

Piper loaded him up with water and he dashed off again. Better than Preacher Jed, who had a halo and wings. That was quite a statement and her grandmother had told her more than once that you can't fool kids and dogs. She bet if there was a dog or a cat or even a pet hamster, it would like Rhett Monroe, too.

But then, the kids at church literally flocked around Jed Tucker, too. Piper was amazed that one of the single women in Cadillac hadn't already gone after him in a serious way. He was sexy, kind, sweet, and loved kids—every woman's dream. So why wasn't Stella interested in him?

"Oh, yeah? That damned old scandal back when she was just a teenager with the preacher's son. We should have rallied around her and hung that boy with a length of rusty barbed wire," she mumbled and then snorted in suppressed laughter. "Besides, Stella would never be interested in a preacher, not after that shit that went on back then."

She carried the hot dogs out to the backyard and Rhett and the boys joined her before she could get the gas grill fired up. He took the platter from her hand and said, "Grillin' is our job. We talked about it and since you've been cookin' all day, we'll do the hard work, won't we, guys?"

Tanner nodded seriously. "Yes, sir. You sit right down here"—he patted the picnic table—"and we'll do the cookin', Mama. Rhett is going to teach us when they are just right, like the street vendors in New York City get them. We'll help you carry out the rest of the food when the hot dogs are done."

Piper smiled. Oh, yes, she would take a very good report back to Stella the next morning. Rhett was a good man and Stella had done well when she started seeing him, even if it was on the sly and she should have told her two best friends all the details.

"New York street vendor, huh?" She sat down and used the picnic table as a backrest.

"Oh, yes. It's a wonderful place to visit for a few days. The guys would love it. They could see a game at Yankee Stadium and take a tour out to the Statue of Liberty, and there are Broadway plays if you like things like that," Rhett said.

Piper smiled. "Sounds like a wonderful trip to take someday."

"You mean a real baseball game?" Luke asked.

Rhett ruffled his hair. "Yes, I do."

"Can we go this summer?" Luke asked.

Piper shook her head. "We'll have to be satisfied with backyard baseball this year, guys."

"Okaaaay," Tanner said. "We really don't mind, Mama, because we got Rhett right here in Cadillac and we got hot dogs just like they make and we can go fishin' with Grandpa and if that Broadway stuff is like them singin' movies, I wouldn't like it, anyway."

Rhett smiled at Piper. "Good kids you got here."

If it had been late enough for stars to pop out, they would have paled in comparison to the flash of his grin. With that kind of charm, it was no wonder that Stella liked him. She couldn't wait to tell her that she'd figured the whole thing out and that she approved.

Chapter Seven

I've been giving this a lot of thought," Heather said from the podium in the fellowship hall where the whole Prayer Angels group had met to discuss the upcoming ball. "I will put the gents' names into one fishbowl and the ladies' into another. They will assemble up in the buyers' loft and as I draw their names they will come down the steps together. The gent will lead the lady out onto the dance floor, where they will wait until everyone is on the floor, and then the music will begin a nice slow waltz and everyone will start dancing together. It's going to be simply lovely."

"What about Carlene and Jack? They're engaged and they sure wouldn't want to dance with someone else," Beulah asked.

Heather sucked in a double lungful of air and blew it out noisily. "Okay, the ones that are formally engaged can have their names put on a ticket in a third bowl. Aunt Violet has three gorgeous crystal bowls that I can use. I'd planned on borrowing two of them, but now the third one can be used also. This is a wonderful idea. It might encourage some of those who are thinking about proposing to get on the ball before the ball." She giggled at her own joke but everyone else just stared at her.

"And the ones who are married already but want to participate in the ball?" Floy asked.

"Maybe the third bowl can just be for all of the already taken people?" Beulah said.

"I'll second that," a lady said from the back of the room.

"Then write it in the minutes." Heather nodded. "One for the unmarried gentlemen. One for the single ladies. And a third for the already taken. It's going to be a grand sight, all the women dressed up and the men in their black ties. I'm planning to talk to the television crew from Sherman and see if they'll come down and shoot some footage."

Floy fiddled with her collar. "Not tuxes. There won't be a single man who'll come if he has to rent a tux. This is small-town Texas, not Tulsa. You've got to take baby steps or you'll never get this idea to take root. You'd better not bill it as black-tie but as jacket and tie. That way they can wear a string tie or a bolo and still be dressed up. You won't have a problem with the ladies. They'll be glad to go buy something fancy."

Heather flashed her new gold fingernail at Nancy. "Is Stella coming? This all started to help her. It would be a shame if she didn't show up."

Nancy wished she could sprout wings and fly out of the room or that she had a hand grenade in her purse. "Yes, ma'am, she will be there."

"And Charlotte and Piper?"

"Yes, and all the girls from Bless My Bloomers and several of their customers, including the Fannin sisters, who are already shopping for fancy dresses. The ladies from Clawdy's are all excited about a ball and Agnes is planning on coming, too, and since she's a single woman you'll have to put her name in that fishbowl."

Nancy deliberately mentioned Agnes just to rile Heather.

"If she pays her fee, I can't keep her from attending, but she'd better be on good behavior or I will have my cousin Ethan escort her right out the door. My poor sweet aunt can't come to the ball." Heather clucked her tongue and shook her head slowly. "Bless Aunt Violet's soul, she will be having a knee replacement very soon and will probably be in rehab during that time. It is so nice of her to let us use her barn for our ball, though, isn't it? Especially since this town doesn't have anything big enough for an event like this."

Yeah, right, Nancy thought. *It'll take someone bigger and meaner than your pussyfooted cousin to toss Agnes out on her ear. She'll have him on his ass so quick he'll wonder what hit him, so you'd do well to steer clear of her.*

Beulah wrung at her hands. Evidently she'd worn out every hankie in her possession and the new order hadn't come in yet.

Floy smiled, which was a miracle. She always looked like she had just sucked all the juice out of a lemon.

Heather went on. "Now, let's go on to the menu. Everett has agreed to smoke all the meat for the ball and we'll serve buffet style. We need centerpieces. Nancy? My aunt, God love her darlin' heart, says you are the best at centerpieces."

"I'm in charge of helping with the buffet table. Someone else can be in charge of centerpieces," Nancy answered. "But if I could make a suggestion. What about a simple jar candle with silk rose petals around it? You could give the candles away to each couple as they leave and since they are in jars they wouldn't drip wax on the tablecloths."

"I like Nancy's suggestion and second the motion to do that. I'll be in charge of finding a good deal on jar candles and silk rose petals," Floy said.

"Good, let's move on to"—Heather dramatically ran her finger down the list inside her angel book lying on the podium—"volunteers for decorating. We'll need to meet at the barn two days before to clean it up and then put up all the illusion so that it looks like a castle. I can just see it all in my mind already and it takes my breath away, it's so beautiful. Nancy, you can be in charge of that committee."

Nancy stood up. "I can't. Remember, I'm on the food committee and I will be helping Everett with smoking the meat. The Fannin sisters called and volunteered to bring the rest of the food and help me cook it. I won't have time to do any decorating. None of them cook so I'll have to oversee every step of the side dishes, but it was very generous of them to offer to donate the food, don't you think?"

If looks could have killed, there would have been nothing but bones and a greasy spot on the church floor where Nancy had been standing.

"The Fannin sisters are not on the committee," Heather said through clenched teeth. "They upset Aunt Violet last year when they took the Easter egg hunt away from her. Poor dear, that's probably the reason her knee has given out and had to be replaced. She's been doing too much since then to show them that she's still able to keep going. She is pushing seventy-five, you know."

"They might not be on our committee, but they are members of our church and they are attending the ball and they want to lend a hand with the supper. They'll be a big help in my kitchen with the preparation. And your aunt is the same age as Agnes, so that makes her every bit of eighty," Nancy told her.

"We can always use all the volunteers that we can get." Beulah spoke up. "And it's time some of the younger ladies in the community showed up at the Angels' meetings on Thursday night, so you might think about a membership drive after the ball is over, Heather."

"Okay, then, Nancy is taking care of the food and nothing else," Heather said in a whine.

Well, while we're blessin' hearts and God-lovin' souls, let's put Beulah in line for some of that heavenly love. If she didn't have a hankie to wring on, maybe her energy would go to her vocal cords and backbone more often. Nancy bit her tongue to keep the words inside her head.

"I could ask for help from Aunt Violet's club," Heather said. "If they saw what a great thing I'm doing, they might agree to join our prayer group on Thursdays. Thank you, Lord"—she looked up at the ceiling—"for sending that idea down through the rafters to me."

"Why couldn't they help? It could be a joint effort," Nancy asked. "I'm sure that Anna Ruth and Andy and several of the other members of club will be attending the ball, so they might have some great ideas."

"I second that," Beulah said.

"We'll have to have a motion before we can have a second," Heather said.

"Then I motion that we ask the Blue Ribbon Society to lend a hand with the barbecue ball," Beulah said.

"And I'll second it," Floy came in right behind her.

Nancy sat down and bit back a giggle. She'd done it. She'd refused to let anyone push her around and it felt damn fine. Now, if only God would toss a husband into Stella's lap when a man came into her shop for a haircut, her life would be perfect.

எ

Piper hauled a container of leftover hot dogs, buns, and all the condiments, along with a bowl of potato salad, one of baked beans, and what was left of a blackberry cobbler to the beauty shop that Tuesday morning. She didn't notice the sign on the glass door with the big neon-green arrow pointing downward. It said, "As of July 1, Men's Haircuts Are No Longer Available at the Yellow Rose Beauty Shop."

She carried all the food to the back room; put the potato salad, beans, cobbler, and hot dogs in the small refrigerator; and set the buns on the table. "I had leftovers from last night so I brought them for our lunch. Lorene picked the boys up today but they're staying for Bible school tonight at their church so they won't be home until bedtime. And Stella, I figured it all out."

"Figured out what?" she asked.

Piper plopped down in the chair at her station and twirled it around so that she could see her friends. "You are sleeping with Rhett. I don't care what people say. I approve. He's good with kids and he cooks a mean hot dog. The boys were still singing his praises this morning. Don't tell Preacher Jed, but they said they like Rhett better than him."

Charlotte dropped her knitting in her lap. The little pink baby hat was coming along fine. "That's yesterday's gossip, darlin'."

"I'm not seeing Rhett." Stella held up two fingers and then crossed her heart like they'd done when they were little girls. "I promise it's not me that he's interested in. He cooked those hot dogs for you, darlin'. I've barely spoken to him . . . oh, speak of the devil . . ."

Rhett's presence filled the beauty shop with enough sexiness to set the whole shop into a hum. His shoulders stretched the white T-shirt and his biceps bulged beneath the two folds on the sleeves. The six-pack leading down to his belt buckle was as defined as if it was bare for all three women to stare at. His jeans were snug and his boots scuffed and when he smiled, the cleft in his chin deepened.

"Good mornin'. Heather and Quinn were having breakfast this mornin' at Clawdy's and she gave me this money order for a free haircut in here," he said.

"Did you see the sign on our door?" Charlotte asked.

"No, ma'am." Rhett grinned and the whole room glowed.

"Well, since you didn't see it, I think Piper is free to do a hair-cut. I've got an appointment that should be here in five minutes and Charlotte's first one is runnin' late but she'll be here . . . there she is now." Stella smiled. "Put away the knitting and get ready to do Trixie's hair."

"I will torture you, Stella Joy," Piper whispered.

Rhett headed for Piper's chair. "I like to keep it short in the summer when I'm coaching the little boys' ball team. It's cooler that way and besides, it sets an example for them."

Stella nodded and smiled sweetly.

Piper vowed revenge. She might start going to church on Thursday nights and praying with the ladies that Stella would find a husband before her birthday.

"Sorry I'm late. We had a big breakfast crew this morning. Gossip must make people hungry." Trixie hopped up in Charlotte's chair. "This barbecue ball and finding Stella a husband are the best things for business since the chili cook-off in the spring."

"I didn't know you was lookin' for a husband. Is that what this southern Kardashian ball is all about? I heard it was to get all the women in Cadillac hitched, not just you. Heather is on some kind of Holy Grail mission about it. Quinn says any time me and Boone are going fishin' he'd love to go just to get away from her fussin' around about the ball and all her ideas for making Cadillac into some big fancy city." He smiled in the mirror at the look on Piper's face.

"What' so funny?"

"Southern Kardashian." She giggled. "Next thing you know the whole thing will turn into a reality television show."

"Hush!" Stella said loudly. "If Heather even hears there's a pos-sibility, she'll jump on it like a hungry dog with a ham bone and turn God into a movie producer."

"Surely to God, they aren't going to pray at the ball, are they? Why don't you just pick your own husband before the ball starts and show them that you're the boss, Stella? I got lots of friends." Rhett chuckled.

"I'm not looking for a husband no matter what they put on the church sign and thank you for the offer to hook me up, but no, thank you. I can do my own finding, my own dating, and my own proposing if I have to," Stella said.

Piper picked up her scissors and started feathering Rhett's hair. She wasn't ready for the sparks that danced around the shop when she ran her fingers through his thick dark hair or for the effect it had on her hormones. She chalked it up to not having sex for more than six months. Hormones could whine around or throw little tantrums because she dang wasn't interested in any kind of relationship: one-night stand, long-term, or friendship. She wouldn't have asked Rhett to supper if she'd known he wasn't the one Stella had been seeing on the sly.

"Hey, what's this about y'all not cutting men's hair anymore?" Alma Grace hiked a hip up into Stella's chair. "If Rhett Monroe isn't a man, then I'm seeing things over there in Piper's chair."

"The Angels had a bake sale to make money to buy money orders for haircuts. Rhett didn't see the sign but he's our last male customer, at least until after the barbecue ball," Piper explained.

Rhett chuckled with a slow Texas drawl that tightened up Piper's gut.

"We just put the sign up and Rhett is the only one we're going to honor," Charlotte explained further.

"I'm not sure I understand any of this. I wasn't at our church on Sunday so I'm in the dark. What's that sign all about, anyway?" Alma Grace said.

"Nancy put Stella on the prayer list for a husband. She's the one that the sign is all about," Piper said.

Alma Grace's light-baby-blue eyes widened until they were about to pop right out of her head.

"Breathe, girl," Stella said.

"What did you do, Stella? I'm surprised with your temper that Nancy is still alive. Why would she do that?" Alma Grace asked.

"What could she do? It was already done before she knew about it," Trixie asked right back. "I heard that she's got a secret boyfriend but she's not tellin' her mama a thing until after the ball because she's so mad at her, though."

"I'm standing right here," Stella said.

Alma Grace's big eyes got wider and wider. "What ball? Lord, what have I missed?"

"The brand-new marriage ministry that Heather is creating is planning a ball." Piper went on to tell Alma Grace all about it.

Alma Grace scarcely blinked through the whole story. "Does Agnes know? I've been on a cruise this past week with my future in-laws and fiancé. Haven't been down to Bless My Bloomers until I ran through here. Do Carlene and Jenny know about this? Lord, I thought that thing with Carlene's divorce was horrible. This has got to be worse."

Piper finished Rhett's hair and dusted the back of his neck with a small brush before whipping the cape from around him. "Whole town knows. It's the newest fodder for the gossip vines. You'll have to buy a brand-new fancy dress for the ball. Agnes says we all have to go."

"Well, I'm not brave enough to fight with Agnes for sure," Alma Grace said seriously. "I bought a couple of formal-type dresses for the cruise. I'll just wear one of them. When is this ball?"

"Last Saturday night in the month of July," Piper answered.

"And you all will be there?" Rhett asked.

"Yes, sir," Trixie said. "Alma Grace spoke for all of us when she said none of us would buck up against Agnes. Are you going?"

"Yes, ma'am. Boone and I've already talked about it. I'm shinin' up my boots and gettin' my hat dusted off. I wouldn't miss a good dance for nothing." Rhett laid the money order on the cabinet. "Thanks, Piper. I appreciate you taking care of my hair. It looks great. Wish y'all weren't going to stop doing haircuts for men. What made you decide that, anyway?"

"Agnes," they said in unison.

"Well, FYI, I wouldn't buck up against her, either." Rhett laughed.

෴

Stella glanced over at Piper. "Well?"

Piper shrugged as she sank down in the chair where Rhett had been sitting. "I thought I was doing my best friend a favor. Now I think I've opened Pandora's box and I'm not sure how to put the lid back on it."

Charlotte raised an eyebrow. "Why would you? Peeking inside what Rhett has to offer might be fun."

Piper threw the back of her hand over her forehead. "Don't give me that look. This is unbelievable."

Alma Grace cocked her head to one side. "Do we need to put you on the prayer list?"

"Good God, no!" Piper almost shouted. "Look what happened when Nancy put Stella on that list. The whole town has gone crazy."

"Crazy is not a new thing for Cadillac," Alma Grace laughed.

Trixie held up a hand. "This will all blow over after the barbecue ball, and something else will take its place. Gossip creates. Time dissipates. That's what Mama used to say before she got sick."

"I don't know if anything can dissolve the gossip since Heather is in town. Lord, the oil boom way back in the last century will be a drop in the bucket compared to this new ministry she's talking about," Piper said.

"And believe me, she is dragging up dirt that I thought was buried more than a decade ago," Stella said.

"You mean about . . ." Alma Grace slapped a hand over her mouth.

"Oh, yes. Fresh scandal from an old recipe. She figures if she can find some poor old fool willin' to marry me with my reputation, she will be well on her way to a prosperous career in marriage ministry," Stella said.

"I've missed a lot. It's going to take a whole week to catch up," Alma Grace said. A short blonde who was almost as religious as Heather, she and her two cousins ran Bless My Bloomers, the plus-size lingerie shop in town. At least, it had started out to be a fancy panty place for the curvy women, but these days it catered to any size. After all, women deserved to have sexy undies, no matter if they were a size 3 or needed three X's on the tag.

Stella finished cutting Trixie's hair and motioned toward the shampoo sink. "Maybe, just maybe, somebody will get married out of the deal even if it's not me. I only want to get past my birthday; then Heather can do whatever she wants. She can re-create the Sadie Hawkins idea if she wants to—as long as my name isn't attached to it."

The front door let in a burst of hot air and there was Agnes looking like she should be pushing a cart filled with great Dumpster-diving bargains.

"Hell's bells, but it's goin' to be a hot one. How many men have you turned away?" She pulled a chair under the air-conditioning vent and slumped into it.

"None. Piper cut Rhett Monroe's hair because he didn't see the sign," Trixie tattled.

"But that's the only one that's getting a money-order haircut," Piper said quickly.

Agnes pulled a blue bandanna from her hip pocket and mopped sweat from her face. "You want to cut your boyfriend's hair, that's all right, but do it at your house. Hell, girl, it would be more fun to cut his hair naked than in a beauty shop filled with women, anyway. And I mean both of you naked, not just him."

"He's not my boyfriend." Piper blushed.

"Bullshit. He cooked on your grill last night. That's more solid than sharing a hymnbook with him in church. And you're all dressed up fancy in them tight things on your legs and that shirt today, so I bet you was hopin' you'd see him. He's a fine-lookin' man. If I was twenty years younger, you wouldn't have a chance with him," Agnes said.

"Agnes Flynn!" Trixie exclaimed. "You old coot. You'd have to be fifty years younger and you know it."

Agnes narrowed her eyes at Trixie. "You should know better than to mess with me, girl. I've put you in your place often enough that you ought to have learned your lessons by now. And FYSA, I was plenty spicy enough to chase down men prettier than Rhett Monroe twenty years ago. Hell, slow as all y'all move, I might still outrun you. I'd done been married more than ten years by the time I was y'all's age."

"It's FYI. The initials mean 'for your information,'" Charlotte said.

"I don't like your alphabet soup world, but maybe I meant *for your stupid ass* when I said FYSA," Agnes smarted off.

"But you are an old dinosaur and you would have been sixty twenty years ago and that would have still been too old to unzip Rhett's pants. What does your snitch say today?" Trixie deftly changed the subject.

"That Piper done read the cards wrong when she thought Rhett was interested in Stella. And that her ex-husband, Gene, already knows that she's got a boyfriend who is taking her boys to New York City to see the Yankee Stadium. Do you need a chaperone, Piper? I always wanted to watch a ball game in that stadium. Y'all got any more of that chocolate cake in the back room?" Agnes headed off in that direction.

Piper gasped. "I'm not going to New York City with Rhett or anyone else. And yes, there's cake in the back room."

"And hot dogs," Stella said.

"Your mama's baked beans?" Agnes looked at Piper.

She nodded. "You can eat whatever you want if you'll tell us who your snitch is."

"I intend to eat some of them beans but I'm not telling you jack shit about my snitch. The FBI or the NASA would come haul my skinny ass off to jail if they knew who I had in my pocket."

"NASA is the place that sends spaceships to the moon and Mars." Trixie laughed.

Agnes waved her hands around. "Well, if they'd stop using letters instead of names, I wouldn't get confused. The FBI or the CBS or one of them god-awful places that listens in on my phone is who I'm talkin' about. Hell, the NASA might be involved. You think they're sending them rockets up there to see if little green men live on Mars? Hell, no, they're sendin' them up there to spy on us. I watch *NCIS*. I know all about that shit."

Trixie paid Charlotte and whispered, "All us at Clawdy's are dropping down on our knees and givin' thanks that y'all got a hornet's nest stirred up down here at the Yellow Rose. Agnes was about to wither up and die. If she and Violet aren't into it about something, chocolate cake can't even make her happy. Now tell me the truth—is that baby stuff really for Cathy?"

"Yes, it is. But Violet isn't stirring up stuff. It's Heather," Charlotte said.

"Heather is her niece, so it's practically the same thing. Agnes will have something to keep her from sinking into depression," Trixie said.

Agnes yelled from the back room, "Hey, did y'all hear that Violet is getting a new knee? Won't be the same without her at the ball, but I'll bet that she manages to show up and make an appearance if they have to push her in there on a hospital bed. Heather is so green that she won't be any competition." They could hear Agnes opening the refrigerator door.

"What competition? Is Heather competing with Violet for the queen bee of Cadillac crown?" Stella asked.

"Hell, no! They'll have to pry that out of Violet's cold, dead hands. The competition is between me and Violet, and if she ain't there, then Heather will be standing in her place and I could out-smart that young'un standin' on my head in hot ashes. It'll be like taking candy from a baby."

Stella laughed out loud.

"It's not funny. I'm bein' serious," Agnes called out. "Now, where's them baked beans, Piper? I can't find them."

"Do you have any idea who her snitch is?" Charlotte asked Trixie in a low whisper.

Trixie shook her head slowly. "We have no idea. She just started talking about her contact or her snitch when all this about Nancy putting Stella on the prayer list came up. I thought it might be Kayla, but then the snitch knows things that happen in places where Kayla doesn't go."

Alma Grace handed Stella a check and said, "I'll walk up the street with you, Trixie. You can tell me all about that doctor you are keeping company with and fill me in on the rest of the gossip before

I go to Bless My Bloomers. That way Carlene and Patrice won't have to play so much catch-up."

Agnes came out of the back door with two plates. One held a hot dog, beans, and potato salad, the other a chunk of chocolate cake. "Hey, Trixie, you'd best be engaged or married to him by the time the barbecue ball takes place. I learned this morning that there's going to be three fishbowls. Heather is putting the gents' . . . and that is her word not mine. Sounds kind of sissified, don't it? Anyway, she's putting the men's names in one bowl and the ladies' in the second one. She'll draw out names from each one and that's who will partner up for the first dance. I hope I get a sexy cowboy."

"The third bowl?" Charlotte asked.

"Will have the names of couples on one piece of paper. Like you and Boone since y'all are already engaged, or Sugar and Jamie Magee since they're already married, and they can dance together for the first dance. I hear it's some shitty old waltz instead of a hoochy-cooch song. Leave it up to Heather to try to turn a barn into a castle and make us all dance like we've got corncobs up our asses." Agnes set about eating the chocolate cake.

"You are supposed to eat your food before dessert," Piper said.

"At my age, you get to eat whatever you damn well please first. I'm proud of your mama, Stella. She stood up to Heather this morning in their meeting. For the first time ever, she didn't let anyone run over her. Your daddy is cookin' and she and the Fannin girls are fixin' the side dishes and that's all she's doin'. I heard that she's quittin' the Prayer Angels soon as this ball is over."

"That's nice, but I'm still mad as hell," Stella said.

Agnes started toward her mouth with a forkful of potato salad. "You'll get over it."

"I'm not so sure. That damned sign is still out there for the whole world to see. That cake looks good." Stella headed to the back room under the pretense of getting a piece of it, but what she really wanted was a moment of peace and maybe to make a phone call.

She poured a cup of coffee and carried it to the small table that they used as a place to eat as well as a place to spread out their papers for business. She pulled out a chair and sat down. Piper and Agnes were arguing about Rhett in the other room. Charlotte, the peacemaker, was trying to change the subject, bless her heart.

There was no way Nancy would ever quit the Angels. She'd be one of those who stuck with it until the day she died. And then the members would all gather in Nancy's kitchen to heat up casseroles and help Everett get through the tough time. Floy and Heather would boss everyone else who stopped by to comfort Stella and Everett.

She slowly shook her head. It wasn't happening like that when her mother passed. No, sirree! She and her father would lock the doors and tell the whole bunch of them to go straight to hell. If it became an issue, they'd post Agnes Flynn on the front porch with her shotgun. She'd gladly take care of turning Violet away if Stella asked her.

After all, redheads stuck together.

A blast of hot air shot across the back room when the door into the alley opened. Only the girls, Agnes occasionally, and the delivery guys came in that way, so Stella didn't even look up. But when Jed wrapped his arms around her from behind and kissed her on that soft part of her neck right under her ear, she jumped like she'd been caught making out on the back row of church during services.

"I've got a free haircut ticket in my pocket," he whispered. "I came to collect."

"Sign on the door says we don't do men's haircuts anymore." She turned enough that she could tangle her fingers in his hair and bring his lips down to hers for a long, lingering kiss.

"Then I guess I'll have to collect on it in private. Maybe tonight at the parsonage?" He picked her up and sat down in the chair with her in his lap. "Or maybe we'll meet back here. Have you ever had sex on the sofa in the shop?"

"No," she gasped.

"Then we'll have to try it out."

"Is someone back there?" Piper yelled. "If it's the delivery guy from the beauty supply, I need six extra perms this next week."

"It's not him, but I'll leave a note."

"Who are you talkin' to? I swear I heard you talkin' to someone." Piper's voice was louder with each word.

Jed quickly set Stella off his lap and stood up. He met Piper halfway across the floor. "Why, hello, Piper. I hope it was all right that I used the back door. I had this ticket for a free haircut but Stella just told me that y'all aren't cutting men's hair anymore." He brushed past her and went into the shop. "Hello, Miz Agnes."

"What are you doin' here?" she asked.

"Free haircut, and I was walkin' down the alley so I used the back door. Looks like you're havin' a fine lunch there." Jed flashed his brightest smile.

"I sure am and I'm right sorry to turn down the preacher, but these girls ain't cuttin' men's hair no more. You'll have to take the ticket back to Heather and tell her to shove it—"

"Agnes!" Charlotte exclaimed.

"Shove it where the sun don't shine. There, does that make everyone happy? I didn't use a single cussword."

Jed patted Agnes on the shoulder. "You did real good, Miz Agnes. See y'all in church on Sunday. I'll be goin' since I can't get a free haircut. You ladies have a wonderful day."

Stella made it to the front of the shop in time to see the door close behind Jed's cute butt, clad in tight-fitting jeans. Stepping out on the sidewalk, he stopped and winked at her and she quickly glanced at everyone else to see if anyone saw it. Thank God, they were all busy either with work or, in Agnes's case, stuffing the end of a hot dog into her mouth.

She glanced at the sofa and high color filled her cheeks. Sex with Jed in all that buttery softness, then cuddled up with him afterward real close because the sofa wasn't all that wide, brought visions to her mind that would shock the cussin' out of Agnes.

"What are you blushin' for?" Agnes asked.

"I had to turn down the preacher. Reckon that will be a scandal?" Stella answered.

"Honey, if it ain't a scandal in the Yellow Rose, then it'll be one at Clawdy's or at Bless My Bloomers. Ain't nothin' Cadillac likes better than a nasty old scandal."

"Ain't it the truth." Stella sighed.

Chapter Eight

The aroma of lasagna and hot bread met Stella that evening when she opened the door to her house. Her last appointment was a permanent that had kept her in the shop until six thirty, so she was hot, sweaty, and hungry.

Jed leaned against the doorjamb in the kitchen, his barbed-wire tat shining beneath the tight muscle shirt. He looked like sex on a stick and she didn't know whether she wanted a shower, sex, or lasagna first.

He made the decision for her. "Bread has ten more minutes. Go grab a quick shower and then we'll eat."

With a couple of long strides he crossed the room and kissed her on the tip of her nose. He smelled like Stetson, soap, and that scent that was all his own, and she had to fight with herself not to drag him down on the floor right there and forget food and a shower.

"This is a real treat," she whispered. "I didn't know if you'd be able to get away tonight. You know this whole town is watching me?" She dropped her denim shorts, T-shirt, and shoes in pile at the end of the sofa and padded to the bathroom barefoot in nothing but her underpants and bra.

He followed her, laid out a towel, handed her a washcloth, and adjusted the water while she finished undressing. "I was careful. I heard that you might be interested in Rhett Monroe. Should I be jealous?"

She rolled up on her toes and kissed him hard. "I'm a married woman who is only interested in one damn fine sexy preacher."

"Good." He grinned.

When she finished her shower, she wrapped a towel around her wet hair and loosely belted a kimono-style terry-cloth robe around her waist. She was almost to the kitchen, where she planned to do a little strip tease with the towel and hopefully wind up having dinner sitting on his lap totally naked.

Piper poked her head out around the kitchen door and said, "Nancy's trying to make up for putting you on the prayer list. I told you that she was sorry."

"Why would you say that?" Stella's heart felt like it was fighting its way out of her chest. Any minute it would throw her left breast out on the floor and land on top of it in a quivering mess. Where in the hell was Jed? Was he hiding in her bedroom?

"*Duh*, girl!" Piper said. "Lasagna is on the bar and I just took hot rolls out of the oven."

"I thought you made all that and had run to the store for salad." Stella was amazed that her voice was not high and squeaky.

Piper shook her head. "I just popped in to see if you wanted to go to the Rib Joint for supper. Lorene called to ask if they could keep the boys overnight so they could take them to a youth rally at their church tonight. But it looks like the magic fairy left supper for us."

Stella's heart settled from a full-out run to a gallop. Where was Jed? She had to get him out of the house, but first she had to find him.

"Well, the magic fairy can come around anytime he, she, or it wants to," she said.

Piper opened the refrigerator. "Nancy is real sorry. You need to forgive her, Stella. There's a beautiful salad all cut up pretty and sliced strawberries for shortcakes."

A rush of hot air blew Charlotte into the house. "What's that I smell? I came by to see if you wanted to go eat somewhere, but I'm staying here if that's Nancy's lasagna. I'd rather eat and then curl up on your sofa with my knitting. I finished the little hat and now I'm working on the booties. When I finish, do you want me to start another one in green or yellow?"

Stella headed toward her bedroom. "Bite your tongue if you are talking to me. But Piper has always wanted a daughter, so you could talk to her. Y'all put supper on the table while I find some clothes."

She shut the door, looked in the closet, under the bed, and behind the drapes. She threw off the robe; jerked on underwear, a clean bright-blue tank top, and a pair of khaki shorts; and swore when she realized she'd left her purse on the sofa.

"Dammit!" She stuck her head out the door and yelled, "Charlotte, will you hand me my purse?"

Charlotte put it in her outstretched hand and said, "Tell her that we forgive her and we love her and if she wants to put us on the prayer list to go right ahead if that means she'll cook for us."

Piper yelled from the kitchen, "I knew you'd made up with Nancy when I smelled the lasagna."

Stella quickly dialed Jed's number. It rang four times before he picked up.

"I'm so sorry. What happened?" she said.

His laughter bounced out of the phone into the bedroom. "Now, that's a story for our old age, darlin'. You'd just gotten in the shower and Piper yelled something from the living room. When she realized that you were in the shower she went straight to the kitchen. I chose my moment and slipped out the door, around the house, across a couple of yards, and came out on the next street over and jogged back to my place. Folks know I run and a couple of cars slowed down and asked if I needed a ride."

Stella's heart settled to a steady beat instead of a gallop.

Even his chuckle had a deep Texas drawl that flat-out set her hormones to humming. She might never forgive those two hussies for interfering with her strip tease and the hot sex afterward. Dammit! They should start sneaking into the beauty shop and using the sofa!

"It's okay, darlin'. A long run and a cold shower will take care of things," Jed said.

"I hate this. I'm almost ready to say to hell with it and tell the world."

"I'm ready to do just that anytime you are."

"We've come this far and it's not much longer." She sighed. "I can endure it until you sign the contract. Besides, they think Mama made supper as atonement for her sins. I'm going to lay the blame off on Agnes because she's been eating everything in sight at the shop. And next week I'm changing the locks on all my doors and nailing my windows shut."

"That'd just cause a bigger problem." He laughed again. "If they leave early enough, call and I'll come back over."

"I'll kick them out in the yard at nine if they aren't gone. It'll be good dark by then," she said.

"Darlin', we don't have to do things this way. I mean it from the depths of my heart when I say that they can take us both or we can both leave Cadillac," he said.

"They didn't ask me before they put their praying panties on, so I'm not giving them any satisfaction until after that damn ball. The hiring committee meets next week. If we get caught after that, it's okay, but it would be nice to put our names in the already-taken bowl at the barbecue ball," Stella said.

What if it comes down to a choice? Leave with your husband or stay with your friends? her conscience asked.

I'll leave in a heartbeat. I love Jed, but please let Jed's next church be close enough I can commute, she answered silently.

"Stella, I'm so ready for you to live in the parsonage with me. I want to be married openly, not secretly," he said seriously.

Her heart flipped twice and her pulse raced. "Me, too, but I know that it will be better for you, for the church, and for Cadillac if we wait until you are hired permanently. I was thinking of announcing it at the ball. What do you think? Are you ready to say that you are married to the town's worst sinner?"

"I will stand up in the middle of Violet's barn and use the microphone so everyone can hear it." He chuckled. "See you later. Love you."

She shoved the phone back into her purse and headed for the kitchen. Piper and Charlotte had the food arranged on the bar, paper plates set at the end, and ice in red plastic disposable cups.

"So was I right? Did Nancy do this for you?"

Stella picked up a plate and cut into the lasagna with a metal server. "No, ma'am, she did not. That's not her recipe. She always uses two kinds of cheese on the top and that's only got one kind. I'm betting that Agnes did it as payback for all the food she's been eating at the shop. I'll thank her the next time she comes in, which will probably be tomorrow morning."

"Tea?" Charlotte asked.

"Yes," Piper and Stella said in unison.

Charlotte filled three cups and said, "How'd she get in your house? We're the only ones with keys."

Piper sipped tea and held up a finger on the other hand until she could swallow. "Hey, that woman can do anything. She's

Agnes-by-damn-Flynn. I wouldn't put it past her to have bugs stuck all over town and that's what she calls her snitch." She took another long sip. "I was spittin' dust. Now, back to Agnes. A locked door wouldn't slow her down a bit, and believe me, she will find out who your boyfriend is before that blasted ball. This sure tastes like Nancy's recipe. I wonder if Agnes talked her into making it without telling her it was for us, or maybe she told her to change it slightly."

"Boone has a late meeting with a new client, but he should be home by eight thirty or we'd watch *Pretty Woman* and have a real girls' night in," Charlotte said.

Piper carried her tea and plate of food to the table. "I'd rather watch *Dirty Dancing*, but my boys will be home by nine, so we don't have time for movies. Besides, I'd rather talk. Rhett called me." She blurted out the last sentence.

"And?" Stella raised both eyebrows.

"He asked me out to dinner, with or without the boys, my choice."

"And?" Charlotte's fork stopped in midair and the lasagna fell back to her plate with a loud plopping noise.

"He'd heard that I thought he was interested in you and just coming around to get to know your friends better. He wanted to clear that up," Piper said.

"Don't pause or stop. Keep talking," Stella said.

"He said that . . ." Piper blushed.

"What? Spit it out," Charlotte said impatiently.

"That he likes tall women with some sass and he admired me for not letting Gene get away with cheating on me. Crazy thing is that I don't know if he did cheat on me—that part could be gossip." Tears flooded her face and dripped off her jaw onto her shirt, leaving wet polka dots on the cotton fabric. "Not knowing is as bad as knowing."

"Cheating on you? Of course he did. He was just sneaky enough that we don't know for sure, but think about it. All those late nights at work and those weekends he went fishing but didn't bring a thing home, not even a sunburn and chigger bites." Stella's voice got higher with each word.

"Honey, we know, but he was careful. If we'd had names and dates, we would have taken his sorry ass out on Everett's boat and made fish bait out of it," Charlotte said.

Stella scooted her chair closer and threw an arm around Piper. "I agree with Charlotte. Besides, what does it matter now, anyway? It's in the past and it's time for you to move on with your life."

Piper took a deep breath, downed half the tea in her glass, and said, "You've convinced me. If you can live with this husband shit plastered on the church sign, I can get my life in order. No more tears and no more worry. It's my life and I'm not going to live it in bitterness and anger."

Charlotte reached across the table and laid a hand over Piper's. "Don't just say it; do it. As long as you are upset about Gene, then he has control, and you are too good to let him control your life."

"Charlotte is right," Stella said.

"You might do well to listen to your own advice," Piper said.

"I'm not mad . . . oh, you mean Mama." Stella did an eye roll and then looked Piper in the eye. "Let it go. We'll make up. I'm less mad today than I was yesterday but you ain't pushin' me into nothing. I'm not in a forgiving mood right now."

"Okay, I've been through denial and anger, what's next?" Piper said.

"Bingeing out on lasagna and strawberry shortcake tonight and talking about this barbecue ball shit. We've got to get dresses. I'm tempted to get one cut down to my waist in the front and up to my crack in the back," Stella said.

"I'll pay for it if you will buy it in bright red. Heather will stroke plumb out," Charlotte told her. "What did you tell Rhett about dinner, Piper?"

"That I'd think about it," Piper answered.

Stella ignored the ringtone the first time her phone rang but when it started again within a minute of stopping, she shrugged and hurried to her bedroom to answer it.

"Hello," she said breathlessly.

"Change of plans. The ambulance just came and took my elderly neighbor to the hospital. They think he's having a heart attack and he's scared. No family left, so I'm headed to the hospital to be with him. See you later."

"I understand," she said. "The girls are leaving by nine, or so they say. Keep me posted. You might still have time to drop by and have some of this fabulous lasagna that Agnes made."

"I'm sure that it's delicious. Don't wait up for me. Love you," he said and the phone went dead.

❧

The boys were still sleeping soundly the next morning when Lorene arrived.

"I'm sorry, Lorene. I should have had them up and dressed, but my alarm didn't go off this morning and I'm running late, so do you mind taking them in their pajamas?" Piper said. "I'm glad you're keeping them. If you weren't, they'd have to be awake and dressed to go to day care." Piper scooped Tanner up in her arms and carried him out to the van with Lorene right behind her. The boys were like rag dolls and didn't know that they'd been strapped into the seats with their stuffed animals tucked in with them.

Lorene patted her on the shoulder. "I'm glad that you let us keep them. We'll see you at the end of the day. If they don't wake up on the way into the house, then I'll let them sleep as long as they need to. They talked a lot about Rhett yesterday and how that he was a great ballplayer."

"They had a great time with him." Piper smiled. "My last appointment is at three today so y'all can drop them early. Just call me if you're coming to the shop and I'll wait there."

"We will." Lorene nodded.

Piper watched the van until it was out of sight, then raced back to the house, grabbed her purse, locked the door, and turned on the air conditioner the first thing when she crawled into her car. When it was already in the high eighties at eight o'clock in the morning, there was no doubt that it was going to be a scorching-hot day.

She'd put the car in reverse and was backing out of the driveway when she noticed the paper stuck under the windshield wiper on the passenger's side. Figuring it was an invitation to a nearby summer Bible school or maybe a flyer for what was on sale at the convenience store in town, she ignored it and drove on to the shop. She was in such a rush to get inside out of the heat that she forgot about it until the hot Texas wind unhinged it and sent it flying across the sidewalk to land right at her feet.

She stopped in her tracks right there in front of the Yellow Rose and read it at least ten times before she put it in her purse. In big scrawling letters it said, "Have a wonderful day . . . Rhett."

Agnes startled the hell out of Piper when she said, "What in the hell have you got there that would make you stand out here in this broilin' heat and stare at it like it was a viper about to bite you on the ass?"

"Where did you come from?" Piper asked.

"I walked down here to see if you brought something good to eat again this morning. The chocolate cake is all gone. I guess I'll have baked beans for breakfast if there's any left since you've let me down," Agnes said.

"Talk to Stella. She might have brought some of your lasagna."
Piper opened the door and stood to the side to let Agnes enter first.

"My lasagna?" Agnes said.

"Is in the back room on the table. Help yourself. The salad is in the fridge with the leftover strawberries," Stella said.

Agnes headed to the back room and returned in a few minutes with a loaded plate. "Well, praise the Lord. I didn't want breakfast food or I'd have gone to Clawdy's. All is quiet on the home front this morning. My snitch didn't have much to report except that the colors for the ball are pastel shades of yellow, which of course is because it's the Yellow Rose Barbecue Ball, blue because the Blue Ribbon Jalapeño Society is helping with it, and pink because Heather's new signature color for her ministry is pink. Sounds like a damn overgrown baby shower to me." She stopped and caught her breath before going on. "I just hope that Heather don't insist that all the unmarried women wear white. If she does, I'll have to bleach out a pair of my overalls."

Charlotte spun around in her chair and caught Piper's eye. "What were you reading out there? You are absolutely glowing."

"A note from Rhett." She pulled it from her purse and handed it to Charlotte.

Stella tiptoed to read it over Charlotte's shoulder.

"Awwww," they both said at the same time.

"I told you he's interested in you," Charlotte said.

"But it makes me so nervous just thinking about the dating world again. I never dated anyone but Gene. We started liking each other back when he sent me one of those notes that said, 'If you like me, check the box with yes,' and I did."

"We'll teach you," Stella said.

"Not me. I'm just like you. I've only dated Boone. Stella will have to teach you unless Agnes wants to," Charlotte said.

"Is that boy stalkin' you? I saw a thing about that on *NCIS* last night. I can put out a hit on him if he is," Agnes said.

"No, he's just trying to take her out to dinner," Stella answered.

"Well, what the hell are you waiting on? He's sexy. He's got money. He's got a job at the fire department in Sherman just like Boone does. He likes your boys and evidently he likes tall women if he's askin' you to dinner. Y'all seen that movie *Pretty Woman?*"

They all stared at her with big eyes.

Agnes giggled like a little girl. "Hell, you think I only watch cartoons. I've seen raunchy movies. What I was about to say is that you remember when the hooker says that about having eighty-something inches of therapy in her long legs, well, maybe Rhett is in need of some therapy."

"Agnes!" Piper gasped.

"I'm old. I'm not dead. Bert Flynn liked that kind of therapy when he was alive even if there wasn't eighty inches of it. I reckon Rhett would, too, and it'd sure put you in a better mood. Plus, it would show that dirtbag ex-husband of yours that you ain't still whinin' around wantin' him to come home," she said. "Who made this lasagna?"

"You did," Stella said.

"Not me. It tastes like what Cathy makes at Clawdy's."

"Guess that's where you got it, then." Charlotte smiled.

"I got it in the back room," Agnes said as she shoveled a forkful into her mouth.

Piper put the note back in her purse and headed for her work-station. Agnes could be secretive about her snitch and the food, but they all knew that she'd figured out a way to get into Stella's house and leave it there. She probably had bought it at Clawdy's, but she wasn't fooling Piper one bit.

CHAPTER NINE

S tella turned the air conditioner thermostat down a few degrees to cool the shop and got ready for a long day. Every slot in her appointment book was filled, which meant she'd hear about what everyone was wearing to the Fourth of July festivities that night, who was coming with whom, who'd never be seen with whom, and who was cheating on whom after the festivities were over.

When the customers had worn that out, they'd talk about the barbecue ball and what kind of dresses they were thinking about or had already bought. To Stella's way of thinking, it was a big girls' prom and Heather was the high school principal who'd keep the kids all in line. Agnes was the rebel who'd bring vodka for the punch bowl, and when the ball was over then the gossips could all settle down until the fall, when the Blue Ribbon Jalapeño Society Jubilee would fire up.

"Hey, I figured we'd be in for a busy day, so I ran up to Walmart and picked up some lunch meat, bread, and staples so we wouldn't starve. I got those barbecue chips that you like and a gallon of sweet tea," Charlotte yelled as she put food away in the back room. "Oh, and I picked up a dozen doughnuts at that little shop for breakfast.

You better get one of the maple-iced ones in a hurry. I think they're Agnes's favorite kind, too."

A movement on the sidewalk outside caught Stella's eye and she hopped out of the chair and made a beeline for the back room. Piper and Agnes were arriving at the same time for the third day in a row and there were probably only three maple doughnuts in the box.

"Give me two of those doughnuts," she told Charlotte.

"One for you and one for Agnes?"

"Both for me. I'm eating one and hiding one in my station drawer."

The phone rang as Stella was stashing one of her doughnuts.

"Good mornin', Yellow Rose Beauty Shop," she said.

"Stella, is Aunt Agnes down there again this morning?" Cathy asked.

"Yes. She and Piper are coming in the door right now," Stella answered.

"I'm just checking on her. She usually eats breakfast here and she's been spending a lot of time at your shop and . . ."

"She's fine, Cathy."

"You sure?"

"I'm going to grow up and be just like her. She entertains us, believe me. Do I owe you something for letting us have her?" Stella dropped her voice to keep Agnes from hearing.

"Oh, no, but if I owe you anything, just send the check or we can take it out in trade." Cathy laughed. "She's happy as a piglet in a fresh wallow right now with all this prayer meeting stuff going on. It's put a brand-new spring in her step."

"Sorry, ma'am, we're all booked solid today. This is the day of the Fourth of July festivities at the football field so I don't have a spare minute, but I could call you if I have a cancellation," Stella said.

"I understand. I'll call back later." Cathy laughed.

"Y'all all goin' to the football field tonight?" Agnes asked.

Charlotte and Stella nodded.

"There's doughnuts and sandwich makings in the back room," Piper said.

"I'll take time for a doughnut if there's a maple one or a chocolate one but then I've got some preliminary work to do before we go to the fireworks show tonight."

"Agnes, you aren't making fudge, are you?" Stella asked.

"Not this year. Violet's on to me, and besides, that was last year's excitement. I can't expect to wring anything more out of that trick. But I heard that she was coming and she's walking with a cane. I told that old bitch she'd wear out before I did. If I wind up in jail, y'all bring me a chocolate cake." Agnes grinned.

"No shotguns, either," Charlotte yelled.

"Well, hell, y'all ain't no more fun than the girls at Clawdy's."

෴

Nancy had barely settled into the chair for Ruby to blow-dry and style her hair when Agnes pushed the door open. The noise level went from a low buzz to dead silence and every woman in the place—those under the hair dryers, the lady getting her nails done, and the four around the table waiting for their turns—looked from Agnes to Violet, who was waiting for her turn to have her hair done. Heather looked up from the table she shared with Violet and rolled her eyes toward the ceiling.

"Good mornin', everyone. Y'all gettin' beautified for the fireworks show tonight?" Agnes pulled up the extra chair beside Kayla's fingernail station and slumped down, kicked off her flip-flops, and rolled up the legs of her overalls. "I want toenails and fingernails both done today."

"I thought you did your business down at the Yellow Rose," Heather said.

"They don't do toenails. I did get my eyebrows waxed last week. They look damn fine, don't they? Yours are getting pretty wild, Violet. Old women have ugly eyebrows and toenails, so they need to take care of them," Agnes said.

"Never you mind about my toenails or my eyebrows. If you didn't wear those god-awful rubber flip-flops all the time, you wouldn't have to worry about yours, either. Bert Flynn would roll over in his grave to see the way you go out in public," Violet snapped.

Nancy held her breath. No one, not even Jesus, would say something about Bert to Agnes. Everyone in town knew that in her eyes Bert had a perfect diamond-studded halo and pure white wings that glowed in the dark.

Kayla broke the silence. "Miz Agnes, you go on and get in the pedicure chair and I'll run some water in the tub for you to soak your feet in. The remote for a chair massage is right there in the pocket."

With the agility of a twenty-year-old, Agnes crawled up into the chair and stuck her feet in the tub. Kayla started the warm water and added a handful of vanilla-scented bath salts.

The whole shop waited in pregnant silence. There wasn't room in Agnes's overalls for her famous shotgun, but there was plenty for a pistol, and Agnes had proven in the past that jail didn't scare her one bit.

"So have you bought your tickets to the barbecue ball?" Heather asked Agnes.

"You mean we got to pay to go to a glorified barn dance?"

"Yes, ma'am," Kayla answered. "Tickets are twenty dollars each and any member of the Angels keeps a supply ready. You need to bring your dress in so we can match your polish to it, Miz Agnes. If

I don't have your color, I'll have to order it. I've got pink, blue, and yellow on hand, though."

"Holy shit, Kayla! Pink is all right but blue would look like someone was about to die, and yellow, my God, would look like dead chicken hide got stuck on a woman's fingernails. You better get in some bright red for me. It'll go with my overalls."

"Miz Agnes, you ain't goin' to really wear overalls, are you?" Kayla asked.

"Yes, I am. And Violet, Bert visits me at night and he says that he likes my overalls and flip-flops. He says that he thinks they are damn sexy. I keep askin' him if I can load up my shotgun and shoot you but he says not until he gives me a sign. Soon as he does I'm going to give you a twenty-minute head start just to give you a fightin' chance. But remember, I can run faster in flip-flops and overalls than you can in a girdle and high heels, especially now since you done wore out your knee."

Violet puffed up like a bullfrog. "Bull crap. Bert was glad to die just so he could be rid of you. And my knee is getting a replacement on Monday. In a few weeks it'll be like new and then I could beat you in any footrace you want to set up, you old bat."

"Y'all heard that," Agnes said. "Nancy, you are my witness. I do believe that is my sign. I'll ask Bert when I get home to be absolutely sure, but there could be fireworks for sure at the football field tonight. Kayla, darlin', paint my toenails the brightest red you got in the shop."

Nancy covered her mouth with her hand and did a fake cough to cover the giggles. What was Agnes thinking? She knew that Violet had her hair done twice a week at Ruby's—on Tuesday and Friday.

"Agnes, I just got one more thing to say. If you do one thing to upset Heather's barbecue ball, you'll be able to talk to Bert up close and personal," Violet said.

"Why, Violet Prescott, are you threatening me? And just when I was about to buy ten of them tickets. Well, Nancy, I'll just buy them from you since Violet, God love her hateful old soul, is in a pissy mood today."

"Why would you want that many?" Nancy was elated. Each member of the Angels was supposed to sell at least ten tickets. She'd have hers sold in one fell swoop if Agnes was serious.

"Three for the girls at Clawdy's, three for the Bless My Bloomers gals, and three for the girls down at the Yellow Rose and one for me. Well, shit, I almost forgot Darla Jean. I can't forget my pastor, now can I, so go on and give me eleven tickets." Agnes counted them off on her fingers.

"Why are you buying for all those folks?" Heather asked. "Can't they buy their own?"

"It's payment for serving as my bodyguards."

Nancy's hair was done, so she got out of the chair so Violet could have it. "You really want eleven tickets, then, Agnes?"

Agnes pulled a wad of money from her pocket, undid the rubber band holding the bills together, and peeled off four fifty-dollar bills and one twenty.

"Miz Agnes, you shouldn't be carryin' around that much money," Kayla said.

"Honey, I'm old but I'm meaner than a junkyard dog. Anyone wants my money they'll have to fight me for it, and I don't fight fair. Thank you, Nancy. What'd y'all do with all them haircuttin' money orders you bought? I heard the men gave them back to you."

"We are giving them as door prizes at the barbecue ball. Since the beauty shop has the same name as our ball, we thought it would be nice," Heather said.

Nancy's laughter broke free when she reached her truck. When sweat began to puddle up around the band of her bra, she remembered to start the engine and turn on the air-conditioning. As she passed Clawdy's she saw Jack Landry crossing the street to his patrol car. She pulled over to the curb and rolled down the window.

"Hello, Nancy." He bent at the waist and put his hands on the side of the truck. "You got a pretty dress for that big redneck ball? I heard that Everett is cooking the brisket. That'll bring in a lot of people in for sure."

"Thought you might like to know that Violet and Agnes are both at Ruby's and they'll be at the football field tonight for the fireworks," she said.

"I'll call in a couple of extra duty volunteers for the evening, then, and thanks," he said.

"Might be a good idea. We don't need a repeat of last year." She smiled.

He straightened up and waved. She rolled up the window and went on her way. She glanced over at the Yellow Rose as she drove past. She missed Stella and couldn't wait until this damned old barbecue ball was over. A son-in-law or a grandbaby couldn't fill the place in her heart that her daughter held.

Chapter Ten

S tella's father waved at her from the second row of the bleachers. Her mother sat on one side of him and Jed on the other. She stopped in her tracks, her feet glued to the wooden steps leading up into the stands.

"Hey, you almost made me dump nachos all over you," Charlotte said right behind her. "What'd you stop for, anyway? Oh, now I see. I'll sit by your mother so you don't have to. You sit by Jed."

Stella swallowed hard. "I'll sit by Mama. It's okay. It won't kill either of us and we'll have to face off with each other someday."

"Someday is not today," Charlotte said. "Get going. Our nachos are getting soggy."

"What's the holdup?" Boone asked from behind Charlotte.

"We're moving," Charlotte said.

Stella could feel every eye in the stands on her as she smiled and waved back to her father. Were they all taking bets as to whether she'd sit by her mother or the preacher? If she sat by Nancy, what wild stories would be setting the phone lines on fire later that night? If she sat beside Jed, would the gossips have a name to go on the church sign?

Charlotte was already making a beeline to sit beside Nancy, so Everett better clean up the shotgun and book the church. But who would do the services, since Jed was the preacher and it probably wasn't legal for him to perform the ceremony for his own wedding? And could the higher powers in the church make them stand up before the pulpit and get married again, or would the courthouse license be legal enough for them? Poor man! He had no idea what trouble he'd brewed up when he decided to keep company with Everett.

"Hi, Daddy. Mama. Jed." She nodded at each person.

"Work hard today?" Everett asked.

"Busiest day of the year. Friday's always tough, but add that to the fireworks festival and it's nonstop," she answered.

"Hello, Stella." Jed smiled.

She sat down beside him. "Hi. I understand you and my daddy have been doing some serious fishin' this week."

He shifted a knee over to touch hers. "We have been havin' a really good time. You should go with us sometime."

"Maybe I will," she said.

Nancy leaned around Everett and touched Stella on the shoulder. "There's enough fish in my freezer for a big fryin'. Why don't you invite your friends and come on over Sunday evening for supper? I'll make banana nut bread for one of the desserts."

"And your famous cream-puff cake?" Charlotte asked.

"That would be good here in this hot weather," Nancy said.

"Boone is bringing his catch of the week and Jed is helping me fry up the fish, so we'll have a big crowd," Everett said.

"How much banana bread are you making?" Stella asked.

"Enough that you can take a couple of loaves home with you." Nancy smiled.

"Can't beat a deal like that. I'll get Piper to bring a pot of baked beans and I'll make that ranch potato salad that Daddy likes," Stella said.

That should give the gossipmongers enough to talk about for the whole weekend. She felt right smug until Rhett Monroe sat down on the other side of her and the whispers started humming like busy bees all around her.

Rhett was dressed in faded jeans, cowboy boots, and a red T-shirt and he smelled like soap and shaving lotion with just a faint bit of beer tossed in the mix. On the other side, Jed wore faded jeans, cowboy boots, and a bright blue T-shirt and he smelled like soap and Stetson with just a faint hint of nachos. The whole scenario was more than a little heady, especially when she overheard someone a couple of seats up from her wondering which one was the answer to the Thursday night prayers.

"Where's Piper? I thought you'd all three be together," Rhett said.

"She's on her way," Stella answered. "Scoot down a little way and we'll save three seats for her and the boys."

"There she is." Jed's hand brushed across Stella's arm when he pointed. "She and the guys are over there beside the hot-dog stand."

"There's lots of room over on this side," Rhett said. "You're asking her to your dad's fish fry on Sunday, Stella?"

Stella leaned forward and answered, "Of course we are. We'd be in the doghouse if we didn't let her make baked beans."

"And those two boys love to come to our place. We'll make a freezer of home-churned ice cream and I'll rig up the donkey wagon so they can have a ride," Everett said.

"So it's a date then, set in stone for Sunday night. The Yellow Rose ladies will be at the fish fry along with Boone, Rhett, and Luke and Tanner?" Jed said.

"And you and me and Nancy," Everett said loudly.

It was her father's grin that melted Stella's heart. She might not be ready to forgive her mother for putting her on that damn prayer list, but she couldn't stay mad at her forever. And her friends were right when they said that Everett missed her.

It was shaping up to be a grand night for the gossip vine. The poor phone company might need to be contacted in advance to be aware that there was a possibility the lines would burn plumb up. Stella had agreed to go to her mother's house for Sunday supper. She was between Rhett and Jed, but Piper would have to sit on the other side of Rhett and that would really throw a wrench into the guessing game. Now they'd all wonder which woman Rhett was really interested in. By morning, the news might be that they'd had a threesome, or maybe an orgy, underneath the bleachers after the fireworks show was over.

Rhett patted the place right beside him when Piper arrived. "Saved you the best seat in the house."

"Look, there's Daddy," Luke said and waved.

Stella reached around Rhett's back, tapped Piper on the shoulder, and leaned back to tell her about the fish fry on Sunday.

"Look, Luke, he's coming up here. Maybe he'll sit beside us. Y'all scoot down. Daddy is waving at us. I wonder where Rita and Grandma and Grandpa are," Tanner said.

The plot thickened further. Much more and Stella wouldn't be a character in the story line. When Gene plopped down beside Luke and ruffled both boys' hair, the static behind Stella buzzed with excitement.

"Hey, y'all make some room for me." Agnes squirmed in between Nancy and Charlotte. "I didn't miss anything, did I?"

That shoved Stella and Jed right up next to each other, shoulders, hips, and legs all touching. Heat came near to setting her on fire right there in the football stands.

"You didn't miss anything, Miz Agnes. They haven't started yet. Put your tote bag right down here beside our feet," Charlotte said.

Gene patted Luke on the knee. "You can sit in my lap and Tanner can sit on Mama's knee to make a little more room."

"I'm not a baby," Luke said.

Tanner shook his head. "Me, neither."

"We're fine down here," Jed said. "No need for anyone to hold one of those boys. We don't mind being scrunched, do we, Rhett?"

"Not a bit." Rhett's chin dimple deepened.

Agnes nudged Nancy. "I hear there's a fish fry going on at y'all's place Sunday night."

"There is and you should come," Nancy said.

"Well, thank you. What can I bring?"

"A six-pack of Coors." Everett laughed.

"I'll bring a case and it'll be cold," Agnes told him.

"Fish fry? Are we goin', Mama?" Tanner asked. "Is Rhett coming, too? Can we bring our bats and gloves?"

"You sure can," Rhett said. "I might even talk Boone and Jed into playing a game with us."

"I thought you guys were coming to my place this weekend," Gene said.

"No, Daddy, last weekend was yours. Remember, you said that you and Rita had plans so we got to stay with Grandpa and he took us fishin'. We love to go fishin' but we love to eat 'em as well as catch 'em," Luke reminded him.

Stella could have kissed that child. It was way past time for karma to bite Gene square on the ass and she was so glad that she got to be there when it did.

"If you ask my daddy, I bet he'll let y'all turn the crank to help make homemade ice cream," Stella said.

"Wow! That's awesome." Luke held up a hand and Tanner slapped it in a high five.

Gene shot a drop-dead look her way, but she just smiled at him. Oh, yes, Madam Karma had made a perfect entrance. It was worth sitting between the two men that her mother absolutely did not want her to be involved with just to see Gene on the hot seat.

Ethan Prescott's voice came through the microphone and the noise level dropped to a dull roar. "Good evening, everyone. We're glad you could all join us tonight for the Cadillac Fireworks Festival. We've got a fantastic show for you, but before it starts, my mother, Violet Prescott, would like to say a few words."

"Well, dammit. She's a perfect target up on that flatbed trailer with the lights shinin' on her," Agnes groaned. "And I didn't bring my pistol. Anyone got a tomato I could throw at her? I've got a good pitchin' arm."

"Agnes!" Nancy exclaimed.

"Well, I do. And, honey, you might not know it, but sittin' beside me will most likely cause Heather to make you give up your angel-prayin' panties."

Stella giggled. "Yes, Mama, you can take my name off the list now, because none of those prayin' women are going to enlist God's help for you since you've thrown in with the redheads."

"I wish to hell—pardon me, Jed—that I'd never asked them to put your name on the list," Nancy said.

Everett patted her on the knee. "I'll all be over by the end of the month, darlin'."

Violet took the microphone from her son and tapped it to be sure it was working. "Guess that you can all hear me all right?"

"We hear her too damned good. No tomatoes, anyone?" Agnes asked.

"I got a little bit of a hot dog left," Luke said.

"And you are going to eat it," Piper said.

"Guess y'all don't leave me no choice." Agnes pulled a bright red megaphone from her tote bag and stood up.

"We thank you for coming and we would like to . . ." Violet started off her speech.

Agnes turned around toward the packed bleachers and shouted into the megaphone, "Let's hear it for the firemen who have donated their time, energy, and money into putting on this show for Cadillac. Put your hands together and stomp your feet for our Cadillac firemen."

Folks over in Fannin County probably looked to the southwest for an approaching tornado when catcalls, yells, and applause joined the stomping that vibrated the wooden stands. Agnes worked the crowd better than any country music star Stella had ever seen. When the folks began to take their seats, she yelled into the megaphone again, "Now let's give a big round of applause to all the vendors who've battled the heat and mosquitoes to make it a wonderful evening for the Cadillac citizens. Let's hear it for the hot dogs, the funnel cakes, and all the good food."

That round was so loud that Luke put his hands over his ears, but he was stomping just as hard as Tanner. Stella glanced over at Jed to find him laughing too hard to cheer.

"Can I have everyone's attention? Please, qui . . . et!" Violet yelled into the microphone. "I would like to say—"

Agnes checked her watch and put the megaphone back to her mouth. "Countdown until the first blast. Ten . . . can I get a ten?"

"Ten!" the whole crowd yelled.

"Nine . . . can I get a nine?"

Nine!"

It went on until she yelled, "Blast off!"

The first rocket lit up the sky in red, white, and blue. Stomping ceased. Everyone took their seats and watched the sparkling display, one after the other, and Violet was left on the flatbed, pointing a glittering gold fingernail up toward Agnes.

Agnes tucked her megaphone back into her tote bag. "Don't worry, Nancy, she won't excommunicate you from the Angels until after the ball or else Everett won't fix the barbecue."

Everett patted his wife's knee. "Damn straight."

Stella nudged Jed. "You are living dangerously, sitting up here among the Baxter heathens and Agnes Flynn. You might not have a pulpit to preach from come Sunday morning. Violet might work the deacons up into a mood to fire your butt."

"Whatever happens with this job, darlin', I'll trust that it's God's will. I survived before he called me to preach. I reckon I can find a job doin' something else if he wants me to quit preaching. Remember, I've still got some acreage and an old mule up around Ravenna. We could always go to raisin' turnip greens and hogs," Jed whispered.

"I like turnip greens," she whispered.

"Did you see that one, Mama? It was your colors. Pink and purple," Luke shouted in excitement.

"Pretty, wasn't it?" Piper hugged him. "Thank you for remembering my favorite colors."

"I always remember. You like pink roses and the purple stuff that looks like feathers. Grandma used to send them to you for your birthday before she went to live with Jesus . . . oh, look at that one, it's red and green like Christmas."

Rhett tilted his head toward Stella. "Pink roses, huh?"

She nodded.

Jed nudged her from the other side. "And what's your favorite?"

"She's always loved yellow roses. Her favorite ones were right off the bush in our front yard. Her grandpa wanted us to name her Stella Rose because his favorite song was 'The Yellow Rose of Texas,'" Everett answered. "That's why she named her beauty shop what she did. She couldn't very well name it Amos Moses after her grandpa."

"So you named her Stella Joy? Why?" Jed asked.

"Joy because I knew when I laid eyes on her that she would be mine and her mama's joy and Stella because that was my mother's name." Everett grinned.

Stella blew him a kiss. "That's so sweet, Daddy."

"It's the damn truth," he said and went back to watching the fireworks.

❦

Violet had both hands on her hips and not a single one of her three chins had the nerve to move an inch when she met Agnes in the middle of the football field. Stella hurried on past Jed and her father to join Cathy, Marty, and Trixie as they circled around Agnes.

"You are a thorn in my side, Agnes Flynn," Violet hissed.

"Well, you are a pain in my ass, Violet Prescott."

Violet's eyes narrowed into slits. "You aren't going to goad me into a fight, but if you think you are going to ruin Heather's ball, you've got another think comin'."

Agnes's smile was laced with equal amounts of sugar and sarcasm. "I thought I was helping, getting the crowd all worked up for the fireworks show. Y'all all see how she reacts when I try to help and be her friend. Some folks just don't appreciate any damn thing you do for them. Help her work up the crowd and she swears at me."

"You knew exactly what you were doing and I did not say a single swear word. You were the one doing the damn cussin'." Violet clamped her mouth shut and took a deep breath. "You are a bitch, Agnes Flynn," she hissed when her lips parted. "You can't leave anything alone, can you? My niece just wants to have a nice event for Cadillac."

"Your niece is just trying to push her marriage ministry shit on us and we don't want it," Agnes said.

"Whoa!" Stella held up a hand. "That's enough, Violet. Let's go home, Agnes, before tempers get out of hand."

"It will be enough when I'm finished talking and I'm not and you, young lady, are the reason for all this crap. If your stupid mama hadn't put you on the prayer list, none of this would have happened anyway," Violet said.

"Don't you call my mama stupid." Stella raised her voice a notch.

"Don't you yell at my aunt." Heather joined the group.

Ethan, Violet's son, took a step forward and Agnes laid a hand on his shoulder.

"You should take your mama to the doctor first thing in the morning. I read up on old people and dementia just this week. There was an article in the AARP magazine that I get every month. It's said that the first sign for some folks is that they get fired up and mad about everything, especially if they don't get their way." Agnes sighed and raised her shoulders a notch before she went on. "I'll be glad to let everyone in Cadillac know that you've got the beginning signs of it so they won't get offended at you. I bet all that glue up under that gold fingernail done caused you to get infected with dementia and I hear there ain't no cure for it."

"Aunt Violet does not have dementia!" Heather yelled over the buzz of cars starting up engines and people talking all around them.

"Bless her heart, Ethan. It's too bad they don't have some little white pills to cure it, but they just don't. It's that fingernail. I just know it is. I'll pray for her. That's the best any of us can do," Agnes shouted.

"You're not a member of my Angels," Heather declared.

"I know, honey. I know. But I can pray to God right out on my front porch. It's tough gettin' old and not even knowin' that you forgot to put on a bra," Agnes said.

Violet looked down at her breasts and hollered so loud that Ethan took a step backward. "I've got on a bra. I have on underpants and a girdle, too, for your information."

"See, Heather, when they get afflicted with that horrible thing, they say the most outlandish things, and I hear that it's hereditary. Do you know what that means?"

Violet's cane sank into a gopher hole when she took a step toward Agnes and she went down on her bad knee. She reached out to grab anything to break her fall and got a firm hold on Agnes's shoulder, bringing her down with her. Everyone in the group heard the loud crack of bones as they fell in a pile of moans and groans.

"My knee!" Violet screamed.

"My hip," Agnes whispered and all the color left her face.

"Call nine-one-one," Heather and Ethan said in unison as they dropped down beside Violet.

"The ambulance is already here for any emergencies. Just hang on, Agnes. They'll be here soon as they can get down the field," Everett said.

Stella knelt beside Agnes. "Don't move. Keep breathing. The ambulance is coming right now."

"Have to tell you something. Come closer," Agnes said.

Stella put her ear to Agnes's mouth.

"Your mama is my snitch. She's sorry she put your name on that list and she's doin' what she can to make it right. You've got to take up the reins and . . . damn, this hurts like hell . . . make sure Heather don't become the next Violet. Remember, it's up to us redheads to save Cadillac from ruination."

"What have we got?" the paramedic asked.

"I think her hip is broken," Stella said.

"Aunt Violet's knee," Heather sobbed.

"Call for the other ambulance," he yelled at his coworker. "I'll stabilize the hip. You work on the knee."

Trixie kissed Agnes on the forehead as they loaded her into the van. "Get well, you old toot. I'll take care of you when you get out.

I'll take you up to my room and you can help me work on a ceramic flowerpot I'm fixin' up for my mama."

Agnes opened her eyes and glared at Trixie. "I'm not going in your damn room. It's so damn messy that the rats won't go in there."

Trixie laughed. "She'll be kickin' ass in no time."

"I'm going to the hospital," Stella said.

"You can ride with us." Trixie nodded.

❧

Stella turned the doorknob, automatically flipped on the light, and hoped that Jed would appear wearing nothing but a towel or a pair of lounging pants slung low on his hips. But a hunky blond-haired preacher didn't poke his head out around the kitchen door.

Charlotte did.

"We were about to give up on you and go home. Shhh . . . the boys fell asleep in the spare bedroom while they were playing with their little video game things. How's Agnes?"

Stella sat down on the sofa and propped her feet on the coffee table. "She broke her hip. They're calling in an emergency team of specialists to replace it tonight. Marty sent Cathy and me home. She said she and Trixie would stay and call us as soon as it was over. The doctor said that she'd be in the hospital a week and then rehab for a few weeks. She's going to love that."

"And Violet?" Charlotte sat down and picked up a ball of green baby yarn.

"She's scheduled for knee surgery on Monday so they're going to keep her, but she didn't do any damage other than falling and making it hurt. They're not in the same room and Trixie already warned them not to put the two old farts in the same rehab room when they get out."

Piper smiled. "Smart woman. What was it that Agnes was whispering to you?"

"Mama is her snitch."

"I'll be damned," Piper whispered. "I knew Nancy was sorry. I just knew it. She already knew she'd done wrong that first morning and the doughnuts were a peace offering. You should have listened to me."

"Maybe so, but she could have told me," Stella said. "And Agnes said that I had to take her place and not let Heather ruin Cadillac."

"And how do you feel about all this?" Piper asked.

Stella raked her fingers through her red hair. "Hell, I don't know. I was so mad at her and she was so sweet tonight and I felt guilty and now I'm mad again. But I don't know if I'm mad at her or at Heather for creating this shit storm."

"She started it when she put you on that damned prayer list, but Heather shouldn't have put up that sign or started all this crap about a barbecue ball." Charlotte pulled a quart of ice cream from the freezer, stuck three spoons in it, and set it in the middle of the coffee table. "I bet this fireworks show goes into the history books."

"Can you believe Gene showed up and had the balls to sit with us?" Piper dug into the ice cream. "I bet that by morning the story will be that we've gone back together."

Charlotte followed Piper's lead by putting her knitting away and dipping deeply into the ice cream. "I heard someone whispering behind us that the baby blanket I'm working on isn't for Stella after all, it's for you, and that Gene doesn't know you were seeing Rhett while y'all were married. And that the twins might not have the same father."

Piper licked the spoon clean. "You've got to stop bringing knitting to work, girl."

Stella picked up a spoon and dipped deep into the rocky road ice cream. "Can you believe I talked to my mama before I knew she was a NASA snitch and agreed to go to supper tomorrow night? I was going to be mad at her until after the ball at the very least. Something's got my emotions all in turmoil."

"It's that damn past gossip about you and that preacher's saint of a son of a bitch son. If you'd let go of that, you could move on, Stella Joy," Charlotte said.

"It's hard to let go of something that's always starin' at you in the face."

"When you see it starin' at you, spit on it," Piper said.

"Lord, that sounded just like Agnes." Stella laughed.

"I'm going to miss Agnes." Piper sighed. "We'll all take turns going to visit her and we'll take some form of chocolate every time we go."

"Can you believe that I'm not home in bed with the sexiest man in Grayson County but I'm here eating ice cream with you two because I want to talk about what all happened this evening?" Charlotte asked.

Stella picked up her spoon. "Let's talk about Rhett now."

Piper fell backward on the sofa and shut her eyes. "What am I going to do? Gene and I had a hellacious argument out in the parking lot. I'm glad the boys were already in the van because I lost it. My language was pretty damn bad."

"And what did the best husband in the world have to say?" Charlotte asked.

"He called me a slut and said that he wouldn't abide Rhett Monroe sleeping with me in the house with his sons," Piper answered without raising her head.

"And what did you tell him?"

Piper jerked her head up and chewed on her lip before she answered. "That I had not slept with Rhett but if I wanted to, it wouldn't be a damn bit worse than what he did when he took them to his new place and slept with Rita."

Stella nodded. "Don't let him walk on you. Remember what Mama told you when you first got the divorce? You can only be someone's doormat if you let them walk on you."

"How could you have ever been mad at her, Stella? I'd give anything to have my mama back to talk to." Piper's eyes misted.

"Mama should have thought twice before she put me on that prayer list," Stella said defensively. "But this is not the first time we've been in a big argument and I don't expect it will be the last. It's just that this one might be the most public what with the sign and this prayer shit."

"Nancy is a good woman." Piper wiped at her eyes with her shirtsleeve.

Stella inhaled deeply. "Yes, she is, but she still should've remembered that we're all talking about Heather and the fact she wants to take Violet's place as Miz Cadillac Head Boss Lady. Besides, you are my friend."

"Yes, I am, and that's why I'm tellin' you like it is." Piper's tears started again.

"No more tears," Charlotte said. "Unless maybe you are crying for your ex-husband and in that case we may drown you in Stella's bathtub."

"I'm not crying for that fool. I can't call him a son of a bitch because his mama is such a nice person. I'm cryin' because I want a mama like Nancy that loves me enough to put me on the damn prayer list," Piper sobbed.

Stella slung an arm around her shoulders. "Then stop it. I'll share my mama. She always wanted more than one child, so you can adopt her and I'll even tell her that she can put you on the prayer list. I'd let you adopt her, too, Charlotte, but you got a mama."

"One is enough," Charlotte said. "All we do is argue these days. I don't need two mamas, believe me. We were into it at her house just before Boone picked me up for the fireworks."

"What about?" Piper filled her spoon with more ice cream.

"My bouquet. I want to carry three roses on my Bible. One for me. One for Boone. One for our life together. She picked out one of those new brooch bouquets with enough bling on it to light up the whole church," Charlotte answered.

"I like those bouquets," Piper said. "I wish they'd been around when I got married."

"Compromise," Stella said. "Tell her that you'll wrap your three roses in satin ribbon and if she or your grandmother has a special brooch, you'll fasten it in the middle of the bow up near the roses. It can be your something old. And if they've got extra brooches, you could ask to borrow them to pin on my and Piper's bouquets and maybe on the little flower girl's basket. Think that will make her happy?"

Charlotte's head bobbed up and down in agreement. "I love it. Absolutely love it and I think she will, too. Only I don't think she's going to be wild about just three roses."

"Then tell her to build you a bouquet out of whatever she thinks is pretty but that you want it to include three roses and tell her why. Irene loves sentimental stuff," Stella said.

"You are a brilliant genius, my friend." Charlotte held up a spoon of ice cream. "Here's to good friends. I'm going to go home to Boone now and hope he's not asleep. And I'm going by Mama's in the morning and tell her what you said. She's going to love that idea."

Stella glanced across the table at Piper. "Did you give the boys a bath before you put them to bed in my guest room?"

Piper nodded. "Towels are in the washer."

"You might as well sleep on the sofa. Call Lorene first thing in the morning and tell her to pick them up here."

"Thanks. I didn't want to go home," Piper said.

Stella locked the door behind Charlotte and pulled out the sofa to make a bed. Piper brought pillows and a set of sheets from the linen closet.

"I had a shower, too. You know I keep a go bag in my van for times like this." Piper smiled. "I'll make the bed, and thanks for always being here for me. You inviting your boyfriend to the fish fry?"

"Why would you ask a thing like that?"

"Well, Boone will be there for Charlotte. And Rhett is coming whether I like it or not. You'll be a fifth wheel."

Stella patted her on the shoulder. "Don't worry about me. I'm just fine the way I am."

Half an hour later, Stella stretched out on her bed and picked up her phone. She sent a text: *Awake?*

One came right back: *Safe?*

She typed in: *No. Piper and the kids are here for the night. Gene problems.*

The next one said: *Good nite, darling. I love you.*

She typed: *Me, too.*

She fluffed up her pillow and went over the whole night's events as she stared at the patterns the shifting clouds created on the ceiling and whispered, "Life can sure get to be a complicated thing, can't it? Thank goodness for good friends . . . even Agnes Flynn!"

She shut her eyes but she was too wound up to sleep. Agnes was in the hospital and Stella's hip hurt with sympathy pains. Thinking about Piper's tears moistened her own eyes enough that she had to blink several times to keep from going into a crying jag. And the business with her mother wouldn't leave her alone. Finally, she picked up her phone from the nightstand and dialed the home phone number.

Nancy answered on the second ring. "Are you all right?"

"I'm fine, Mama. Did I wake you? Oh, my Lord!" Stella glanced at the clock and realized it was almost two a.m. "I didn't realize how late it is."

"If you are all right, it's fine. I was watching an old movie because I couldn't sleep. What's on your mind?"

"All this shit going on in town."

"This, too, shall pass," Nancy said. "We've lived through worse. I'm glad to hear your voice, Stella Joy."

"Are we okay, Mama?"

She heard her mother yawn. "I think we're workin' on it and that's the first step. You aren't backin' out of the fish fry, are you?"

"No, ma'am. Piper and Charlotte might unfriend me if I did."

A long pause made Stella check the phone to be sure she hadn't lost the connection. "Mama?" she asked.

"I love you, Stella. Now I'm going to say good-night and we'll talk more at the fish fry when we can do it face-to-face."

"Okay, Mama. Good night."

Stella ended the call and shut her eyes. Sleep came immediately and with it dreams of Jed sitting beside her in rocking chairs on the porch of the parsonage. Children played on the grassy lawn and the sound of their laughter put a smile on her face, both in her sleep and in reality.

CHAPTER ELEVEN

Something gnawed at Charlotte's soul. It was more than the wedding bouquet, and Boone had made a big breakfast that morning before he went to Sherman for his shift at the fire department, so it wasn't hunger. Still, she couldn't put her finger on the reason she was so antsy that morning as she drove to the Yellow Rose.

Stella and Piper were already there, waiting on their first customers and talking about Gene. She sat down in her chair, spun it around, and the more she heard, the worse the jittery feeling inside her felt. She thought about knitting but she'd probably drop so many stitches she'd have to start all over again. Her head was going to explode if she heard another word about secret boyfriends, a barbecue ball, or cheating ex-husbands.

"So what's your last appointment today?" she asked when she could sneak a word in edgewise.

"Noon. Most of my regulars scheduled for yesterday," Stella said.

Piper checked her book. "One o'clock. Why?"

"I'm to the saturated point with everything. I'm either going to start crying or kill someone if I don't get away for a little bit," Charlotte said.

"Afternoon at the lake?" Piper asked.

"More," Charlotte said.

Stella picked up her purse and riffled through it. "Spa and girls' night out at the bar in that hotel we went to for Piper's bachelorette party?"

"I'll call Lorene and see if she wants the boys for the night. We can be back in time for the fish fry tomorrow, right?"

Charlotte nodded. "That might work."

"You said that your knitting relaxes you," Piper said.

"I threw three balls of yarn at the walls this morning and ripped out every bit of that green blanket I started working on," Charlotte said.

Stella picked up her phone, hit a few icons, and said, "Check-in is at three and checkout at noon tomorrow. Will that keep our shop from going up in flames?"

"Barely," Charlotte answered.

"Want to talk about it?" Piper asked.

"I'd love to, but I don't know what it is. I just know I've got to get out of the forest or the trees are going to swallow me up and I can't breathe. I want to curl up underneath my desk and cry or else kick the hell out of something," Charlotte said.

Stella quickly went to hug Charlotte. "Then by damn, we'll get out of the forest. We haven't had a girls' weekend out in forever. It'll be good for all of us."

"Good mornin'," Cathy hollered from the door. "It's going to be another hot one and being pregnant sure doesn't lower the temperature a bit. You ready for me, Stella?"

"Waddle right on over here and get in this chair," Stella teased.

Cathy and Marty were twins and if they didn't wear their hair different—and if Cathy wasn't as round as a beach ball—folks wouldn't be able to tell them apart. Marty had always been the extrovert who spoke her mind, slept with cowboys, and didn't give a damn what anyone said or thought. Cathy had been the good-girl peacemaker up until Ethan Prescott pushed the wrong buttons the year before. They'd been engaged but she broke it off when he insisted that she sign a ridiculous prenup. Now she was happily married to John, who owned the Rib Joint, and was fast becoming a rising star in mystery writing. They'd eloped a couple of months before and the baby was due in the next few weeks.

"Hey, now, it might be your turn next," Cathy said.

"Not me. Charlotte is knitting for you, not me. How'd you get away from the café?"

"I've got the roasts in the oven to put out on the noon buffet. Marty and Trixie are running the breakfast crew and Darla Jean came over to help at the cash register. With the crowd we've got, I should have called and canceled. Everyone wants to talk about Violet and Agnes," Cathy answered.

Piper giggled. "I wonder if Ethan will put her in a home after her knee surgery on Monday. I mean, what with the dementia and all."

"Shame on you. Agnes just said that to start a rumor. Trixie said she's awake and bossy already this morning. They're going to get her up and make her walk this evening. Sassy as she is, she could probably walk all the way home." Cathy laughed.

Piper slapped her thigh. "I wouldn't doubt it, and then she'll crow about how she beat Violet home."

Stella whipped a cape around Cathy's shoulders and laid her back in the shampoo chair. "So y'all think she'll sabotage the ball from her hospital bed?"

Cathy shook her head. "No, she told Marty this morning she was passing that torch to you and if you don't pass the test, she's going to make you dye your hair black. Hey, Piper, I heard Gene had him a boy hissy in the parking lot at the football field last night."

Piper nodded. "And I had a girl hissy right back at him. The folks around here get the news faster than those telecasters who get to the story seconds after it happens."

Cathy laughed. "That's the gospel truth. I'm glad that you didn't let that man back you down and you stood your ground."

"We married too young. He'd just finished his freshman year in college and I graduated from cosmetology school one week and we got married the next. He didn't get the running around out of his system and now he's regretting it," Piper said.

"Other guys marry young and don't act like that," Cathy said.

"You're right, but they aren't spoiled little boys who got tired of playing husband and daddy games with a boring, plus-size wife," Piper said.

"And if you say anything more like that, you don't get to go to the spa day," Charlotte said.

Cathy groaned. "Oh, a spa day sounds wonderful! I'd almost clean up Trixie's room just to have a spa day, but things are too busy for me to take any time off right now, especially when I'll have to be off when the baby comes."

Stella giggled. "Hey, Agnes was fussing about Trixie's room last night. What was she talking about?"

"Trixie is not a neat freak. She does ceramics and scrapbooking and her room looks like a trash truck exploded in it most of the time," she explained. "Agnes says that the only way she'll go in there is if the hazmat team goes in before her. Trixie really loves that old fart, but I'd never tell her that. She wants to grow up and be just like her. Full of piss and vinegar and giving everyone hell."

Alma Grace arrived at the shop and quickly shut the door behind her and said, "Don't want to let this good cold bought air out. It's going to be a scorcher. Weatherman says it'll hit a hundred and fifteen by noon. Thank God it's Saturday and we don't work tomorrow. I'm so ready for a day off. The shop is overflowing already this morning but I snuck out anyway." She crossed the floor and sat down in Charlotte's chair. "Just a shampoo and style. I hear that Violet Prescott has been diagnosed with dementia and has gotten so violent that Ethan might have to put her in a nursing home."

"Agnes broke her hip, had emergency surgery last night, and will be elated to know that the gossip she started is spreading, but Violet does not have dementia. She already had knee surgery scheduled so they're keeping her until Monday when they'll do the surgery," Cathy said.

Alma Grace laughed out loud. "God bless the gossiping mongers. They do keep Cadillac interesting. I got to give them that. And as long as they're spreading rumors about Violet and that horrible Heather, then they're leaving us alone down at Bless My Bloomers."

Cathy shook her head. "We were in the hot seat a while back when I was engaged to Ethan."

"You dodged a bullet there," Alma Grace said.

Cathy shuddered. "Don't I know it! Violet for a mother-in-law? I get hives thinkin' about it."

Charlotte shivered. Mother-in-law? Sweet Jesus. Two mothers interfering with everything. No wonder she had the jitters.

⁂

Soft, soul-soothing music played in the background and a lady with magic hands gave Charlotte a facial straight from the courts of heaven. Her mind drifted from Boone to the wedding, to Piper and her problems, and then to Stella and that stupid prayer list that had started another uproar in Cadillac. Some of the anxiety had subsided when Piper drove east and then south toward Dallas, but there was still something stirring up her insides like butterflies fluttering around a flame.

It was a miracle but Stella had managed to get all three of them into the Ultimate Spa Day program if they could be in Dallas by one thirty. It took some fancy packing and faster driving, but they handed the valet the keys to Piper's van and the bellboy their room number with five minutes to spare. Charlotte looked at the clock when they entered the spa and it was exactly one thirty.

They'd been led to a changing room, where they donned white robes that Stella swore were made from clouds that were harvested in heaven's courts. As soon as they finished their facials, they would be taken to the garden for a late lunch.

"I'm starving," Piper mumbled.

"Ten more minutes. They are preparing your lunch now," the lady doing Charlotte's facial said.

Right on schedule they sat down at a small table for three with a beautiful lunch consisting of cold gazpacho, finger sandwiches, fruit, and salad. A tray of petits fours and tiny bite-size cheesecakes waited on a rolling tray beside the table. A woman dressed in a soft white caftan poured wine into stemmed glasses.

"I feel like a princess already. Can we come back to this place the weekend before my wedding?" Charlotte asked.

"Then you aren't ready to blow up the shop anymore?" Stella asked.

"No. I'm still jittery like I've had too much sugar and caffeine, but it's not physical. It's in my soul," Charlotte said.

"I got like that before I married Gene," Piper said.

"Wrong thing to say," Charlotte groaned.

"I'm sorry."

"It's normal. Stop fretting and enjoy the day," Stella said.

Charlotte shrugged. "Easy to say. Hard to do. What if my marriage turns out like yours, Piper? What if someday Boone has papers served to me at the shop like Gene did and I fall apart? What if he decides that he wants to chase other women? We've been together since we were kids and we were each other's firsts. We've never had sex with anyone else. What if when he's middle-aged he regrets not being wild like his brother?"

"Can't answer a single one of those questions," Stella said. "All I know to tell you is what Daddy tells me. Follow your heart. What does it say?"

"That I love Boone. That he's my soul mate and I want to spend my life with him," Charlotte said.

"Then that's what you do," Piper told her. "Confession time. Two weeks before I married Gene I caught him with one of my cousins. They didn't have sex, but they were at the river in his car making out in the same spot where he and I always went. She swore to me that he said I had called off the wedding or she wouldn't have gone riding around with him that evening. She was just trying to console him. He swore that she was lying and it had been her idea to go get a snow cone over in Bells. I believed him and didn't speak to my cousin again until last week."

"You didn't tell us? Why?" Stella asked.

"I was too embarrassed. Now I wonder if he'd been a little older if he would have gotten all that out of his system. So I know the feeling you have, Charlotte," Piper said.

Charlotte touched her arm. "You should have told us."

"I know, but I wanted to trust him so bad. Do you trust Boone?"

Charlotte nodded. "With my whole heart, but what if he changes?"

"What if you do?" Stella asked.

"That's what scares me."

☙

Stella picked up a grape and popped it in her mouth.

Piper poked her on the arm. "You are awfully quiet."

"Just thinking about what Charlotte said."

"Which time?" Charlotte asked.

"That a woman doesn't change at our age."

"Drink some more wine. Get drunk and tell us who your boy-friend is and then we'll tell you how much change is needed. You plannin' on putting in a beer joint next door to the Yellow Rose or maybe a house of ill repute? I suppose that would require that you change a whole lot." Piper giggled.

"Maybe I'm going to marry a preacher and lead the choir at church," Stella said.

"Yeah, when pigs fly. You'd never, ever in a million years be a preacher's wife, especially in Cadillac." Charlotte giggled.

"I might be," Stella said.

Piper leaned back and studied her. "Don't tease us, girl. I don't see you married to Darla Jean. You never have shown signs of that persuasion and neither has she. And Jed ain't your type."

"Maybe he's not from Cadillac?" Stella said.

"Naw." Charlotte shook her head. "After that shit with the preacher's son, you said you'd never, ever get tangled up with any form of religious man again. That bad experience done broke you from suckin' eggs, girlfriend, so we ain't buyin' that brand of bullshit, as Agnes says."

"Okay, enough talk of preachers and their worthless sons. Charlotte, what you have is bride's jitters and not fear," Piper said.

Charlotte raised her glass. "Amen, sister."

Crystal glasses touched and Piper said, "To friendship. It has survived puberty, marriage, childbearing, PMS, and pure old bitch-iness. There's nothing that can knock it down. Not scumbag hus-bands or bride jitters or a few secrets that we didn't or won't tell."

Stella smiled. "Yes, ma'am. You covered it all. And now it's on to a massage, a mani-pedi, and a shampoo and styling. Then we're dressing for dinner and drinking the night away in the hotel bar."

Chapter Twelve

Nancy met Stella at the door and wrapped her arms around her in a fierce embrace. "I'm sorry for putting your name on that list and creating this whirlwind of a mess. I told Heather to take it off but she'd already gotten bit by this damn marriage ministry bug and wouldn't do it. I want you to know I had nothing to do with that sign or the one about a prayerathon that's going up this week for a stupid thing they are having on Sunday, which I will not be attending."

"Oh, yes, you will." Stella hugged her mother back, relief flooding through her. How in the holy hell had she managed to survive without her mother in her life? Sure, she had a healthy dose of anger to feed upon, but it didn't satisfy a daughter like a hug from her mama. "I still need a snitch inside the camp."

"Agnes told you?" Nancy whispered.

"Yes, she did, and if I don't sabotage this crappy idea of a barbecue ball, she's going to make me dye my hair black."

Nancy stepped back, reached out, and touched Stella's hair. "Why would she do that?"

"I have to earn the right to be a sassy redhead and this is my first test to see if I can handle the responsibility," Stella answered.

Nancy's laughter bounced off the walls and echoed through the house. "If we could buy Heather for what she's worth and sell her for what she thinks she's worth, we'd be rich as Midas."

Stella led the way to the kitchen. "It's just three more weeks, Mama, and we'll take her down. Doesn't she realize that we like Cadillac just the way it is and we don't want an opera house on Main Street?"

"A grocery store would be nice, though, wouldn't it?" Nancy said. "Oh, no! Agnes probably won't be able to go to the ball and the only reason she was going was so y'all would. Now what?"

"We're going, Mama. I wouldn't look good with black hair like Heather's," Stella said. "Just promise me that you'll be there."

"We've given our word that we'll provide the barbecue. And, honey, if you want to be an old maid, then promise me you'll at least get a cat or dog so I can have grandcats or granddogs," Nancy said.

"And what would that make you . . . a grandpussy or a grand-bitch?"

Nancy laughed harder than before. "A dog, please, then. I'd rather be a grandbitch. I can't wait to tell your daddy what you said. But not now. Preacher Jed is already out in the backyard, so we'll keep that joke between us until he leaves. And your daddy likes him so well that he said next week he'd sit on the front pew. I was shocked beyond words."

"He really does like Jed, doesn't he?"

"Yes, he does. So how was the spa?" Nancy asked.

"Oh, Mama, I'll take you for Christmas. You'll love it," Stella said.

Nancy's eyes twinkled. "If I don't put you on the prayer list again?"

"Maybe I'll put you on it. They can pray that I get just the right puppy," Stella told her.

"We'd better go join the crowd accumulatin' in the backyard. Piper and her boys arrived a little while ago. Rhett came with Boone and Charlotte. I was about to give up on you. I'm so glad that we're good again. I missed you," Nancy said.

"Me, too. Now where's my banana bread?" Stella's throat closed off with a lump as big as a grapefruit. Damn that Heather, anyway, for coming between her and her mama.

It wasn't all Heather's fault. Agnes's voice was so clear in her head that she looked over her shoulder to see if the old gal was right behind her. *It was your anger and your mama's stubbornness that kept the fires fueled. Nancy wants a grandbaby before she's too damned old to enjoy it. And you want total acceptance in this town. Suck it up, buttercup. You probably ain't goin' to get that, so be happy with what you've got today.*

Nancy popped her on the fanny. "Get on outside with your friends. You have to eat your supper before you get dessert. And don't flirt with the preacher, neither. Just because you and him are both here as fifth wheels don't mean that I want a grandchild from him. I'd rather have the puppy as that."

"I thought you liked Jed."

"I do, but you know what they say about preacher's kids. They're the orneriest kids that ever lived and I want a sweet little grandbaby, not a hellion. I done already raised one red-haired spitfire and that's enough," Nancy told her.

Stella could tell that the incident from her sophomore year passed through Nancy's head but she didn't mention it. Back when the rumors started and Stella came home crying about the way she'd been treated at school, Nancy had told her to hold her head up high and not let anyone take her dignity. And then she'd said that they would forget what happened and never mention that boy's name again.

∽

Rhett had traded his signature tight-fitting jeans for loose khaki shorts, his cowboy boots for sandals, and his western-cut shirt for a three-button knit the same color as his dark-brown eyes. He kept up with two Frisbees flying at him from Luke and Tanner, laughing and joking with them the whole time.

Piper sat in a lawn chair and watched. She'd worn cutoff jean shorts, a flowing gauze shirt with swirls of bright blue and hot pink, and flip-flops that evening. She was glad for the shade trees in Nancy and Everett's backyard and the cool breeze that barely ruffled the tree leaves.

Charlotte brought a couple of those church fans out of her purse and handed one to Piper. "When I was a little girl, I wondered why they put Jesus on one side of these things and a funeral home advertisement on the other side. Sitting out here in this god-awful heat I've figured it out."

"It's to remind you that if you haven't done something about your soul by the time you die, you're goin' somewhere seven times hotter than this, right?" Piper asked.

Charlotte stirred the air with the fan. "You got it. There's Stella. Looks like she and Nancy made up."

"Now how do you know that? Stella is by herself," Piper asked.

"It's the look on her face. She doesn't look like she could chew up railroad ties and spit out Tinkertoys. She absolutely looks happy," Charlotte answered.

"I hope you are right. Praise the Lord, and I mean that from the depths of my heart. I hate it when they argue. I love them both," Piper said.

"Hey, you boys ready to do some serious ice-cream makin'?" Everett called out.

Both boys dropped their Frisbees and ran toward the back of the yard with Rhett right behind them. He shot a wink toward Piper on the way and high color filled her cheeks.

Stella and Nancy each pulled a chair close to Piper and Charlotte, creating a semicircle. Before anyone could say a word, Everett yelled, "We're puttin' on music to turn the crank by. We're listenin' to Collin Raye here first."

"My Kind of Girl" reverberated off the trees and Boone grabbed Charlotte by the hand and danced around the yard with her while singing at the top of his lungs. The lyrics said that he asked her if she'd like some music and she asked if he had any Merle, and that's when he knew she was his kind of girl.

Charlotte was hot and breathless when the song ended and Boone returned her to her chair, kissed her on the tip of her nose, and bowed deeply. "Thank you for the dance, ma'am." He went back to the fish-frying kettle.

"My pleasure." Charlotte giggled as they locked eyes. "Now please tell me that you two are right again and promise us that this won't never happen again." She looked at Stella.

"We're okay," Nancy answered. "You got a good man there. It's in the eyes."

"For real? What do you look for?" Piper asked.

"If you can't see to the bottom of his soul, then walk away," Nancy said.

Rhett crossed the yard and held out his hand to Piper. "May I have this dance, ma'am?"

She stood up and he slipped his arm around her waist for a two-step to "Love, Me." Collin sang about reading a note that his grandma wrote back in 1923. The lyrics said that if he got there before she did not to give up on him, that he wouldn't let her down and it was signed, "Love, me."

Rhett whispered, "If I get there before you do, I'll wait for you, Piper. I'm not in a hurry and I'm not rushing you, but I like the way I feel when I'm near you. Like Collin is singing, I won't give up, because this feels right."

Piper's pulse raced and her heart skipped a beat or two. She nodded and whispered back, "I really don't even know what to say other than to tell you that it feels right to me, too."

He drew her closer and buried his face in her hair, brushing a hidden kiss across her forehead. "That's enough for today."

He returned her to her seat, bent, and kissed her fingertips before he jogged back to take a turn cranking the ice-cream maker.

"Oh, my! You must've stepped in front of Stella and my prayers hit you," Nancy said. "That boy's eyes say it all."

"And now for some Restless Heart and then we'll listen to some George Jones," Everett said.

"Everett loves company. We should've had a dozen kids, but God only gave us Stella," Nancy said.

"He loves people almost as much as he does fishin' and country music," Stella said.

Everett came across the yard and held his hand out to Nancy. "What do you say, Mama? Shall we show these kids how it's done?"

The song was a fast one titled "The Boy's on a Roll." Everett showed off some fancy footwork as he and Nancy swing danced in the grass. The lead singer sang that they were livin' and lovin' a day at a time and that they had something they could feel in their soul.

Everyone in the yard, including the two boys, stopped what they were doing, quit talking, and began clapping to the beat of the music.

Everett blew kisses to Stella and winked at all the men. Nancy was beaming through the whole song. When it ended, he returned her to her chair and kissed her smack on the lips. "Now that's the way it's done, boys, when we're on a roll. And me and Mama, we stay on a roll."

Everett had barely gotten from where the ladies were sitting to the ice-cream-making business at the back of the yard when Jed started toward Stella. He stopped in front of her and said, "You are too pretty to be a wallflower, ma'am. Might I have this dance?"

"I didn't know preachers danced." Piper clapped a hand over her mouth as soon as the words were out. "I didn't mean—"

Jed chuckled. "I can't speak for all preachers, but this preacher likes to dance. Especially in the backyard on the green grass in his bare feet."

Piper looked down and sure enough, he and Stella both had kicked off their shoes.

The first chords of "Dancy's Dream" started when Stella put her hand in Jed's. It was a semifast dance and Jed mixed up a two-step with swing dancing. The song talked about the devil coming every night and dancing through Dancy's dreams.

"So does the devil really dance in your dreams about a dark-haired beauty in New Orleans?" Stella asked.

"No, the woman who dances through my dreams is a redhead and she's from Cadillac, Texas," Jed said.

"Really? Who is she? Someone I know?"

"Maybe, but we were keeping our relationship a secret, remember? But I do have good news. Want to guess what it is?"

"Agnes didn't break her hip but just threw it out?"

"No, she did break it but she came through the surgery just fine. Guess again."

"They called off that damned barbecue ball—sorry, I'm trying to stop cussin', I really am."

"Nope, it's still on the docket. Try again." He drew her close to his chest and her heart swelled up so big she thought it would burst out of her chest. There was Jed Tucker holding her right there in front of her friends and her parents and it felt so right.

"Rhett told you that he's in love with Piper?"

"Don't know about that, but he didn't tell me anything. Try one more time."

"I'm out of guesses and the song is almost over. Tell me, please, darlin'," she whispered seductively.

"The hiring committee met early and they hired me permanently today. I signed the contract just before I came over here," Jed said.

"Dammit, Jed! You tell me that when I can't even kiss you," Stella said.

"Payback," Jed said. "Let's announce it right now to your family. This is a special night and that would be the icing on the cake."

"Not until we've had time to talk about it and process it," she said.

"And celebrate?"

"That, too. I'm so happy, darlin'."

The song ended and Jed escorted Stella back to her chair with his hand on her lower back. "Thank you, ma'am."

"Thank you for not leaving me to be the only wallflower of the evening," she said.

"What were y'all talking about out there?" Piper whispered when Jed had rejoined the guys. "Your eyes lit up like a kid at Christmas. Is he the boyfriend?"

"I can honestly tell you that Jed is not my boyfriend."

"George Jones," Everett yelled, "is in the building, or maybe I should say his spirit is in the yard. These guys and these young boys are in for an education in real country music. Y'all listen to this now. Mr. George taught a lot of singers like Vince Gill to sing with a broken heart. It takes somebody with a heart to do that."

Nancy wiped a tear. "I'll go to my grave mourning for not seeing to it that your daddy at least had a back-row seat at Mr. George's funeral. He went to the river with his little player the day that they had that funeral at the Grand Ole Opry. He had completely filled up the player with George's music and didn't come home until the thing needed recharging."

"Who's Gonna Fill Their Shoes?" played and everyone was respectfully quiet as Everett pulled off his hat and held it over his heart.

"Now let's get happy," Everett said, "with a little 'White Lightning.' Nancy, get out of that chair and dance with me to make me happy."

Nancy came out of the chair so fast that Piper only saw a blur and the dancing began on the grass. Stella started clapping and whooping and the rest followed suit and pretty soon the whole area was alive with energy and happiness.

"That's what I want," Piper said.

"If I can't have that, then I don't want anything," Stella agreed.

Charlotte nodded. "Don't ever get mad at your mama again."

Stella whistled through her teeth and Nancy sashayed around Everett, teasing and flirting like a young girl. Everett's eyes glittered with love and pride when he brought her back to the chair.

"Okay, folks, we'll be listenin' to 'Good Hearted Woman' while we finish up this ice cream and work on fryin' fish," Everett said when the CD played the last George Jones song.

Jed grinned and headed across the yard again.

"I do believe you are not going to be a wallflower," Piper said.

"This is the song I sing to my secret wife," he said as he swung Stella out and then brought her back into his arms. "Only I'm changing the words up a little bit. I'm a good-hearted preacher in love with a good-timin' gal. Through good times and bad times we'll pass through this world hand in hand and I love her in spite of her wicked ways she says she has."

"Oh, you do?" Stella asked. "You want to tell me her initials? The ladies over there are dyin' to know some new gossip. They're sick nigh unto death of hearing about that prayer list, the barbecue ball, and Violet's dementia."

"Not until she's ready to tell the world. Then I'll be glad to give y'all her full name. She's said something about tellin' the news at the barbecue ball," he said breathlessly when the song ended.

The music stopped at the same time Everett picked up the first pan full of fish and dropped it into the bubbling-hot grease.

"I'm sure glad I'm just a little boy," Luke said with a snarl on his six-year-old face.

"Why's that, son?" Everett asked.

"Because I don't want to dance with no sweaty old girl."

Tanner snarled and shivered. "Me, neither."

"You'll get over that one of these days, but right now I'm glad you're just a little boy, too," Everett said seriously. "You boys might want to steer clear of this kettle. I don't want you to get burned, and it pops sometimes."

"Yes, sir. We'll go toss the Frisbee some more, but could you hurry that fish up? We're pretty near starved plumb to death. Mama wouldn't let us have a taste of them beans she cooked."

"We sure will. Soon as the fish floats, you can be the first ones to get fed," Everett said and then yelled, "Nancy, these boys are hungry. You gals want to get the rest of the food brought out to the picnic table so they can chow down on the first batch that comes up?"

Nancy touched Stella on the shoulder. "I don't think a puppy is going to do the trick for your daddy, darlin'."

☙

Stella barely got the door open to her house when strong arms picked her up and carried her through the kitchen and out the back door. She laid her head on his chest and whispered, "Where are we going?"

"Away until tomorrow evening. My truck is waiting over on the next block. I packed a suitcase for you. If I did it wrong or forgot a single thing, we'll buy it at the Walmart," he said softly.

"I should tell Piper and Charlotte in case they need me," she said.

"It's Piper's turn to clean the shop tomorrow and if they need you, they'll call. Your phone is in your purse. I want to sleep with you in my arms and wake up tomorrow beside you. This week has lasted for an eternity, and we are celebrating the hiring of Jed Tucker at the Cadillac church," Jed said. "I made reservations at a cabin on the banks of Lake Murray just west of Durant. We don't have to check out until Tuesday morning at eight o'clock."

"We get to play house for almost two days?" she asked.

"We will play house forever in exactly three weeks or we could start on Tuesday morning at eight o'clock. Your choice, darlin'."

"Is that a second proposal?" she asked.

"Sweetheart, I'll get down on one knee again any time you want me to. Right under the only red light on Main Street at high noon if you just say the word. I'm not ashamed of loving you."

"I might make you eat those words." She sighed.

"Just hand me the salt and pepper and I'll go to chawin' with a big grin on my face," he said. "And remember, I intend to announce it with a microphone at that barbecue ball."

She snuggled down tighter into his arms. "Not if I get it in my hands first."

CHAPTER THIRTEEN

"Mama, Mama, look who's making pancakes for us," Luke squealed.

Piper definitely had a case of bedroom hair going on with a tangled rat's nest at the back of her head, her faded nightshirt barely covered her underpants, and she was busy rubbing sleep from her eyes.

How could it be Tuesday morning already? And why would Stella be at her house that early?

"Pancakes sound wonderful," she mumbled.

"I'm glad," Gene said.

Her eyes popped wide-open and would not shut. Her head set up an instant throb and her gut clenched up into a pretzel.

"What are you doing in my house?" she asked.

"Making pancakes," Tanner said innocently. "He woke us up and helped us pack. We're goin' to Grandma's for two whole weeks."

Her eyeballs were dry and her brain close to exploding. "Were you going to tell me?"

"Sure, we was going to bring you breakfast in bed," Tanner said. "But now that you are in here, we can sit down at the table all together, right?"

"A word, Gene?" she said.

"I got nothing to say that my sons can't hear." He smiled. "Might I add that you look fetching this morning?"

"No, you might not. And what is all this about?"

Gene was an inch shorter than Piper, had thinning hair that he kept cut short, hazel eyes, and a square jaw. He'd played football in high school but slowly over the years he'd put on a few pounds here and there and now he had a spare tire above his belt.

"Divorce papers say that I should have had them for the July Fourth holiday and then for my two weeks in the summer. I can't reclaim the time from Friday until now, but they're mine for the next two weeks from right now until the twentieth of the month. Then we will begin our every-two-week schedule, which means they come with me on July twenty-fifth, so you might want to write this down. I wouldn't want to surprise you again," he said with a wicked gleam in his eye. "I should bring them home Sunday at six o'clock on the twentieth, but my folks have plans that Sunday to go away and I have plans for the company picnic so I'll bring them to you on Saturday evening at six o'clock. I do get them for Thanksgiving this year and you have them for Christmas, but I get them for Christmas Eve until six o'clock that evening. I will be going strictly by the papers from now on, Piper." He spouted off the words like he was reciting a school lesson that he'd memorized the night before.

She sat there in stunned silence. The company picnic was a family affair. Whom was he taking and why couldn't he take the boys?

"There's nothing you can do about it, Piper. Your only option is to let me move back in here and we can be a family again. What do you say, guys? Want us to be a family again?" he said.

Tanner tiptoed across the room and whispered in Piper's ear, "Is he teasing?"

She hugged Tanner and whispered back, "I don't know."

"I see that you've turned them against me," Gene said through gritted teeth.

"You haven't been around much the past six months. Their trust is a little slim," she said. "But they do have a little bit left. I don't and this family idea—it ain't happenin'." She chose her words carefully since the boys were in the room.

"Okay, guys, we'll be spending two weeks at Grandma's house after we have pancakes," Gene said.

"Will you be there?" Luke looked from his mother to his father.

Gene flipped two pancakes onto a plate and set them on the bar. "In the evenings I will be. I have to work in the daytime."

"And Rita?" Tanner asked.

"Rita and I are not together anymore, so I'm living with Grandma and Grandpa until your mama comes to her senses. But I do have a new friend I want you to meet. She has a couple of little boys a little younger than you are and she goes to church with your grandma," Gene said gruffly.

"What's her little boys' names?" Tanner asked.

"Her name is Ramona and her boys are Tommy and Freddy."

"How much younger?" Luke asked.

"Tommy is three and Freddy is two," Gene answered.

Tanner rolled his eyes at his mother. "They're babies. They can't play ball with us."

Luke popped his forehead with his palm. "I bet they still wear diapers."

"Are you using them for bait or babysitters?" Piper asked Gene.

He pointed an egg turner at her. "You did the same thing."

"Not hardly," she said. "Hey, guys, I'm going to make sure you've got everything you need to spend two weeks at Grandma's. Y'all enjoy your pancakes. I'm not hungry this morning," she said and then said out the side of her mouth for her ex's ears only, "I'm having the locks changed tomorrow. You can drop the boys off at the shop when you bring them home, and from now on that's where you will pick them up and drop them on your weekends."

"I paid for this house," he started.

"No, we split the payment every month and I bought you out in the divorce settlement between us. It's mine. Hey, guys, do you want to take your gloves and baseballs so your dad can play catch with you?"

Luke popped his head again. "We forgot that. And our Frisbees, too, Mama."

"I'll pack up a duffel bag of your favorite things," she said around the lump in her throat.

"Stuffies?" Tanner asked.

She smiled at him. "Oh, yes. I wouldn't want you to go to bed without your Hoppy Bunny."

Tears were flowing down her cheeks when she reached her bedroom. She picked up her phone from the nightstand and dialed Charlotte's number first.

∽

Boone left a sweet note on Charlotte's pillow saying that he'd just spent five minutes watching a princess sleep and that he was going to work and he'd see her that evening for dinner and a movie in Sherman.

She hummed the song that they'd danced to on Sunday while she applied her makeup. It had been a glorious weekend and she couldn't wait to talk about it with Piper and Stella.

"I'm going to miss Agnes popping in and out of the shop telling us the latest gossip," she muttered and smiled. "I wonder what kind of devilment she's been up to at the hospital this weekend."

Her phone rang and she picked it up with one hand and kept brushing on blush with the other. "Hello, Piper. Are you already at the shop? I don't have an appointment for another hour so I didn't get in a hurry. Want me to pick up food for the week on my way?"

Nothing but sobs came through the line.

Charlotte held it out from her ear and there was Piper's picture.

"Piper, what's wrong?"

"Brussels sprouts." The words were barely audible through the tears.

"I'm on my way," Charlotte said. She dropped the brush, grabbed her work shoes and purse, and ran barefoot to her car.

She couldn't remember when any one of them had used the code words they'd invented when they were seven years old. It was the one thing they all hated worse than spiders and mice, and the only time it was to leave their lips was if they were in big trouble. Then the other two were to drop everything, even if it got them grounded or sent to prison forever and ever, and go to help the friend in need.

"Please, God, don't let one of those boys be hurt or dead," Charlotte prayed out loud as she ran the red light in town and ignored three stop signs.

ↄ

Stella missed seeing Agnes out on her porch as she jogged past her house. She'd had a glorious weekend at the lake with Jed and they'd talked about what they were going to change when they remodeled the parsonage. She didn't have a problem with any of his ideas as long as they didn't give Charlotte and Piper keys. She checked her watch as she slowed to a jog a block from her house. She'd have to rush to get a quick shower and her makeup on if she was going to beat her friends to the shop. If she was late, they'd ask a million questions and it was getting harder and harder to keep quiet about Jed.

Her phone rang as she hit the first step on her porch. She fished it out of the hip pocket of her jean shorts and breathlessly said, "Hello, Piper. Are you already at the shop?"

"Brussels sprouts," a sobbing voice said.

Stella's blood ran cold. They'd teased about that code word for years but things had to be really bad for Piper to use it.

"I'm on my way. Do I need to bring a gun or dynamite?" she said as she sorted through her key ring for the right one to start her car.

"No, just you," Piper said between sobs.

The light was green but if it had been red, Stella would have shot through it like a cannonball. She slid through two stop signs and used up a hundred miles of rubber on her tires getting stopped at the curb in front of Piper's house. Charlotte pulled in right behind her and they had a footrace to the porch.

"You know anything?" Stella panted as she opened the door.

"Just that it's an emergency," Charlotte answered.

"What in the hell are you two doing here?" Gene stood in the middle of the living room floor. "Did she call you?"

Stella glared at him. "We might ask you the same thing."

Dammit! She should have brought both dynamite and guns or at least a fish fillet knife.

"I'm here to get my boys for their summer visit. I asked you if she called you." Gene's tone dripped with ice.

Tanner ran out from the kitchen with Luke on his heels. "Guess what? Daddy woke us up this morning and we're going to Grandma's for two whole weeks and guess what else? We had pancakes for breakfast."

"And Mama is packing our baseball gloves because we forgot so she's in our room," Luke said.

Charlotte bent down and kissed each boy on the forehead. "Y'all have a wonderful time at your grandparents' ranch. But don't forget to call your mama. She's going to miss you."

"I'll miss her, too." Luke's eyes went all teary.

"Now look what you've done," Gene said.

Tanner hit Luke playfully on the arm. "Grandma will let us call every night. She says that we don't have to ask, that if we want to talk to Mama just go in there and hit the number one key on her kitchen phone. And I bet she'll come get us for ice cream any time we get to wishin' for her."

"These two weeks you will need to ask me before you make calls to your mother. This is my two weeks and I'm the boss and she's not going to see you at all during my time," Gene said.

Stella shot him a look that was meant to turn him into a big fat lazy slug, but he just smiled sarcastically. She stooped down and kissed Luke on the forehead. "You ask Grandma while your daddy is at work if you can call your mama. Now I'm going to help her find all the stuff that you will need. We sure don't want you to forget your favorite pillow, do we?"

Luke did another head-popping gesture. "Forgot that, too. Daddy, you aren't much good at packin', are you?"

Stella left Gene to explain that to Luke and headed back down the hallway. She peeked into Piper's room but it was empty, so she knocked gently on the twins' door, cracked it open, and peeked inside. Piper was holding a stuffed bunny in one hand and a stuffed giraffe in the other.

Charlotte pushed past her, pulled Stella into the room, and closed the door. She led Piper to the bed and gave her a gentle push and then she and Stella flanked her in a three-way hug.

"It's all right. Lorene has them all day anyway and they're used to the place and two weeks will go fast. The only way I can see out of it is to shoot the bastard, and then you'd end up in jail and never get to see the boys," Charlotte said.

"He was in the kitchen making pancakes like this was his house and he could just waltz in here and he said that we should be a family again and he and Rita broke up," Piper said in one breath.

"And you told him to book the next flight to hell, right?" Stella asked.

Piper nodded. "And then he told the boys he had a new friend already. Someone named Ramona that goes to his mother's church and she has two little boys that are three and two—or was it four and two? I don't remember. I'm a mess. The boys can't see me like this before they go. What if he runs away with them?"

"He's not going to run off with those kids," Stella said sternly. "He's punishing you for sitting beside Rhett and not falling all over yourself to let him come back here. In a week he'll be ready to bring them back, trust me."

"You got those things ready? Mama is expecting us and I have to be at work in half an hour," Gene yelled down the hall.

"Suck it up. Put a smile on your face. Don't look at the bastard," Stella said. "Just focus on the boys and tell them to call you every day because you'll miss them."

"I should have brought the shovel," Charlotte said.

Stella shrugged. "I offered a gun or dynamite."

"Were you going to shoot him or shove the dynamite up his ass?" Piper tried to smile but it was evident that it was forced.

"Shoot and then shove and then use Charlotte's shovel to bury whatever was left. Right now we've got to get through the next five minutes and then you can fall apart," Stella told her.

"Put these in that duffel bag and we'll each carry out a piece of luggage." Piper handed the stuffed animals to Charlotte. "I can do this now that you are here with me."

They marched out of the room single file and set two suitcases and the duffel bag on the floor. Gene gave them all a smug smile and said, "You aren't going to carry them to the truck?"

"That would be your job," Piper said.

Stella tapped him on the shoulder. "And my job is to inform you that there will only be two times in the complete history of the world that hell will be closed. That is when Agnes Flynn dies and when I do. And that is because we are so mean that the devil doesn't want us in hell, so my advice to you is to be very careful or you will face the wrath of one or both of us. Piper is my friend and you do not want to upset her ever again. This is the last time you pull something like this."

"Don't threaten me and I'm not afraid of you," Gene said.

"It's a promise, not a threat, and believe me, it would be a big mistake not to be afraid of me," she whispered and then squatted down in front of the boys. "You guys have a good time and when you come back we'll all have another fish fry or maybe a barbecue at my daddy's. Two weeks will give him enough time to catch a whole bunch."

"And ice cream, too?" Luke asked.

"And can Rhett come? I like him a lot," Tanner said.

"Yes, to all of it," Stella said. "Now let's get you out to the truck. Your daddy can carry the bags and you can hold your mama's hands."

Piper kept a stiff upper lip as she walked Luke and Tanner out to Gene's truck, strapped them into the backseat, and kissed both on the forehead. "Y'all mind your grandma and call me. She has my cell phone number and the shop number, so I'm just a phone call away. And have fun. Remember your manners and brush your teeth after you eat."

"Grandma tells us all that." Luke laughed.

She waved until they were out of sight.

"You going to make it?" Stella asked from the porch.

"Yes, I am. This is just an ordinary day and I'm going to pretend that was Lorene who drove off with them. I'm going to wash down my whole kitchen with bleach and then I'm going to change the locks on all my doors. Thank you both."

"Hey, I agree, it was a brussels-sprouts day." Charlotte looped her arm into Piper's. "But the rest of it is going to be good. I feel it in my bones."

Chapter Fourteen

Nancy came through the door of the shop like a whirlwind, talking as she made her way to the sofa and plopped down. "What is this I hear about Gene driving away from your house with your boys this morning? It's Tuesday, for God's sake, not Friday, so what right does he have to Luke and Tanner? Piper, you look like warmed-over sin on Sunday morning. Talk to me."

Piper stretched her long legs out in front of her. "He came into my house, in my kitchen, and woke the kids up. I didn't know he was there until I woke up."

"How did he get inside?"

"He has a key. I'm changing the locks later today," Piper answered and went on to tell the rest of the story, including the brussels-sprouts part.

"Know what Stella told him?" Charlotte asked.

"That she was going to cut him up into pieces for fish bait?" Nancy answered.

Stella groaned. "I didn't think of that."

"Takes age to perfect the meanness." Nancy's smile got wider. "What did you tell him?"

"She whispered in his ear that there would only be two times that hell would be shut down, the day Agnes Flynn dies and the day she dies. It will be closed for three days while the devil talks God into letting them into heaven because they are both too mean to have a place in hell," Charlotte said.

"You weren't supposed to hear that, and I didn't say it just like that," Stella whispered.

Nancy cackled. "I don't care how you said it, I'm using that line on Heather next chance that I get. When she tells me to go to hell, I'm tellin' her that the devil won't have me but he's still got hopes for her sorry old hide."

"Mama, you remind me of Ouiser in *Steel Magnolias* talkin' like that." Stella steered the subject away from Gene and the twins.

Piper mouthed, "Thank you."

"I liked that movie so much that I bought it and watched it a dozen times in a week." Nancy laughed.

"Changing the subject here. We've had all of that sorry bastard Gene that we can stomach for one day. What's going on with the barbecue ball?" Charlotte asked.

"It's comin' right along. We've got to go to Violet's this week to check out the barn and make suggestions about how to decorate it. It's a barn"—she raised her voice and flapped her hands around—"it ain't goin' to change into a castle just because Heather points that ridiculous gold fingernail at the walls. If me and your dad weren't doin' the cookin', I wouldn't go out there."

Piper's first client arrived, so she got up and headed toward her station. She was glad it was Tuesday. Good hard work among good solid friends who dropped everything and ran to her side would keep her mind off that son of a bitch.

"How you doin', Carlene?" she asked.

"I'm doin' great, but my hair looks like crap and the church over in Luella is giving Alma Grace a wedding shower tonight and I want it to look nice. So give me the works."

"When is the shower here in Cadillac?" Stella asked.

"Next Sunday afternoon. Aunt Tansy is having it out at her place. Y'all will get your invitations in the mail today, I'm sure. I hear they're having some kind of praying deal at the church all afternoon. Is it at the same time as the shower?" Carlene asked.

Stella nodded. "The prayerathon will be all afternoon and I doubt that any of us will go to it. We'll all be at the shower. Is Alma Grace getting the jitters yet? I can't believe we're having so many weddings before Christmas."

"Oh, yes, she's getting the jitters. Everyone I talk to says it's normal. Hey, is Agnes going to be able to come to that ball they're all planning? I heard she's doing real good since the surgery, but hips do take a while on the elderly folks," Carlene asked.

"I dropped in to see her early this morning and she says she'll go if she has to use a wheelchair and that she's wearing her overalls," Nancy said.

"Hey, I just got an idea," Carlene said. "I'm going to talk to Marty and have her bring a pair of overalls to Bless My Bloomers. We will fancy them all up and Agnes will love them. She'll put enough bling on them to make everyone at the rehab place jealous."

Nancy clapped her hands. "I love it. That'll cheer Agnes right up. Lord, she'll act like Elvis Presley. I wouldn't be a bit surprised if she doesn't practice a lopsided grin in front of the mirrors."

Stella popped a hip out, snarled one side of her nose, and said, "Thank you very much, Carlene."

Piper laughed so hard that she dropped the hairbrush. "You sounded just like her and it wasn't a bad impression of Elvis, either, especially if he had red hair. Maybe Carlene ought to make you some overalls to wear to the ball."

Stella smiled. It would be good enough for Heather if she showed up at the ball in overalls, but she wanted to look beautiful for Jed, maybe in something like ivory lace.

Nancy started for the door. "Stella is not wearing overalls to the ball, not if I have anything to say about it. I'll see you girls later. I've got to make a run to Sherman for cattle feed."

"We'll be right here if you've got time to run back by." Piper nodded.

Carlene reached out and touched Piper on the arm. "Honey, I heard about Gene takin' your boys for two weeks and how he did it. Alma Grace will be all for putting your name on the prayer list right along with Stella's."

"I'll dye her hair purple and give her a spike hairdo if she does," Piper declared.

Carlene slapped a hand over her mouth. "I would love to see that."

"I wish you would put her name on the list. It's lonely at the top," Stella said.

Charlotte shook a comb in their direction. "Hey, I heard about Alma Grace's prayers. Y'all might want to reconsider. I heard that she flat-out put one on Kitty Lovelle last year when she prayed for her."

"Yep, that woman can sure do up a prayer right. She asked God to do everything but strike Kitty dead as a roadkill possum." Carlene grinned.

"I may ask her to pray for Gene," Charlotte said.

"Or for Heather," Stella said.

Carlene lowered her voice. "Well, truth is, not even Alma Grace can stand Heather. She's a self-righteous gold digger, according to my cousin."

"Join the club. If she keeps putting down Cadillac and calling it names, she's not going to have a single friend in town other than her aunt Violet and maybe Annabel," Stella said.

"I know she hates you, Stella. What happened?" Carlene asked.

"She declared war on me when I wouldn't join every organization she's invented," Stella said. "She's moved in here and thinks she can change everything about the town, and we love it just the way it is."

"You do know the whole town is watching you. I heard that Violet has hired a private detective to tail you so that she'll know who your boyfriend is before Agnes finds out and he's been told to bring his reports to the hospital," Carlene said.

Stella groaned.

Carlene laughed. "Maybe we should dye your hair and give you a spike hairdo. The PI wouldn't recognize you that way."

"It's a thought. Know where I could buy a couple of bozo wigs?" Stella asked.

Piper worked the lather into Carlene's curly blonde hair and let her mind wander as the girls talked about ways to avoid detection. Stella's first appointment of the day arrived and the talk again veered over to Alma Grace's wedding shower planned for Sunday. Then Charlotte's client Rosalee, an elderly lady who had moved from a farm into town when her husband died, turned the talk to her garden and canning tomatoes.

"I've got some peppers coming off," she said, "but they won't never be as hot as what Claudia Andrews grew up there beside where Clawdy's is now. That woman had a secret with jalapeños that made them almost as hot as a habanero. I'd just love to know what it was, but she's passed on and Cathy said that the seeds she saves from them are still hot but she has no idea how her mother and grandmother put the fire in them to begin with."

At least they weren't talking about Gene anymore. Piper would rather hear talk about Rhett—she let his name stick in her head and didn't try to kick it out. She glanced at her appointment book as she put the finishing touches on Carlene's hair. She had a fifteen-minute break. That would give her enough time to sneak to the back room and forage for something to eat. There was no way that she would have touched one of Gene's pancakes that morning and now that the jitters had passed, she was starving.

"I love it, Piper." Carlene smiled. "You've outdone yourself. I'll expect to see you at the shower on Sunday?"

"Of course, but let's get something straight. This is a wedding shower, not a bridal shower, right?" Piper asked.

"Yes, ma'am."

Rosalee raised a hand out from under her cape. "What's the difference?"

"A wedding shower is where we take things like sheets, towels, blenders, and food processors. A bridal shower is where we take sexy underbritches and see-through nighties from down at Bless My Bloomers," Stella said.

"I'm glad that it's a wedding shower, since I bought a set of sheets. Do they really take sexy things to showers for brides these days?" Rosalee asked.

"Yes, ma'am, and they buy a lot of it at Bless My Bloomers," Carlene said. "What did they bring to your shower when you got married?"

"Brooms, mops, towels, and sheets. My mama gave me a high-necked flannel gown that buttoned all the way to the top, but she didn't give it to me right out in public. It was better than something skimpy, let me tell you."

"Why?" Stella asked.

"Honey, a man likes to unwrap pretty presents. It's your job to rope the present down real tight to give him a challenge. It turns them on a lot more than a scanty-wrapped present, believe me. I'm speaking from experience, so if some of us old dinosaurs bring high-necked nightgowns to your bridal shower, we know what we are doing."

"I'm not having a bridal shower," Stella said.

Carlene nodded seriously. "But I am, and thank you for that advice."

Nancy pushed through the door, threw herself on the sofa, and waved at Rosalee. "How's your garden? Got any tomatoes left or has the heat done burned them all up?"

"I'm pampering them, so they're coming out my ears. Did you know that Violet started a fuss about backyard gardens at the chamber of commerce meeting last week? Someone said it wasn't in the chamber's business to worry with the physical beauty of the town, so she said she'd go to the city council meeting next month. She says they're a terrible blight on the town. Truth is I'm glad that she's laid up and won't be at the meeting. I hope she forgets all about it and it don't come up again," Rosalee said.

Nancy shook her head from side to side. "She's about to cut off her nose to spite her face. Cathy grows her peppers right out beside Clawdy's and those are what won all those ribbons and what make the festival such a big thing. If she says no one can grow vegetables in their yards, then Cathy won't be able to grow her peppers."

"You might tell her that. I didn't mind leaving all the work of a full-fledged farm, but I'd sure hate to give up my garden," Rosalee said.

"I will when I get the chance. Oh, I got news."

"About?" Rosalee asked.

Nancy sat up straighter. "Beulah called and said that Heather has been working on more rules. But anyway, the big news is that it's now been written in stone that the women have to wear a dress and the gents—that's Heather's words, not mine—have to wear a jacket and a tie. They were going to make it black-tie and the men would have to wear tuxes, but we managed to get that overturned in the last meeting. The one that Heather called this morning put the rules down as gospel."

Piper stopped at door into the storeroom. "So no overalls for Stella?"

Rosalee's laughter filled the whole shop and bounced off the walls like a sugared-up six-year-old who'd just spent the day with her grandparents. "I've got a pair of overalls. I think I'll take them down to Bless My Bloomers and get her to make me a ball gown out of them. She could cut the legs off and sew a skirt tail on them, put all them shiny stones on them like she's doing Agnes's overalls, and it would be a fancy dress, right? I hadn't planned on going, but y'all done got me excited about it. Heather didn't make a rule about nobody over fifty not being able to go, did she?"

"Hell, no!" Nancy said. "Just call Carlene and tell her what you want. Maybe you ought to have her stick a label on the bib pocket that says Bless My Bloomers so everyone can see where you got your custom-made ball gown. Kind of like them fancy labels that the hoity-toity folks like to show off."

Piper could have kissed Rosalee and Nancy. They'd taken her mind off her troubles and given her something to laugh about.

Chapter Fifteen

The temperature gauge on the dash of Nancy's truck said that it was a hundred and one degrees, but until the air-conditioning kicked in, it felt like six degrees hotter than hell's furnace. She'd barely cooled down when she parked in front of Violet's house that Friday afternoon, quickly crossed the well-manicured lawn, and rang the doorbell.

Two weeks and the whole damn thing would be over. Well, two weeks and a day, since the ball was planned for the last Saturday in the month.

With eagle eyes, Heather scanned her from toes to head before she stepped aside and said, "Come in, Nancy. You are the last one. We went ahead and started the meeting without you but we've only had time to discuss one thing and we'll fill you in."

Nancy felt like a kid on the way to the principal's office as she followed Heather down the short foyer and into the den. She'd worn her best slacks and ironed her shirt. Maybe the fact that it was sleeveless didn't set well with Heather, who was dressed in a pink suit with short sleeves, a silk shell under it, and high-heeled shoes. And holy shit, the woman was wearing hose on a hot summer day.

Heather took her place behind her aunt's massive desk, shuffled some papers, and motioned for Nancy to sit beside Floy on the sofa. "I was just telling Nancy that we discussed the mode of dress that will be acceptable to the barbecue ball. At our last meeting, we had voted that the gents must wear a coat and tie and the ladies have to wear a dress, and it was in the minutes for old business. Today we'll talk about new business."

"Coat and tie. They'll suffocate," Nancy gasped.

"We have ordered several commercial-size portable refrigerated air conditioners to keep things cool." Heather did a little huff that said she didn't really appreciate Nancy's comments.

"Do all the dresses have to be white?" Nancy asked.

Annabel looked up from a chair right in front of the desk and frowned at her. "This is not a debutante ball but the first annual Yellow Rose Barbecue Ball. Heather has decided that we will use pastel blue, pink, and yellow for our colors. Yellow for the idea of the roses, blue since the Blue Ribbon Jalapeño Society is helping us out, and pink because it's the signature color for the marriage ministry. I do believe that you already knew that, Nancy."

"I suppose you're going to change the name of the Angels to the Yellow Rose Prayer Ladies?" Nancy wondered how that thought had gone from her mind to right out in the room for everyone to hear, but once it was out there wasn't a thing she could do about it.

"Of course not. I wish we would have given our ball a name other than the Yellow Rose, but since it is a popular Texas song and since this all started to find a husband for *your* daughter, it seemed appropriate." Heather inhaled and let it out slowly. "And to answer your question, the ladies can wear whatever style dress they want in whatever color they wish. Hopefully the Angels will try to find something suitable in yellow. I have chosen a pink dress screen printed with Texas bluebells on the silk. The fabric and pattern is at my seamstress's place of business even as we speak and"—she paused for effect—"I shall save each of my gowns from all the balls we'll have through the years so that when my ministry is really big they can be auctioned off to make money for more elaborate balls in the future. I foresee a huge ballroom on the ground floor of a gorgeous hotel in Cadillac within the next ten years."

Shit! What had Heather been smoking right before the meeting? They'd be lucky if one or two of the boarded-up buildings on Main Street had new life in them in the next ten years.

"So the color scheme is now formally decided?" Floy asked.

Heather put a finger next to her lips. "I think so. No, I know so. And for everyone's information here, I want to tell you that Aunt Violet is doing very well after her surgery and that any mention of dementia is just gossip. Now that rumor is buried, we will go on. Annabel, will you please be in charge of the petits fours we will serve for dessert at the ball?"

Annabel glowed. No, that was understating the look on her face. She lit up the whole damned room with her smile.

Can I please kiss your fingernail for letting me work my fingers to the bone on little cakes for the first annual Yellow Rose Barbecue Ball? Nancy didn't say those words, but she could hear them rattling around in her head like marbles in an empty soup can.

She'd far rather be sitting in her daughter's beauty shop basking in the glory of having their argument settled. But oh, no! Everett had told her that if he was going to be responsible for smoking enough brisket, turkey, chicken, and pork tenderloin to serve the whole town of Cadillac, then by damn she was going to every meeting between now and the ball.

"I want you damn good and tired of all that shit so you won't back out when it comes time to quit," he had said.

When she got home, she intended to kiss him smack on the lips for making her go. This was better than a circus.

"Nancy, are you listening to me?" Heather asked sternly.

"I'm so sorry. My mind drifted. Now what was it you were saying?"

Heather did one of her dramatic inhale-deeply-and-blow-it-out-slowly rituals, but this time she added a glare in the mix. "I said that we will need equal amounts of pork loin and brisket, half as much chicken and turkey."

"That's what Everett planned on," Nancy said. "He wants to know if it's going to be open bar or bring your own beer or bottle."

"This is an Angels affair," Annabel gasped. "There will be no liquor of any kind or shape at the barbecue ball."

Oh, Everett is going to love that idea after cooking for days. Why couldn't they at least have beer?

"That's right," Heather said. "This is a formal affair. We will offer lemon-infused water and sweet tea and of course there will be a punch bowl on the table with all of Annabel's gorgeous petits fours. And a smaller bowl on a little round table for those of us who are allergic to red punch and prefer the kind made with white grape juice and lemon-lime soda. I shall be in charge of the smaller one since I'm the one who can't abide red punch."

Nancy made a mental note. *I'll just bring a cooler and leave it in the car. Everett has one of those fancy can covers so no one will know. I'm not asking him to help me serve all night with nothing but lemon-infused water to drink.*

"Now, on to the next item on the agenda. I'd like to get this all settled before we drive down to the barn and look it over. Ideas will just pop right out of our heads when we see the inside and figure out what we can do to make this the best affair in Cadillac. I can foresee people coming from miles away like they do for the jubilee." Heather's eyes actually went misty.

"Are you plannin' on a carnival next year?" Nancy asked.

Annabel's quick intake of breath said that Nancy was sure walking on thin ice. "Of course not! This will always be Cadillac's formal affair. The jubilee is for families. The chili cook-off is to make money for the firemen's fund and it's also for families. But this is a holy affair."

"Well put, Annabel." Heather nodded.

A holy affair? Did that mean they would offer up a virgin on a hay bale at the end of the festivities? If that's what Heather had in mind, she'd best start advertising for one real soon, because Nancy was pretty sure that none of the over-eighteen women in Cadillac would qualify.

Heather held a hand up toward heaven. "This will be Cadillac's way of telling our Lord and savior that we appreciate his answering our prayers all year. The money that we take in will go straight into the church's brand-new marriage ministry fund. I've talked to Reverend Jed about it and he said that we could keep whatever money we made for future projects for my ministry."

"I'd like to see it used for a fund to help folks in need. Like broke people who have car trouble near Cadillac. Or young, single mothers who have trouble paying the rent," Nancy asked.

"I've decided this is going into the MM fund, which stands for marriage ministry fund if you don't understand the world of initials," Heather said. "Why would you want such a fund, anyway? I asked you earlier if Stella was pregnant. Has that changed?"

Every eye in the room cut toward Nancy. "Not that I know about, but y'all remember that I asked you to pray for a husband first and then a baby. I don't think God will get it backward. He's pretty good at keepin' things straight."

Heather ignored her and shuffled a few more papers. "We will have music playing and the dance will go on from six to eight. I would like to be able to hire a harp and have a piano brought in, but it's not possible this first year. So we have a sound system and CDs, but there will be none of that twangy country music. We'll have true waltz instrumentals. That way there won't be any of that sinful rubbing-all-over-each-other type of dancing."

"Are you kidding me? Not a single one of the men in Cadillac will stay past the first dance," Nancy said bluntly.

"Yes, they will, because the ladies will love it," Heather protested.

"Have you got rocks for brains, woman?" Nancy asked.

She'd promised Everett she'd go to the damned old meetings. She had not promised to be good and not speak her mind.

"You are being contentious, Nancy Baxter, and you know what the Bible says about that. We are going to dance the waltz like civilized people, so get used to it."

Before Nancy could answer that snide remark, Annabel raised her hand like a little first-grade girl in pigtails. "Miz Heather, I had a vision of all the single women being sent to the buyers' balcony on one side and the single men to the other balcony. When you call out their names, then the guy . . . I mean, the gent . . . crosses the whole barn and offers his hand to the lady at the bottom step of her side."

"That's lovely." Heather clapped her hands. "I'll write that down and we'll do it just like that. I knew you'd have some wonderful notions. Now shall we go to the barn and see what else we can come up with? Annabel, I'm just sure you'll picture all kinds of scenarios. I'm eager to know how you think we should arrange the tables. Would you be in charge of that the day we set them up?"

"Oh, yes, ma'am. I'd be honored to take care of that. Would you like me to rent the tablecloths as well?" Annabel asked.

Heather left her throne behind the desk and looped her arm in Annabel's. "That would be lovely. Dinner will be served at eight, then, and the couples will be announced right before that. They will have their first dance together and then sit together for their dinner and then dance some more. Oh, I could just swoon thinking about it. Just keep the receipts for the tablecloths, honey, and the ball fund will reimburse you for your expenses."

"And the meat that Everett is cooking?" Nancy asked.

Heather threw a drop-dead-and-fall-in-fresh-cow-poop look over her shoulder. "I thought that was your donation. It is tax deductible since it's for the church. But if you are too poor to buy it, then by all means keep the receipts."

"Thank you. I will bring them to you the day we buy the meat. The Fannin sisters and I will be donating the potato salad, the baked beans, and the coleslaw. You might want to ask someone else to volunteer for the condiments," Nancy said.

❧

A rooster crowed and Agnes fetched her phone from the bibbed pocket of her hospital gown. "Got to take this one, Stella," she said.

She listened for so long that Stella was sure she'd forgotten to hang up when the call ended. But finally she hit a button and shoved it back into her pocket.

The rehab room was nicer than the hospital room that Agnes had been in for less than a week. And over there hanging on the front of the closet door were her brand-new fancy overalls. The sunlight filtering in through the miniblinds caught the stones and flashed spots of color on the walls.

"They're downright beautiful, ain't they? Alma Grace brought them yesterday and said that they was supposed to help me get well. I done took them to the therapy session so Violet could see them. I'm going to remake my will and be buried in either them or the dress that Carlene is making for me to wear to the ball. I hope to hell Violet and Heather wear something that requires a corset and a girdle and they're miserable all night," Agnes said when she tucked the phone back into her pocket.

"I bet Carlene could sell those things faster than hotcakes if she'd put some in her store window." Stella smiled.

"Oh, no! Them is one of a kind. Me and Rosalee has got the only ones and we ain't sharing," Agnes told her. "Now listen to me. That was Nancy on the telephone. You already know about the dress rule. There will be no liquor of any kind, not even beer. We will be drinking lemon-infused water, whatever to hell that is, sweet tea, and of course there will be a punch bowl on the table with Annabel's petits fours. I hope she makes chocolate ones because I intend to eat about twenty."

"I'll pale in comparison to a redhead who'll be wearing an overall formal with that much bling."

"Bullshit! Don't you try to weasel out of going. I need my bodyguards," Agnes said.

"But Cathy, Trixie, and Marty will be there," Stella said. "And you'll be in a wheelchair, Agnes, and that's only if you are lucky and get out of rehab."

"I'm going if I have to go in a damn hospital bed. You should see what Carlene is doing with my ball gown. I've had some curtains up in a trunk that I took down out of my kitchen about twenty years ago. Yellow sunflowers on a green background. Carlene is using the material for the bottom of my new formal," Agnes said.

Stella laughed out loud. "That should bring down the house. You reckon the newspaper and television station will interview you and take pictures?"

"Hell, yeah, they will, if I have to pay them to do it."

"Okay, then, I promise I'll go shopping and buy a dress. What do I need to do to take care of things from my end?" Stella asked.

"I'll do most of it with my telephone, but there's a couple of things I'll need help with. Nancy needs to make a trip out to old man Hinton's. That's all you need to tell her," Agnes said.

"To buy moonshine?" Stella asked.

191

"How'd you know about that?"

"If you grew up in Cadillac, you knew about old man Hinton. You leave a twenty-dollar bill on the stump out near his smoke-house. There's a thumbtack in the stump and an hour later you go back and there's two jars of 'shine sittin' there in place of the money," Stella said.

"Well, I'll be damned. You ever drink any of it?"

Stella shivered at the memory. "One time. But Mr. Hinton has gone out to El Paso to live with his son. He is ninety now, you know. They moved him out there last week, Agnes."

"Well, shit!"

"Hey, hey." Piper poked her head in the door. "Did Stella upset you about something?"

"Hell, no! Old man Hinton did. I need moonshine."

Piper pulled up a chair beside Agnes's hospital bed. "You can't have moonshine in here. You might have a reaction to whatever medication they're giving you if you mix it with liquor."

"It ain't for me." Agnes's eyes settled on Piper and she nodded. "Liquor? Yep, that's it. Your job is to go to a liquor store and buy whatever looks and smells like moonshine. Whiskey won't do. It'll make the punch taste funny."

"Agnes Flynn!" Stella gasped.

"It's just for the little punch bowl. The big one is going to have red punch in it. Nancy already told me so. But there's going to be a little one on a second table for folks like Heather. She tells people that she's allergic to the pineapple juice that goes into red punch. The smaller punch bowl will have something made out of white grape juice, so whiskey would sure show up in it."

"Vodka," Piper said.

"That'll work," Agnes said. "Just don't let nobody see you gettin' it or it might set off an alarm. She has to drink it for my plan to work."

"And what is this plan?" Stella asked.

"To make this the only Yellow Rose Barbecue Redneck Ball in Cadillac. The jubilee and the chili cook-off are enough. And I sure don't want it to have the name of your beauty shop," Agnes answered.

Stella was just glad that it wasn't her job to buy liquor. It wouldn't bode well for the preacher's wife to be seen in the liquor store and someone would be bound to see her even if she tried to buy it in Sherman or Denison. Then when she and Jed announced that they'd been married more than two months, someone would remember that she'd bought liquor after they were married. Gossips were very good at remembering dates and times!

Agnes pointed at her. "Your job is to get one of them flash-point-drive things that you put into a computer and get someone to fill it plumb up with country music. I want that kind that you can do the hoochy-cooch to. Ain't no way we're goin' to be bored to death with a bunch of waltzes from the Civil War days."

"Yes, ma'am," Stella said.

"And Charlotte's job?" Piper asked.

"You tell her to come see me tomorrow. We've got some discussin' to do. Now I'll be goin' to my therapy here in about five minutes, so y'all best scoot on out of here."

"Does Violet go to the same therapy?" Piper asked.

"Hell, yeah, she does." Agnes grinned. "But she's a big baby. I hope she whines around until she loses every bit of her clout in Cadillac."

"Heather is going to be just as bad," Stella said.

"I can handle that girl with one hand tied behind my back and I'm about to prove it. Y'all know that she ain't from Tulsa like she says. She's from a little bitty place that ain't got five hundred people about fifty miles west of there. Town called Ripley. She went to college in Tulsa and wants everyone to think she's big city."

"Well, how about that?" Stella smiled.

Agnes pointed at the door. "They'll be comin' to take me to the therapy room any minute now, so it's really time to go, girls. Y'all come back anytime. And tell Charlotte I want to see her tomorrow."

"Yes, ma'am," Piper said.

ↄ

Charlotte had a cancellation late in the day so she reached the rehab center by five thirty. Stella and Piper each had a job to throw wrenches into the barbecue ball. With Heather tipsy and country instead of classical music playing, there didn't seem to be much else that was needed. But if Agnes summoned her, by golly, there was no way she wasn't putting in an appearance.

"I brought you a chocolate cupcake from that fancy shop down the street," she said as she entered the room.

"Thank God! Bring it over here and I'll eat it while you call in a large pizza. They brought liver and onions for supper. I like onions but I hate liver. We'll share us a pizza and visit a spell," Agnes said.

"Only if the nurse says it's all right," Charlotte said.

Agnes pushed her call button and a lady poked her head inside the door. "Yes, ma'am?"

"I want pizza. Y'all got a problem with my friend going to get it for me?"

"No, honey. You can eat whatever you want, and between you and me, I wouldn't have eaten that supper they brought in here, either," the duty nurse said.

"Thank you." Agnes peeled the paper from the cupcake and talked between bites. "I bet Violet ain't got a cupcake. If I had the energy, I'd get in my wheelchair and go past her room with chocolate on my mouth."

"Agnes Flynn! Breaking a hip hasn't slowed you down a bit."

"Hell, no, it didn't slow me down. It just gave me more time to plot and plan for the barbecue ball. You know we ain't got but two weeks to get it all planned out and ready to go."

A smile turned up the corners of Charlotte's mouth. "You are incorrigible, woman. What kind of pizza do you want?" Charlotte dug her phone from her purse and flipped through the contact list to find the number for the pizza place.

"Supreme with extra bell peppers," Agnes said. "And a side order of jalapeños. They won't be as hot as what Cathy grows, but they'll do. And I want the biggest sweet tea they sell. The tea they got in here ain't got a bit of sugar in it. And yes, I'm incorrigible. If I hadn't been, Violet would have destroyed Cadillac years ago with all that bullshit she puts out."

Charlotte ordered the pizza and then sat down in an easy chair beside the bed. "Stella tells me she has a job and Piper has already bought the vodka."

"I guess you heard that Heather is planning on each feller coming down the stairs from the buyers' balcony on one side and crossin' the barn to take his lady's hand in his. Then he'll lead her out to the dance floor and wait until all the names are called out before the first dance commences?"

Charlotte nodded.

"Your job is to convince her to let you do the name callin'. I don't give a shit if you have to knock her out and drag her back behind the barn. But I want you to call out the married and engaged people first and then go on to the single folks."

"Why?" Charlotte asked.

"Stella is going to goad her into eating her chicken some way or she's by damn going to dye her hair black. I swear it on my mama's Holy Bible. If she can't get Heather to eat chicken, then she don't deserve that mop of red hair."

"What if Heather hates chicken as bad as red punch?" Charlotte asked.

"I already know that's her favorite kind of barbecue and I've already had a talk with Cathy, who will be delivering a dozen peppers to Stella the day before the ball. Her chicken is going to be extrahot, so that will send Heather straight for the punch bowl once she samples it. Since she's got holy blood flowin' in her veins, I reckon she ain't never had much to drink. It shouldn't take much liquor to make her dizzy, and by that time she's going to be real worried about the money."

"What money?"

"She's spending too much and there ain't no way the admission money is going to cover it all. So there's no doubt in my mind she's going to be real worried," Agnes explained.

"Okay," Charlotte said and waited.

"Now this is where you come in. I want you to offer to give her a thousand dollars to let you call out the names."

"A thousand dollars?" Charlotte whispered.

"I'm donating that to the cause. She'll jump on it; believe me. I been keepin' tabs on what she's spending."

"Why?" Charlotte asked.

"I want you to pull out Stella's name from the women's bowl and Jed Tucker's from the fellers' bowl," Agnes said.

Charlotte sat straight up in the chair and said, "Why?"

"You sound like a damn parrot, girl. Because Stella has a boyfriend and she likes him a lot or she would tell y'all who he is. For some reason she don't think she's good enough for him. If he's there, it won't bother him if she's dancin' with a preacher. I don't want her to lose someone that she loves, Charlotte. And while you're at it, fix it so that Piper and Rhett wind up together, too. The rest of it is up to you," Agnes said.

"You old toot." Charlotte laughed.

"You'd do the same if you'd have thought of it. She just looks so happy and sad at the same time. I couldn't bear it if she lost her boyfriend because her name got put with Rhett or some other sexy feller and the boyfriend got all jealous," Agnes said. "But you can't tell her what your job is. You just say that I said it was one of them FBI things."

"Yes, ma'am. Pizza should be ready. I'll be back in ten minutes," Charlotte said.

"Walk real slow past Violet's room with it," Agnes said.

Chapter Sixteen

The strong aroma of bleach preceded Piper into Stella's living room. She looked up from the sofa where she was watching *Steel Magnolias*. "You ever realize how much Agnes and Ouiser are alike?"

Piper hauled her suitcase toward the guest bedroom. "Of course. How come you didn't see that before now? I'm here until the boys come home. I've tried staying at my house and it's too damn lonely. Send me a bill for room and board at the end of the time."

"Hey, if you clean, I'm sure we can work something out," Stella yelled and went back to her favorite movie.

She heard the bathroom door shut and the shower start. Thirty minutes later Piper carried a blanket from the linen closet to the recliner, threw the side lever, and covered up.

"You smell better, but you do know this is summertime in Texas," Stella said.

"And you keep this house at sixty-five degrees and I'm cold-blooded. His spirit is still in my house. When he filed for divorce and moved all his things to Rita's place, it was gone. But it's back now. That leer on his face is there every time I turn the corner.

I wish he really was there and the boys were outside playing. I'd knock him flat on his ass and enjoy doing it."

Stella didn't take her eyes off the screen. "I like this part. They're in the locker room of the football team." ·

"Are you hearing me, Stella?" Piper raised her voice.

"Yes, I heard every word, but you don't have to worry about a thing. It's taken care of, and short of moving out of Texas, which Gene won't do because it would mean leavin' his mama, he's going to get a lifelong dose of karma chewing holes in his ass."

"What did you do?"

"Me, not one thing. I just had a long visit with Mama."

"Good God!"

"Oh, yeah. We'll get some garlic and a roadkill armadillo and perform an exorcist thing on your house if he don't reclaim his spirit and leave you alone. We'll put butcher knives into an effigy of him and send the video right to his e-mail box," Stella said.

"You know how superstitious he is. That would cause him to have an acute coronary." Piper laughed.

"If he dies, he dies. Oh, I can't watch this part without crying. Shelby should have never gotten pregnant," Stella said.

"She lived the way she wanted to. It took risks but she did it," Piper said.

"Hey, shove them words right back into your mouth and eat them. Rhett wants to take you out and you're afraid to take that little risk."

"Sometimes I don't like you," Piper said.

"You are evil and you must be destroyed," Stella quoted from the movie.

"You can't be Ouiser. Agnes is Ouiser. You have to be Annelle."

"Hell if I will. I don't pray if the elastic in my panties is shot"— Stella quoted lines from the movie—"and I damn sure wouldn't ever pour out a good can of beer. I'll be Clairee but I'm not being Annelle. Besides, I'm not tall enough. You can be Annelle."

The giggle started low in Piper's chest but soon it was a full-fledged laugh that would have put a three-hundred-pound trucker to shame. "She *is* divorced and the elastic in my panties is shot and I am tall like her," she said when she could catch her breath.

Charlotte pulled a suitcase inside and quickly shut the door. "What is going on in here? I thought someone was crying or dying."

Stella put the movie on pause. "Holy shit! Did you and Boone break up?"

"No, but Nancy called and said that Piper had moved into your house after she hosed hers down with bleach. Y'all ain't havin' a house party without me. I might go for a sleepover with Boone but hey, if Piper is going crazy it'll take both of us to keep her out of a straitjacket. She's one tall woman, I tell you," Charlotte said.

Stella pointed. "See, I told you so. You are Annelle."

"Is that *Steel Magnolias*? Sometimes I think we're reliving that thing down at the shop. Agnes is Ouiser." Charlotte left her suitcase in the middle of the floor, kicked off her shoes, and curled up on the other end of the sofa with Stella. "Start it all over again and let's watch it from the beginning. If Piper is Annelle, who are you?"

"I'm Clairee," Stella said proudly.

"You are not! You're not that old and you've got red hair."

"Then I want to be Truvy," Stella said.

"You'll have to bleach your hair and get a boob job to look like Dolly Parton. You think this new boyfriend that you won't talk about would like you as a blonde with big boobs and a smart mouth?"

Stella's laughter came close to breaking the windows. "Darlin', my new feller likes me any way he can get me, but he likes me best naked and hot and he thinks my smart mouth is right fine."

"He don't mind the past thing or have you not told him?"

"Oh, he knows, and he says the same thing that Truvy says. If you can achieve puberty, you probably have a past."

"And what is his past?" Piper asked.

Stella tossed a throw pillow at her. "I'll tell you after that rotten ball is over. I'm really starting to look forward to it since Agnes has spiced up the party with her ideas."

Charlotte smiled. "I'm serious as a heart attack. I want to grow up and be like Ouiser."

"You'll have to dye your hair and get a pair of overalls." Stella laughed and it felt so good.

∽

Stella had just gotten into bed when her brand-new ringtone, "Good Hearted Woman," started playing.

"Hey," she said softly.

"I drove past your house and saw two extra cars. I guess Piper doesn't like the quiet," Jed said.

"Gene's ghost in the house is spookin' her more than a quiet house. She's moved in until the boys come home. And Charlotte couldn't stand it so she brought her suitcase and she's here for the duration, too," she said.

"You know what they say about familiarity."

She nodded even though he couldn't see it. "We'll practically be together twenty-four/seven. By the time they leave I'll be ready to yank all my hair out, but tonight it wasn't too bad. They're my friends, Jed."

"You got a lock on the bedroom door?" he asked.

"Yes, I do. Why?"

"Got one on the window?"

"Yes, I do," she answered.

"Then unlock the window right after you lock the door. I'm comin' in. No way I'm going that long without sleeping with you." He chuckled.

She bounded out of the bed and quietly turned the lock in the middle of the doorknob and then raced across the room to open the window. He slipped in effortlessly, bringing a small duffel bag with him.

She took the bag from him and tossed it on a chair, wrapped her arms around his neck, and rolled up on her toes for the first kiss. "This may keep me from yanking my hair out."

"I'm sure it will keep me from going insane." He marched her backward across the floor until the back of her knees hit the bed. "Turn on some music to mute the sound."

"I can be very quiet."

"But I can't. Not with you in my arms."

"I feel like a naughty teenager."

"I just feel like I've got the woman I love in my arms."

❧

Nancy followed the girls into the shop on Wednesday morning. She brought two loaves of banana bread, a plastic container of chicken salad, and a loaf of fresh homemade bread. "Thought y'all might like something other than takeout for dinner today. We're on count-down starting today. It is ten days until we get this ball over with, then the sign can come down off the church and I can plan Stella's birthday party. What do you think, girls? A fish fry or a steak cook-out. We're already sick to death of the idea of barbecue, so I'm not fixing that the week after the ball."

Stella clapped her hands like a little girl. "Thanks, Mama. That all looks scrumptious and I want steak and one of your cream-puff cakes for my birthday cake."

"I brought some tomatoes to go with all that and I'll be glad to bring something to the party if you'll invite me." Rosalee followed Nancy into the shop.

"Of course you are invited and Agnes should be out of the rehab place, so you can bring her along, too," Nancy said.

Stella adjusted the thermostat, turned on the lights, and headed toward her station to do some minor cleanup before her first client arrived that morning. Rosalee trailed along behind Nancy to the back room and came out with a chunk of banana bread.

"Your mama is making a pot of coffee," she said. "From the looks of them dark circles under your eyes, Stella Joy, you done stayed up too late last night, so the caffeine might be just what you need."

"We stayed up and watched *Steel Magnolias* to see if Agnes is like Ouiser. You been to see her?" Stella glanced in the mirror. Yes, she did have dark circles, but they were so worth the night she'd had.

"Of course I have seen Agnes. I go every day before she goes to therapy. I'm surprised that she hasn't bitched about going. But she loves it because she gets to show Violet up in the therapy sessions. She's doin' so good they're already sayin' she won't have to stay the whole time. And Stella, when I first saw that movie, I asked Agnes if they'd interviewed her for the character." Rosalee cackled.

"What did Agnes say?" Piper caught the last part of Rosalee's comment.

"She said that of course they did and asked her to play the part but she was too busy keeping Cadillac on its toes," Rosalee answered.

"I don't doubt it for a minute. Now why do you have dark circles under your eyes, Stella Joy?" Nancy turned her attention to her daughter.

"If she wouldn't play that music so loud, she could probably sleep better," Piper said. "It was going at two o'clock when I got up to raid the refrigerator. Oh, I forgot to tell you, I got the last piece of banana bread, so it's a good thing that Nancy brought more today."

Stella picked up all the brushes to run through the sterilizer. "I like music. It helps me sleep."

"We called it sex in my day," Rosalee said. "Who was in the bed with you that you had to cover up the noise with music?"

"Really!" Piper almost choked on the banana bread. "Was there a man in your bedroom?"

"Well, shit! I gave up Boone to stay with y'all and you get sex?" Charlotte shook her finger at Stella.

"Quit grinning and talk," Nancy demanded.

"I'm not saying a word." Stella felt the heat of a deep crimson blush crawling up her neck all the way to her face.

Rosalee winked at Stella. "Looks like we need to leave Stella alone with her secret, but darlin' girl, the whole town is snoopin' around tryin' to find out who is puttin' that smile and that blush on your face." She turned toward Nancy and said, "Tell me more about these god-awful rules Heather has made up for the ball. Did she really say it was going to be an annual affair?"

Nancy nodded. "She did. Why?"

"Anyone want to bet me five dollars that this is a one-time-only shindig?"

"Not me," Nancy said. "Not when Agnes has passed the torch to Stella."

"Well, damn. I withdraw my offer. If Stella is going to take Heather down, then it's a onetime thing for sure."

A cold shiver inched its way down Stella's spine. They were sure enough putting a lot of pressure on her. "What makes you so sure?" she asked.

"Age and experience," Rosalee said. "And speaking of music, why didn't you just go in there and turn the music down after Stella was asleep, Piper?"

"The door was locked," Piper said.

"Aha! I knew it." Nancy slapped her thigh. "You did have a man in your bedroom, didn't you? Even though I disagree with the way you young people go about things, I might get a son-in-law before your biological clock runs completely out of power yet."

"One never knows," Stella teased.

"I'm going down to Ruby's now and get my nails done. Had my toenails done last week and they ain't chipped yet. But I want pretty fingernails for Sunday when I go to Tansy's for Alma Grace's party. Y'all are all going, right?" Nancy asked.

"Yes, ma'am," Stella said. "And Mama, thanks for dinner and the bread."

"You are so welcome. Now I've got to go take care of my spy business or Agnes will have my scalp."

&

Annabel was sitting at Ruby's station with permanent rods in her hair when Nancy arrived at the beauty shop. Heather was at Kayla's nail table and Floy was getting a shampoo.

"You got an appointment this morning?" Ruby asked.

"No, I just came for Kayla to do my nails," Nancy said.

"They need doing," Heather said bluntly. "Tacky is always noticeable and there's nothing tackier than chipped fingernails."

"Oh, I could argue that point, but not today. So, anything new on the barbecue ball? If we'd been truly smart, we would have made each lady bring her special recipe of barbecue and put out pretty jars for donations for the best one," Nancy said.

Heather clapped her hands and squealed. "I love that idea. Let's do it. It's not too late to announce it and it'll save us a bunch of money having to pay for the barbecue. Oh, we must do this! Let's draw up the rules. Each lady has to bring her favorite recipe and a side dish to go with it. We'll have the food paid for that way. I'll make cute little boxes for the donations with the ladies' names on it. It sounds so Victorian, don't you think?"

It still sounded like a redneck thing to Nancy, but she wasn't saying a word. She'd never figured she could get Heather to fall for the job Agnes had given her so quickly. Everett wouldn't have to cook for two days. He could smoke a roast for her and a couple of chickens for Stella and that would do it. Stella could make her ranch potato salad and Nancy would take a bourbon-banana cake for the dessert table. Heather didn't have to know about the cup of bourbon in the recipe. The baking process did, after all, remove the alcohol.

Kayla picked up the pink fingernail polish and shook it. "You sure you don't want the gold fingernail this week?"

"Yes, I want you to leave it off," Heather snapped at Kayla. "Aunt Violet told me when I visited her yesterday that she's had hers removed and she's just sure that's what made her knee go bad. Something in the glue seeped into her blood and ruined her knee, so I won't be wearing a gold nail anymore until I do some more research on the adhesive. After all, I have lots of work to do if I'm going to turn Cadillac into a cultural city."

"I heard that it can cause dementia and terrible gastroenteritis." It came out so slick that Nancy wondered if she'd said the words out loud.

"Oh, my! I really can't afford that. With Aunt Violet ailing, this town needs me so much." Heather sighed loudly.

"What do you want me to do with this fingernail?" Kayla asked.

"Put it in a nice little box and I'll keep it until they invent glue that is guaranteed not to make me sick."

"So it's all right to tell folks about the new idea for the barbecue ball? You know that will make it somewhat like the chili cook-off," Nancy said.

"Oh, yes, tell them. I'm making an executive decision right now. It will save my ministry a lot of money and it will be fun. Who can come up with the best barbecue in town? And I went to that chili cook-off. My beautiful ball will be dignified. It won't be anything like an outdoor thing with beer and kids running around like a bunch of hoodlums," she declared.

"Be sure that's what you want, because once the story gets out, there won't be any going back. Tickets are still twenty dollars but the ladies have to bring barbecue and a side dish, right?"

"That is what I said." Heather shot her a dirty look.

"All done," Kayla said.

"Oh, and each person has to bring their very own barbecue. It can't be from the Rib Joint and it can't be made by someone else," Heather said.

"You mean Everett can't make Stella's?"

Heather's mouth turned up in a wicked grin. "That's right. She has to make her own or be disqualified. I do hope someone brings pulled chicken, because that is my very favorite."

"Then you will simply have to save room for Stella's chicken. Her pulled chicken and her ranch potato salad are her specialties," Nancy said. "What are you bringing, Heather?"

"Darlin'," she said sarcastically. "If you will remember, I'm making the punch for the small table."

Was it really a sin to slap a woman right out in public? And was that considered assault and battery, which was a felony, or would Jack call it disturbing the peace and let her off with a fine?

CHAPTER SEVENTEEN

On Friday morning, eight days before the ball, Annabel showed up at the Yellow Rose with a poster in her hands. Not just a little legal-size paper poster someone had generated on the computer, but a full-size glossy one showing something like Tara of *Gone with the Wind* in the background, stating the event's time, from six to midnight with dinner (not supper) served promptly at eight following the drawing to unite the couples.

Annabel's dark hair was laced with streaks of gray and if she didn't keep a healthy supply of rocks in her pockets, a good, strong Texas wind could have blown her plumb away. She never left home without perfect makeup, hose, and heels and most of the time she wore a cute little suit. That day she was in perfect form, smile pasted on and high heels clicking against the tile floor.

"Good morning. I'm the poster girl today for the Yellow Rose Barbecue Ball." She giggled. "Aren't these simply divine? Heather did such a wonderful job of designing them. I'd like to put one in your window, Stella."

She couldn't say no but she damn sure didn't want to say yes, so she nodded. Poor Annabel was grooming herself to take on Heather's job, but Annabel would never be the second coming of

Violet Prescott. She simply did not have enough mean in her bones or ice water flowing through her veins. Heather, with or without the fingernail, could fit the bill, so Annabel might as well learn to love the backseat.

"You want to leave it with me or hang it up yourself?" Stella asked.

Annabel flashed a smile. "I'll be very happy to put it up myself. Y'all just go right on about your business. Don't mind me. I'll be done in just a second."

She looked at the big display window with "The Yellow Rose" written in a half circle and "Beauty Shop" tucked up toward the top, but shook her head. "Not there."

For two whole minutes she paced across the front of the shop, her heels making a noise on the tile floor like ducks flying south for the winter. Stella kept an eye on her while she combed out and teased up Lillian Thomas's thin gray hair.

"What is she doing?" Lillian asked.

"Trying to decide where to put that poster. If she takes this much time with every one, it'll be over before it's advertised," Stella whispered. Suddenly, her stomach knotted up and she barely made it to the bathroom before she upchucked everything but her toenails. When she returned, Annabel was still trying to find the perfect place for her poster.

She stopped what she was doing and glared at Stella. "I heard you are the cause of all this craziness. You look a little pale. Are you all right?"

"Yes, she is the reason for the barbecue ball. If she would have just gotten married right out of high school, she could already have her first divorce under her belt," Piper said.

"Or if she would have chosen her own husband six months ago or picked one of those poor beggars that Nancy drugged and dragged to Sunday dinner, she wouldn't have been in this mess.

And I might add, we wouldn't be searching for barbecue recipes," Charlotte said. "And she is pale because she didn't have time to put on her makeup this morning."

Stella started counting backward and almost fainted right there in the floor. Holy mother of God! How was she even going to buy a pregnancy test without someone seeing and reporting back to the gossip hounds? Surely she was not pregnant. She was on the pill and it was more than 99 percent effective. Her stomach clenched again and she had to swallow hard to keep from rushing back to the bathroom a second time. She'd only missed one period and she could chalk that up to stress, right?

Annabel whipped around. "Nancy might have started something with her prayer request, but this is going to be the beginning of a whole new wonderful thing called marriage ministry and it will be a cultural affair for Cadillac. Miz Heather is working very hard on it."

A blast of heat flooded the shop when Nancy pushed through the front door. "Wow, those posters look expensive," she said.

Annabel was truly flustered. "This is going to be a wonderful event. We couldn't have anything less than professionally done posters to advertise it. After all, this first ball is the foundation for something bigger and better each year." She quickly removed the sign saying that there would be no more men's haircuts given at the Yellow Rose and taped the sign in the window of the glass door. "Good day, ladies. Thank you for letting me put a poster in your window."

If Agnes is grooming you to be next in line for her title and Heather is dethroning Violet, what's going to happen to Cadillac? Stella's inner voice asked.

Who gives a shit about Cadillac? What if I'm pregnant? Stella argued with the voice.

"Will Jed be upset or happy?" Stella mumbled.

"What did you say, honey?" Nancy asked. "I was watching Annabel and didn't hear you."

"I was just thinking out loud."

Nancy pulled out the side of the poster, laid her cheek on the glass, and peeked at the bright colors.

"Hey, you can go outside and look at it from there," Charlotte hollered.

"Oops," Nancy said when the poster fell off the window and landed on the floor. "Guess the heat and me messing with it made the tape let go. But don't worry, I can fix it. When I get done it will stay up there until eternity dawns."

She jerked a partial roll of duct tape from her purse, held the poster back up to the window and ripped off long strips of gray tape. When it was firmly in place, it was slightly askew and looked like crap from the outside, but she seemed quite happy with her work.

"Good thing I'm following Annabel around. She means well but she just doesn't have the equipment to work with. I done fixed the ones she put on the door at Clawdy's and at Bless My Bloomers. I reckon I'll have to check the one at the convenience store and over at the community center soon as she gets them put up," Nancy said. "So, Lillian, how's your garden this summer? Grasshoppers got your cucumbers yet?"

ఴ

Piper flipped through the hangers at the Ross store in Sherman. She found a cute little black lace dress that might have worked for the ball, but only the outer skirt came to the floor. The lining was supposed to stop at midcalf and let the lace show legs from there down. Piper held it up to her body—the lining would have had trouble covering the elastic in her underpants, so she put it back on the rack.

"I refuse to pay a lot of money for something I'll only wear once. We should have started looking before it was only a week before the ball. Remember when we were in high school? We fretted about our prom dresses for months on end," she told Charlotte and Stella.

"But you might get to dance with Rhett again," Stella said. "Can you believe that Mama duct-taped those signs all over town? Heather is liable to go up in flames and throw her out of the Angels."

"Hey, I'm just happy she didn't use a Magic Marker to draw mustaches on the gent and the lady pictured on them. Did you see the way they were dressed? That man looked like a sissy from the last century with those knee britches and buckled shoes," Piper said.

"And the lady with her hair all done up two feet high and that ball gown with a hoop skirt sure don't look like she's going to a Texas barn dance, does she?" Stella laughed.

"I'd have liked to see Nancy use a Magic Marker to turn the mansion in the background into a barn or a one-hole outhouse." Charlotte held up a lovely pale-green halter dress with a rhinestone clasp, which would show off cleavage. "Think Boone would like this?"

Stella motioned toward the empty cart they were sharing. "Put it in here and we'll take it to the dressing room. I'm not going with less than six and I'm not leaving without a dress."

"And I'm not spending a lot of money," Piper said.

Charlotte smiled. "Darlin', we're in the discount store of the South. I don't think anything in here would knock too big of a hole in our checking accounts."

"But after the dress, we've got to buy shoes and jewelry," Piper reminded her.

Stella held up an off-white ankle-length lace dress with spaghetti straps. "I might forgo the jewelry and get one of those temporary tats on my shoulder just to rile Heather."

Piper picked up another off-white lace dress and held it up. "You should buy this one or at least put it in the cart to try on. Look, it's got a little train in the back and oh, I do like the satin buttons all the way from shoulders to train. It's gorgeous and it's been marked down three times, so it's a steal."

"And you are not getting a tat, not even a temporary one. Everett would throw a fit," Charlotte said. "I think a strand of pearls is what you need with that dress. Borrow your mother's. Those that belonged to your grandmother. Then you won't have to buy jewelry."

Stella took the dress from Piper and put it in the cart. "I like it and it's in my size."

"So you are making pulled chicken and potato salad. I think I'll make broccoli salad and barbecued pork chops," Charlotte said.

"How in the hell am I supposed to make her eat my chicken? She hates me and sure won't trust me not to dose it with something," Stella mused aloud.

"First, you tell her that it's much too spicy for her delicate nature. Then you tell her that you really made it for Quinn because he has always loved it so much. Believe me, she'll eat it then." Piper tossed two dresses into the cart. "I don't know why we're buying dresses. If it was billed as a barn dance we'd be wearing tight jeans and western-cut lace blouses."

"Cultural affair, my ass. This is Cadillac, Texas, where folks get excited about hot peppers and chili, not dancing some fancy waltz shit in a barn. I can't even picture Boone in knee britches," Charlotte fussed.

Stella held up a dark-green dress in Piper's size. It was chiffon over satin with a shorter underskirt, but this one was designed to stop at midcalf, which would put it about knee length on Piper. The halter top was draped in soft folds that would draw the eye to her long, graceful neck.

Charlotte took the hanger from Stella and draped the dress over the cart. "Put your hair up in a messy French twist with a glittery clasp, and Rhett is taller than you so you can wear high heels."

Piper tossed another dress into the cart. "Y'all are forgetting something very important here. Charlotte automatically gets drawn in with Boone because they are engaged, but there's no tellin' who Heather will draw out for me and you, Stella."

Stella patted her on the arm. "Not to worry. Agnes can do magic from a hospital bed. If she swears you will be dancing and dining at the ball with Rhett, then it will happen."

Nancy rounded the end of the long dress rack and waved. "Hey, y'all out huntin' down a cheap dress for this ball?"

"Yes, we are." Piper raised a hand to high-five with Nancy. "Good job on all those posters."

Nancy slapped her palm and said, "I used up a whole roll of duct tape fixin' those posters, but by golly, it'll take a muscle man to bring them down off the windows."

"Are you sure Agnes hasn't recruited you to take her place in Cadillac instead of Stella?" Charlotte asked.

"Oh, no, I don't have red hair. I'm just a minion for the new queen." Nancy bent her knees in a bow to Stella.

"Stop it. When she springs that joint, she'll want her crown back." Stella laughed.

"You mean her horns?" Nancy said. "I'm surprised, Stella. I thought you might take Agnes's lead and wear overalls redone into a dress."

Stella held up the lacy dress. "What do you think of this one? Agnes and Rosalee are the only ones who get to go in fancy overall dresses. Rest of us have to be properly attired."

"It's beautiful. My mama's pearls would look good with it."

Charlotte pushed the cart closer to Nancy. "Throw whatever you find in here and we'll all go to the dressing rooms together. We've already told Stella that your pearls would be good with the dress. I'm leaning toward this pale green and Piper is looking at the dark green."

"Well, I'm damn sure not wearing pink or blue or yellow, since that's the colors of the whole shebang. So it could be that green will be my color, too." Nancy started going through the dresses in her size.

Stella held up a cute little white eyelet lace sundress with a defined waistline and a full skirt. "I like this for the shower on Sunday. What do y'all think?"

"It's cute, but it's a wedding shower. You think you should wear white?" Nancy asked.

Piper pulled another one from the rack. "Here is the same dress in green. It matches your eyes and you could wear your cowboy boots with it. The ones that have that green Celtic cross in relief on the front."

"That's a great idea. Y'all buyin' something for the shower?" Stella asked.

"I've got a new capri set I'm wearing," Nancy answered.

"I'm buying. You know how I love clothes, and a shower is a wonderful excuse to get something brand-new," Piper said.

Stella saw a grass-green dress on the rack and pulled it out. "Mama, what about this one?"

"Oh, honey, I'm too old and my arms are too flabby to wear something sleeveless, much less a spaghetti strap like that." Nancy smiled.

"How about with this?" Piper held up a short-sleeved off-white jacket trimmed in satin ribbon the same shade of green.

"It goes with it," Stella said. "See, right here, it says that it's a two-piece outfit. Someone must've knocked the jacket off and then

215

it got hung on a separate hanger. And for the record, Mama, you work too hard on the farm to ever get baggy arms."

Nancy beamed. "Thank you, honey. Let's go try on all this finery and then go across the highway and have us some catfish. I'm treating tonight because y'all are helping me buy something I don't want to go somewhere I don't want to go."

Stella had been planning on finding a way to buy a pregnancy test that evening, but with both her friends and her mama in her company that wasn't going to happen. She hadn't mentioned a word about it to Jed and she hadn't thrown up again, so maybe, just maybe, it was nothing more than nerves that kept her from having a period. And hopefully it was eating leftovers that had made her sick.

Charlotte pulled the cart back and quickly added two more dresses. "Thank you, Nancy. But don't forget we have to buy shoes to go with these dresses or we'll have to come back again."

"Well, crap! I forgot about shoes. Good thing you remembered, Charlotte, because I'm not wasting another night on the most boring thing we've ever had in Cadillac." Nancy sighed.

"It could turn out to be a riot." Stella laughed.

"Maybe we should have an ambulance there just in case?" Nancy followed the three women and the cart to the fitting rooms at the back of the store.

"Heather has the television station from Sherman coming down to cover it," Piper said.

"Was that girl born stupid?" Nancy frowned.

"It's the big-city ideas coming out of her. She has visions of grandeur because she moved from Tulsa to little bitty Cadillac," Piper said.

"Honey, that girl lived in Ripley, Oklahoma, population less than five hundred. She went to college in Tulsa but she wasn't raised there," Nancy said.

"So Ripley." Stella giggled.

"Believe it." Charlotte laughed with her.

"Or not!" Piper finished the sentence.

CHAPTER EIGHTEEN

Alma Grace wore a chin-length wedding veil attached to a glittering tiara with a cute little floral sundress. Rick was decked out with a bow tie, a garter around his arm, and a top hat. They had the place of honor under a decorated arch in the huge living room.

Tansy swept across the room and hugged Nancy. "I'm so glad you and Stella came today. Come over here and sit beside me."

Tansy was a self-proclaimed psychic and her predictions were right about 50 percent of the time. The other half she blamed on her crazy cockatiel not doing his part in being her muse. As usual, she looked like a gypsy in a flowing multicolored skirt, dozens of gold bangle bracelets up her arm, and fancy sandals that laced around her ankles.

Charlotte and Piper arrived and Tansy ushered them to seats right behind Nancy and Stella. "This way we can all be in a group. I've got dozens of questions about the ball."

Stella took one look at three eight-foot tables stacked full of presents and whispered to Nancy, "Mama, swear to me that you won't let anyone give me a wedding shower. I'll allow a bridal shower with lots of pretty things from Bless My Bloomers, but I don't need ten toasters."

"No, ma'am. We like our parties in Cadillac too well for that, but I will promise you that I'll help write thank-you notes. And so will Piper and Charlotte. That's what bridesmaids are for. Do you have a fellow or maybe a date in mind?" Nancy asked.

"Maybe," she answered.

Carlene passed presents to Alma Grace and Rick. Sugar, Alma Grace's mama, wrote down each gift in a pretty white book. Jenny strung the bows on a velvet coat hanger and stuffed trash into a white plastic bag imprinted with wedding bells.

Just watching them gave Stella an acute case of imaginary hives. She held her hands in her lap to keep from scratching at bumps that weren't there. She was so glad that she and Jed had simply gone to the courthouse in Durant, Oklahoma, one Monday afternoon, bought a license, and got married by the judge. It had taken thirty minutes from the time they walked into the court clerk's office until they were back in Jed's truck. They'd spent the rest of the day and the night in a hotel room and she hadn't been late to work the next morning.

Tansy leaned back and said in a low voice, "Isn't it all lovely? Now, about this ball. I hear it's like a renaissance fair and a pre–Civil War ball all mixed up together. The poster at Bless My Bloomers looks like a movie advertisement. Are the men really supposed to wear knee britches? If they are, we'll have very few guys to dance with. This is Texas."

"It's renaissance and redneck with lots of crazy thrown into the mix," Nancy said. "All profits will go to Heather's marriage ministry but if she doesn't stop spending so big, she's liable to be in the red for a long time with her new-founded ministry."

"She's got a lot to learn, doesn't she?" Tansy whispered.

"Hello, everyone." Heather waved from the doorway. "I'm a little late so I let myself in. I did my fifteen minutes of prayer at the prayerathon first so I could attend." She slid a sidelong glance toward Stella. "Now the rest of the prayer folks are doing their duty."

"Well, ain't that nice," Tansy said.

Heather had barely parked her fanny in a chair when the doorbell rang. Tansy popped up and headed in that direction and brought Annabel and Floy back with her.

"We prayed together. There is strength in numbers." Annabel smiled at Stella. "You will be in line for all this real soon, Stella. We were talkin' about your wedding shower on the way over here."

Tansy returned the next time the doorbell rang with Rosalee right behind her. Her overalls were amazing, with sparkly stones creating a floral design up the outsides of both legs as well as across the bib. She wore a shiny red satin shirt underneath them and red rubber flip-flops with bright-colored stones glued to the straps.

She sat down beside Charlotte right behind Tansy, leaned up, and whispered, "What do y'all think? Agnes says for someone to send pictures to her phone."

"You look amazing," Stella said. "Can I borrow those sometime?"

"Anytime until I die, but then I'll be buried in them. Me and Agnes decided when I went to see her this morning that we'd be buried in our new overalls or else our ball gowns. Damn, this is more fun than I've had in years." Rosalee grinned.

"They are opening Heather's present," Charlotte said softly.

"Oh, Heather, how thoughtful of you," Alma Grace said. "And it's got a wide slot in the top for bagels. Rick and I are addicted to bagels with cream cheese. Thank you so much and please thank Violet for us, also, for sharing in buying the gift. We are so sorry that she couldn't come and we hope that she's feeling better real soon."

Said like a true southern girl, although there were six more boxes the exact same size on the gift table. Stella wasn't sure she'd have that much grace, not even as a preacher's wife.

Gigi handed Alma Grace an envelope and said, "This is from Agnes and Rosalee."

Alma Grace opened it and squealed, jumped up, and ran across the room. Tears welled up in her eyes as she threw her arms around Rosalee and hugged her fiercely. "You and Agnes are such sweethearts. Bless her heart, I know she wants to be here. You shouldn't have done this, but I'm so happy that you did. Oh, and I adore your outfit. You may have just started a brand-new fad."

"Your dad is delivering it to your new house right now, so it's there," Rosalee said. "It was mostly Agnes's idea but I wanted to help, so we shared the gift."

Alma Grace hugged her again. "I can't believe that she remembered. Thank you, thank you! Everyone, I want to tell you a story. Last month, I was in an antique store in Sherman and Agnes came in to browse. I'd been admiring a gorgeous old burled-oak washstand. It was in perfect condition with the original hardware still on it and I said that there was a place in my house that it would fit right into. She has bought that lovely piece of furniture for us. Isn't that the sweetest thing ever?"

Rosalee shooed her away. "It's not a big deal. Not many girls your age appreciate good solid furniture, and we wanted you to have it. There's something tucked inside the drawer that is a little extra surprise. Now go on and unwrap the rest of those presents before you have me cryin' with you."

Piper poked her on the arm. "What's in the drawer?"

"Just a little hand-crocheted runner that she admired. My mama used to crochet that pineapple pattern and I thought she should have it to go with the washstand," Rosalee whispered. "But don't tell anyone. Heather can wonder if I put a check in there to pay for her honeymoon."

"Lord, you are almost as ornery as Agnes." Piper giggled softly.

"Well, thank you, honey." Rosalee beamed.

☙

The window was unlatched. The door was locked. Music played. But Stella was in bed alone and she couldn't sleep. She rolled to one side and checked the clock.

It was early and she hadn't heard from Jed, so he might still show up. He had called the night before and said he had to sit with an elderly member of the church in the hospital. Two nights in a row wasn't fair, not when they'd found the perfect place.

In plain sight couldn't be beat. So far folks didn't seem to be interested in what Preacher Jed was doing out jogging around town in the early morning and late night hours. They were too busy spying on Stella.

She slapped his pillow down over her face and inhaled deeply, filling her lungs with air and the remnants of his cologne. It just made her miss him all the more. She held the pillow up and imagined that it was his face with the angles, his definite jawline, firm but sexy lips, and those lines in his cheeks when he smiled.

"I'm so much in love," she muttered.

The rising window made a slight noise but she'd imagined hearing that all evening, so she didn't believe that he was there until he sat down on the edge of the bed. She squealed and threw herself into his arms.

"It's true," he said.

"What, that I love you?"

He kissed her on the tip of the nose. "No, that absence makes the heart grow fonder."

"I hate sleeping alone," she said.

She took his hand and wiggled out of his embrace. "I have a surprise."

"Is it edible? I'm starving."

"No, but I'll go to the kitchen and get you something," she said.

"I'll need energy to do what I've got planned for tonight," he whispered. "Are you going to wrap yourself in something from Bless My Bloomers?"

She led him to the chest of drawers and opened the middle drawer. "Something far simpler than that. You are now the proud owner of your very own drawer, darlin'."

He picked her up and carried her back to the bed. "I've changed my mind about food."

"I don't mind making you a sandwich," she said. "Are you disappointed?"

"No, I'm amazed. That is the best present you've ever given me. If I have a drawer, it means we are a step closer to being a real married couple. I want to make love to you until the sun comes up, Stella."

The laughter that bubbled up from her soul was soft and sweet. "I love you and yes, we are a step closer and I'm getting used to the idea of being a preacher's wife, but I still want to wait until after this blasted ball is over, if you don't mind."

He sat down on the edge of the bed with her in his lap. "We can wait that long as long as I have a drawer and can hold you in my arms. Have I told you today that you are beautiful?"

"I haven't seen you today," she reminded him.

He slipped her gray tank top up over her head and kissed the hollow spot in her neck. "You didn't get my telepathic messages? I sent one every ten minutes while you were at the shower and since you've been home."

"So that's what my heart was hopping around about all day," she mumbled just before her lips met his.

"Stella, we need to talk," he said.

"About?" Her blood ran cold. Surely Annabel hadn't thought she was pregnant and was spreading more tales.

"About this dark cloud hovering over your head. I want us to get it out in the open and"—he paused—"I need to get my past out, dust it off, and be honest about it, too. We should have done it before we married, but I was afraid I'd lose you."

"You first," she said.

"Okay. Baring souls and confession time, and then we'll put it all in the past and not visit it again. But when you meet the folks where I grew up, I don't want anything they say to ruin our marriage." He kissed her on the forehead.

"What could you have possibly done that was worse than my past?" she asked.

He toyed with a strand of her hair. "I was as wild as a tornado when I was young."

"So was I, especially after the preacher's son ruined my name." She touched his face.

"I was that preacher's son," Jed said.

"No, you weren't," she argued.

"My father was not a preacher, but I was just like that boy. The first time I had a girl, I went to school and bragged about it. Her reputation was ruined and we were both only fifteen. I didn't even learn my lesson then, either. I smoked. I drank. I didn't do drugs because I was afraid my daddy would kill me for that, but he lived by the old rule—boys will be boys and they have a different set of rules than girls. I made it my business to sweet-talk lots of pretty girls into the backseat of my old car."

"Why are you telling me this?" she asked.

"Because when we go home to visit, folks are going to say things and I want you to know now," he told her. "Your past isn't nearly as bad as mine, so you need to let it go and forget about the gossip that this town hangs on to."

"You're not fixin' to tell me that you have AIDS or children hiding in your past, are you?" she asked.

He slowly shook his head. "Neither one, but only by the grace of God. I was tested for everything before I met you and I'm clean, and there are no children. I should have told you before, but I was afraid I'd lose you and I'm not sure my heart could keep beating if I didn't have you in my life. But that barbecue thing is getting close and I want to give you the opportunity to—"

She laid a finger across his lips. "I don't want to end our marriage. I love you, Jed. And you didn't get a saint, either. I'm glad you fessed up, but I want to spend the rest of my life with you. Can we please bury the past and go on with our lives?"

"No one has ever accepted me like you have, Stella," he whispered. "I've been living in fear that you'd tell me you couldn't stay with me since I have that much baggage."

"And I lived in fear that you'd tell me to hit the road when I told you about the scandal in Cadillac, so we're even. Now kiss me and let's don't waste any more of this night."

"I can do that," he said.

His lips closed over hers and she finally let go of the past and looked forward to the future.

Chapter Nineteen

"I t's almost time for Stella's birthday," Charlotte commented as she checked her appointment book.

"I can't believe that my boys will be home soon. Lorene has been wonderful to let them call every day, sometimes several times," Piper said.

"I truly believe that Lorene loves those boys." Butterflies fluttered around in Stella's stomach. By her birthday, everyone would know that she was married. The thought of being a preacher's wife would be scary even if she'd had a halo and wings, and Stella Baxter had neither. Marriage alone was a sobering venture and being a preacher's wife . . . well, that added an extra dimension, then throw in the fact that she still hadn't found a way to get her hands on a pregnancy test. Since she hadn't had any more nausea since that day, she forgot about it sometimes for a whole hour, but then something like Charlotte's knitting would remind her.

Piper grabbed the broom and dustpan. "Blasted crickets. Little demons are worse this year than they've ever been. And Stella, there never was a question about Luke and Tanner being all right with Gene's folks. It was me that would have gone to pieces and turned into an alcoholic if you hadn't let me move into your house while they are gone. Oh, and they've offered to keep them the night of the barbecue ball. They're going to take them to the waterslide in Wichita Falls that day, spend the night in a hotel, and the next day they're going to a movie. It's their little vacation with the boys."

Charlotte carried a basket of white towels to the front and they all started folding. "It wasn't a matter of *letting* us move into her house. She couldn't do a thing about it."

"Hey, y'all know you are welcome anytime, just like I know if a sumbitch ghost of a preacher's son that drinks too much beer invades my house, I can go pack my suitcase and be welcome at your homes," Stella said.

The bell rang and a stranger looked around, taking stock of the beauty shop. She was one of those delicate women with near-transparent skin, dishwater-blonde hair, and blue eyes, which now darted from one of the three friends to the others. "Hello, I have an appointment for a shampoo and comb-out with Piper. I wasn't expecting three of you."

"I'm Piper. This way to the shampoo chair. You are"—Piper ran a finger down the page in her book—"Katy, right? I don't think you've been here before."

"My first time." She almost smiled. "Alma Grace Magee said that I should come see you."

Piper whipped a cape around the woman and touched the foot pedal that leaned the chair back. "She is so sweet. I'll have to thank her for the recommendation. You've got lovely thick hair."

"Thank you. Sometimes I wish the powers that be would have given me less hair and more height, though. I go to the same church that Rick does and got to know Alma Grace when they started dating. We all love her," Katy said.

"This is virgin hair, isn't it?"

Katy smiled. "Yes, ma'am. No dyes for me. I'm much too busy to keep up with all that. I've got two little boys and a full-time job. You have children?"

"Two boys, twins. They keep me in line pretty good. They're with their dad for his two weeks' summer visit right now and though they get to call home often, I feel like my world isn't right," Piper said.

"I'm a single mom, too, but my husband hardly ever sees the boys. He said that he'd think about having them come visit when they were both fully potty trained." Katy's tone went from warm to icy. "At least your ex is a good man who loves his boys."

"Yeah, right." Charlotte stuffed towels into the cabinet above the shampoo sink.

"He has them for his summer visit, right?" Katy asked.

"Yes, he does," Piper said.

"And his name is?" Katy asked.

Piper's Spidey senses went into the red danger zone. Who was this woman and why was she fishing?

"Gene Stephens."

"Small world. His mama goes to my church, too," Katy said.

Piper rinsed Katy's hair and then poured in the conditioner. "It's a small world especially around this part of Texas. If you aren't kin to someone, then one of your relatives knows someone who is, and if the gossip isn't juicy enough when it gets started, believe me, it will be by the time it filters down to the last person to hear it."

"How old are your boys?" Stella asked.

"There's only a year between them, so it's a lot like raising twins when they're two and three. They sure grow up fast, don't they? Alma Grace said that y'all have been friends since you were little girls. I bet you know all the gossip," Katy said.

"We've been best friends since we were in kindergarten, but if you want the down and dirty gossip, you'd have to go to the old gals like Agnes, Rosalee, and Beulah," Stella told her.

Piper wrung the water from Katy's hair and wrapped her head in a towel. "And Violet Prescott. They're the ones who know the history and the stories."

"Hey, y'all would be about the same age as Trixie Matthews, then? She's part owner of Clawdy's with Marty and Cathy Andrews," Katy said.

Stella nodded. "We were all in high school together. The Clawdy's crew and the Bless My Bloomers bunch. Where did you go to high school?"

Katy hopped up into Piper's chair and crossed her legs at the ankles. "In Harlan County, Kentucky. I came out here and went to work in the nursing home that my uncle owns when my husband left me. That's where I met Trixie. Her mother is in the nursing home. I'm the activities director."

"So how do you like Texas?" Stella asked.

"It's not so different from Kentucky, but the only people I really know are my uncle and aunt and the folks at the church. I would've stayed in Kentucky, but I needed a fresh start."

Piper combed through Katy's long hair and wished that she'd had the nerve to pick up and go east or west or, hell, even north or south for that matter. If it hadn't been so convenient for Gene to just waltz into her house, then he wouldn't have the boys right now. And if she didn't live in Cadillac, he wouldn't know that she'd been talking to Rhett.

Her phone rang and she pulled it from the pocket of her khaki shorts, checked the ID, and said, "Excuse me, Katy. It's my kids."

"Hello, what's going on today?" Piper said and then giggled. "Is that right? I can't wait until you get home to see it. And you're going back today? What fun. Guess what? I found out that Bible school is at our church next week, so you guys might want to tell Grandma that you'll be staying with the sitter so you can go."

"But Grandma already knows that, Mama," Tanner said. "She wants us to tell you that she's going to be a teacher at Preacher Jed's church, so she's goin' with us, too. And guess what, we're helpin' Grandpa in the garden and he said we could bring home a whole sack full of vegetables."

"And you're going to eat them?" She laughed again.

"We'll eat the potatoes and the corn. We told Grandpa not to put them old nasty squashes in the sack," Luke yelled.

"You don't have to holler. She can hear us," Tanner told him.

"Are you guys on speakerphone?" Piper laid her phone down on the countertop and pushed a button so Stella and Charlotte could hear.

"Yes, we can both talk that way," Luke said.

"Tell me again what you made in Bible school," she said.

"Well, we stirred some water into a white powder and made a glob of it on this waxy paper. Then we took a pencil and wrote a Bible verse in it. When it got hard, we chipped off the knots and painted it," Tanner explained.

"And then we glued a thing on the back so you can hang it on your wall," Luke said.

"What's your verse?" Charlotte asked.

"Well, I wanted to write 'God is good, beer is great, and people are crazy,' but my teacher said that's a song, not a verse, so I just wrote 'The Lord is my shepherd,' and Luke wrote . . ." Tanner said, and there was a long pause.

"I took it off speakerphone on this end and I'm here," Gene said. "Have you come to your senses? Are we going to be a family again?"

"I never lost my senses, Gene, and no, we are not." Piper reached to pick up the phone.

Charlotte slapped at her hand and shook her head.

"You've got five days to make up your mind," he said.

"My mind is made up. I've moved on and you have, too, Gene. This is your second move. You left me for Rita and you've left her for Ramona. I hope you find happiness, but it's not going to be with me. Good-bye," Piper said.

"Don't hang up! Ramona is just a bed partner until we are back together, just like Rhett is to you. You boys go make your beds or you won't be doing a bit of fishing this afternoon. You're not talking to your mother again today. They won't be talking to you the rest of the week except at bedtime. I've been too damned lenient on them."

The phone went dead.

"I'm not sleeping with Rhett." Piper's voice cracked.

Stella took the brush from Piper's hand. "You won't mind if I take over, will you, Katy? I'm really good with long, thick hair. We all work with Alma Grace and your hair reminds me so much of hers."

"That's fine. I'm sure you'll do a fine job," Katy whispered.

Piper ducked her head and headed for the back room, where she melted into a chair and laid her forehead on her arms on the table. She cried until her ribs ached and her lungs burned, but it wouldn't stop.

"It's not fair for him to take out his anger toward me on the boys." The words came out a couple at a time between sobs.

Charlotte sat down beside her and patted her shoulder. "Shhh. He'll go to work pretty soon and Lorene will take care of them. He won't be around except in the evenings. They'll be home in five days."

"It breaks my heart," Piper said. "I wish he'd marry that Ramona and get on with his life."

"If she's smart, she'll run the other way," Charlotte said.

"Who'll run which way and who's smart?" Nancy came through the back entrance and set a pan of brownies on the table. "Are you talking about Gene and his new woman?"

Charlotte told the story while Piper dried her eyes and fixed her makeup using a small hand mirror.

Piper's chin quivered but she took a deep breath and said, "I wish he'd not only get married but that he'd move right on out of this state." She pushed the chair back and returned to the front part of the shop. "Is there room in Kentucky for another worthless ex-husband, Katy?"

"There could be. Round 'em all up and put them in one place so they can't sweet-talk their way into breaking another woman's heart."

Charlotte cut two brownies from the pan, put them on a plate, and whispered, "Maybe brownies will help everyone. Thanks for bringing them, Nancy."

"Hi, Mama." Stella smiled. "Any rain on the horizon?"

"Hell, no, there ain't no rain in sight all week. Gardens would wither up and die if folks didn't water. Cadillac has always produced a patch of hot jalapeños up by Clawdy's and Cathy will see to it that there is a good crop this year, but it's takin' lots of water. I hear she's making candied ones from an old recipe she found in her mama's things to enter in the fair. Who is this you are fixin' up? I don't think we've met. I'm Nancy, Stella's mama."

"Right pleased to meet you, ma'am. I'm Katy. Alma Grace recommended this shop and I have to agree with her; these ladies do a fine job. My hair is so thick that most hairdressers just want to thin it out and cut it off," Katy said.

"Brownies? Nancy brought them." Charlotte slid the plate close enough that Katy could reach it.

Katy reached for one. "That is so sweet."

Nancy sat down in Stella's swivel chair and stared at Katy. "Fresh out of the oven just before I left."

"So what brings you into town this mornin', Mama?" Stella asked.

"I've got to make a run up to Sherman for sugar. Peaches are coming off the two trees in the orchard so fast that I can't keep up with them," she said.

"Puttin' them in the freezer or makin' peach pie filling?" Stella asked.

"Freezer today," Nancy answered.

"Delicious brownie. I didn't take time for breakfast, so it's really hitting the spot. I miss my granny's peach cobbler. She uses a little bit of cinnamon and for special times like weddin's or birthdays she makes homemade ice cream to go on top," Katy said. "Thank you so much, Stella. I've got just enough time to get to work. Piper, it might be awkward for me to come back here, but I did enjoy meeting all of you."

Piper slid into the chair next to Nancy. "I want to apologize for not finishing my job. I hope you don't hold that against us. I don't usually get emotional, but ex-husbands can be trying." Piper frowned and asked, "Why would it be awkward for you to come back?"

Katy waved her hand in dismissal. "Alma Grace did me the biggest favor of my life in sending me here. It's not that I don't want to come back but that I shouldn't. I wasn't totally honest with you. My grandmother called me Katy since my middle name is Catherine, but when I came out here from Kentucky I decided to make a clean change and I've gone by my first name, Ramona, ever since." She took a deep breath and her chin quivered slightly. "Y'all and that phone call sure opened my eyes, so thank you, and Piper, believe me when I tell you that you don't want Gene back in your life. I thought you were a witch from hell who'd cheated on him since the month after you got married and kicked him out when he wouldn't let you go on a singles cruise with your two friends here. I'll thank Alma Grace on my way out of town." Ramona/Katy put a bill on the counter and swept out of the shop without looking back.

Nancy's sudden intake of breath was the only sound in the beauty shop. "Well, don't the world go round."

Stella was speechless for all of thirty seconds and then she whispered, "I bet Gene is in a bitchy mood the rest of this week. I wouldn't be surprised if he doesn't bring the boys home early."

"That would be a blessing," Nancy said.

"Now he'll really be grouchy with the boys," Piper groaned.

"Don't you worry one bit about it. Karma is a bitch and his mama ain't goin' to let him get too mean. Those are her grandkids and believe me, if I had boys like that, I'd fight a forest fire with nothing but spit to protect them. Now pass me one of them brownies and who are you sleeping with, Stella?" Nancy said.

Stella opened her mouth to spit out his name and then shook her finger at her mother. "You are sneaky this morning."

Piper squeezed the bridge of her nose between her finger and thumb. "I love you and I want to know who your boyfriend is, but right now I wish I could have what Ramona got—a fresh start."

"Please don't leave Cadillac," Charlotte whispered.

"I couldn't leave my friends, and the boys have roots here, but it don't keep me from wishin' I could do something different."

"You could sell your house and buy another one. Leave his ghost there and move on for real," Stella said.

Piper dropped her hand. "Now that sounds like something we should talk about."

CHAPTER TWENTY

The phone was right beside her on the end table and Piper was stretched out in the recliner under the air conditioner vent. Charlotte and Stella shared the sofa, one on each end with their legs stretched out across the middle. Piper's favorite movie, *Something to Talk About*, was in the DVD player.

"I can so relate to this movie, only Gene isn't as nice as Eddie Bichon. By the end of the movie I'm hoping that he and Grace get back together, but I never want to look at Gene again. If I poisoned him like she did Eddie in the movie, I'd add enough that he'd be in the morgue, not the damned emergency room," Piper said.

"Hey, anybody in here want a cinnamon roll right out of the oven?" Nancy yelled as she made her way to the living room. She set the pan on the coffee table. "Your daddy is fishin' and hey, I like this movie. I am Georgia King, the mother. I'll get some paper towels to use for napkins from the kitchen."

Stella reached for a warm roll. "Daddy never did flirt with another woman, did he?"

"He's still alive, isn't he?" Nancy ripped two paper towels from the roll and handed one to Stella. "Gossip has it that Gene's girlfriend came into the shop with a gun and threatened Piper today. I was there for part of it so I know it's not true, but it does make for a juicy story."

"That ought to be real good for business," Piper groaned.

"Gossip also says that you are thinkin' about a fresh start and you are moving to Harlan County, Kentucky." Nancy put the rest of the towels on the coffee table and then pulled a wooden rocking chair closer to the end of the sofa.

Piper ripped off two towels and reached for a cinnamon roll. "It would be nice if everyone could get the story right if they were going to tell it. We're going to send every two-timin' husband to Harlan County, not the poor old wives who get their hearts broken."

"Sounds like a plan to me. Maybe they could have a season on their sorry asses, kind of like deer season. Two weeks out of every summer women could buy a license to hunt them down," Nancy said.

Piper smiled. "I'd have to take shootin' lessons."

"I could teach you," Nancy said. "I'm a fair shot with a pistol and I can take the eyes of a snake out at fifty yards with a good rifle. Which brings me to a proposition I got for you, Piper. I got to thinking about you sellin' your house and startin' fresh. I went home and talked to Everett about it first and he agreed that would be a good thing for you to do."

Piper picked up her second sweet roll. "It would be nice, but the market is down right now, especially in a small town like Cadillac. We only bought it five years ago, so there's not much equity. I doubt I'd get enough to put a down payment on another place."

Nancy kicked off her sandals and drew one knee up in the chair. "I don't want your answer tonight. I want you to sleep on it first. As you know, my mama refused to move in with us when she got to where she really shouldn't be livin' by herself. Wouldn't be a burden, she said. So we put a trailer on the farm about a quarter of a mile back behind our house. Fenced it in so she could have her dog and the cows wouldn't eat her roses. She said she couldn't live in a place where there wasn't roses, so Everett planted ten bushes in front of her trailer."

"I remember that story." Piper smiled.

"What if you was to move in that trailer and let us watch the boys for you? It would give Everett something to do. I don't know what I'll do with him once he gets tired of fishin'. Wouldn't cost you a dime for the trailer or the babysitting, unless you want to charge me for the boys keepin' Everett. You could rent your house out here in town. We got some new teachers comin' in that's already lookin' around for houses to rent so it shouldn't be hard to do. Of course, you'd have to pay your own utilities, but there is a good clean well that provides free water," Nancy said.

Tears streamed down Piper's cheeks and dripped onto her shirt.

"Now, don't bawl like a baby. You can tell me to butt out and mind my own business," Nancy said. "I just figured since I don't have no grandbabies that me and Everett could kind of adopt yours. And since Gene can pop into Lorene's anytime and be hateful to the boys, then maybe it would be best if they only saw him on his weekends."

Piper popped the leg rest of the chair down and crossed the room in three long strides, knelt in front of Nancy, and put her head on her lap. "That is the sweetest thing anyone has ever offered me. You are an angel straight from heaven. Do I have to wait until morning to give you my answer?"

Nancy patted her on the shoulder. "I just figured that it would give me and Everett more time to hope you'd say yes. Don't know why we didn't think of it sooner. He really loves Luke and Tanner."

"Yes, yes, yes." Piper hugged Nancy tightly. "I can't ever thank you enough."

Nancy patted her on the head. "Havin' someone out there to take care of the trailer so it don't get vandalized or fall down in a heap will be nice. In a few years you might want to sell your house and move back to town, but we'll cross that bridge when we get to it."

Charlotte wiped away tears with a fresh paper towel and threw the roll at Stella, who peeled several off and passed it on to Piper.

"Now that's settled, we'll start packing tomorrow night, right?" Charlotte asked.

"Before you change your mind," Stella said.

"I'll get Boone and Rhett to move the heavy stuff on Thursday evening. We can pack in two nights and the boys will have a big surprise when they get home. Now they can have a puppy, right, Nancy?" Charlotte asked.

"They can have dogs, cats, ducks, or rabbits and chickens . . . it's the country," she answered.

"My head is spinning." Piper finally laughed. "They'll be so excited. I'm not telling them or Gene anything about it. He's already been told he has to bring them to the shop, so he won't know."

"I'm supposed to help teach Bible school next week so the first week, me and the boys will be real busy. Everett is already pouting because he says it's not fair that I get them more than he does right at first," Nancy said.

"It just gets better and better," Piper said.

"Okay, we've settled Piper's problem, Nancy. Now help me with mine. I'm getting married in a few months and I've got second thoughts about it." Charlotte spit the words out in a rush.

Nancy clutched her shirt at heart level. "Your mama . . ."

"I know," Charlotte exclaimed.

Letting go of her shirt, Nancy exhaled loudly. "I feel like my life has come around in a circle right now, Charlotte."

"Why?" Stella asked.

"It was about two months until my wedding day. We didn't have a lot of money but Mama had bought the prettiest white satin and did hand embroidery on the dress she made for me until her fingers were raw. She was scared to death that they would bleed and she'd get a drop of red on that dress. And there I was wondering if I should marry Everett Baxter. I felt so guilty and I imagine you do, too," Nancy said.

Charlotte's eyes misted up again as she nodded.

Stella reached for the paper towels. "Lord, help us all. This is sure a cryin' jag night."

"Are you prayin'?" Nancy teased.

"I might be at that." Stella smiled.

"What did you do, Nancy?" Charlotte asked.

"Well, I sure couldn't talk to my mama, not with that dress almost finished and the fabric for the bridesmaids' dresses all ready to cut out next. I couldn't talk to the Fannin sisters, who were barely past the honeymoon stage. And Claudia was in the same boat as Sugar, Tansy, and Gigi. We had a whole bunch of weddings those couple of years just like we're havin' right now in Cadillac. Trixie's mama was my special friend, but she'd run off to join a commune and, honey, we didn't have cell phones to call people like y'all do. So I went up to Claudia's mama's house," Nancy said.

"That would be Agnes's sister, right?" Stella asked.

"That's right. I remember knockin' on the door and then breaking down into sobs and she took me into a room. It was hot summertime but that room was so cool and so dark. She turned on one little lamp and sat down beside me on an old blue velvet sofa and asked me if my mama had passed."

Stella slung her feet around and planted them on the floor, propped her hands on her knees, and asked, "Why would she ask that?"

"She said that she'd never seen me cry before and thought it had to be a death to cause it. Well, I told her how I was feeling and I'm going to tell you the same thing and make you do it. It will seem crazy, but it will work," Nancy said.

"I will do anything," Charlotte said. "I need some peace."

"Stella, do you or Piper need to go to the bathroom for any- thing? It's going to be locked for the next half hour," Nancy said.

Piper raised her hand and raced down the hall.

Stella shook her head.

"When Piper gets out, Charlotte, you go in that bathroom and lock the door behind you. Sit on the floor with your back to the door and don't turn on a single light. Clear your mind and don't think about anything for at least a whole minute, and then I want you to imagine life without Boone," Nancy said.

Charlotte sucked in a lungful of air and started to speak, but Nancy put up a palm.

"Think about coming home without him in the house. You won't ever feel his arms around you again. Don't think about him dead, because that's a whole different feeling. If you didn't marry him, you'd still be sad if he died so that's not what you get to think about. Once he's out of your life—although it will just be in your imagination—I want you to think about all the things you will do without him," Nancy said.

Charlotte cocked her head to one side as if she was already thinking about it.

"Trips. Other boyfriends. Other men to sleep with . . . don't look at me like that, I know y'all live different than we did at your age. I'll knock on the door in half an hour and you can come out. Give me your cell phone," Nancy said.

"Why?"

"You have to stay in there thirty minutes and you can't talk to anyone but yourself. You can yell, rant, rave, or just sit there with your thoughts, but I'll guarantee you, just like Claudia's mama promised me almost thirty years ago, that you will have your mind made up when I knock on the door," she answered.

Charlotte handed over her cell phone. Piper stepped to one side when she started down the hall.

"What's that all about for thirty minutes?" Piper asked.

"She's gone to do some serious soul-searching," Nancy answered. "Now, what time are y'all going to start packing tomorrow night? I'll bring over a Crock-Pot of potato chowder and a loaf of fresh bread so you don't have to stop and eat. You don't have to move appliances. We left those in the trailer in case Stella ever wanted to live in it but she's bought the house in town."

Stella thought about life without Jed. Seeing him around town with another woman. Her feelings with another man after having slept with the love of her life. Her heart was as empty as the drawer had been before he put his things in it. Suddenly, she wanted to tell the world that they were married. That she was a preacher's wife and she trusted Jed to never break her heart—but would she ever have second thoughts?

She shut her eyes and tears welled up at the horrible feeling of never seeing him again, or worse yet, seeing him with another woman. Thinking of his hands roaming on someone else's body the way they had touched Stella's was agony. Thinking of life without him tore her heart into a million pieces.

God, she prayed earnestly, *please don't ever let me experience this pain for real. It's excruciating in thoughts. I can't imagine it in reality.*

Suddenly a visual of him lying beside her, sleeping with those thick lashes fanned out on his cheekbones, appeared like an answer to the prayer. Then he woke slowly and a brilliant smile covered his face as he looked up at her, like he'd done dozens of times. All the ideas of second thoughts were gone when she felt someone poke her on the shoulder.

"Stella!" Piper raised her voice.

"What?" Stella didn't want to leave that picture of Jed behind but she had to open her eyes.

"I asked you what time your last appointment is tomorrow so we'll know when we can start packing." Piper reclaimed the recliner but she didn't prop her feet up.

"Five o'clock." Her voice sounded hollow.

Nancy nodded. "Then I'll have supper at your house right after that and you can eat when you want as we all four get some work done. I'll get Everett to break down a bunch of boxes and put them by your back door. I'll bring the tape and the Magic Marker."

Ten minutes later they heard mumbling coming from the bathroom. Five more and the weeping started.

Nancy checked her watch. "She's tough."

"It's only been fifteen minutes," Stella said.

"I lasted fourteen and Claudia's mama said that I was the toughest she'd ever seen. That she'd about decided I was going to call off the wedding and give that pretty dress to my sister when she got married," Nancy said.

"Then you aren't going to make her stay in there thirty minutes?" Piper asked.

"If she does, y'all better be ready to go tell her mama there won't be a wedding after all," Nancy answered.

Stella couldn't take her eyes off the clock. Dammit! She didn't want to deliver that kind of news. It might be the only time in history, but she had no doubt she'd never leave the Miller property alive after all the money that had been spent and the work that had already been done.

Twenty-eight minutes after she went into the bathroom, Charlotte came down the hall. "I'm going home to Boone right now. I won't be staying here another night, Stella. And, Nancy, thank you." She held out her hand for her phone, wiped her wet cheeks, and marched out the door.

Stella wiped the sweat from her forehead. "That was a close call."

"She's tougher than she looks. That don't mean she won't argue with him, bitch at him, or make him sleep on the sofa some of the time. It does mean that she's in this for the duration and nobody better mess with her marriage because she's sure about what she wants now." Nancy sighed.

"Why the sigh?" Stella asked.

"Doesn't that make you happy?" Charlotte asked.

"Yes, it does. I care about all three of you girls and I want you all to be happy. I was just thinking, though, that I thought Claudia's mama was ancient when she gave me that advice. Now that I look back she was about my age."

"And you're thinkin' you are old?" Stella slung an arm around her mother's shoulders.

"Hell, no, I was thinking that Claudia's mama was pretty young to be that smart." Nancy laughed.

Chapter Twenty-One

Stella woke at midnight and reached for Jed. She opened her eyes and realized he was gone, picked up his pillow, and threw it against the wall. She was wide-awake, her stomach growled with hunger, and she had to go to the bathroom.

Slinging her legs over the edge of the bed, she heard a noise at the window and her heart did one of those crazy dances like always when he arrived. She quickly turned, but it was just a tree limb scratching the window.

With a moan, she headed toward the door and to the bathroom. She didn't turn on the light when she washed her hands because she didn't want to see herself in the mirror above the sink. She made her way from there to the kitchen as quietly as possible and opened the refrigerator.

"You couldn't sleep, either?" Piper said from the table.

Stella squealed, slammed the refrigerator door, and jumped six inches straight up off the floor. "You scared the shit out of me. What you doing sitting in the dark?"

"Trying to figure out a way to apologize to you and disappoint your mama," Piper answered.

Stella turned on the light above the table, pulled out a chair, and sank down into it. "My heart is still racing. You scared me so bad that I saw the pearly gates in the distance. Thank God, I'd already been to the bathroom."

"I probably would have seen the biggest bonfire Lucifer could get going instead of hearing angels singing and playing harps if you dropped dead," Piper said.

"Enough of the lame jokes. What are you doing sitting in the dark and why are you saying that about disappointing Mama?"

Piper shrugged. "I didn't think to ask you when Nancy made that offer. They're your parents, not mine. And I'd be overstepping my boundaries to move out there. I can't do that to our friendship. I love you too much, Stella."

Stella pushed her red hair out of her face. "What in the hell are you talking about?"

"I keep saying this but it's the truth. You and Charlotte have helped me get through the tough times. Remember that old saying about how a good friend will double your joy and half your sorrows? That's what y'all do. And you'll wind up resenting me if I move that close to your folks. Your dad will get even closer to the boys than he is now and when you have children . . ." She let the sentence trail off.

Stella reached across the table and laid a hand on Piper's. "I get so mad at my mama that I could strangle her, but believe me when I tell you she's got a big heart and there's plenty of room in it for all of us." She paused to get the next words right. "And FYI, honey, it was my idea in the first place. I suggested that she offer you that trailer house and that she bring up the idea of renting your place to a teacher. Rosalee asked me last week if I knew of any rental property available. Her friend's great-niece, or was it her neighbor's son's dog walker's cousin's boyfriend's cousin by marriage—you know

how it goes in Cadillac—is one of those new teachers that Mama
mentioned."

Piper giggled. "You can always make me laugh with that line."

"It's not a line. It's the gospel truth according to Rosalee and is
probably one of the lost books they talk about sometimes in church.
If truth was known there's a cousin's camel walker who married a
niece's maid somewhere in there, but it got lost in the uncle's tent as
they crossed the Red Sea."

"Hush or I'll laugh so hard I'll start snorting," Piper said and
then got serious. "Are you absolutely sure? I can turn this around
in the morning and find another place. Hell, we could convert the
top floor of the building we rented for the shop into an apartment.
Darla Jean lives in the back of her church a few doors down. The
boys and I could turn the back of the building into livable space."

Stella shook her head hard enough that her hair was soon back
in her eyes. "I won't have Luke and Tanner living above a beauty
shop and playing on the sidewalk. Kids need fresh air and sunshine.
So yes, ma'am, I'm sure."

ↄ

Rosalee followed Stella into the shop, set a paper bag of tomatoes on
the coffee table in front of the sofa, and eased down into the corner.
"Y'all have to share them but I guess the whole bunch of you are
livin' together most of the time anyway. When do Piper's boys come
home?"

Stella smiled. "You are sitting in Agnes's favorite spot."

Rosalee waved a hand in a gesture that said Agnes wouldn't care.
"Arthritis is acting up or I'd help y'all pack tonight. Don't look so surprised. Nancy and I had breakfast together at Clawdy's this morning
and she had to tell someone or she'd blow up. And I can keep a secret
for at least two days. I did tell Agnes, but that don't count."

"I want to surprise the boys," Piper said.

Rosalee put a finger over her lips and closed her eyes. With the heavy silence, the shop was as eerie as the music in a horror film. Finally her eyes popped open and her mouth turned up in a wide grin. "Agnes left the story about you moving out up to me and I just figured it all out."

"What?" Stella asked.

Rosalee just smiled. "If you want a diversion to work, even in gossip, it's got to have just enough truth in it to shock the shit out of everyone. Y'all just go right on about your business and don't try to be all secretive about a damn thing. I'll take care of the rest," Rosalee said. "I'll call Agnes after a while and we'll hash it out to see if I'm on the right track. I've had more fun this summer than I've had in years."

"You can tell us so we'll be ready for whatever you two old gals cook up," Charlotte said.

"Y'all just get on about your jobs tonight and trust me to do mine. Now, let's talk about the barbecue ball. I've rented a limo to take us and Agnes and Nancy and whoever from Bless My Bloomers and Clawdy's wants to go with us," Rosalee said in the same tone that she'd told them they had to share the tomatoes.

"Holy shit!" Stella said.

Rosalee rubbed her hands together. "It's the finest limo you've ever seen. It's camouflage and it's one of them Hummer things. I wanted a pickup truck, but it was already taken for a wedding over in Tom Bean. We'll meet at Darla Jean's church and go from there. Give y'all plenty of room to park your cars and trucks that way."

"Is Darla Jean going?" Piper asked.

Rosalee tucked her chin down to the top of her overalls and looked up over the top of her bifocals. "Sure she is. I told her if she didn't, I'd quit going to church and that God sure enough wouldn't let a former hooker in heaven if she couldn't keep her congregation in attendance."

"Well, thank you. I will be honored to ride in a camo limo." Stella laughed. "But why go to the expense? Heather will be inside and won't see it."

Rosalee smiled. "Done got that covered. The newspaper in Sherman is sending down a reporter to cover the ball and she will be there in time to photograph the limo. Hell, I wouldn't pay out them big bucks if it didn't bring me some happiness. And I bet with all the hoopla we can get Heather outside long enough to see the limo."

"Does Heather know about this reporter?"

Rosalee adjusted her glasses. "Oh, yes, and the television station. We want her to spend lots and lots of money, and she'll do it if she thinks she's got something flashy happenin'. Marriage ministry, my ass. That girl thinks she can make God into one of them Internet dating services."

Stella sat down beside Rosalee. "What else have you two got up your sleeves?"

"Lots of wonderful surprises. Piper, you will be dancing with Rhett, so wear high heels if you've got a mind to," Rosalee yelled across the room.

"How can you promise that? I might get paired up with one of those McKay brothers and they barely come up to my shoulder. If I wear high heels, their noses will get buried up in my boobs when we dance," Piper said.

"Trust me and FYI—or is it SYI? I can't ever remember them alphabet soup things you kids say these days. Oh, Lorene says that Gene bought a ticket to attend the ball," Rosalee said. "Just thought you should know."

Piper groaned. "What if Heather draws his name and then mine?"

"I told you to trust me. You will be dancing with Rhett. As for the rest of it, there ain't no tellin' what might happen at the barbecue ball." Rosalee patted Stella on the knee.

"Can you tell me who I'm dancing with?" Stella asked.

"I could, but I ain't. If you don't stand up and testify about that man that's sneaking in your bedroom window at night and out again in the morning, then your dance partner will be a big surprise," Rosalee told her.

Stella's cheeks immediately flooded with crimson. "How did you know about that?"

"Grasshopper, you have a lot to learn before Agnes dies and leaves Cadillac to you." She giggled. "I'm off to Ruby's to see what kind of trouble I can stir up. Agnes has given me the job of pestering Violet."

"But she's in rehab," Piper said.

"They're bringing her to Ruby's in a special van to get her roots done this morning," Rosalee said.

Silence once again fell on the shop after the door closed behind Rosalee.

Charlotte stared at Stella.

Piper couldn't even blink.

"Is it true that your boyfriend is sneaking in the window at night? We were teasing about the music. We thought you were using it to cover up Charlotte's snores," Piper said.

Charlotte air slapped her on the shoulder. "Mine aren't as loud as yours."

"Back to the window and the man sneaking in and out," Piper said.

"Yes, he does," Stella said, "and the music isn't to cover up your snores. And no, I'm not telling who he is until after the barbecue ball. And now he won't be coming in the window because one of you would be hiding to see who he is. And if I get bitchy, you can blame yourselves. So there," Stella said.

"Why wait until after the ball?" Charlotte asked.

"Because that's my mother's punishment for putting my name on that damned prayer list and starting all this and because . . . it's a secret," Stella answered.

"But you and Nancy made up at the fireworks show," Charlotte said.

"We did, but that doesn't mean she doesn't get punished."

"Stella Joy Baxter, your mama loves you," Charlotte said.

"Don't triple name me. I know she loves me and I love her, but the man I've been seeing and I have decided to wait to come out of the closet. You will be one of the first to know, I promise," Stella said.

Chapter Twenty-Two

The curb in front of Piper's place looked like Piper was either having a garage sale or else she'd turned her place into a used-truck lot. Nancy and Everett had come in separate trucks with Jed parking right behind Everett. Boone brought his truck and cattle trailer and Rhett showed up in a truck with a flatbed trailer hitched to the back. Rosalee and Agnes had better have their stories down real good, because when the first piece of furniture went out the door, the stories would start flying around Cadillac.

"I brought the preacher with me," Everett said. "He ain't got church tonight and he volunteered."

"Thank you," Piper yelled from the kitchen. "I'll take all the help I can get."

Everett touched his wife on the shoulder. "Okay, Nancy, you're the organizer. What do we do first?"

"The living room. Take all the furniture out and put it in Boone's trailer and truck. Those"—she pointed to the boxes lined up on the wall—"are to go in the same truck and trailer. We'll unload that one last when we get there. When that's all done, I'll tell you what to do next and y'all can grab a bowl of soup while you rest."

Stella poked Piper on the arm. "See, I told you. Controlling."

"You say ta-mah-toe while I say to-may-toe. You say controlling. I say organizing," Piper said.

Charlotte removed the lid from the enormous Crock-Pot and took a whiff of the vegetable beef soup. "I say I'm hungry and we should eat. That way us four ladies will be done and the guys can have the kitchen table to sit at before they load it up."

Nancy nodded. "Sounds like a plan to me. Cut that pan of cornbread, Stella. Piper, you can put ice in glasses and pour sweet tea. Charlotte, you get the disposable bowls out of the sack I brought. There's also plastic spoons and a soup ladle and napkins in there."

"Want me to cut the brownies, too, boss lady?" Stella asked.

Nancy cut her eyes around at Stella. "I'm leaving my organizational skills to Charlotte instead of you."

"That's a good thing, Mama. I'm going to be busy filling Agnes's shoes," Stella shot back.

"You do remind me of her, but those are some big boots for you to fill."

"Agnes wears flip-flops, not boots," Charlotte said. "And to my thinking, I'll have some big ones to fill, too, if you leave me your skills. There's no way we could have packed everything in one evening without you."

Piper nodded. "And I thank you all. I can't believe we are getting it done so fast."

Nancy patted her on the shoulder. "Now let's get to work. When the guys get it all loaded, Piper will drive her van and go with them. That way she can tell them where to put things. You two"—she pointed at Stella and Charlotte—"will stay behind with me and we're going to wipe down countertops, vacuum, and be sure everything is completely ready for the new renters. That way Piper doesn't have to come back here for anything. They can bring her rent money down to the shop."

Piper hugged Nancy. "Thank you."

Nancy yelled into the living room, "Jed, come in here and bless this food before we eat it and then there will be room at the table for you guys."

Jed set down the box that he'd just picked up, dusted his hands on the seat of his jeans, and headed toward the kitchen. He bowed his head, said a quick grace, and inhaled deeply. "Just smelling that good soup will make us work faster. We do get to eat right after we get the living room loaded, don't we?"

"Yes, you do," Stella said. "We'll be finished by then and you can have our chairs."

"Come on, Jed. You've had time to say four graces by now," Everett yelled. "I need help with this sofa. Holy shit, Piper! Is this damn thing made out of concrete?"

Piper swallowed and yelled back, "I bought a sturdy one. I've got two boys, remember? You sure you want me to move to the country?"

"Jed, call in the other two. It'll take all four of us to get this damn thing in the trailer," Everett said.

"Guess Preacher Jed is getting an earful of cusswords," Stella whispered in her mother's direction.

Nancy sighed. "I imagine he prays for your daddy's soul every night. I heard today that your boyfriend has been slipping in the bedroom window at night. That's a little bit juvenile, don't you think, Stella? He could come right in the front door."

"Mama!" Stella's eyes popped wide-open.

Nancy smiled. "Don't look at me like that. Rosalee told me and when I asked her how she knew, she said that was an FBU secret. I get a big kick out of the way that she and Agnes get things turned around. I'm sure she was talking about the FBI, but I didn't say a word."

"I'm not sayin' a word. She's coverin' for me tonight about why I'm moving," Piper said. "But I did hear down at the convenience store this afternoon that Stella's boyfriend is an ex-con and she don't want her mama to know she's fallen in love with a man who has tattoos and a record."

"Oh, my God!" Nancy's voice carried all over the kitchen.

"He doesn't have a record," Stella protested.

"Tattoos?" Nancy raised an eyebrow.

Stella shrugged. "You didn't tell them to put that on the billboard at the church. You just said a husband. You should've been more specific if you don't like tats. And, Mama, now that the whole town knows he's visiting me, I guess I gave him his own drawer in my dresser for nothing." She hadn't meant to say that last sentence, but there it was hanging over the table like heavy smoke in a cheap honky-tonk.

"You have a boyfriend and you gave him a drawer in your bedroom. This is serious, Stella Joy." Nancy clapped her hands like a little girl. "I'm going to get a son-in-law and I don't give a shit if he's got a dozen tattoos as long as he treats you like a queen."

Piper's spoon was halfway to her mouth with soup dripping back into the bowl. "Yes, it is, and you didn't tell us until tonight?"

"I didn't mean to tell you tonight. It just slipped out. Not that it matters now," she said.

"I'll be gone after Saturday night. He can come on in the front door after that for sure," Piper said.

"With the whole town watching every door and window in my house? Hell, I wish I had moved out to Granny's trailer. At least there were no neighbors for miles."

"Announce who he is and the gossip will die down," Nancy said.

Piper scooped up more soup. "This is delicious, Nancy. What's your secret?"

"Half a cup to a cup of homemade picante sauce in it after it's cooked. Who is it, Stella Joy?"

Stella wanted to tell her mother but she flat-out couldn't that night. Not while they were moving Piper and not until she talked to Jed. They should be together when they announced to the world that they'd been married before that sign went up at the church. "I will tell you the night of the barbecue ball, I promise."

Nancy's eyes twinkled and she wiggled her shoulders. "The Angels did a good job after all."

"Don't give them an ounce of credit for anything but creating a big mess over all this. I"—she stopped midsentence before she said "married him" and quickly finished—"was seeing him long before you put my name on that damned old list."

"And you didn't bring him home to meet me and your dad. Shame on you!" Nancy fussed. "All this could have been avoided if you'd just told me."

"Oh, but Cadillac needed something new to fuss about, so it's not all in vain," Piper said.

"Sometimes it takes magic to make things clear." Charlotte smiled. "Who would have thought a half an hour in a dark bathroom could turn my life around?"

⁊

Rhett was the first of the guys to make it to the kitchen. He washed his hands in the sink and dried them on a paper towel. "Soup looks good. Did you make it, Piper?"

"Nancy did," she said.

Their eyes met and the heat in the room went up twenty degrees. Not even when they were young and their hormones raged had she felt like that with Gene. He smiled and she did the same.

"You still going to the dance out at Violet's barn?" he asked.

She nodded. "She's calling it a ball and it's a cultural affair."

Rhett chuckled. Lord, he even chuckled with a deep drawl. "She can call it those things if she wants, but it's a barn dance. Want me to pick you up for it? Since it's formal, shall I bring a corsage?"

"Agnes and Rosalee have rented a limo for us ladies."

"A chariot will bring you, then. I'll be there to help escort you inside," he said.

"It's a far cry from a chariot, Rhett. It's a Hummer that's painted camouflage."

Rhett laughed out loud. "That ought to cause a stir. What color is your dress?"

"Dark green, but it's not camo."

He blinked a few times but his eyes never left hers. "I'll have your corsage delivered to the shop."

She looked down at the floor. "What if my name isn't drawn with yours?"

"I'll cut in on every dance and manage to sit beside you at dinner anyway. I'm sneaky that way," he whispered.

"Hey, don't eat all the soup," Jed said. "We worked as hard as you did."

According to the clock, the conversation had lasted less than two minutes. If that short time brought on the jitters, she wondered if her heart could take a whole evening with Rhett.

"Hey, Piper," Stella called from the back of the house. "Come help us. We forgot to pack up the bathroom last night."

"See you later," Rhett said.

She nodded and floated down the hall toward the bathroom.

"I flirted with Rhett and it didn't feel awkward," she whispered.

"It shouldn't. Boone says that he really likes you," Charlotte said.

Stella whipped the shower curtain back. "Mama, your prayers bypassed me and hit Piper."

Nancy was carefully setting everything from the medicine cabinet in a small box. "Well, I'm glad someone is benefiting. I may not ever forgive you for having a boyfriend who gets a drawer in your bedroom and you don't tell me about him. But at least someone is benefiting from the shit storm I unleashed when I asked for prayers. Maybe God thinks y'all are all my daughters. And Stella, darlin', I guess you know that I intend to look through that drawer when you are at work tomorrow."

"You go into my bedroom and I won't tell you his name until Christmas," Stella threatened.

"I'm going to the kitchen to help those guys with their supper before y'all get out the guns and knives," Charlotte said.

"Hey, we don't have guns and knives," Nancy said.

"But we've got fingernail files and hair conditioner, and believe me, those can be deadly. This is Piper's night so let's talk about her, not me," Stella smarted off.

Charlotte tightened her ponytail and headed for the kitchen. She stopped at the table long enough to drop a kiss on Boone's forehead before she picked up the tea jug and refilled their glasses. "Y'all ready for brownies?"

"Got any coffee?" Everett asked.

"Yes, darlin', I brought a thermos. I knew you couldn't eat brownies without coffee," Nancy shouted from the bathroom. "When y'all get done eating, start on the boys' bedroom."

Charlotte set the pan of brownies in the middle of the table. "They're cut and ready. I'd best go help carry the kids' clothes out to the back of Piper's van so all she has to do is take them out and hang them up."

As she was leaving, she heard Boone say, "I'm the luckiest man in the whole world."

Everett said, "You just keep thinkin' that, son, and you'll have one of them marriages that lasts past the time the wedding bells stop ringin'."

Charlotte stopped in the hallway and eavesdropped.

"So what's your secret?" Jed asked.

"There's two secrets, son. One is to love your woman, not with your whole heart but with your soul. If you got an inklin' that you aren't finished chasin' skirts, then you ain't ready to settle down anyway. The other is to respect your woman." Everett poured coffee from the thermos into his cup. "That's different from loving her. That means you don't belittle her, not in front of other people or in private. Your job is to not only make her feel like she's gorgeous but to know in your heart that she really is and to drop down on your knees every once in a while and thank God that he put her in your life. You do those things and you'll be just fine. If you don't, somebody else will and you'll lose the best thing that ever happened to you."

"Good advice," Jed said.

"Yes, it is. Now dig into those brownies and I'll pour y'all up a cup of coffee and then we'll go load up the boys' room."

Charlotte hurried on to the bedroom and grabbed an armload of little boys' clothing. As she was going out the door, Rosalee parked her old car across the street and made her way to the porch.

"I thought you were going to see Agnes," she said.

"I did but thought y'all might need some supervisin'."

"Nancy is doin' a fine job of that," Charlotte said.

"I'm older than she is and I got more experience." She smiled. "Besides, she said she was bringing soup, and I want a bowl."

"And brownies," Charlotte whispered.

"Honey, I can do a hell of a lot of supervisin' for some of Nancy's brownies. Besides, I'm here to check out the—what is it y'all call them things? Now I remember—the vibes between Rhett and Piper. Agnes said I'm to report to her tonight after y'all finish up here no matter how late it is." She lowered her voice to a whisper. "Agnes says I'm supposed to spy on Stella, too, and to call her if I smell a rat."

"You got the story going about why Piper's moving?"

"My friend is on the phone right now. I only have to tell my next-door neighbor a little bit of something and she's like that television show where they said, 'Take it away.' By morning the stories will be wild and woolly, believe me. Now step aside before them men eat up all the brownies," Rosalee said.

"You and Agnes sure do have a chocolate sweet tooth," Charlotte said.

"Comes from growing up poor. We can just smell chocolate and our noses follow the scent. Anything going on between Piper and Rhett? I've got to report to Agnes and I need something."

Charlotte smiled. "I thought you and Agnes were both like God and knew everything."

"No, that's Heather, not us. And the big man is going to strike her graveyard dead with a lightning bolt one of these days for thinkin' like that. Marriage ministry! If that ain't the biggest crock of shit I've ever heard." Rosalee headed toward the kitchen, mumbling the whole way.

That Rosalee was a hoot—not as big or as flamboyant in her ways as Agnes but still a woman to be reckoned with. Maybe Charlotte could grow up to be just like Rosalee. Then she and Stella could grow old together and keep Cadillac from falling apart.

Chapter Twenty-Three

Heather had never shown her face in the Yellow Rose but that was the only explanation that crossed Stella's mind when the buzz in the shop stopped so fast. Stella carefully peeked out from around the partition in front of the shampoo sink to see what was going on.

"Well, hello, Irene," Stella called out, relieved that it was Charlotte's mama and not Heather coming to stir up trouble. She had enough on her plate as it was, what with still not being able to find a way to sneak off to Sherman and buy a test. Not that she really needed the thing, because she hadn't been sick again and she had been under a lot of stress. Still it would be great to see that thing say *not pregnant* for sure.

Charlotte's mother raised her free hand. In the other one she carried a plastic bag with what looked like a bull-necked football player's head inside. It didn't look heavy enough to transport something that big, but then, Irene was a big strong woman. Tall, raw-boned, with short brown hair, she looked like she wouldn't take a bit of sass from anyone: male, female, or rowdy steers.

"How are you girls? I heard that you moved last night, Piper. I brought the bridal bouquet. I worked on it all night and I want your opinion, ladies."

Agnes was sitting in Charlotte's chair getting her roots touched up. Piper was busy trimming Alma Grace's hair and Stella had just finished shampooing Trixie's hair. They all six stopped and watched the bouquet come up out of the plastic by degrees.

"I never had a wedding," Irene said. "When I married Charlotte's daddy, we just went to the courthouse and came home to a tiny little garage apartment down south of town. I wanted a bouquet or a corsage, but we barely had the money for the marriage license after we paid a month's rent. What do you think?"

"It's beautiful!" Alma Grace squealed. "That is spectacular."

"I thought about making it out of real flowers, but if she has silk, then she can keep it forever." Irene beamed.

"That's a hell of a lot of work," Agnes said.

Stella couldn't take her eyes off the arrangement of pink hydrangeas, three lovely silk roses, baby's breath, ferns, lace, and satin. It was a work of art but she was still glad that she and Jed had decided to go the courthouse when they got married.

"Oh, Mama, it's beautiful," Charlotte gasped.

"Really? You aren't just saying that?"

Charlotte left Agnes in the chair and hugged her mother. "No, Mama, I mean it. It's the prettiest bouquet I've ever seen. You did an awesome job on it." She reached out to gingerly touch a bit of lace. "I love the little touches of lace and satin you've tucked into it. And is that Grandma's cameo on the stem?"

Irene's smile lit up the whole shop. "Yes, it is. Here, you hold it. See how it feels in your hands. Pretend you are walking down the aisle with it. Is it too heavy?"

Charlotte took the bouquet from her mother and carried it all the way back to the door, then she turned around and nodded at Stella. "Music, please."

Stella began to hum the "Wedding March" and Charlotte held the bouquet at waist level and slowly strolled across the tile floor to her station. "It's not too heavy, Mama. Real flowers would have weighed a lot more. Now can I keep this one or do we have to make a dozen more?"

"Oh, hush." Irene wiped her eyes. "You looked like an angel carrying that, but when you are coming in the church, walk a little bit slower. Boone needs time to catch his breath. If you go too fast, he'll still be stuttering when you reach the front."

Charlotte handed the bouquet back to her mother. "Yes, ma'am. Now, why don't you sit down and wait until I get done with Agnes and then I'll pamper you a little bit today. How about a haircut, shampoo, and set?"

"With real rollers and the hair dryer?" Irene carefully tucked the bouquet back into the plastic bag. "Put this in the back room. We don't want anyone else to see it."

"Miz Irene, I thought I wanted real flowers for my bouquet, but after seeing what you've done, I've changed my mind. Would you make me one of those?" Alma Grace asked. "And smaller versions for my bridesmaids? Maybe you could go with me to buy the flowers and give me some ideas?"

"What would Sugar think?" Irene asked.

"You've got to show her that bouquet. She's going to love it. And when my wedding is over, I'm going to have a shadowbox made for mine so I can hang it on the wall above the credenza in the foyer. Pink and silver are my colors. I want lots of bling, so be thinking along those lines. Will you do it for me?" Alma Grace begged.

"I would love to," Irene said.

"You want a cup of coffee?" Piper asked. "It's brewing in the back room and there's what's left of a pan of brownies back there."

"I'd love both," Irene said.

Charlotte leaned down and whispered into Alma Grace's ear, "That was so sweet."

"Sweet nothing!" Alma Grace exclaimed. "We've searched and searched for silver flowers and pink only comes in roses and gladiolus. I want something unique that no one else has ever had or will ever have. Your mama is a genius."

Piper poked Charlotte on the arm. "Did you know that about your mama's wedding?"

Charlotte shook her head. "But from now on this one is hers to do with what she wants. I want to be married. The wedding isn't as important as the marriage. Nancy taught me that."

Irene carried a brownie on a napkin in one hand and a cup of coffee in the other. She sat down at the table at the same time Stella wrapped a towel around Trixie's head and the two of them went back to Stella's station.

"Well, Trixie, I didn't know that was you over there," Irene said. "How is your mama? I always loved Janie. She always had a lovely smile for everyone, no matter who they were."

"She has good days and bad days. Seems that lately the good ones are few and far between," Trixie said.

"I need to go see her. We grew up right next door to each other. Played paper dolls in my front yard lots and lots of days. Do you think she'll know me?" Irene asked.

"Seems like she knows folks from that time more than those she knew in her twenties or thirties," Trixie said.

"There was less stress in those days," Irene said.

"But still just as much scandal and gossip," Trixie said.

"Some things never change, honey." Irene nodded. "But I always admired your mama for doing what she did. She might have thought that boy was her soul mate when she left town with him, but when she figured out he wasn't, she didn't just marry him because you were on the way. Town might always remember her for that, but me, I remember her pretty smile."

"Thank you." Trixie flashed a smile.

"Some folks like to relive the negative gossip. We'd all be better off if we had one of them delete buttons like on a computer on our memories. We could hit it when the gossip is malicious like it was with your mama, and like it was with Stella." She paused and looked around the room that had gone quiet. "Never could figure out why folks acted like they did with either one of them. And I'm right sorry to bring this up, Stella, but Charlotte says it's been worryin' you lately."

"Thank you." Stella hugged Irene. "You are so sweet."

"Just callin' it like it should be. Now let's talk about this barbecue ball. I swear I ain't never heard of anything so silly in my life."

"You gossipin', Mama?" Charlotte chuckled.

"No, I am not. I'm statin' my opinion. Gossip is unfounded bullshit. Opinions are ours by rights of the Constitution."

❧

Nancy parked close to the door into the fellowship hall and hurried across the hot parking lot inside the cool church. Heather was already standing behind the podium with her minions sitting around a long table. She shot a dirty look Nancy's way and tilted her head up.

"We had given up on you. This is our last meeting before the ball and we're just going over our duties one more time," she said.

Without the gold fingernail, she didn't look nearly as authoritative. She wore a navy-blue pantsuit with a red-and-white-patterned silk shell under the jacket, a sparkly red crystal cross pin on her lapel, and red high-heeled shoes.

Nancy sat down in the only empty chair. "So how are we doing with the expenditures and the sold tickets? Are we working in the black or the red?"

"Floy." Violet frowned.

Floy opened a hard-sided briefcase and brought out Heather's notebook. She handed it to her and Heather flipped open the cover. "As of today we are a thousand dollars in the red, but we will make that up with tickets sold at the door and with the donations for the best barbecue. We only have a few more things to purchase—the angel candlesticks for the winner, and of course we will have to pay the bills for some of the inside decorations. The air conditioners and the tablecloths are paid for."

Annabel raised her hand and said, "We will sell lots more tickets. Folks often wait until the last week to buy and I know several people who've bought dresses but haven't bought tickets. You were a genius, Heather, to come up with the idea of each girl who buys a ticket bringing her own special barbecue."

That was the last straw and she'd done her duty, so Nancy stood up and said, "I am resigning from the Angels. I will not be attending any more Thursday night meetings. I'm going to be too busy. I was going to wait until after the barbecue ball but since Everett and I are not responsible for the food, I'm resigning now. Good luck, Heather, with the rest of the preparations. I'll be bringing my own special recipe for pulled pork in a Crock-Pot and I'd appreciate any donations y'all want to put in my can."

"You can't resign." Heather raised her voice. "One does not simply resign from praying."

"I'll continue to pray, but not on Thursday nights with all y'all."

"I forbid it. I will not accept your resignation," Heather said in a louder voice.

Nancy started for the door. "I can damn well do whatever the hell I want."

Heather's voice raised another octave and got downright squeaky. "Don't you swear in the church. You aren't fit for the Angels."

Nancy smiled. "You got it, darlin'."

Beulah went to wringing her hands. "Please tell me you aren't going to change churches."

"Hell, no!" Nancy said. "I'm staying right here. It's where I've gone my whole life, but I'm finished with committees and clubs. I've got a life to live and I don't need any of this drama."

"Well said, Nancy," Rosalee said from just inside the door.

Heather turned her attention and fury in that direction. "What are you doing here? You don't go to church here anymore. You go down to that one on Main Street with Agnes."

"Making sure that you don't shoot Nancy or scratch her eyes out since Agnes is laid up and can't take care of the job," Rosalee said.

"The both of you can get out of here. That is an order," Heather said. "I heard you were down at Piper Stephens's place last night helping her move into the house with Rhett Monroe. Anyone that sanctions that kind of immorality shouldn't be allowed in our church."

Rosalee grinned so big that her eyes disappeared. "Hell, Heather, if we kicked out all the sinners, who'd pay the tithes to keep this place runnin'? It does require a lot of money to pay the electric bill, the water bill, and buy toilet paper. And I bet you dollars to cow shit that you and Quinn did some hanky-panky before you got married. We just didn't know it because it went on in Ripley instead of Cadillac."

Nancy picked up the cue. "I thought she was from Tulsa? Where in the hell is Ripley?"

"It's a suburb of Tulsa," Heather stammered.

"I see. Well, I'll be leaving. Y'all have a good day," Nancy said.

"Ripley is fifty miles from Tulsa. That's too damn far to be a suburb," Rosalee said. "It's a little bitty town that's only a third the size of Cadillac, so stop puttin' on airs."

Heather tossed her head back in a defiant gesture as she flipped on the overhead projector and showed everyone the table placement. "I'm not discussing where I was raised. Now, this is the way that the tables will be arranged. The buffet tables will be lined up at the back. I did it that way so the traffic could flow down both sides, so you might keep that in mind as you get set up. And right here will be a curtained-off place to use as a workstation. We don't want trash cans and such cluttering up our lovely ball."

"Sounds like you have everything under control, but you didn't answer my question about hanky-panky with Quinn," Rosalee said.

"You don't deny that Piper is living with Rhett?" Heather glared at Rosalee.

"I didn't say that and it's none of my business or yours," she answered.

"Well, I'm not dignifying your question with an answer. But I did hear that Piper has been seeing Rhett for years and there's a possibility that the twins don't belong to poor Gene, who is just heartbroken over the way he's been treated. You do know that he's a distant cousin of Quinn's and that we are familiar with the situation. I'm telling all of you right now that the marriage ministry will not include divorced or loose-legged women," Heather said.

Rosalee made a big show of heading toward the door. "Darlin', if your ministry is going to get its big butt off the ground in Texas, you'd best reconsider that statement. Divorce is part of the culture these days, especially since women have learned that they don't have to put up with rascals. Y'all have a wonderful day now, and I'll see you at the barbecue ball. It should be a lot of fun."

Rosalee giggled the whole way across the parking lot to her car.

Nancy was leaning against her truck. "Well? That was fun, wasn't it?"

"Oh, yeah. How much is she in the hole for? Agnes will want to know for sure," Rosalee asked.

"A thousand dollars to date. There ain't enough people interested in a damn ball to come for miles around like they do for the jubilee. So it'll mainly be the townspeople with a few from Luella and Sherman, but not enough to pay for what all she's doing. Someone is going to have to bail her out. I expect that it'll be Violet," Nancy said.

"Agnes is going to love that news." Rosalee got into her truck and drove away.

Chapter Twenty-Four

Piper crawled out of bed early and sang off-key at the top of her lungs while she took a shower. She could be staying at her new home, but she wanted to share the first night there with the boys, which was tonight, so she was happy that morning.

Stella was scowling on the sofa when Charlotte came out of the guest room and Piper opened the bathroom door.

"What are you doing up this early? You don't have to go to the shop until midmorning," Charlotte said.

"You are both mean old bitches," Stella said. "How can a woman sleep through all the noise y'all make? And what are you doing here, Charlotte? I thought you weren't spending another night away from Boone."

"He's on a twenty-four-hour shift and the house got too quiet for me to bear, so I let myself in after y'all had gone to bed," Charlotte answered.

Piper bent at the waist and towel dried the underside of her hair. "I haven't heard music in your room the past couple of nights."

"I'm not having this conversation." Stella covered her head with a throw pillow. "I'm going to go for doughnuts and fried pies at that new shop in Luella. I shouldn't be nice to either of you since you woke me up so early, but I'll bring breakfast to the shop."

"Why don't you run on up to the rehab center and check on Agnes before you come in? We can wait on breakfast that long and you can take her a couple of fried chocolate pies. I bet she's going into withdrawals if they haven't served chocolate in a couple of days," Piper suggested.

∽

Agnes was in therapy, so Stella left a chocolate pie on her bedside table and drove back to Cadillac. As she passed the church with that horrible sign still shining for the whole world to see, she noticed that Jed's truck was parked around back, so she whipped in beside it. She slipped in the back door and heard him whistling in his office. Peeking in the glass she could see him, leaning back in the chair, eyes closed, hands locked behind his neck.

She eased the door open and quietly crossed the room. She was in the process of throwing one leg over his lap when he sat up suddenly and grabbed her butt firmly in both hands.

"Caught you." He chuckled.

"Do you always greet the women of the congregation this way?" she asked.

"Only the ones I'm married to, and just for the record, I don't believe in polygamy." He kissed her hard on the lips, the kiss lingering for several moments before he broke it. "And darlin', I heard you drive up and you played right into my hand, quite literally."

"I love you and I'm ready to tell the whole world that we are married today," she said.

"I'm glad, but we're going to wait now until the barbecue ball. The ball will be a perfect place to announce our wedding to the

THE YELLOW ROSE BEAUTY SHOP

whole county at one time." He strung kisses from her nose to her lips, to that soft tender spot at the hollow of her neck.

"But I'm ready to announce it now and move into the parsonage with you," she said.

"Me, too, darlin', but I really like the idea of announcing it at the ball. You deserve more than word-of-mouth gossiping that can get things all twisted up. You deserve a big moment." He teased her mouth open with his tongue.

"I love you, Jed Tucker." Her heart swelled with pure love for the man she'd married a few months before.

"That doesn't mean we can't go to the parsonage and play house for a little while right now," he whispered.

"And ruin the surprise if someone caught us? No, thank you." She got up and locked his office door, pulled the blinds, and sat back down in his lap. "I've got thirty minutes. What's on your appointment book?"

"Nothing until noon, and that sofa is inviting us to move over there."

☙

"I hear your kids are coming home this evening and that you've moved in with Rhett Monroe," Trixie said. "Good for you, Piper. I'm glad to see you moving on with your life. Gene was never the man for you. We all knew he was a mama's boy."

"Why didn't you tell me that before I married him?" Piper asked.

"Would it have done any good?" Rosalee asked from the sofa. "Y'all may have to start charging me rent on this couch as much as I stay here anymore."

"You are welcome to run in and out and stay as long as you like," Charlotte said.

271

Piper used a curling iron on Trixie's light-brown hair. "I did not move in with Rhett. We aren't dating."

"Then where did you move?" Trixie asked.

"It's a secret until this evening. I don't want Lorene to find out and tell the boys. I want to surprise them, but getting out of that house with all the memories was a big step in moving forward with my life," she said. "There. All done."

"Good for you," Trixie said. "On a different note, I should forewarn you, Alma Grace has been in the café bragging about Irene working up a custom-made bouquet. Charlotte, your mama is liable to have her hands full, because there's a lot of wedding fever going around. And there could be more after the barbecue ball."

Charlotte picked up the broom and started sweeping hair from around the chairs. "It really did make her feel good for Alma Grace to ask her to make her bouquet. Maybe it'll work into a second job for her."

"Time for me to go. Me and Agnes and Violet, oh, and Beulah, are about the only ones left from our graduating class here in Cadillac. Y'all won't know Bobby Dalhart, but he died, and they're having his funeral today in Sherman. I haven't seen him in forty years, but I feel like someone from our class should pay our respects at his funeral." Rosalee stood up slowly. "When I die, I want you to come to the funeral home and fix my hair just like this, Charlotte. You do such a wonderful job." Rosalee threw the shoulder strap for her purse over her head and nodded toward Piper. "Your secret is safe with me. But, honey, I'm a little disappointed. If I'd lived in today's world as a young woman, I would have moved in with that handsome Rhett in a heartbeat."

All of them, including Trixie, were stunned into speechless silence as Rosalee made her way out of the shop.

"Holy shit! I can't believe all that's gone on since Nancy put Stella's name on that list. I thought Rosalee was one of the last survivors of the old school and would crucify one of us for moving in with a boyfriend," Piper said.

"I don't care how much I like someone, I'm not doing a dead person's hair." Charlotte shivered from head to red toenails.

"One of you will have to do mine when I go," Stella said. "I wouldn't trust another soul to do it, and if you don't do it right, I'll come back and haunt the hell out of you."

"Where did you come from? And you aren't dying, so don't talk like that. It gives me the shivers," Piper said.

"Down the back alley and through the storeroom. I'm practicing my Agnes skills." Stella laughed.

"You could easily share DNA with Agnes," Piper said.

Stella cocked her head to one side. "Does that mean I'm the Cadillac Irish mob? If so, then all y'all and Bless My Bloomers and Clawdy's all are my mob family like in *The Godfather*. And Darla Jean, I can't forget Darla Jean. We might be the Cadillac eleven, kind of like that George Clooney film."

Charlotte pulled a tissue from a fancy little box at her station and dabbed her eyes. "You are a female godfather for sure. Don't you think so, Trixie?"

"That sumbitch wasn't Irish," Trixie said.

"Well, if he had been, then Stella would be his kinfolk," Piper said.

"Hey, Luke and Tanner are coming home this evening. I just remembered," Stella said.

"Well, duh! We've been talking about it for two whole days and I've moved into a new place and tonight I'm leaving your house. You'd think you would have . . . okay, where have you been and who have you been doing it with? You've got that glow that says you had sex and you've forgotten everything we talked about for two days," Piper said.

"And I smell Stetson again," Charlotte said.

"And I don't deny or affirm one thing, so there," Stella said. "Trixie, has Piper been watching the clock like the end of the world was coming?"

Trixie leaned forward so that Piper could get to the last bit of hair with the curling iron. "Yes, she has. And the news in the café this morning is that Gene's new woman broke it off with him, changed churches, and told him to never call her again. And this is for your ears only." She lowered her voice.

"Oh?" Stella leaned closer.

"What's said in the Yellow Rose stays in the beauty shop, right?" Trixie asked.

"Only a psychiatrist's office is more sacred than this place," Piper said.

Trixie went on, "He thinks he's getting a promotion at the company picnic and he's goin' to win a trip to Hawaii. But neither one is happenin'. He's still got a job but he ain't gettin' no fancy office with his name on the door. He's still just a cubicle person at that company where he works and his hours are being cut so he won't be working full-time," she said.

"How do you know that?" Piper asked.

"Agnes isn't the only one with a snitch on the payroll," she said.

"Trixie!" Stella exclaimed.

"Well, I haven't had to hire one for wet work, as they call it on the television, but I do have a little fund earmarked for that if it becomes necessary." Her phone rang and she took it from her pocket, put it to her ear without saying a word, listened for a minute, and then hit a button and put it back in her pocket. "I've got to run up to Bless My Bloomers. Alma Grace heard something that she can't or won't repeat on the phone."

As soon as Trixie had left Charlotte singsonged, "One week until the ball and then we'll know who Stella's seeing."

"Nine hours until my boys are home and I hope they like what I've done." Piper's off-key voice came right in behind Charlotte's.

"This has been a month to remember, hasn't it?" Stella sat down in her chair and fluffed at her red hair. She was so ready to be Jed's wife, to live with him and wake up every single morning with him beside her. She was ready to take on the battle of being his wife, if she had to knock Heather square on her ass to get the job done. It was long overdue and Stella was up to the job.

"Agnes will be so proud when she finds out." Stella could hardly wait to share the news of her marriage and really start a new life with Jed, right out in public for the whole world to know about.

"What's that about Agnes? I'm wondering what she'll say about me getting sexy things from Bless My Bloomers for my bridal shower. Earth to Stella! Where is your mind?" Charlotte snapped her fingers in front of Stella's face.

"My mind was on telling y'all who I've been seeing. To answer your question, Agnes will entertain us for hours about sexy underwear," Stella said.

"I've got a confession," Piper said. "I hated the idea of you having a man in your life when Nancy put your name on that list at the church. I didn't ever want you to get hurt like I did and I couldn't bear for you to ever get married. I prayed that God wouldn't hear the Angels and that he'd make Charlotte see that she didn't need to get married, either."

"That was mean," Charlotte said.

Piper's head bobbed up and down in agreement. "I know and I apologize."

"Y'all know I'm about half-superstitious," Stella said. "So I'm wondering if your prayers is why Charlotte felt the way she did. Up until my name got on that list, Charlotte was floating around in bridal cake heaven."

Piper clapped a hand over her eyes. "Oh, no! I didn't think my prayers got past the ceiling. They sure didn't when I prayed that Gene would come back to his family that week he divorced me."

"Sometimes God says no when it's for your own good," Charlotte said.

"Are you still my friends?" Piper asked.

"We've been through worse. Hell, we've been through wars, not piddlin' little arguments," Charlotte said. "Y'all have held my head up when I upchucked because I was so worried that Boone would break up with me over that floozy that moved in here from Dallas when we were seniors in high school."

"And you held my hair back for me when I turned twenty-one and got so damned drunk and when I wanted to die when that damn boy bragged all over church and town that we'd had sex in his truck." Stella smiled.

"And we didn't tell Nancy, either," Piper said.

Stella put her head in her hands. "Believe me, she knew. I can still see her peeling peaches at the kitchen sink. She told me that we live with the choices we make and learn from them and when I made a mistake to hold my head up and not make the same one twice."

"She might have been talking about one of your short skirts or you wearing too much makeup to church," Piper said.

"No, she knew."

"My mama would have harped on it for a week," Piper said.

"Mine would still be fussin'," Charlotte told them.

The door swung open and Stella looked up, expecting to see her first appointment of the day. But it was a lady with a floral delivery.

"Hey, how are y'all this morning? It's going to be another hot one. I've got a rose for Piper and a balloon for Stella." She handed them off and asked, "Y'all goin' to this barbecue ball? I see you've got a poster in your window. The previous owner over at the flower shop let them put up a poster and left a ticket in the cash drawer for me. But it sounds a little boring. By the way, I'm Gloria."

"Oh, believe me, it won't be boring," Stella said. "I'm Stella. This is Piper and that would be Charlotte."

"Pleased to meet y'all. I just bought the flower shop and this is my first day. A woman named Heather was my first customer. She hired me to make a centerpiece for the head table at the ball."

"Where are you from?" Stella asked.

"I moved here from Wichita Falls. I've got a shop over there, too. I'll probably send my niece over here to take care of this one when I get the inventory all straightened out. Well, got to go. I left the door open," Gloria said.

Piper opened the card attached to the single pink rose in a gorgeous cut-glass bud vase: *Your beauty far exceeds that of this perfect rose . . . RM.*

She held it to her chest until Charlotte grabbed it and said, "I think I'm going to swoon. That is the best pickup line I've ever heard."

Stella opened her card carefully and held on to it tightly. It read: *Saturday night I'll float higher than this balloon . . . yours through eternity.*

She didn't fight with Charlotte when she slipped the card from her fingers and sighed. "I didn't get sweet words and prizes, but I got to admit I'm so happy for you both that my heart is singing and it's not off tune like Piper was this morning."

"You've been getting flowers and balloons and presents for months. It's our turn," Stella said.

"I see weddings and happy ever afters," she sang.

Stella tied the balloon to the back of her chair and stared at the big red heart with *I Love You* written in the middle. Yes, she was finally ready, and it had taken every bit of the turmoil since that damned sign went up at the church to get her ready.

"How in the hell did Gladys sell the flower shop so slick? I haven't heard a word about it," Piper asked.

"She has her hair done at Walmart in Sherman and she goes to church up there, but we should've heard something," Charlotte said.

"Blame it on the barbecue ball and that church billboard. That's what everyone is talking about these days," Stella said.

Chapter Twenty-Five

Nancy's backyard was filled with laughter, friends, and the faint odor, still lingering, of smoke. She'd gone inside to refill the sweet tea pitcher and took a moment at the kitchen window. God might work in mysterious ways but prayers did get answered.

Boone leaned down and kissed Charlotte on the forehead. Their gazes caught so solidly that it was evident that for a moment there was no one else in the backyard but the two of them. Nancy nodded. That's the way it should be. They needed to hold on to that moment and remember it when the times got tough.

Rhett collapsed in the grass with two boys hanging on him. He shook them loose and jogged over to the picnic bench to cop a seat by Piper. She was still skittish even after the rose he'd sent the day before, but she would come around. Luke and Tanner loved him already and Everett always said that you couldn't fool kids or dogs. Nancy giggled when Jonas, their big old yellow Lab, laid his head on Rhett's knee. He began to scratch the dog's ears but his eyes kept shifting over to Piper.

Stella was sitting in a lawn chair, her phone in her hand and her thumbs moving like lightning. Most likely she was talking to her boyfriend. Nancy frowned. Was her daughter ashamed to bring him home because of them or because of him? Either way, the whole situation worried her.

Jed rounded the end of the house, waved at Everett, spoke to everyone, and sank down into a lawn chair beside Stella. He was the best preacher Nancy had ever known. He always delivered a down-home message on Sunday that got right to the point and that she had no trouble understanding. There didn't seem to be any of that stiffness in him that some preachers had. Maybe that's what made the strange friendship between him and Everett work so well.

"Sinner and saint," she whispered. "It's like Everett's swearin' just rolls off him like water off a duck's back. And it's like him being a preacher don't faze Everett."

Her phone rang and she pulled it from the hip pocket of her jeans. Without looking at the ID she said, "Hello."

"We're spittin' dust out here, Mama. You need some help with that tea?" Stella asked.

"I'm on my way out the back door." She hit a button and shoved the phone back into her pocket. "Rotten phones. Time was when a person yelled. They didn't call their mama from the backyard to the kitchen. Damn technology will be the death of all of us." She was still fussing under her breath when she set the pitcher on the table.

"What are you mumbling about?" Stella asked.

"Them damn phones. They're good in their place but good Lord, Stella Joy, calling me when I'm standing in the kitchen window and not fifty feet from you? That's ridiculous."

"I didn't know that you were in the kitchen. I thought you might be in the back of the house. Get a glass of tea and come sit beside me and Jed. Don't get so worked up over a phone call that your blood pressure goes up," Stella teased.

"Hey, Nancy, make Everett tell me his secret about smoking the brisket for your part of the barbecue. I can't get a thing out of him except that he's using some peppers in the water when he makes it this time," Boone yelled across the yard.

"See! Yelling works. He didn't have to use a phone."

"He won't tell anyone that secret," Nancy said. "I'm surprised he doesn't keep it in his gun safe under lock and key. I'm just grateful he only has to make one brisket for my contribution instead of cooking for the whole crowd."

Stella raised her voice above the kids, dogs, and conversation floating around the backyard. "Daddy, I really need to know the secret to good smoked chicken so I can win the prize at the barbecue ball."

"I'll leave it to you in my will, but I'm not telling you today. And besides, you don't need that ugly set of angel candleholders. They look like shit." Everett nodded.

"I'm going to go throw a Frisbee for Luke and Tanner so Piper and Rhett can have some time to talk," Jed said. "Hey, guys, y'all come on over here and show me how to throw this thing. I've forgotten how you hold it."

"We'll show you," Tanner said. "And we'll show you the right way since we like you."

"Piper, can I buy this kid from you?" he asked.

"Sorry, he's not for sale today, but there might be a day when I'll give him to you and not charge a dime if you've got a good barbecue recipe for country ribs." Piper laughed.

Tanner covered his ears with his hands. "Mama! Don't think of it."

Piper pulled Tanner to her side and kissed his sweaty little cheek. "Honey, I'm not getting rid of you. I kind of like you."

Tanner hugged her tightly. "I love you, Mama, and I'm so glad to be home."

"So you like your new house?" Rhett asked.

"Wow, man! It's like heaven and Poppa Everett said me and Luke can each have our own puppy. We done picked out the ones we want and we get to take them home tonight. This is the best day in the whole world. It's okay if we call him Poppa Everett, isn't it? He said we could. It's kind of like a grandpa but it really ain't," Tanner answered.

"That's just fine," Piper said. "Now that you've had time to think about it and slept in your new room, you aren't disappointed not to go back to your old house?"

"Heck, no!" Luke answered for his brother. "That was just a house. This is heaven. And starting on Tuesday, we get to stay right here with Poppa Everett and Nanny. Miz Nancy said we could call her that since she's kinda like a nanny. We'll miss Grandma and Grandpa, but we'll see them every other weekend like before. Now we got to go teach Preacher Jed how to throw a Frisbee." He lowered his voice. "Don't worry, Mama, we'll be nice. He is the preacher, you know."

He went from standing still to a blur as he and Tanner raced to the other side of the yard, where Jed twirled the bright-red Frisbee on the tip of his forefinger.

"I remembered how to do this, but you guys need to show me how to throw it," Jed said.

"They'll be practicing that for weeks now," Piper said.

Nancy dragged a chair across the yard and sat down at the end of the table. "Everett is really excited about having them stay with us. He's already talking about making and painting birdhouses and doing some pond fishing with them."

Rhett chuckled as he watched Jed with the Frisbee. "He's really good with kids. Do I need to worry about losing my place?"

"I don't think so. The first thing they asked me last night was if you knew we'd moved," Piper told him.

Rhett's smile covered his sexy face. "Wow!"

Piper nudged him with her shoulder. "To them you are ten feet tall and bulletproof, too."

What on earth that handsome man saw in a big, gangly woman with legs that were too long and who shopped at plus-size stores was beyond Piper. Not that she was griping one bit. Sitting beside him with the hot summer breezes fluffing up her hair, she felt like a dainty princess about to be rescued by the handsome prince.

"Now that my ego is properly inflated, I'm going out there and see if I can help Everett," Rhett said.

Boone stood up. "Me, too. Those two will wear Jed out in a while and we'll need to rescue him."

"Y'all are crazy. Luke and Tanner will tire out before Jed," Charlotte said.

Stella joined them at the table and the guys went to the back of the yard where the smoker was located.

"Hey." Charlotte poked Piper. "Where's your mind? I asked you if you slept well last night in your new place."

Piper smiled. "I'm sorry. I was woolgathering. The boys were like live wires last night. I didn't realize how much they needed a fresh start, too. But yes, we all three slept better than we have in weeks."

"I was afraid they'd be sad," Charlotte said.

"Not one bit, and when they heard they were staying with Everett and Nancy, they about brought the house down with their squeals. They love their grandparents but things are very tense over there right now."

Charlotte refilled their tea glasses. "How did Lorene take the news?"

"She was relieved. Said that since she'd offered to keep them, she didn't feel like she could tell me to put them back in day care but that things were kind of tough since Gene came back to the ranch," Piper answered.

Stella downed the rest of the tea in her glass and reached for the pitcher. "Mama, you are awfully quiet."

"I'm just thinking that it's less than a week until you reveal the name of that man who has a drawer in your bedroom," Nancy said. "You could just tell me now. I've already quit the Angels."

"And ruin all the fun," Piper said. "Stella is enough like Agnes that she'll be dramatic about the introduction."

"Hey, you're supposed to be my friend." Stella wanted so bad to tell them but the faintest mention of his name and the wind would carry it right back to everyone in Cadillac.

"I am, and friends are honest with friends. You won't tell us and we have been best friends forever and the way I see it is that after the way things have gone in the past, Stella deserves a big moment."

Charlotte turned around and put her legs under the picnic table. Piper did the same so that they were all facing each other. "You could tell us his initials," she whispered.

Stella flashed a brilliant smile. "Okay, darlin' friends, his initials are *SF* and they stand for 'Stella's feller.'"

With a long arm, Piper reached across the table and smacked Stella on the forearm. "You are downright mean."

"Nancy, you might have to put them in opposite corners of the room if they're going to fight," Charlotte teased.

"Or make them sit on the porch and hold hands." Nancy giggled. "I'm glad y'all stayed so close. I miss Janie so much. She was my best friend and when her mind started going, I thought I'd go crazy. I can't imagine how Trixie must feel. I didn't realize how much we'd depended on each other. Y'all don't take any of that for granted, not ever."

Stella bit her tongue to keep from whispering Jed's name in her mama's ear at that very moment. She'd been so busy living her own life and worrying with the drama in her friends' lives that she'd never realized how much her mama had missed Janie since she was diagnosed with early-onset Alzheimer's. Now Janie might not even know it when Trixie did have children. Thinking of that brought her full circle back to Nancy's grandchildren.

Well, shit! Stella looked around to be sure that she hadn't said it out loud.

The Internet, Agnes's voice said loudly in her head. *You can order dog food and all kinds of kinky things from the Internet, so order those damn test things and they'll bring them right to your door.*

While her mama and her two best friends went from one conversation to another, Stella dragged out her phone, ordered three pregnancy tests, paid the extra for shipping to get them there the next day, and then laid the phone down in her lap.

"Who were you texting that time?" Charlotte asked.

"We don't need to ask. It was SF." Piper laughed.

"You'll know at the ball. If I had to endure Heather all month, you can endure a few more days until I make the announcement." Stella reached over and laid a hand on her mother's knee. "Instead of a party here, let's all go out and eat somewhere for my birthday, Mama. You don't need to cook all day and wait on everyone all evening. After all, you were the one who gave birth to me that day and who has spoiled me most of my life afterward."

Nancy reached across the distance and hugged Stella. "I can't say I enjoyed that labor room when you were coming into the world or the first months of your junior year in high school, but the rest of it has been as much fun for me as it was for you. I like cooking. I like having all this noise around, and we'll have your birthday right here. But only if you promise me you'll bring your new fellow. I can't decide if you are ashamed of him or us."

"Neither, Mama. It's complicated," Stella said.

"That word sure comes up a lot in today's world."

"But I do promise that he will be here for my birthday."

Nancy reached up and grabbed a Frisbee floating toward them. Luke ran over to retrieve it, bringing the smell of sweaty kid with him. Nancy waited until he was ten feet away and tossed it back to him.

"I would like a dozen grandkids. Boys. Girls. A combination of all. But if these two are the only ones I ever get, I'll live with it, Stella. I just want you to be happy," Nancy said.

"Thank you, Mama. I'll let you in on a secret. At my birthday, I'll bring my fellow and we'll make an important announcement," she said.

Nancy scooted away from Stella and stared at her face so long that Stella blushed. "That's good enough for me, but I can't wait until you tell me it's time to look at wedding cakes and flowers."

"What if I just elope and there are no wedding cake and flowers?" Stella laughed.

"I'd even be happy with that if you were married and there were grandkids on the horizon," Nancy said.

"Ahhh, Stella is in love," Charlotte said.

"We've known that for a long time. She cried, remember? And Stella gets mad. Stella gets even. But she doesn't cry," Piper said.

"You cried?" Nancy asked.

"I was mad and I vowed I'd get even with Heather over that sign. With Agnes's help I just might get the job done, and yes, Mama, I cried," Stella said.

"She thought her new boyfriend would see that church sign and be offended by it," Piper said softly.

Nancy hugged her again. "I'm so sorry I started all that by asking for prayers. I had no idea I was turning loose a monster."

"Oh, she's not turned loose yet, Mama," Stella said. "Heather doesn't have what it takes to step into Violet's shoes. She's started off too big and too quick. And Agnes has given her just enough chain to hang herself."

Stella hoped that the wind carried that right back to Heather's ears.

೧೨

Trixie carried a tray of pecan tarts in one hand and a disposable pan of fried chicken in the other as she backed her way into the Yellow Rose. It was almost noon and the smell of still-hot chicken quickly filled the room.

"To what do we owe this wonderful visit?" Stella asked.

"I don't care what you want, you can have it. I didn't eat breakfast and I want a piece of that chicken," Piper said.

Trixie took it to the table in the back room with the three hairdressers following behind her like beagle pups on the trail of a rabbit. "I need a favor, so this is a bribe."

Charlotte reached for a pecan tart. "Up to a fourth of my kingdom is yours."

Trixie sat down at the table and spread her hands out. "We have a problem. Agnes is doing very well in rehab, so well that they are going to let her out at the end of the week. The trouble is that she cannot do steps, so we wanted to put her in the assisted living place in Sherman."

The other three pulled up chairs around the table and Trixie went on. "I know lots of folks come through here, so I was wondering if you'd ask around to see if there would be a small house we could rent for a couple of months. She swears she won't go anywhere but home when she gets out of the rehab center. We'd take her in at any of our places, but they all have as many steps and stairs as her place, so that's not a possibility. We need a house here in Cadillac that's been built on a slab instead of pier and beam."

"Sure we will," Charlotte said. "I'd let her come to my place, but it's got steps up to the porch."

"My trailer is full and it's sure not conducive to handicapped folks," Piper said.

Trixie laughed. "Don't say that word in front of her or she'll scratch your eyes out."

"She can come to my house," Stella said. "Remember the McKays built it on a concrete foundation because Miz McKay's knees had gotten so bad she couldn't climb steps anymore, and they had the whole place fixed for her wheelchair. What day is Agnes blowing that joint?"

"Saturday morning," Trixie said. "She swears that she's coming to the ball that evening. Are you sure about this, Stella?"

"Couple of questions first. Can she live alone?"

"Sure. It won't be a problem for you to leave her for work. We'll check in on her through the day."

"I mean as in all the time. As in if I'm not living there?" Stella asked.

Three sets of eyes immediately fixated on her. She straightened her back and stiffened her resolve to keep quiet a few more days, but it wasn't easy.

"Where are you going to be?" Charlotte asked.

"I plead the Fifth, but Agnes can live in my house for a couple of months until she can climb steps again and go back to her place. It's furnished and I'll help y'all run in and out and check on her. I love that old fart," Stella said.

Piper cupped Stella's cheeks in her hands. "You aren't leaving the shop for two months, are you? Promise me that you aren't running away from us."

"No, I am not. I'll be here Tuesday morning to open up, but it is your week to clean the shop on Monday," Stella said.

"I knew this was the place to come. I just knew it," Trixie said. "I'm on my way up to take her some chocolate cake, so I'll tell her the plan."

"Tell her that I'll have clean sheets on the bed, but she's on her own for food unless she wants to cook," Stella said. "I'll get everything ready for her homecoming. We'll be too busy at the shop to have a real party, but we'll have the ball that night so it can be her homecoming party."

"I'm telling her that you are moving out and I don't know where or with whom. You might want to steer clear of the rehab center or she'll pester the hell out of you until you tell her what she wants to know just to get her to shut up," Trixie said.

Nancy came through the back door talking as she crossed the floor. "The countdown continues. Four days until all this shit is over. Oh, hello, Trixie. Is that fried chicken? It's too early to order our lunch, so what's going on in here?"

Piper spoke up with the newest story. "And Stella is pleading the Fifth and won't tell us any more than that."

Nancy laid a hand on Stella's shoulder. "I expect that you are moving in with someone. I knew that giving a man a drawer in your bedroom was a step in that direction. And you've promised to bring him to your birthday party. Trixie, you and all the girls at Clawdy's plus the Bless My Bloomers girls are invited to the party. So with that in mind, I think it is wonderful of you to let Agnes borrow your house. I'll stop in and take her with me when I have to run up to Sherman so she doesn't go stir-crazy."

"You aren't going to make her tell you anything more?" Piper asked.

Nancy shook her head. "It's need to know. Right now I just need to know how many steaks to thaw out for her birthday."

Chapter Twenty-Six

Every dryer was blowing hot air, the styling station chairs were full, two women on the sofa leafed through magazines, and two others sat at the table eating ice cream on a stick. The noise level wasn't as loud as it had been when there was lots of gossip flying around, but it was a far cry from being quiet in the shop that Wednesday afternoon.

Then Gene plowed into the shop, slammed the door behind him, and yelled across the whole room at Piper, "What in the hell have you done?"

It took a few seconds, but every bit of conversation stopped. Not a single magazine page turned, and the lonesome cricket that Stella had tried to track down for two days stopped chirping.

Piper laid down the curling iron and met him halfway across the room, right in front of the yellow sofa. "This is my place of business. We will step outside or go to the back room, but this is not the place to yell at me," she said softly.

He folded his arms over his chest. "I'm not going anywhere. You really did move in with Rhett Monroe, didn't you? The stories are true."

She looked him right in the eye without blinking or tiptoeing. "What I do or do not do is none of your business."

"It is when it affects my sons, or are they my kids? Do I need to get a DNA test run to see if I really owe child support?" he asked coldly.

"I'll take care of that for you next week," she said. "Anything else?"

"I want to know where you live. It's my right."

"No, it is not. The divorce papers say if I move from the county with the boys, I have to let you know. If I take them out of the country for a vacation, I have to make you aware of when we leave and when we return if it interferes with your visitation dates, which are now on my calendar. Other than that, where I live is my business, and since I live in Grayson County, I don't have to tell you jack shit, boy."

One of the women started clapping and the others followed suit.

Gene tried to glare at all of them, but there were too many. "I'll have you declared unfit and take the boys away from you," he hissed.

"Tell me the court dates and I'll be there to fight you, but since your hours have been cut at work, you might want to be aware that if you lose, you get to pay the court fees as well as all the lawyer fees," she said.

"The house is empty," he shouted.

"Yes, it is. The locks will be changed this week. I'm leasing it to a new teacher and his family. They will be moving in the first week of August, so you might not want to be breaking and entering or you'll wind up in jail."

"My mother will not be babysitting for you ever again. The boys can't go with them this next weekend if you are going to be like this. I'll have her call you," he said.

"I can pay a sitter. I was just letting your mother have them because she asked. Now if that's all, I've got to get back to work, and I'll see you the weekend after next on Friday at six right here. And then you will bring them home to me Sunday at six right here."

He stormed out without another word.

Piper took a deep breath and went back to her station. "Sorry about that. Some men are . . ."

"Just born stupid," Carlene said from the sofa.

"You got that right," Piper said.

⁓

Stella roamed through the house that had been her home for more than a year. It wouldn't be difficult to leave it and move into the rambling old two-story white parsonage on the south side of the church. The ground floor was bigger than her entire little brick house, and there were three bedrooms and a bathroom upstairs.

The furnishings were old and worn and the whole place needed a coat of paint, inside and out. The hiring committee had told Jed that they wouldn't be out money on the parsonage but it would be a good sign in their books if he invested some of his in renovating the place.

He might need a gold star in their books when they found out he'd married Stella Baxter, so she'd already picked out paint colors and had no doubt that all her friends would gather for something like an Amish barn raising if her mother and daddy offered to furnish the food.

She was eager to move and ease into her new role as Jed's wife— more than ready to sit with him in a restaurant or on the front pew in church where the preacher's wife sat while he delivered his sermons. She wasn't ready for him to crawl out of her bed in another hour, put on his running clothes, and jog across the backyard to the next street over. And she damn sure wasn't ready to dance with another man at that damn ball the next night out at Violet's barn.

Tears welled up in her eyes at the thought of Jed's name being drawn out with another woman's. She really should wait to pee on the stick in the bathroom until the whole thing was over. Knowing wouldn't help and she damn sure couldn't tell anyone if it was positive. If Jed knew that she was pregnant, he'd take the microphone out of Heather's hand and announce it to the whole world so they wouldn't have to be coupled with anyone else.

"Agnes would be disappointed if we don't follow her instructions to the letter, and I really don't look good in black hair." She managed a smile through the tears. "Piper cried a lot when she was pregnant, so is that a sign?"

"Who are you talking to?" Jed asked from the dark hallway.

"Just mumbling, darlin'. Happy barbecue ball day. My bags are packed. I'll put them in the car before Agnes gets here and I get to go home with my sexy husband tonight."

He raked a hand through his blond curls. "Think I might sneak into the shop today for a haircut."

"We don't do men's haircuts anymore, remember?"

He wrapped his arms around her shoulders and pressed her back to his chest. "Not even if I beg?"

She whipped around and kissed him passionately. "Run by anytime between twelve and one. We don't usually book anyone for that time and I'll take care of this lovely mop of curls. Do you realize that our children don't have a snow cone's chance in hell of having anything but curly hair?"

"I hope the girls are all red haired and pretty as their mama." He kissed her on the tip of her nose. "Now, I'm off to jog to the church. I'll see you at noon and then tonight. Just one more day and that blasted sign comes down. It will say something totally different tomorrow morning, I promise."

"'Blessed are they that endure until the end'?" She quoted Scripture.

"I'm working on something better than that," he whispered.

Piper and Charlotte arrived promptly at eight o'clock to help her load her suitcases and clothing and say good-bye to the house. It was crazy, but they'd done the same thing when they moved from the apartment complex where Charlotte and Stella had shared an apartment and where Piper, Gene, and the boys had lived a few units down.

Piper brought in two colored sheets done in little boys' ideas of what the sky and dogs should look like and taped them to the front of the fridge. *Get well, Miz Agnes* was scribbled across the bottom of each. Charlotte put a chocolate cake from Clawdy's inside the cake keeper on the bar and a gallon of milk in the refrigerator.

"I see you've put sweet tea and cans of root beer in here for her, too," she said.

"I did, and the bed is made with fresh sheets. The bathroom is clean and I think she'll be just fine here until she can go home. I gave Trixie my keys last night. Y'all want to put yours on the counter?"

Piper laid hers beside the cake. "Good-bye, house. You've been good to me, keeping all the ghosts at bay this past six months when I needed a place to stay."

Charlotte wiped at a tear when she laid hers beside Piper's. "So long, house. You've been a good friend and I'll never forget the revelations I had in your bathroom."

"It's been fun, house, but it's time for us to take a leap of faith into the future, where neither of my friends will have a key to my new house." Stella smiled.

"Good God!" Piper threw the back of her hand over her forehead in a dramatic gesture. "We've done grown up."

Piper and Charlotte left and Stella roamed through the rooms one more time. She found herself in the bathroom, making sure all her toiletries were packed, when she found the pregnancy tests hidden safely in an old shoe box full of sponge hair curlers. Taking a deep breath, she pulled one out and held it in her hand. It wasn't much bigger than a pencil, and yet it held the answer to the question of that one morning's nausea. She sat down on the potty and followed the instructions.

It was one of those new fancy ones that was supposed to say "negative" or "positive" and then give the approximate weeks of pregnancy. She laid it on the counter, washed her hands, and put the potty lid down.

She picked up the instructions again and reread them to see if it would say "negative" or "not pregnant" or "you are one lucky girl today." It showed her the clear sign of what it would say and her breath caught in her chest.

Jed had said he hoped their daughters had red hair like hers. Her mama had said that preachers' kids were hellions. She'd understood that years ago, when that preacher's kid went to school and bragged about taking her virginity in the back of his truck—and Jed had told her he'd been like that boy when he was a teenager. Lord, what would she do with a son like that? Or with a red-haired, sassy daughter?

You will raise them up to love their mama like you love Nancy and their daddy and hope like hell they turn out right. Agnes's voice was back in her head. *And you will love them with your whole heart.*

She shut her eyes tightly and fumbled for the stick, but then she couldn't force herself to open them. She wanted Jed's children, lots of them, and suddenly, she realized that she'd be disappointed as hell if she wasn't pregnant. The nausea was a fluke and the missed period had to be because of all the stress but still, she touched her stomach and wanted a baby to be growing there.

She finally opened her eyes and reached for the phone, hit speed dial for Jed's number, and said, "Where are you right now this minute? I need to see you."

"Jogging about half a block from your house."

"The back door is open and the house is empty."

"Three minutes." He chuckled.

"Run faster and get here in two," she said.

She laid the stick on a paper towel on the kitchen cabinet and met him at the back door. Wrapping her arms around his neck, she rolled up on her toes and kissed him, long and lingering on the lips.

"If your neighbors saw me barrel into this house, there'll be talk before the ball," he said. "But I do like the gleam in your eye."

"I'm pregnant," she blurted out. "I thought that one morning with nausea was something I ate and that the lack of my period was stress and the pill is supposed to be ninety-nine-point-whatever effective so I didn't think I could possibly be pregnant but the test is over there and you can see for yourself . . ."

He picked her up and swung her around the kitchen floor until she was even more breathless than ever. "This is the best wedding present ever. I feel like I'm floating on air. I love you, Mrs. Tucker, and now we've got a double announcement to make."

"I love you, Jed. Are you sure you're not disappointed? We talked about waiting two years to start a family."

"No, my darlin', I'm so happy that my heart is about to explode."

With her feet dangling off the floor, Stella felt as if she was floating on air for real. Gossip, scandal, malicious lies. None of it could touch her when she was in Jed's arms.

Chapter Twenty-Seven

The camo limo left the church parking lot and drove slowly out to the Prescott place. Stella had purposely sat beside her mama at the back of the limousine, and while the rest of the ladies carried on a lively conversation, she took Nancy's hand in hers and whispered in her ear.

"Mama, I want you to know before the announcement is made at the ball. I've been married to Jed Tucker since May." In her wildest dreams she'd never thought that it would feel so good to say the words.

Nancy's quick intake of breath was so loud that Stella looked up at the other passengers to make sure they hadn't heard.

"Holy hell, Stella! The preacher," she gasped.

Stella nodded. "I fell in love with him, but all that scandal when I was young—and don't tell me you didn't know—scared me. I was afraid the church wouldn't give him a contract if they knew we were married."

"I'm speechless. Does your daddy know?"

Stella's head moved from side to side. "Not yet. You want to tell him or should I?"

"News that big should come from you. I can't wrap my mind around it. You were married when he came to the backyard parties?"

Stella nodded.

"When he danced with you? Hell's bells, girl. I'm losing my inner sense. I should've seen it. Lookin' back, he had a special way with you. I should have seen it, but he's the preacher." Nancy's voice got louder.

"Shhh. This is for you only because I love you and want you to know before we get out of this limo."

Nancy squeezed Stella's hand. "I'm fighting tears of joy. I'd go on and cry, but I spent an hour on this makeup."

"Me, too, Mama. It feels so good to tell you. I wanted to say something before, but . . ."

"You deserve the big announcement after everything that has happened, including that rotten sign. I hope it's taken down by morning."

"Oh, it will be. Jed promised."

The limo arrived amid flashing photographers' lights and rolling cameras from the television station in Sherman. Rhett stepped up to the doors and lifted Piper down like a gentleman helping a lady out of a chariot, his hands firmly around her waist and hers on his shoulders.

She whispered something in his ear and he nodded. Then he turned, took Agnes's crutches from her hands and handed them to Boone, and picked her up like a bride, carrying her to the door of the barn and setting her down gently before handing the crutches back to her.

"You are a gentleman and I never did believe all that shit about you," Agnes whispered.

He blushed and said softly, "It was probably all true, ma'am, but sometimes a leopard can change its spots if the right woman comes along."

It was Boone's turn to help Charlotte from the limo next and he did so with a flourish, kissing her fingertips when he set her down. "Oh, my!" she said.

"You are lovely tonight, m'lady. Shall we?" He crooked his arm.

She slipped hers inside it, and Agnes held the filmy curtain back for them with the tip of one of her crutches.

Rhett picked up Piper's arm and tucked it inside his. "I hope my little brother knows what he's doing. I've never been to something with a princess before and I'm following his lead."

Piper smiled. "That, Sir Rhett, is the best pickup line I've ever heard."

Everett poked his head inside the limo. "Well, I'll be damned. This thing looks like a hooker wagon to me. Where's my lovely wife?"

"She's right here, Daddy, and you are so right. I was just whispering secrets to her before we go inside," Stella said.

"I might have known it. Y'all been thicker'n thieves since the day we brought you home from the hospital. Well, come on, woman. Let's go see what in the hell them prayin' women done got cooked up inside there. I'm hungry and we got to wait until they get the names all called before we can eat. That Heather girl is out there talkin' to some reporters, but they're more interested in this big contraption than they are what she's got to say," Everett said.

When Nancy put a high-heeled shoe on the first step, Everett scooped her up in his arms and said, "You'll be the prettiest one in there tonight, Nancy darlin'. There ain't a woman in Cadillac who can hold a candle to you." He didn't put her down until they were inside the barn.

Stella was the only one left in the limo and when she started out the driver held out his hand. She reached for it but Jed appeared out of the shadows and took her hand, helped her down, and looked deeply into her eyes before tucking her arm into his. "I love you, Stella Tucker."

"That sounds real good," she said.

"It does, doesn't it? Miz Agnes, darlin', could I escort the two loveliest women in the county into this ball?" he asked when they made it to the door.

"You are full of shit, Jed, even if you are a preacher, but I'll gladly walk into this barn dance with you and Stella. Oh, my God!" Agnes said.

"What? Did you hurt your hip?" Stella said frantically.

"Hell, no! I just now figured the whole damn thing out. It's been right there in plain sight the whole time. It's Jed. And you are both wearing bright shiny new gold bands, which means he ain't your feller but your husband. I can't believe you pulled the wool over my eyes," Agnes said.

"Yes, he is, but don't let the cat out of the bag just yet." Stella laughed.

"Does Nancy know?"

"I just now told her."

"I bet she don't know whether to wind her ass or scratch her watch." Agnes cackled.

"That pretty much sums it up," Stella said.

෴

The big tin building was still a barn with a cracked concrete floor, wooden rafters, and buyers' balconies on either side. It smelled like dozens and dozens of kinds of barbecue. No matter how many scented candles burned brightly on the tables or how many rose petals were tossed on the serving tables at the back, those were still slow cookers and disposable aluminum pans back there. And those really were red plastic cups for sweet tea and lemon-infused water.

The yards and yards of filmy illusion netting blown backward by the noisy air conditioners did little to keep the cold air in and the hot air out. Heather's floral dress with its wide skirts looked like something out of a pre–Civil War museum.

"Well, Stella Baxter, here you are," Heather said. "And the rumors have it that my marriage ministry has worked and you will be telling your family the name of your future husband tonight?"

"You look lovely, Heather, but"—Stella lowered her voice to a whisper—"you shouldn't eat any of my pulled chicken. I made it special for my feller and he does like it a bit spicy. A delicate little flower like you could never handle the heat, but I do understand that Quinn loves it, so maybe he can have your portion."

Heather's beady little eyes squinted nearly shut. "Are you making fun of me?"

"No, ma'am. It's just that city folks can't eat my chicken. It upsets their delicate nature. Down here in the backwoods, people are stronger. They are able to handle the jalapeño peppers we grow here because they've been eating them their whole lives, but you, comin' from the city, honey, it's just a warning. Don't take offense, now," Stella said.

"Are you implying that I can't handle as much as you can? I've eaten food with jalapeño peppers in it. Mexican food is some of my favorite," Heather said.

"No, I'm telling you straight up that you can't. You might think you are taking Violet's place in Cadillac, but darlin', I'm the new Agnes. And FYI, Violet couldn't get ahead of Agnes and you will always be two steps behind me." Stella laid a hand on Heather's shoulder and looked her right in the eye. "And I'm giving you fair warning, my pulled chicken is not for you. You can thank me later when you come down off your high horse. Now I really must get on up into the balcony before you start drawing names."

Heather headed straight for the food table holding Stella's bright-red slow cooker of pulled barbecued chicken. She laid the lid to the side, picked up a plate, put a hamburger bun on it, and loaded it with the chicken. The expression on her face said that she would show that hussy just who had more steel in her backbone.

Stella watched from the shadows near the stairs leading up to the balcony where the ladies were gathered. Sheer determination made Heather eat every bite of the sandwich, with her eyes watering and her face flushed by the time she finished it.

Then she took off in a big-skirted waddle toward the table that held her special white grape juice punch. Piper, bless her heart, had offered to serve until time for the drawing and she filled a pink plastic cup to the brim and handed it to Heather.

"Someone should have told you that Stella puts a lot of jalapeño peppers in her barbecue. You poor dear," Piper said sympathetically.

"I can take the heat," Heather said stoically, but she downed the whole cup of punch and held it back for more. "I'm not a pansy."

"I'm sure you are strong, darlin'," Piper said. "The tables look lovely with all the candlelight flickering."

Heather put down the second cup faster than the first and handed it back to Piper. "One more time. I've been working very hard and I'm thirsty."

Piper was more than willing to oblige her. "You've done such a lovely job. Why, no one would ever believe this is a common old sale barn. Everyone in the whole county is going to be saying that it's the best barn dance they've ever been to."

Heather tilted up the third cup and gulped it down. When she set it down, her eyes were glazed and she grabbed the edge of the table. "This corset is really tight. I . . . oh, my sweet Gee . . . Gee . . . shus . . . what in the devil is Agnes Flynn wearing?"

"It's cute as a button, ain't it," Piper said. "Carlene down at the Bless My Bloomers store created it from some old kitchen curtains and a pair of overalls for her. Have you shopped there? I do all the time. They have the sexiest things for us tall folks as well as chubby ladies. I'm sure you could find something that would turn Quinn on."

Heather's nose snarled as she tilted her chin up a notch. "That is a naughty panty store. I wouldn't be caught dead in there. I do believe this corshit is cutting off my cirsulation."

"Hello, Heather, darlin'. Are you havin' trouble breathing?" Charlotte was suddenly at her side, hooking an arm through hers and leading her to a nearby table. "Come on over here and sit beside me."

Floy wandered up to the punch table and nodded at Piper. "I do believe it's almost time for you to join the ladies. I will take over from here."

Piper handed her the ladle and headed toward the stairs. If anyone ever questioned the punch, Floy would swear on a stack of Bibles that it didn't have a drop of liquor in it. And she'd be right. The three cups that Heather sucked down so quickly had come from behind the punch bowl and Piper had already poured them about a fourth full of vodka before she ever added the punch to them. The empty vodka bottle was tucked away safely in her purse and she'd leave it under the balcony seats. Now it was up to Charlotte to do the job Agnes had assigned to her.

"Heather, darlin', I have a huge favor to ask of you. You can say no, but it will make me so sad, and frankly, honey, with this onset of the vapors I don't think you're up to reading the names anyway," Charlotte said.

"I do feel a bit faint," Heather said. "But I am not delicatsh. I'm strong enough to be a marriage minishter."

Charlotte decided to go bold instead of sneaking up on Heather's blind side. "I will give you one thousand dollars to let me call out the names. I have it right here." She pulled out an envelope with ten one-hundred-dollar bills in it. "You can count them if you want. That will go a long way toward getting your marriage ministry out of the red."

"I can't. It's my job as the marri . . . marri . . . the minishter to call the names."

"I happen to know that you are more than a thousand dollars in the hole on this party," Charlotte said.

"It's a ball. A fancy dress ball. Why, there is my aunt Violet. Doesn't she look pretty in her black sha . . . sha . . . satin?" She finally spit the word out properly. "Even in the wheelchair. I should go talk to her." She looked at the envelope lying in front of her and back at Charlotte. "Why do you want to do this so bad?"

"Because I heard that someone put Violet's name in the single women's bowl. I wouldn't want to call it out with Rhett Monroe and start a bunch of rumors about her liking younger men and paying them to go to bed with her," Charlotte whispered.

Heather covered her eyes with her hands. "Oh, no! They wouldn't say that about an old woman."

"I heard that she's been flirting with him and the way you are feeling faint, you might say her name before you think. I'll make sure that if I pull her name out I hide it in my bra," Charlotte said.

Heather picked up the money. "Go on. Just protect my sweet aunt."

Charlotte made her way to the middle of the dance floor, where a small table had been set up with three fishbowls on it. She picked up the microphone and said, "Good evening, folks. Let's give a big round of applause to everyone who has made this barn dance possible."

"Barbecue ball," Heather mouthed from across the room, but no one heard her above the noise.

"And we need to thank all the ladies who've brought the barbecue and the side dishes, which we will turn y'all loose on here as soon as we draw up the names of the couples and they enjoy their first dance. So let's have another round for the cooks," Charlotte said.

Agnes gave her the thumbs-up sign.

"I saw some of the ladies all dolled up and I know you menfolks are champin' at the bit to get this show on the road. I'll be drawing the married and engaged folks' names first. Sugar and Jamie Magee, come on down!" she yelled like a game show host.

Heather had her hands over her ears.

It took ten minutes to get through the slips of paper in that bowl and then she started on the next two bowls. "Rhett Monroe and . . . let's see . . . will you be dancing with Violet Prescott or maybe Agnes Flynn?"

Everyone laughed and then it got quiet. "Looks like I was wrong. Your date for the evening is Piper Stephens. And the next bachelor is Gene Stephens. How's that for luck folks, two Stephenses in a row? And your date for the evening is Macy Bardeen. Come on down here on the dance floor. Don't be shy, Macy darlin'."

Stella sat down beside her father, close enough that she could whisper in his ear much like she'd done in the limo with her mother. "Daddy, I need to tell you something before Jed makes an announcement here."

"He's your husband." Everett chuckled.

"Yes, he is," Stella said.

Everett slapped his knee and then gathered Stella to his chest in a bear hug. "I knew it! I just damn sure knew it! The way his eyes go all soft when he looks at you. It's the way I look at your mama. I couldn't be happier for you, sugar. I like the man and he'll be a good son. Does your mama know yet?"

"I told her in the limo."

Everett let go of his daughter and grinned so big that it lit up the barn more than the candles on the table could ever do. "I knew she was hummin' with excitement and now I know why. I hope to hell they choose y'all's names so you can dance together. If they don't, I'll have to say something that might make a lot of folks real mad. Y'all looked so happy when you danced in the backyard."

"You're really okay with this?" Stella asked.

"Are you happy, sugar?"

"Very."

"Then I'm okay with it. Now they'd damn sure better draw out y'all's names so you can be together for this first dance. You'll be right out there on the floor with me and your mama just like it was your wedding day."

Charlotte went through a dozen more names before she finally drew out Jed Tucker's name. "And who will be dancing with the preacher tonight? Aha, it is the lovely Stella Baxter, in whose honor I do believe this barn dance is given. And the last name belongs to me, and since I'm engaged, I'd like to call upon my fiancé to join me in the first dance of the night. Boone Monroe, honey, where are you?"

Heather was rolling her eyes toward the rafters. Violet was shaking her finger at her niece and Agnes was smiling like she'd just been given the keys to heaven.

"Music," Heather mouthed toward Charlotte.

"The lady who put all this together for us tonight says it's time for the music to begin. So if our DJ will plug in the flash drive I do believe we . . ."

Jed led Stella to the middle of the floor and reached for the microphone. Heather shook her head emphatically at Charlotte.

"Hold off on that music, Mr. DJ. I guess before we dance, Jed would like to say a few words. So take it away, Preacher Jed," Charlotte said.

"Stella and I have an announcement to make," he said in his deep Texas drawl.

"Oh, my Lord," Charlotte gasped.

Stella smiled at her and winked.

"As you all know, this barn dance came about because of the sign on the church lawn, which will be changed to something else tomorrow. For those of you who might not have seen it, it says, 'Pray for My Daughter. She Needs a Husband.'"

Laugher echoed through the whole barn.

"I know it's funny," Jed said. "But when Heather asked the prayer group at our church if they had someone that they wanted on the list, Nancy Baxter did not think it would be broadcast for the world to see when she asked the Prayer Angels to ask God to bring her daughter a husband." He stopped and slung an arm around Stella's shoulders. "Stella has been a real trouper about the whole thing, folks. I wanted to take the sign down the next morning but she thought it was a hoot, especially in the light of the fact that she already had a husband at that time, so the ladies were praying for something that had already come about." He raised his voice and brought the microphone all the way to his lips. "And I am that husband, folks. Stella and I were married at the Grayson County Courthouse a month before that prayer meeting, which means we have been married two months and one week tonight."

Applause rocked the barn.

"So this can be our wedding party. We'd like nothing better than for y'all to enjoy the barbecue. I would advise you to go easy on Stella's pulled chicken. I like it spicy, but it might be too hot for some folks. And I'd like to invite all y'all to church tomorrow morning. There will be a potluck in the fellowship hall afterward, so if you've got any leftover barbecue, bring it along. My whole family will be there to celebrate my job at the Cadillac church and my marriage to the most wonderful woman in the state of Texas."

Stella reached for the microphone.

"Thank you all for the applause. It means a lot to us. It was my idea to keep the marriage a secret because of my past. I didn't believe Jed would be hired as the preacher for the next two years if anyone knew he was married to me. But just a few days ago the committee voted to give my new husband a contract, so we'll be in the parsonage for the next year at least, maybe longer if our prayers are answered and we can make Cadillac our home." There, she'd said it right out in public for the whole town to hear.

Jed moved closer to the microphone and said, "I do believe there is an old adage about not throwing stones at glass houses, so if any of y'all got a rock in your pockets, either throw it or toss it on the ground right now."

Violet and Heather inhaled and then let their breath out noisily, but not another sound was heard in the whole barn.

Everett made his way to where Jed and Stella stood and took the microphone. "Y'all all raise your plastic cups. This is a toast to my new son, not son-in-law, but son, because when he joined our family, he became a part of it as surely as if he was blood, not in-law. To my precious daughter, Stella, and to my new son, Jed Tucker. May their marriage be happy and as my old Irish grandmother said when I married Nancy"—he raised his red plastic cup higher—"may God be with you and bless you. May you see your children's children. May you be poor in misfortunes and rich in blessings. May you know nothing but happiness from this day forward."

"Hear, hear! To Stella and Jed," Rosalee yelled, and everyone tossed back a few gulps of whatever was in their cups.

Nancy had already started to the front of the building, accepting hugs on the way. When she reached the center, she hugged Stella and then Jed before she reached for the microphone. "I know you're ready to get this show on the road, but I have to join Everett in saying that I'm so happy tonight. And the fact that that damn sign—and yes, I did cuss, because it has been a damn thorn in my side for weeks—will be down come morning makes this a double blessing."

"Hear, hear! To the damn sign coming down. Now let's start the dancing," Agnes hollered, and the catcalls, foot stomping, and applause came close to raising the roof right off the Prescotts' old weathered sheet-metal barn.

Trisha Yearwood's voice came through the speakers as she sang a slow country two-stepping song, "How Do I Live." Jed wrapped his arms around Stella. Her arms went around his neck and the wide gold wedding band flashed in the light of fifty flickering candles.

In the middle of the song, Stella felt a bump on her shoulder and her father leaned over and whispered, "I'm right proud to have that damn preacher in our family. Don't know of a man that I'd rather keep company with."

"I love you, Daddy," Stella mouthed.

The barn was full of gorgeous women clad in lovely dresses, but none could hold a candle to Piper in her dark-green chiffon-over-satin dress with the shorter underskirt. It had been beautiful in the dressing room, but tonight Piper was absolutely stunning. It had more to do with the way Rhett held her possessively close and the way he kept whispering in her ear than the dress, but still, when he swirled her around and the chiffon moved so gracefully . . . well, the happiness Stella saw on her friend's face made her go misty-eyed. She had to blink several times when she saw him singing along with the words saying that without her there would be no sun in his sky.

Stella glanced to her left and there were Boone and Charlotte, who wore the lovely pale-green halter dress with a rhinestone clasp that did indeed show off enough cleavage to draw the old stink eye from Heather. Boone, bless his heart, would never know that Charlotte had had second thoughts, and that was good because he was truly in love with her.

"Penny for your thoughts," Jed said and then sang along with the lyrics asking how would he live without her, how would he breathe without her, how would he ever survive without her.

"Only if I can use the penny to buy some hot sex tonight," she said as she brushed away one tear that found its way down her cheek.

"I think that could be arranged, Mrs. Tucker," he said.

"I was thinking about how beautiful and happy my friends are right now," she answered.

"They're not as pretty as you, darlin'. I swear when I saw you in that gorgeous lace dress with all those buttons, all I could think about was undoing them one at a time and kissing you after each button. You are stunning, my bride."

"I'll look forward to it, but darlin', I'm your pregnant wife now." She smiled up at him.

He bent forward, kissed her on the earlobe, and whispered, "Stella Baxter Tucker, you will be my bride until the day you die. And if you go first, walk real slow, because like this song says, I can't live without you and I'll be joinin' you on those steps up to the pearly gates within twenty-four hours. Did you tell your mama and daddy about the baby?"

Every word of the song, his hands on her back, his soft sweet words set loose a roller coaster of emotions so deep that she wanted to hold them close to her heart forever. "Not yet. I want us to have a little while, just a day or so when it's ours alone."

"Let's tell them together after the party tonight. I don't think I can wait a day or two," he said.

"And to think I was afraid you'd be disappointed."

"Never. I want lots of kids, and this is the icing on the cake."

Piper tapped her on the shoulder. "I understand why you couldn't tell us and I forgive you."

"Me, too." Charlotte poked her on the arm.

Jed took a step back and let the three of them have a group hug just as the song ended. Three gorgeous women, one in ivory lace, two in shades of green, with three tall, handsome men surrounding them as the song ended with the lyrics asking, "How do I live?" Friendship, family, a wife. He couldn't live without them, but most especially Stella. His heart would stop beating without her.

The whole barn rocked with another round of applause and then "Good Hearted Woman" started playing and Everett grabbed Nancy for a second dance as the people started a reception line to greet both the bride and groom. Heather and Violet sat at the back of the barn and seethed, but Rosalee and Agnes were first in the line.

⌘

Heather was mortified that the Sunday morning newspaper called her glorious ball a barn dance and didn't mention her marriage ministry at all, and the article, barely two inches long, was buried under the obituaries. The fifteen-second news clip on television right before the weather the night before showed Rhett Monroe carrying Agnes Flynn to the door of the barn with a short sentence about *Duck Dynasty* not having a thing on Cadillac, Texas, with its fancy barn dance and camouflage Hummer limos. There wasn't a single picture of Heather or a mention of her marriage ministry. It all gave her a raging headache and she didn't make it to church.

But Annabel sent her a picture via cell phone of the new church sign. It said: "Jed Tucker and Stella Baxter Married May 21." And right below that it said, "First Baby Due March 21."

She'd teach them all a lesson. They would not have a Yellow Rose Barbecue Ball ever again. They'd ruined their chance at rising up out of their backcountry ways. They'd miss her desperately when she moved her membership to a larger church in Sherman. Some people simply could not appreciate the finer things in life.

❧

Stella was glad that she had a seat at the piano that Sunday morning. The church was packed so tightly that elbows, knees, and shoulders were crammed together on the pews. She'd never realized his family was so big. There must be close to a hundred new faces out there and the only ones he'd had time to introduce her to before services were his mother and father. Jed might be an only child, but good grief, he had cousins and aunts and uncles by the score and there were babies everywhere.

She hoped that in days to come, listening to the sermon would be easier, but that Sunday morning, she was either fretting about his family or letting her mind drift to the glorious night they'd just had together in the old parsonage.

Then suddenly the benediction was over and it was time for the potluck in the fellowship hall. She and Jed stood in an informal greeting line and he introduced her to his family as they came through. Evidently, his mother was no stranger to church potluck dinners. She and Nancy were over there in the kitchen supervising and organizing.

Charlotte tapped Stella on the shoulder. "Are you serious about not giving me and Piper a key to your new house?"

"Very much so. You have to knock on the door."

Piper touched her other shoulder. "Heather wasn't in church. You reckon she has her first-ever hangover?"

"I'd like to know if she's planning another ball for next year," Stella said. "Save me a place at whatever table you've got saved."

Finally, the last hand had been shaken and Everett clapped his hands loudly. The noise died down and he raised a red plastic cup of sweet tea. "Before Jed graces this dinner, I'd like to propose a toast to my daughter and new son. I'd also like to welcome his family to Cadillac. Y'all make yourselves at home and come back often. You are always welcome. And I'd like to toast to our first grandbaby, who will be born next spring. I hope it's a red-haired girl just like my Stella Joy. Now, Jed, bless this damn food so we can get to it."

"Thank you, Daddy," Stella said.

"Yes, sir." Jed nodded.

Agnes pushed a walker up beside Stella and whispered, "And I'd like to report there will be no more barbecue balls of any name or description in Cadillac, and that next week Heather will be moving her membership to a church in Sherman. Here's to Cadillac. May it never change and may you never dye your hair black."

ABOUT THE AUTHOR

Photo © 2014 Charles Brown

Carolyn Brown is a *New York Times* and *USA Today* bestselling author and a RITA finalist. Her books include historical, contemporary, cowboy, and country music mass-market paperbacks. She and her husband live in Davis, Oklahoma. They have three grown children and enough grandchildren to keep them young. When she's not writing, she likes to sit in her gorgeous backyard with her two tomcats, Chester Fat Boy and Boots Randolph Terminator Outlaw, and watch them protect the yard from all kinds of wicked varmints like crickets, locusts, and spiders.